$2.50

P6

69147.

THE BLUE GATE OF BABYLON

Paul Pickering was born in Rotherham and educated at the Royal Masonic Schools and Leicester University. He has been a columnist for *The Times*, the *Sunday Times*, the *Evening Standard* and *Punch* and has worked as a journalist all over the world. He lives in London and loves Berlin. *The Blue Gate of Babylon* is his third novel.

THE
BLUE GATE
OF
BABYLON

Paul Pickering

PENGUIN BOOKS

PENGUIN BOOKS

Published by the Penguin Group
27 Wrights Lane, London W8 5TZ, England
Viking Penguin Inc., 40 West 23rd Street, New York, New York 10010, USA
Penguin Books Australia Ltd, Ringwood, Victoria, Australia
Penguin Books Canada Ltd, 2801 John Street, Markham, Ontario, Canada L3R 1B4
Penguin Books (NZ) Ltd, 182–190 Wairau Road, Auckland 10, New Zealand

Penguin Books Ltd, Registered Offices: Harmondsworth, Middlesex, England

First published in Great Britain by Chatto & Windus 1989
Published in Penguin Books 1990
1 3 5 7 9 10 8 6 4 2

Copyright © Paul Pickering, 1989
All rights reserved

Made and printed in Great Britain by
Richard Clay Ltd, Bungay, Suffolk

Except in the United States of America,
this book is sold subject to the condition
that it shall not, by way of trade or otherwise,
be lent, re-sold, hired out, or otherwise circulated
without the publisher's prior consent in any form of
binding or cover other than that in which it is
published and without a similar condition
including this condition being imposed
on the subsequent purchaser

To my mother, and Alice

So we beat on, boats against the current,
borne back ceaselessly into the past.

FITZGERALD

I would like to thank Jonathan Burnham, Rupert Lancaster and Carmen Callil; also Caroline Dawnay, and all the people who helped and encouraged me, especially in Berlin.

1

The instant the night Express from Hanover jolted into East Germany on its way to Berlin, the door opened and the window blinds were pulled down by two brusque men, who from their sly zeal appeared about to commit some intense and irresistible sexual act before me on the dusty green seats. Both wore baggy uniforms verging on the military that could as easily have belonged to bus conductors as border police. They stank of stale sweat and diesel oil. In mute explanation through the gloom, one used a stubby torch to illuminate a sign above the window. A notice in Gothic script forbade any contradiction of the ridiculous gesture with the blinds, or indeed anything else.

'We draw your attention to the fact that this train is the territory of the German Democratic Republic. We expect you to refrain from any provocation on this territory. Otherwise we will take the security measures necessary.'

I was entering a land where the very act of witnessing the scenery was a provocation. In some overheated office in Potsdam it had been deemed essential, no doubt by someone who thought himself in excellent mental health, that travellers by train to West Berlin should not see the snow and mud meadows of the East. Dim electric lights flickered into a grudging life and, an instant after the two officials left the stifling carriage, which now smelt of damp overcoats, old shoes and Balkan cigarettes, she slipped into my world like a mist. It was her cologne that I noticed first, as I peered around the corner of the blind to catch a glimpse of the grey railway siding, a view that had been so boring a moment before but which had suddenly acquired a certain cachet; even the pavement is magical in a Forbidden City. In the half-light, in the claustrophobic space of that blinkered train, I was inches away from a more provoking vision; from the most beautiful girl who had ever walked into my world.

Believe me, I never intended to meet Magda. I never intended to meet the most enchanting girl I had ever seen, and I am not usually given to exaggeration. Well, not very much, as I read the Classics at Oxford. In fact, not half as much as that old liar Herodotus . . . But I was ripe for falling under the spell of the Magdalenas of my dreams. I did not, as yet, glimpse my own blood sacrifice in the dimple by rouged lips, in the winky-slink of a walk, in the black seam of sheer stockings, in the promise of a caress between crisp linen sheets . . . I had fallen before. As my train crashed towards dawn on a foggy morning at the fag-end of the first year of the 1960s I had no thoughts for caution. I was mad for life. I was still child enough to believe in happy endings (even though my idol, Buddy Holly, had just rock-and-rolled into a mountain). The bright future seemed possible, and usually was, especially if you were single, free, and only twenty-one.

Well, perhaps not everything in my garden was rosy, which is why I happened to be on this train. Perhaps I too was a great pretender. All the same, most of me wanted to shout: Look out, tomorrow, here comes Toby Jubb. Watch out for yourself, *schmierfink*, clattered back the points, but I didn't hear them. Diddle-de-dee – Diddle-de-dum. Watch out Berlin, here I come. If I had known exactly where that road of Prussian iron was taking me, I might have jumped from the speeding locomotive, or at least pulled the communication cord. There again, I might not. Some of us poor mortals do seem fated to go whistling cheerfully though the fabled Blue Gate of our Babylons, seeking the object of our desire, greedy for whatever we find in that lush oasis, amid the bleak deserts of our limitations. We never believe we will fall victim to what squats in the mysterious darkness of the citadel beyond.

As she started to put a large, heavy bag on the roof rack, I got up to help her, and the violent shunting threw her into my arms. The apparition had form. Inadvertently I grazed one hand on a brass light fitting stamped with a Prussian Eagle. My first meeting with Magda was engineered in the shabby rolling stock of the old German Imperial Railways, tupped and buffeted by a modern Russian locomotive. I always preferred cars to the totalitarianism of a train.

'*Danke*,' she said, wriggling away from me and into her seat. There was a wickedness growing in the partial darkness that surrounded us.

'*Bitte. Zigarette?*'

But she shook her long hair, which was honey fair, and fell in languid curls upon her slight shoulders. At the corner of a large, lazy mouth there was a suggestion of a smile. She unbuttoned a cheap raincoat to reveal a tight white woollen dress which hugged her breasts and narrow waist and showed a lot of her slender legs. They were long legs. What my father called American legs. Her stockings rustled as she reached into an old handbag. There was a flash of a lighter and she lit a cigarette of her own. Perhaps the stockings were silk. As she exhaled the smoke, it created a halo around her teasingly knowing but angelic face. Her eyes, enormous and a vivid china blue, were amused and seemed to feed off the carriage's shadows and my amorous confusion. We were moving again, and I peered around the side of the blind.

'I can see a farmer on a tractor,' I said, with the unintentional fervour of Christopher Columbus' lookout sighting land. Her throaty chuckle through a cloud of Caporal made me wobble slightly at the knees.

'*Ja* . . .' The girl drew the word out as if talking to a child or an idiot. 'This is farmland,' she added in English. 'Do tell me if you see a cow.'

A surge of power as the train picked up speed made the lights brighter, and I noticed a small scar at the base of her neck; unmistakable, even to someone just down from university, as a bullet wound. The scar was puckered and ugly. Yet from another angle the ridges of the penetration had the ruddy beauty of the labia. However much I looked for flaws, it was quite easy to imagine men becoming murderous over her, though it was not easy to say what exactly made her so special. In the brighter light the high cheekbones and definite German jaw gave a cruel, predatory impression. Her nose was too sharp, and the eyes not quite the

3

colour I had imagined them. Yet, hers was a seditious smile, the sort that can sabotage ten years of happy marriage through a chance meeting; a walking bomb ticking, clicking into a room on high heels, an adulterous grenade sent rolling into a cocktail party. Perhaps the girl in front of me was too worldly to be truly beautiful. Many women in Ancient Greece must have been as lovely as the fabled Helen, but only she had that magical, devastating quality which, provided the giddy excuse to attack poor Troy (though of course, as that old liar Herodotus notes, the lady was probably eating lotus in Egypt throughout the siege). And, for me, there was something else. In the eyes of the girl who sat across from me was both a terror and a greed for everything around her; she looked at the world with the longing of a priestess, conscious of the perils in the divinities she invokes. I felt faint.

'Are you all right?' she asked, as, without warning, we jolted to a halt for another bout of shunting. 'Are you in pain? If you wish to vomit there is a toilet along the corridor,' she said with that frank brutality which is so uniquely German.

'No, thank you. I mean yes, I am all right,' I replied rather breathlessly, trying hard to be cool. I had read endless magazine articles at my desk in Paris on how to be oh so cool. Such wiles never work for impatient youth. I caught my reflection in the glass door to the corridor. I was so big and clumsy beside her. At six feet four and three-quarters my school had decided I was too Gothic for the cricket team. My mother, claiming to be several parts Russian, had buttonholed the headmaster and said I was too big for England. My chin was a little too large, my nose crooked. I have one of those unfashionably earnest nineteenth century sort of faces which look out of place in coffee bars. My smile felt like a death mask. I turned away. Sexual confidence is a fickle thing. Best foot forward, Jubb. (It had always been the unofficial family motto, based on a priapistic uncle's novel way of knocking on ladies' doors at house parties.)

'. . . Quite all right, really. I say, your English is jolly good.'

'You like my legs better, I think,' she said, raising pencil-thin eyebrows. A hint of face powder had fallen onto her dress. 'Or are you attracted to a girl by her vowels? How lucky you are to be interested in farmers on tractors and the way people say things.'

She purred the words and I wanted to disappear through the

floor. I also wanted to touch her. To run my hands up her legs. To kiss that delicious mouth and those languid eyelids. But the door was opened and our shrine violated. The drab men who pulled down the blinds were back, questing like disgruntled moles. As with most public officials, they looked quite unsatisfied with the discomfort they had already caused and were sniffing the air for other ways to upset. They hated the girl's beauty. Anger showed in every line of their cheese-coloured faces.

'Papers,' one demanded. I reached into my pocket and pulled out my Four Powers military warrant, which had already caused some confusion as I was in civilian clothes, plus a virgin diplomatic passport.

'Papers,' they repeated. Now they were addressing the girl. She appeared frozen. A pearl-pink nail fingered the old scar.

'Where are your papers, Fraulein?'

'I'm travelling with my husband here. He is English. The rail pass is for both of us, isn't it darling? We are going to Berlin for our honeymoon,' she cooed in German. The voice was that of a little girl.

'Berlin for your honeymoon?'

The jaded officials were unconvinced. Her mood changed. 'Aren't you going to congratulate us?' she added accusingly, the hard rasping edge returning to her voice. The aggression was perfectly timed. I had just put my warrant away. All they had to do was ask for it. I would then be required to explain why her name was not written next to mine. Would they question the word of a diplomat? Their eyes indicated that they certainly would. Indeed, it would make their day. The hairs on the back of my neck began to prickle, as they always had when I did something wrong at school. To be flung into jail on the way to doing what, after all, was diplomatic penance would be the end. They would let me rot.

'Is there a problem?' I ventured in German, as innocently as possible. They hesitated, and then one leered and nudged the other. The second did not smile but, with a stiff nod, slid the door open.

'Every happiness,' he muttered morosely, and then was gone, arguing with his comrade. I felt like a spy.

'Bloody hell,' I said quietly. We had been lucky. They must have been told to avoid incidents over Christmas. The girl's mouth dimpled slightly at the side as she looked across at me. I coughed. My chest felt tight.

'What would you have done if I'd said you weren't my wife?'

She shrugged.

'You look as though you should be married, big boy. Or at least be with your mother. Anyway, I think I could have won those two idiots over . . . I mean if things had become difficult.' She waggled a long finger. As I leaned forwards she kissed me gently on the lips, then pulled tantalisingly away. I was changing my mind about trains.

'Perhaps now we should be introduced,' I said. 'Perhaps we should know to whom we are married?'

'Why?' she smiled. 'Most married people do not.'

'My name is Toby, Toby Jubb.' I was suddenly deeply infatuated. Mother always said my passions would be my undoing.

'I'm Magda, and very pleased to meet you, Toby Jubb. A moment ago I did not have a ticket and now I have a husband.' We were both looking at the thin gold ring on her left hand. 'Don't worry, Toby Jubb, my first husband is dead.'

'I'm sorry.'

'I'm not. He was a shit. They shot him for looting a children's hospital. He had found the morphine and chocolate but stopped for a Red Cross box of teddy bears. It said so in the paper. They would never have caught him if it wasn't for those bears. He was a very small man, but usually very nimble.'

'Who shot him?' I asked, wondering from her bullet scar if she too had been on the raid to steal morphine and soft toys. Stealing candy from sick babies inexplicably added to her allure.

'You did,' she said matter-of-factly, lighting another cigarette. 'You English.' She blew smoke in my face. 'Please be my husband until we get to Berlin, Toby. You were so sweet. I lost my purse and my pass is still being processed. Now I am saved by a giant Englishman.' With a movement that came mostly from her hips she was sitting beside me. 'How clever of a war baby to grow so big, Herr Jubb. What adorable blonde curls. What big blue eyes.'

She touched my forehead. A low shudder went through my body, and it was not the shaking of the train as we rattled intimately towards Berlin.

'My-er-father had an interest in some butchers' and grocers' shops.'

'Oh, yes, the black market, always the black market. Even in honest England where you have a Queen and Beefeaters.' In another theatrical change of mood and position she was sitting opposite me again, a stranger as she pulled an astrological magazine from her bag. I saw a desolation in her eyes and it wasn't for her husband. Her eyelashes were naturally long. She pushed the magazine aside after a while and turned back towards me with a pout.

'You are too young to go to Berlin, Toby. Why do you go to Berlin?'

'I've no choice. I've been sent. I was working as a diplomat in Paris.'

'Ahhh Paris. How could you leave such a city. Nothing matters in Paris. Everything is fun.'

'And there is no fun in Berlin?'

She paused. Magda was no longer smiling.

'In Berlin everything has to be paid for. It is a city built on sand by evil people. It is a crossroads. The devil has always liked crossroads. Witches meet at crossroads. I hate the place. Nothing good can grow there. Everyone seems to want it, even the holes. Everyone has guns. At a crossroads one is always forced to choose. It is so exhausting. Except now in my city all the roads lead to nowhere. Whatever we choose, it is usually bad.'

A passion had entered her voice. I was about to hold forth on what I knew about the goddess Hecate, and how she too was linked with cities built at crossroads, as indeed was Ishtar, the female deity of love and war in Babylon, my speciality. But then I noticed the garish cover of the astrological magazine and decided against such a course.

'Berlin can't be so bad,' I mumbled in the end.

'My, Toby, you are so big. So big and so innocent. So big for a little Englishman. You will look after me until we get to Berlin, no?' I nodded. I would find it hard to refuse her anything. Her soft, light olive skin accentuated the whiteness of her teeth. The barman at the Crillon had confided that you could tell a lot from a girl's teeth. Many of the girls in Paris have such putrid mouths. Great gaps punctuated by decaying teeth, or the cheap gold of a dentist lover. Magda had learned to look after herself very young. If she were twenty-five she would have only been ten when the war ended. Twenty-five seemed so impossibly sophisticated. Laughter-lines had begun to etch the corners of her eyes, but it was impossible to say for certain how old she was. Did I like her because she reminded me of my mother? In the woman that sat across from me there seemed to be the same combination of an almost masculine resolution with a disarmingly feminine enthusiasm and daring. An energy in her steady stare seemed to probe all shadowy plans and made me ashamed of my artless complexity. I thought of the envelope in my pocket containing a letter written in the waiting-room of a Paris station to my mother. An attempt to explain why I was moving from the plum posting of Paris, to the dour fortress of Berlin. I always told my mother everything. She was my confessional.

Gare de l'Est
Paris   December 27, 1960

Dear Mother,
It's Christmas, the snow is falling and your only son is in disgrace again. I was not in love with her, mother, although I did like her and felt sorry for her. One feels pity for anyone married to a tyrant. The most unsuitable people appear to be selected to represent their country's honour and interests. The affair started so innocently. She wished to learn Greek, and asked one night to come and listen to my records. Now His Excellency's wife (whom he quite often thrashed with a carpet beater bought for the purpose in Istanbul) has been packed off to an aunt near Angers, as her ladyship is French, apart from being delightfully pretty in a Pre-Raphaelite sort of way. The abominable aunt lives in a chateau, and to prevent my swimming the moat and scaling the towers, they are sending me to Berlin, although not to the Legation. I'm to help in 'Personnel' for the Allied Kommandatura, whatever that means. In other words, I am being sent to Siberia. Oh woe, how the sins of the flesh pull us down. My ailing career has taken a turn for the worse. To add insult to ignominy, I am under the military I took such pains to avoid, and have an honorary commission; so if I step out of line this time, someone will probably put me up against a wall and shoot me. But seriously,

your Toby is a soldier boy now, *me miserum*, though no one has issued me with a uniform of ours or any army, and one should be grateful for that small mercy. Yes, it's Christmas, Mother, the snow is falling and I give you a big kiss under the mistletoe, even if I am dished. I'm sure Berlin will not be that bad. Burn a candle for me,

Love and kisses,
Toby

'What do your parents do?' I asked Magda, thoughtless and very English.

'Putrefy, I think is the correct English word, Toby. Like Berlin, I am an orphan. Is that not exciting? One day I shall be an actress. I will be able to tell such outlandish and embroidered stories to the newspapers and people will say, "Ahhhh . . . poor girl". I love to think of such things when I have a bath. I have a friend who has a huge apartment with a big marble bath I fill with bubbles. I give interviews to *Time* Magazine in that bath. In that bath I am as famous as Pears soap. I shall then fill the bath with emeralds and pearls and drown in them. I shall be rich and powerful and still beautiful.'

She blew me a kiss, and without another word lay back in her seat and closed her eyes. It was not until near our arrival that she opened them again. I watched her all the way. My mother had the same guilty fiddles with her fingers. Mother said she loved father, but her first love was for her dancing and then just for life; a powerful, celebratory emotion never to be confused with caring. She made him cry and I seemed to love her all the more, even when I saw him shedding tears over the tiny wooden ballet dancer in a musical cigarette box. I did not want to be like Papa who constantly lied to himself. The Jubbs had been enthusiastic builders of bridges and dams throughout the British empire, but dear Papa saw more of a future in being a cabbage king in the retail trade when the world was hungry, and made a small fortune through what he claimed was Christian hard work. He also liked to labour under the impression that my mother was taking piano lessons, while even I, the large and awkward only child, knew she was with her current lover, who usually did something more interesting (she once was seen in Wallingford taking tea with a notorious armed robber). Papa never went to war, as he said his business could not spare him. His consoling passion was a model village he built in a corner of our huge garden, a project equal in its way to any Jubb construction of the past. He began with a painstaking copy of the village of Faringdon, but as my mother's adulteries increased he progressed to the Pyramids, the Great Wall of China and the Hanging Gardens of Babylon, although I am sure every brick and stone was a secret tear. Perversely, it awoke my interest in the ancient world. But I always had to know the uncomfortable truth about those I loved; even when it stung in the eyes like school carbolic. I hated pretence and pretenders.

One cannot easily explain an obsession. I sat watching as Magda looked down at what were obviously brand-new, white high-heeled shoes. She frowned for an instant, peering at the hardly-scuffed soles to see if they were worn. From that moment I loved her.

'Can I see you in Berlin?' I began nervously. 'We could go dancing. What sort of music do you like? Buddy Holly? I have all his hits. Even Peggy Sue on American import.' Perhaps there was something odd and a little naïve about a junior diplomat seconded to the military authorities in Berlin, who had read Classics and Ancient Persian at Oxford and written a well-received paper on his hero, the fifth century B C Greek traveller and rogue, Herodotus of Halicarnassus, not to mention a bit of archaeology on the side, yet whose brown leather suitcase bulged with Buddy Holly, the Everly Brothers and Sam Cooke. I always joked to my mother that I had to seek the shelter of a college or an embassy because of my size. No one takes you seriously when you are seriously outsize in a shrinking country. Magda delayed her answer for as long as possible, underlining my impetuousness. She understood the virtue of drawing down the blinds; of using every wall and border.

'Of course,' she eventually replied. Shouts could be heard coming from either side of the track. A horrible grinding noise shuddered through the floor. 'We are getting near,' she observed, fumbling in her bag and scribbling on a piece of paper.

'I will be there from tomorrow night. Ring or call if you want to. If you don't, it doesn't matter. We have had a wonderful marriage.'

'Have you time for a coffee?'

'I'm meeting someone. He's French.'

'Is he your boyfriend?'

'My what?'

Magda put her hand to her mouth and muffled a tinkling laugh. I felt myself blushing. My military-style raincoat seemed more than a nip and a tuck too small. But something inside registered that my young, though not entirely innocent world, had really begun to turn.

'Oh, I understand,' I said, lifting down the heavy leather suitcase she hardly seemed big enough to carry. Excited, I tried to imagine what contraband lay inside. 'By the way, what do you do in Berlin, Magda?'

'What do I do, Toby? I make people happy. It's the most marvellous job in the world.'

I wondered how she was going to get through the ticket barrier as we slid into Berlin Zoo station. Suddenly, Magda moved close to me and planted a kiss at the corner of my mouth which sent a shiver through my body. She clutched at my lapel as we came to a halt. I closed my eyes. When I opened them she was part of the shuffle and shove of the corridor, dragging the suitcase after her with a feline strength, like a cat dragging a hare. She vanished in a heaving sea of gaberdine and khaki. I felt very anxious for this girl who travelled free and made people happy.

Only as I reached to get my own case did I notice my wallet containing fifty pounds in English notes was missing. Mercifully, she had left my passports. Jubb had been shunted, no doubt like many before him, into a siding. Slowly, I tugged my bag onto a platform in a station that really was the end of the line. Yes, I had never intended to meet Magda, but she had certainly been looking for someone like me.

If I was not careful, Berlin would be the end of my limitations.

2

Magda, if that was her name, was long gone. Berliner Zoo station, so called because it is near the zoological gardens in the Western sector of the city, was an anomalous part of the GDR. A notice reminded the traveller of the fact. So did the East German soldiers, looking as if they had been recruited that day and were still heartbroken about leaving the family pig. A small boy was peering at a dead rat being buried between the rails by snowflakes. Moon-faced women sat on bags of grain and chewed, content as cows despite the sub-zero cold, while what appeared to be half of Europe pushed and shoved along the platform. For an unnerving second I glimpsed a man with a black top hat and monocle. He was as unexpected as the modern rectanguloid city of West Berlin which blew in through the open sides of the windy station. A sharp-edged city with no time for curves. I blinked at the light. An advertisement for Mercedes on an office block dominated a landmark I remembered from newsreels, the church without a spire, the Kaiser-Wilhelm-Gedächtniskirche, blasted half down by the best intentions of the Royal Air Force. The frenetic process of rebuilding was going on next to the ruin. An open-topped, camouflage green Buick drew up to disgorge American servicemen. One kicked a can as they made for a group of waiting girls. The concrete and glass and bustle were not the city I had expected. A fat woman with bloated apple cheeks struck me on the chest with a ham. I had stepped on her toe. I made for the ticket barrier, while trying to apologise to the woman who began to hit me again and pursued me along the platform, swearing. A third blow made me stagger as practised hands took my bags.

For a moment I thought I was being robbed for the second time in half a country.

'Quit, lady, or I'll shove your baby where no light shines. Bastards, if you ask me, the average German,' began my rescuer, giving the woman an expert push in the direction of the grain sacks. 'Give them a bit of food and they're soon too big for their boots again. You should have been here after the war. The chicks would sleep with you for a pack of Chiclets. Meek as apples. Kind as rice pudding. Now they got money again. We should have sent them up the chimney . . . You'll be Jubb. Pleased to meet you, I'm sure. My name's Weitz. Your car is waiting, your lordship. I'm your driver. An American taxpayer who was a millionaire last week is your driver. Shift your butt, Hermann.' At the barrier they obviously knew my new companion and waved us through. Mr Weitz gave the guard a cigar.

'I take it you don't like it here, then?' I said, trying to keep up with the much smaller man.

He stopped and glared at me. 'Like it, I love it,' he said accusingly.

'But I thought you . . .'

'No buts in Berlin. No ifs, either. You gets on with it. Everyone loves Berlin. As a posting it sounds seriously hazardous to the girls back home, but it's safer than being blown apart by some Chink or Arab, take it from me. I've seen genuine hundred per cent warfare and believe me, this cold war stuff is far better. Less danger of getting dead. Here is the car. Now, nice Colonel Midwinter told me, take the new man down for a quiet smoke and a coffee at the Kranzler while I do my shopping, so that's what I'm going to do. Then bring him up to Kindergarten Number Nine. We'll wash his balls in turpentine. Make them shine. That's one of the Colonel's little jokes. In between times he races horses.'

'Kindergarten what?' I was beginning to feel at sea.

'Number Nine. None other than the headquarters of the slimy limey British Military Intelligence and wick dipping. It's in Wedding, near the Red sector border. In Berlin, Wedding's a district, not a misfortune. The Kindergarten used to be for growing Hitlers.

13

Part of it is still for Allied forces brats. No kidding. Fools no one though, everyone knows it's spooktown.' ·

'But I'm a diplomat . . .'

The American grinned.

'Well, you are halfway there. Halfway there already. Polite lies are all part of it. All part of it . . .'

He left me on the pavement outside a café made of glass; an aquarium of sleek creatures whose thick-lipped mouths opened and closed around things much sweeter than what lay behind their frowns. I needed to stretch my legs, and dodged around a tram and across a highway even I knew was called the Kurfürstendamm. In a few moments, I was in a district of little streets and squares which had never been touched by blast bomb or incendiary. Houses from the comfortable half of the last century, in leafy avenues which seemed almost surprised at the occasional blemish of war on their impeccably bourgeois façades. Yet they held a mystery for me far greater than Paris, which, because of my mother, I was almost as familiar with as London. Berlin was different. I reached forward and touched the dark stones of a doorway which on the year I was born had felt the rumbling shock of the first RAF bombs. As I suckled at my mother's breast – a mother who was part Jewish but, like most Russians, hid the fact like a guilty family secret – men in black uniforms, with strange armbands emblazoned in crosses with black and white and red, visited sweethearts in these quiet streets away from the storm. Berlin to me was as exotic as the ancient Babylon I had studied at Magdalen only six months before. The girl on the train was right. Berlin was still an evil place. A thrill ran through my hands on the stones of the doorway and under the cobblestones beneath my feet though I was nowhere near a U-Bahn underground station. Was I imagining things? Yet a city cannot change in a few short years. One cannot easily erase such wickedness.

'Young man? Young man? Are you American?'

I glanced down into the fat and happy face of a middle-aged lady who was beaming up at me. She carried a heavy shopping basket. Her terrier barked at my turn-ups.

'If you take my advice, you'll forget her. No use mooning around closed doors at your age,' she continued in German. 'Would you like to come in for a cup of tea?' she added in English. 'I do so like

American boys. My husband is American. He is an engineer.' I wanted to retreat to the reassuring brash modernity of the Kurfürstendamm, more than a little confused. Our dreams of places can sometimes change the scenery.

'No, thank you. *Guten Tag*.'

'*Guten Tag*, American.'

The Café Kranzler was full, and martial carols played over slatted wood loudspeakers. A matronly waitress brought me a pot of coffee and a slice of chocolate gateau without my asking, as if I were a small boy, or an American. Outside, the cold and grey was ripped apart by a barrage of electric light. Across the street the art nouveau Café Möhring looked decidedly underdressed and old, as the crowd pushed past on the Kurfürstendamm. Several girls in summer dresses and high boots shivered in the bitter wind, and took turns to shelter in a battered Ford with their pimp. Down a nearby alley, a sign in purple neon unambiguously winked: Sex, Sex, Sex.

I was quickly beginning to realise, within the warm glass womb of the rebuilt Kranzler, with the black-stockinged, white-pinnied girls rushing back and forth, that even the little I had seen of Berlin did not square with the 1940s travel book I had purloined from the Embassy library in Paris. I knew from school history lessons that the sandy infertile soil of the Mark of Brandenburg wasn't really good for growing anything except bayonets, marching bands and the odd equestrian statue. Berlin had to expand because there was nothing at home worth stealing. The Prussians fortified their sandcastle with the perverse pride of people who have fuck all. Defence very soon became attack and Berlin the hub of a German Empire, the living cliché of a German Industrial city, always more polyglot than Paris, the cradle of cabaret, satire and inflation, a gallery of rogues who became little princes in the golden twenties. Men not unlike my father, except they had more fun. All before Mr Hitler reduced it to sand again. Now the Allies had got out their buckets and spades. From my seat I could see the chromium palace of an American car showroom which displayed an election poster. On the horizon of my *Schokoladentorte*, the bear of Brandenburg appeared to have been tamed.

'Do I have to learn all this half-assed crap?' A deep Texan voice came from behind thriving spider plants which divided my booth from the one next door. The well-tailored, carefully pressed

15

uniforms of the United States army were arranged neatly between the burgers and old ladies as if for the purpose of decoration. 'I don't believe there was a German fucking resistance.'

'Please, Major,' came a tremulous answer as I peered through the leaves. 'Let's go over it again. You have to address Herr Brandt and the others in an hour. We have to show we understand them, colonel. At the moment, history is all these folk have. It's dangerous to take away a person's pride in his past.' I caught a glimpse of a chaplain's crosses on the earnest man's shirt collar. The Major had started a cigar.

'Oh yeah. Founded in the eleventh century by a bunch of river pirates . . . You know, preacher, the only bit I really like is those Dadaists with that loony painter George Grosz organising races between sewing-machines and typewriters and where everyone got their oats at the Central Dada Sex Office. They certainly knew how to have fun. But do you know the only thing that matters, preacher?'

'No, Major.'

'We fucking beat them. No, they can kiss my ass if they think I'm learning about some Elector of Brandenburg just to please some phoneys. Any resistance went up the chimney at Auschwitz. Yes, sir, we beat them.' Silence and smoke drifted through the spider plants with a desperate finality. The waitresses neither turned to left nor right as they sprinted with the orders. No one had heard the Major, it seemed, except me, the preacher and whatever gods haunted the Café Kranzler. The speakers were playing the German version of Silent Night.

Sex, Sex, Sex, winked the neon sign, down the sidestreet.

'All is calm, all is bright . . . Sleep in heavenly peace . . . Sleep in heavenly peace,' commanded the carollers on the loudspeakers, as another hundredweight of cake was dispensed to the respectable multitude with a clockwork precision.

My Gallic travel book much preferred Berlin beaten, with the old Prussian sandcastle marooned in a hostile sea. A plague victim effectively quarantined. The author was as viciously sympathetic as only the French can be about someone they truly hate. 'Berlin, as you will see is a city shattered to cobblestones . . . doubtful whether it will rise again . . . famous for its sausages and for an uninteresting type of doughnut known as a *Berliner* . . . the uncertain political climate makes it a place of ambiguous charm for the more adventurous tourist. But, kind traveller, pity poor Berlin . . .' The fifty-year-old woman opposite me in her black mink coat did not need any help consuming her third slice of cake as strong jaws worked rhythmically behind an over-made-up mask. A giant sea anemone sucking down her prey in a favourite rock pool. I shuddered. Lipstick stuck to her dentures. The diamond ring on her index finger could probably have bought a modest chocolate factory. Magda's late husband had been shot for less than the woman consumed in a week.

'My stars, Jubb.'

'Parr.'

'Captain Parr said he knew you,' muttered the returned Weitz, who looked suddenly smaller and furtive, like an animal conscious of the beast stalking it. I knew how Mr Weitz felt. Anthony Selwyn Parr was the last person I wanted to meet under the Christmas decorations of the Kurfürstendamm.

'Hello, Parr,' I said as coolly as possible. Politeness made me take the bony hand, which pumped mine enthusiastically though I could not imagine why. On the boyish face with its lank, straight fair hair falling across the forehead was a deceptively cheerful look, as if a five-year-old had been given the keys to a toyshop. He was wearing a British Warm and his pink face was reflected in his shoes. At school I had been Parr's fag. He had made me do everything.

'Not as clean as when you did them, I'll bet.' Parr effortlessly said the wrong thing. He had that infuriatingly superior English manner that would have driven St Francis of Assisi to homicide; a straight-bat, stiff-lipped defensiveness born more of a feeling of inferiority than power. 'Hear you were at college, Jubb. Always were a bit of a brainbox. Hope there are no hard feelings about school. One had responsibilities. Spot on, you've joined up. The army needs big chaps. Clever chaps too.'

'Glad to hear it. Actually, I'm not in the army, Parr.' I replied as casually as I could but the angular man ignored me. He was insufferably optimistic, always poised for the final victory; no valley of death was long enough to make him think twice. At school he wasn't so much a sadist as a moral eunuch; the gelding on which the Empire once galloped. He was four years older than me and should have been as extinct as the dinosaur. His mouth opened slightly and

I could see his large front teeth. He wrinkled his nose in what passed for a smile.

'Been back to the old Alma Mater?'

'No, Parr, I've been in Paris.'

'And now you've come to help us win the war in Berlin?'

'Help you?'

'You are under Colonel Midwinter in Kindergarten Number Nine. Well, I am too. Terribly exciting. I was hoping for Malaya but Berlin is vital, really vital. We can be pals if you like. Pals now, Jubb. Hard cheese about school.' He hit me playfully on the shoulder and insisted on settling the bill. Parr's nature was to control, whatever the cost.

'Let's give him the guided tour, Weitz,' he said as we settled back into the leather seats of the Mercedes. The winter's day was darkening. Parr rattled off landmarks and I did my best to ignore him. I was beginning to feel bilious.

'Down there is Unter den Linden. Over there is what is left of the Reichstag. Here is the Tiergarten. A real killing ground once. Growing again now. Must be all the bodies. Jolly good manure.' In front of us stood the Brandenburg Gate. Soldiers in capes were stopping cars as it started to sleet.

'Wanna cross?' asked Weitz. But Parr was still in a world of his own.

'. . . do you know, nearly half the buildings were flattened? Pretty efficient job of work by the RAF. Really bashed up the old Hun. Now fifteen years later, thanks to all the king's men, Humpty is nearly back together again . . .' I felt Mr Weitz wince. Parr loved statistics. At school he had spent hours poring over text books and re-fighting the battle of Waterloo while everyone else had been devoted to Health and Efficiency and self-abuse. His father had been a general.

'Do we cross or don't we?'

'No, thank you, Weitz. Take us to the Kindergarten. I have work to do.' Parr sounded irritated at being interrupted. When we left the leafy parkland the increasing number of bomb sites gave an inkling of what inspired Parr's enthusiasm. Entire blocks were missing. Like an archaeologist one had gently to search for clues in order to piece together the past.

'Are they strict about crossing over to the East?'

'Crossing's far too easy at the moment,' retorted Parr. 'Too many smugglers and racketeers. Scum. But we do what we can, don't we, Weitz?' The American remained silent and Parr did not elaborate. At the corner of one bombsite we drew up outside a long, low grey building all on its own. Above the entrance one could still make out the 'Kin' of Kindergarten. Two plump women were both thrashing children as they emerged from inside. They passed us on the steps.

'You dirty boy. Wait till I get you home. You shouldn't put poo-poos in Mrs Big Bunny's basket. I don't know what we are going to do with you. You'll grow up to be a Teddy boy, mark my words . . .'

Parr looked appalled. 'Civilians . . .' he began, opening the car door. 'Remember, it's a challenge here, Jubb,' he added and then mercifully was gone, bounding up the Kindergarten steps. Mr Weitz breathed again and I followed him into the building. What caught my eye, below a noticeboard with several berserk drawings of the Queen Mother, was a six foot rabbit painted on hardboard. The animal had cruel, flat blue eyes which followed you around, and strangely twisted limbs. Emblazoned on a basket decorated with paper fruit and flowers hanging around the demented animal's waist, and containing a collection box for war orphans, was the legend 'Mrs Big Bunny Loves Good Children'. Mr Weitz noticed my interest.

'One of the teachers found an old Hitler Youth Swastika with a young stormtrooper painted on it down in the basement. She daubed over it using a Mrs Big Bunny colouring book as a model. That's why the legs are twisted on account of them being part of the swastika. She said she could not improve on the eyes of the original.' He smirked, and left me in a classroom with tiny chairs and pictures of Hertfordshire villages, which had long since become towns, adorning the dingy walls. I found it hard to imagine I had ever been that small. Chalkdust covered everything.

'Ah, Mr Jubb? My Mr Jubb.' Before me stood a man who could have easily passed for a headmaster of a public school. He had the same, bruised, slightly shop-soiled superiority which puts any pupil off teaching for life. He looked formidable enough to be a don. Yet there was an amused sparkle behind the pince-nez.

'My name's Midwinter. Do come through. Drop of sherry or Scotch perhaps?' He beckoned me into a room across the hall.

'Sherry would be nice, sir.' I hadn't intended to call him sir. He looked me in the face for a full half-minute, his pale eyes never blinking.

'Jolly well done, Jubb.'

'Sir?'

'Jolly well done to grow so big, Jubb.'

As I stared at him he handed me a Fernet Branca. 'Jolly well done, I'd say. Shows British spunk. It's what we fought a war for, my boy, so that people can grow as tall as they want without some short-arse megalomaniac interfering. Bit of a drawback when it comes to covert operations though, spying and that sort of nonsense. Sherry all right, is it?' His piercing stare made me look away. On the wall behind the desk were photographs of racehorses, two of which were upside down.

'Fallers, Jubb. Two of my best yearlings. Necks broken. Crack! they go like a pistol shot. It's a hobby of mine. Bloodstock, I mean.' A copy of *Timeform* lay open over a leather-bound volume of Rupert Brooke. He picked up a file with my name on it and began to turn the pages and shake his head.

'I'm not so sure I'd breed from you, Jubb. Not sure at all. Not from reading this . . .'

I took a sip of warm Fernet Branca and wished I hadn't. Midwinter was holding the folder as if it contained rotten fish.

'I particularly like the bit where you try to hide in the armoire when the ambassador comes into the bedroom and the bloody thing falls over. Shades of *Tartuffe*, what, though someone of your size would have a job hiding behind ladies' crinolines. Don't be embarrassed, old boy. At least you prefer the fillies. It's almost unique for me to get my hands on someone intelligent and sexually ordinary. Homosexuality is so fashionable. I have a theory it's something to do with wartime powdered egg. Anyway, that's why I rescued you. Remember, Mrs Big Bunny Loves Good Children.' He lit an untipped Players Senior Service and offered me one, snapping the gold case shut before I had time to reply.

'Did you say you rescued me, sir?'

'Yes, Jubb, that's exactly what I said and did. They were going to rusticate you. His Excellency began making inquiries about having you doctored under the Official Secrets Act, not to mention charges of espionage and criminal damage over the armoire. Perhaps it would have helped if his wife had not been tied to the bed with her stockings . . . Mrs Midwinter has not asked me to do that for many a year.'

'I didn't think they would mention the intimate details, sir. Is it on my file? I mean will it remain on my diplomatic service file?'

'Black stockings, Jubb.' Midwinter licked his thin red lips. 'Afraid so, Jubb, all that and more. Frilly, French bedroom fancies, Jubb. Things that would spice a wet weekend at Bognor but nobble you in public life; even if they would be thought quite the thing in the public bars. Damn lucky I was in Paris and able to calm His Excellency down. Remind him of his own intemperate youth. Then he told me all about you. *Alles*! I said you were just the chap for my dubious purposes and bought you with a mediocre lunch and a bottle of forty-five Lafite at Maxim's.' He waved the file in front of him. 'If you're a really good boy, Jubb, this can go into the dustbin and you can save it all for the memoirs. I understand you are particularly hot on Persian culture; brilliant first class honours. Your tutor Pennington filled me in. That's good too.' He beamed at his own mysteries like a cat in front of a fire.

'What is it you want me to do, sir?'

'Well, that's delicate, Jubb. So delicate it's hard to find the right words. Our little secret. But I don't want to keep you guessing.'

'They said administration.'

'Yes, in a way . . .'

He paused. I had depressing visions of translating the Colonel's entire filing system into ancient Persian for security purposes.

'Promise me it will be our little secret?'

'Naturally, sir.'

'I want you to run a brothel.'

The statement made time appear to stand still and hang in the air like the layers of blue-grey smoke from the Colonel's Senior Service. I was reminded of when, after a few spoonfuls of blancmange, my maternal grandmother had experienced a lucid moment and had gone on to describe the private parts of Edward, Prince of Wales, in stunning detail. The silence was the same, except for a tumble of coke in the grate. Outside, it was still just light and snowing heavily. On a piece of wasteland stood a single tree and in its branches, silhouetted against the white, was a crow. The bird hopped down to forage among the frosty rubble. Midwinter moved nimbly around the desk and put his hand on my shoulder.

'We don't want to be a faller at the first fence, do we, Jubb?'

'No, sir. A brothel, sir?'

'A brothel, Jubb.'

Her Majesty the Queen looked enigmatically down from a photograph over the fireplace.

'But why . . . Why me?'

'Do you know, I said exactly the same thing when they parachuted me into France during the last war. Couldn't speak a word, not a word, but learned a lot about horses. Only chaps to talk to. More or less ended up running the national stud, by complete accident of course. Do you remember the Berlin airlift, Jubb? We really got caught with our pants down that time and when I took this job I said to myself, Midwinter, that's not going to happen to you.' The voice had lost its donnish friendliness. 'The thing is, all this American lolly floating about has made West Berlin too damn attractive. Hermann the German realises it's not very smart to be a good comrade in the East on cabbage stew when you can come to the West and eat steak, or at least watch other people doing it through restaurant windows and decide to become a criminal. At present we are getting one refugee a minute through a border with virtually no restrictions. It cannot go on. East Berlin is bleeding to death, Jubb. Even that silly little sausage-eater Walter Ulbricht who pads around in fluffy women's slippers and pretends to run the show will have to do something. Personally, I don't think the man could organise a point-to-point. The thing is, I want to know what and when and how. I want a man in the opposition's stables. We know their senior soldiers sneak across here for a bit of tail once in a while. You will provide it, Jubb. Then we can reckon up their handicap.' He stubbed his cigarette out and quickly lit another as he returned to his desk and consulted a second file.

'If you catch me a really big fish, Jubb, one who will talk and come over to our side of the track, well, the slate is wiped clean. Not to beat about the bush, I'm interested in a character called Baron Rollo von Hollmann. A protégé of Rommel. One of the Nazis' brightest young tank commanders. Iron Cross with oak leaves and double sauerkraut, that sort of monkey. The Eastie Beasties have pulled him out of prison and put him in charge of a tank unit. They have conveniently forgotten the man's penchant for the odd atrocity. Rollo is a very capable man, but he does love the good things in life and we have been keeping an eye on him. We know, from our resident racketeer Mr Weitz, he has even visited the famous Blue Angel, popping over with a few senior officers among the thousands who come to work in the West every day, but he always returns. Weitz has all the dreadful details. In particular, Rollo has a weakness for women, which is why we want to be in a position to be able to offer him and others like him the services of a discreet knocking shop. You and Rollo should get on like a house on fire. Don't let me down, my boy. Please don't be a faller!' One look into those grey eyes removed any possibility that this was some sort of bizarre initiative test.

'You've no idea what the airlift and subsequent blockade was like,' he added after a few moments. 'The town was full of every sort of mad hatter ringing Liberty Bells against communism. Do you know they even brought over the Royal Shakespeare Company to give us Webster's *White Devil*? I opened my door one morning for a step around the Grunewald to find a delegation of American women Baptists dressed as crusaders wanting to pray with everyone in the street. Had them arrested. How on earth one is meant to look after one's horses while trapped in a lunatic asylum I don't know. Do you think you're up to it, Jubb? Do you think you can organise an orgy in a brothel, if not for the benefit of freedom and democracy, at least for the St Leger, this poor soul's Hampshire stables and the sport of kings? Help me, Jubb. Be a good boy. Let me down, and you could find yourself on your way to the knacker's yard.' For the first time since school I felt that telling pang of fear in my solar plexus. High up on the walls of Midwinter's study was a frieze of nursery school characters; transfers on paint yellow with tobacco. We were both looking at Mr Wolf. Mr Wolf had big teeth and was about to eat a chicken.

'What exactly does Parr have to do with all this, if you don't mind my asking?'

'Oh, but I do, Jubb. Parr's talents lie in a different direction. We call on him at our peril. Now, have I made things quite clear?'

'Yes, sir.' In the circumstances there seemed little else to say. I did not have deep-seated moral objections. To me, sexual morality seemed rather like trigonometry; a back-of-the-envelope sum where sinners calculated the angle of society's design while following their own sweet tangent.

'Where is the place, sir? Does it come equipped with a staff?' The idea of being in the front line of the Cold War was depressing: something I associated with the older generation like toupees, bunions and, to put it plainly, brothels. Brothels are positively Babylonian.

'Thinking like a professional already, Jubb. The place is in the Kreuzberg area. Yes, it has a staff and is run by a Frenchman. Horrid man, horrid. Made of syphilis scabs and old cloakroom tickets. Since the war the Frogs have been claiming diplomatic rights on this building in the British sector. The place was originally a brothel for high-ranking staff of the Luftwaffe and before that had played host to the crowned heads of Europe. There is also another reason why I chose you, Jubb. The old diplomatic residence and adjoining building, which is I believe a bakery, is to be officially handed over at midnight. Rather like one of our old colonies going wog. With your knowledge of the French this should not present a problem. Disgusting man, *le patron*. Here, have some money.'

Midwinter tossed a wad of notes across the desk and they came to rest against the glass of Fernet Branca.

'What if *le patron* doesn't want to go?'

'Weitz will come along and hold your hand. He is an extremely low-lived American we were going to send to prison but he should be of some use. Here's a copy of his PF—22 personal file. Weitz is a clever little man. He alone knows what the fornicating Baron looks like, as we have no current picture. Don't worry about le patron. His own people will take care of him. We are a little island in a sea of troubles, Jubb. However, the occupying forces have tremendous powers. Berlin is a colony. Think of it that way and you can't go far wrong. The military here are the direct successors to Dönitz, the last Chancellor of the Third Reich. We can shoot a housewife for having a carving knife. I can shoot you.'

With a magician's dexterity he conjured a pearl-handled revolver of the type used by Roy Rogers from behind the desk. He had cocked the hammer and pulled the trigger on an empty chamber before I could feel surprised.

'Bang, bang, Jubb. Do give this to the reprobate American. He tells an amusing story about how he stole it from General Patton.

Another of his elaborate lies. He is waiting for you. He has all the minor details.' Midwinter was watching me closely. On his finger was a Masonic ring. He stood up and so did I.

'Did you like your sherry, Jubb?'

'What do I do with the money I make, sir?'

He sighed.

'I want information, Jubb, not the profits of pimpery. Do what you like with it. Plough it back into the business. Spend it on a fancywoman in Baden Baden for all I care. By the way, any communication, and I discourage it, is to be on British Council notepaper and never specific and, if possible, in crayon. We try to maintain the pretence we are educational.'

I lingered.

'What is it now, my boy?'

'Why did you say it was an advantage I knew about the ancient Persians?' Midwinter sat down at his desk and put his feet up on the table. His shoes were solid English brogues.

'In espionage, Jubb, we have to be allowed some surprises ... Oh, and Jubb.'

'Yes, sir?'

'Do beware of Mr Wolf ...'

Later, since I had an hour to kill as Mr Stigi Weitz was otherwise engaged with Colonel Midwinter, I cadged a lift into the centre and was dropped again by the Kaiser Wilhelm Memorial Church. Building work was in progress next to the sooty old memorial. The dirt was in contrast to the surrounding concrete and glass and neon. Dirt from another era, which if the passers-by noticed at all they possibly regarded as quaint. A yellow crane was lifting a large crate into place. A man in a leather jerkin waved it to the ground, and two important-looking colleagues in suits clutching papers watched nervously as it was opened with a crowbar. The wooden door removed, the workman pulled out packing to reveal a statue of Christ. The men in suits shook hands. Yet the figure was unlike any image of the Son of God I had ever seen. I walked nearer the barrier. The statue had obviously been in the bombing. Shrapnel wounds still complemented those made by the centurion's spear and the crucifixion nails. Christ had been away for refurbishment. The holes left by the casings of blast bombs had been filled in; His marble skin smoothed. Yet they could not change the expression in those eyes. The most angry, scalded, incensed eyes in the world. The anger was not with His own wounds but directed outwards. He was angry with the fat, complacent Berlin which passed Him by. He seemed angry that nothing had been learned.

He was looking at me. He was looking directly at me.

I could not get those eyes out of my mind as I sat in a bar, drinking a small glass of lager. Burly men of the 89th Airborne Division were talking loudly of a football game they had won against another unit. Two crumpled old locals watched them from underneath Homburg hats, bought cheap and too big at the pawn shop. They drew on thin cigarettes. I amused myself by reading Stigi's file which Midwinter had given me as I left, and I had tucked in my brief-case. Stigi was coming to join me. In another corner sat a man in an expensive overcoat, staring into space. I could sit and dream like that. In the Bodleian library in Oxford I used to dream my way back into the Classics. Characters turned out to be quite different from the personalities revealed in dry pages. I often imagined I was Herodotus' clerk, or the man himself. My tutors said my essays sounded as if I had been there. In a way, I had . . .

'Hey Stigi! Get me a chick . . .' shouted an American.

My new friend ignored the order.

'Come along, Mr Englishman. I'm gonna show you your place of work. Let's take a ride. Let's take a ride to Babylon. Easy . . . you'll soon see what I mean.'

3

'Dr-e-e-eam-Dream-Dream-Dream,' sing the Everly Brothers. Sometimes I dream when I'm standing up. By the banks of the Isis I would often go to Babylon. I dream all the time. I just can't help myself . . .

The worn stones of the old caravan road are hot under my new sandals. In the indistinct precision of a mirage towers the fantastical Blue Gate of Babylon, the sacred gate of Ishtar, the dark Venus of the East. For a moment I cannot catch my breath, but from wonder (and I am not prone to exaggeration), not the choking dust stirred up by the pilgrim crowds, who are milling outside the city walls in a fetid, singing, shouting mass and forcing me into Babylon. If only I had had the sense to buy that horse in Palmyra . . . But the Gate. Ten thousand, thousand tiles the colour of the deepest sea rise abruptly from the desert adorning cliff-like portals taller than twenty grown men. From that unforgiving, adamantine surface leap the guardians of the city; the sacred bulls of Raman and the sirrush, the dragon of Babylon with the head of a snake and the legs of a cheetah and the talons of a hawk and the sting of a scorpion . . .

'I used to have a sirrush for a pet when I lived in Scythia,' says a poxy-looking Chaldean, pulling at my cloak. 'You're a Greek aren't you, mate? Yes, a sirrush is ten times more vicious than a mastiff. Keeps you safe, a sirrush does. Folk respect a sting in the tail. Do you want to buy one, mate?' I ignore him.

A Massegetae, from his headdress, hysterical in the heat-and-rib-bending crush suddenly bites the man in front and pushes for all he's worth. A worrying occurrence, as the tribe have the habit of including their senior citizens in a general sacrifice of cattle and then gobbling them up, boiled in vinegar and water.

'Stop pushing, can't you?'

In front of me a child is coughing and crying at the dirty rivulets of milk on his distracted mother's breast. The woman is having her fortune told from the contours of her ear. A beggar, hand outstretched for the charity of the babbling, shin-kicking tide is knocked from his palm-wood crutches and does not rise. Make a wish when you go through the Blue Gate, and legend says it will be granted. (I only wish you would believe me, or I will be condemned like my kinsman, Herodotus.) The sun glints on the golden helmets of Persian archers, stretching their bows on the battlements. Now we are inside. I advance with more than a little of the numbing dread a sacrifice feels on the way to guarantee the water and crops of the most wicked, enchanted city in the known world; the perfumed city of the fallen Nebuchadnezzar. In a gentle breeze, above the dull smells of common man are those of myrtle, sandalwood and sweet dates, of the quiet gardens said to lie beyond. The cool flowing water and laughter among the many fountains . . .

'Bastards! Unbelievers! Idolaters! Whoremongers!' I am now in the Processional Street of Lions, a street where the same brilliant lapis-lazuli tiles are decorated with scores of life-size cats: proud beasts who are no one's servants, curling their tails as if to pounce on the unwashed pilgrims to the sacrifice. 'Back to the desert, you stinking cunts. The best bit of you ran down your mother's leg . . . You only came here for the whores and to see the blood flow. I, Daniel, chief satrap of Babylon and servant of the only true God, Jehovah, say this . . .'

The speaker, a small, proud man with mad eyes, sways under a silken awning where vendors are selling fig and palm wines and other strong drink. The piercing note of the drunken Daniel's voice seems to subvert the blast of the ram's horns and the beat of the sacred processional drum, made, I am told, from infant's buttock skin. Women supplicants of heartbreaking beauty laugh behind their hands, their dark eyes streaked with Kohl; their black hair laced with blue ribbons and hung with tinkling silver bells. By them,

28

between two enormous eunuchs, is a trussed youth. His hair is full of flowers. His fear on that road to certain death will be heavy with the scents of sandalwood and myrrh. A priestess beckons. In the dark of the temple of Bel Marduk it will be misleadingly cool and peaceful beneath the immense golden statue of fantastic worth as she reaches for the knife, the flaying, butchering knife, hidden in a veil of silk.

'You are all going to fucking well burn in the eternal fires of hell. Frightened by Bel Marduk's furnace? My brothers walked out of that. But wait till you see hell and your eyeballs melt down your pretty cheeks. Free that boy!' shouts the small brown man, determined to spoil the occasion. 'Hasn't what Daniel says always been the doom of tyrants?'

'He's well pissed,' says a voice angrily.

'Well pissed.'

'Let's stone him.'

'Stone him! Stone the Jew!' cry other souls in the crowd. But before anyone can hurl anything at Daniel, the pissed chief satrap of Babylon, trumpets blow on the azure battlements. There is a terrifying sound of whips and chariot wheels. The dust settles and the pilgrims flee as best they can, and I am crouched looking at the Persian battle chariots of King Darius's regiment of the Immortals. A woman lies whimpering, crushed by an immense spiked wheel. No one moves to help her, except drunken Daniel the satrap. Worse still, the dignified man in the leading chariot, on which hang the carcasses of two lions, wears the sacred helmet of boar's tusks. He is Darius, King of Kings; the greatest ruler the world has ever seen. A cohort of his Immortal Guard swarm through the gate. A man who runs in disorientated panic towards the dignified figure of Darius is impaled on a sword. A spearhead forces me to kneel. Only Daniel is left standing, swaying slightly.

'The king has been hunting!' says the captain of the guard in the second chariot. It is simply a description, not an excuse for the dead and injured. 'Bend your knee before the greatest of rulers . . .' The greatest of rulers looks almost embarrassed. What is more he has a bandage round his head. He has toothache. Few things are more dangerous than an absolute ruler with toothache.

Daniel, of course, ignores the command to kneel.

'Look what brought in the cat . . . or look what the fucking cat brought in . . .' says Daniel, leaving the woman who has stopped whimpering and taking a step towards the chariot.

The air seems to stiffen. We all expect the Jew's death.

'O great King . . . Great King? The biggest bastard that ever walked on the one God's earth. I know you, Darius the Mede. I see into your heart. I see the colour yellow . . .'

The king sighs. He does not have a reputation for tolerance except in religious matters. Perhaps he has a soft spot for Daniel. He fingers the bandage, stiff with the pus of an abscess and winces. The captain of the guard eyes his monarch for a sign.

The dark eyes of Darius never leave the capering prophet.

'O great King. Slayer of pretenders. Hah! I know the truth. You were a chicken herd.'

The dark eyes narrow slightly. Daniel beams. At last he has found his mark. He seems so careless with his life. He is relentless.

'And while we're at it, what's this about a new edict? All this bollocks about worshipping you? Eh? Bit too proud, eh? Look what happened to old Belshazzar, my son, if you go down that road. And don't preach me any of your Zoroastrian one-god piety. My God's the only true God and don't forget it . . . excuse me,' he belches. 'I'll tell you one thing, oh greatest of monarchs . . . People that come after will only remember Darius, King of Kings, as a passing acquaintance of Daniel. Worship you? I'd rather worship a lion's bum . . .'

And with a weary nod of Darius's head and an almost inaudible whisper, Daniel's wish, as every schoolboy knows, was granted. Things hardly ever turn out as we expect . . . History has become a science of lies, practised by those pretenders who seek nothing more than their own advantage.

'You all right?' said Stigi Weitz taking hold of my arm. I was shaking.

'Good God, it's splendid. I felt I was . . . I was dreaming. I can hardly believe it. Absolutely splendid. Don't you find it one of the most incredible things you have seen in your life, Mr Weitz?' The man before me looked disturbingly like the prophet Daniel. He had the same insanely driven expression. He also had the power to convince people entirely of what he was saying. Isn't every preacher a confidence trickster to some extent?

'The Gate is truly magnificent, Mr Weitz . . .'

'If you say so.'

'Don't you like it?'

'You wanna buy it?'

'Buy it? Buy It? This is one of the wonders of the ancient world. The Blue Gate of Babylon, dedicated to Ishtar, a very powerful deity, a goddess of war as well as love. But it should be in the Pergamon-Museum in the Eastern zone. What on earth's it doing in a doughnut factory?' We were in a disused and gutted bakery, the size and shape of an aircraft hanger. Too large in fact for the lights which illuminated the Gate of Ishtar to reach to the other end of the massive utilitarian structure. In the cold distance there was a thunderous clanging as a caretaker slammed one of the doors to a remaining bread oven, making the damp air vibrate. The building stood beside an ornate nineteenth century house in the French style on what had been a street. The two hulks formed a craggy, ill-matched island in a rubble-strewn wasteland at one corner of the Tiergarten. In front was what Mr Weitz said had been Berlin's equivalent of Piccadilly Circus, the Potsdamer Platz once prowled by the shaven-headed, shark-jawed men from an expressionist canvas, now as much phantoms of the past as the priests who walked the gardens of Babylon. We had entered the bakery first because a light was on. I felt somethng of a trespasser. I could not take my eyes off the Gate.

'Sure you don't want to buy it? Tiles ain't my style but it's a great piece of work and it's a hundred per cent genuine. Except for a few bits and pieces in that vastly inferior reconstruction in the Pergamon this, friend, is the real McCoy. Brought to Germany at the time of the Kaiser on a railway he had specially built to Baghdad. Go on, touch it. Smell it. Run your hands over an antique more than twenty-five centuries old. What's it doing here, you ask? Well, old Hermann Göring, who lived over the road, had it moved while it was undergoing refurbishment. It was to be the backdrop for a wild party. Over there is even the actual section of tiles where the moving finger of God wrote warning Nebuchadnezzar – or was it Belshazzar? – of impending doom. Yes, a prime piece of history. The whole lot comes apart in easy sections. Go on, amaze your friends. How many people can say they own a piece of old Babylon? What a talking point it would be at a family barbecue. Make me an offer. Name me a price!'

31

'A single tile is priceless,' I replied, as we stood in a yellowish pool of light from one of the bare bulbs dangling from the roof above. The individual attempting to sell me one of the treasures of the ancient world, with all the salt of a second-hand car salesman, had slicked-back dark hair, thinning at the temples. Mr Stigi Weitz only came up to my chest. He was slightly built but held himself very straight with the fragile dignity of a Vatican count, his black leather coat hanging from his shoulders like a cloak. He appeared constantly in motion and his brown eyes twinkled as if he was enjoying a personal joke with the devil. His was the kind of energy that made one feel tired. His American accent was discernible but not strong, and his tanned face had a deeply-lined attractiveness which reminded me of an old boxing-glove.

'Call me Stigi. Everyone does,' he continued. 'I like idealism. One can sure use idealism. The Gate should be under safe-keeping, but if the Pergamon is happy with what they got, why stir up trouble? As I said, parts of their Gate is kosher due to it all being in pieces when it was being done up. As it is, private buyers already have their eyes on this little beauty. Men of means. The sort who can really appreciate Babylon. A month ago I was a rich man and I'll be up there again. But I bet Belshazzar said that. You a college kid?'

'Actually, I read Classics and Ancient Persian at New College, Oxford . . .'

'You don't say . . .' He laughed out loud and shook his head. 'But will it help you run a whorehouse?'

Stigi Weitz aimed a kick at a tin can and wandered over to examine a fire hydrant. He did not seem to expect a reply. After my one actual affair with Simone, the ambassador's wife, and a handful of very amateur nights on the tiles I was only starting to learn the ropes myself, let alone ladle rumpy-dumpy and custard out to the public. Well, if in doubt fall back on the Classics.

'Oh, they knew a thing or two in Babylon, to say nothing of the Persians,' I said, feeling rather pompous and awkward.

'Tell me about it.'

'Well, for a start the goddess Ishtar, or Astar or Astarte, was the guardian of all prostitutes. The high priestess, who always lay ready on the golden couch in the great ziggurat for her lord god, Bel Marduk – although because of smoke, incense, heady perfumes and the like she could occasionally confuse him with the odd mortal –

has first to be a city prostitute. In one ritual she wears seven veils of light blue silk which she tantalisingly discards, as Ishtar did before Hell's guardians in a bargain to rescue Tammuz, her lover and the lord of rebirth . . .'

'So she invented stripping?' said Stigi, interested.

'Yes, er, I suppose she did. I can think of no earlier reference . . .'

'And they were big on cat houses?'

'Brothels? Oh, yes. I'll say. There was absolutely no hypocrisy. Really, you couldn't get away from prostitution, as such. The law of Nebuchadnezzar states that every woman, rich or poor, had to go and sit by the Blue Gate or outside the temple on the eve of her marriage and wait until a man, any man, except perhaps a leper, threw a silver shekel into her lap and claimed her in the name of the goddess. She then had to give herself joyfully to the man in a sacred union that lasted one night, to bring prosperity to the wheatfields. She was a kind of sacrifice and her body the altar. They were very religious.'

'I bet they had a lot of wheaties too,' sniggered Weitz, totally missing the significance and gravity of — if human love and understanding were present — a charming and enriching custom, and I turned back to the Gate.

'We must find out the legal owner. I'll have to consult Colonel Midwinter.' Mr Weitz looked more than a little dismayed. Midwinter obviously had plans for the Gate himself.

'Have you ever run a brothel before, Stigi?'

'Didn't that horsetrading bastard show you my file?'

I tried to hide my pleasure at getting a reaction. My mother said everything showed in my eyes. I did not count myself guileless. But by the side of Stigi Weitz I was a cherub. In fact, reading the closely-typed pages in the buff folder as I had waited for Stigi, I had begun to feel somewhat outclassed. In the circumstances it was akin to a village cricketer playing alongside someone who has been selected for England. I was playing out of my league.

'I'm sorry. Midwinter said I should read your file. It was jolly interesting. I only read it once and there is such a lot of it, but I think I can manage a précis. You grew up near the Chicago stockyards of mixed immigrant parents possibly from Italy and lost an uncle in the St Valentine's Day massacre. By twenty-three you were already suspected of white slavery, narcotics trafficking, strike-breaking, fixing the Kentucky Derby, and being a Bolshevik agent because of an affair with a female stevedore from Archangel. Right so far?'

'She wasn't a stevedore, she was first mate.'

'Then, as Mr Hoover's G-men closed in, you volunteered for the American Legion to fight in Europe and were sent as a quartermaster clerk to North Africa, where you were accused of stealing the Desert Rats' morphine allocation from Montgomery's headquarters. To save a scandal you were transferred to the logistics staff of General Patton. In return for them turning a blind eye to your helping yourself to money from banks where you didn't have an account, you helped Patton win the race through Sicily, with the help of an old friend Mr Lucky Luciano. Patton was so pleased at beating Montgomery as well as the Germans he made you munitions and procurement officer for his army group, a post which virtually allowed you to print money; even though some reports suggest a certain culpability over Old Blood-And-Guts' demise.'

Stigi shook his head and did his best to look offended.

'Next, you used your position to found the Babycake Charity – slogan, Let's Give Baby A Break You Guys. In the wage packet of every GI was a leaflet with the picture of a bouncing baby and a message pleading that he should go without cake and candy bars to help war-orphaned children and apply for the money to be deducted from his next wage packet, which you then pocketed. You supplemented this by a black market trade in army PX stores, in particular with East Germany through your company Trans Rio Grande Verlag S.A., and you were soon able to found leisure complexes and country clubs in Dusseldorf, Frankfurt and Cologne as well as golf courses and hotels. Investigation into this multi-million dollar fraud began when General Clay tried to give an Enterprise Against Communism award to the head of your parent company Six-Shot Services, only to find it was registered in the name of a beagle called Six-Shot Otto the Hound. Your Bolshevik past was also catching up with you via the Committee for Un-American Activities and you were facing a prison sentence when the Colonel rescued you, no doubt swayed by your prowess with the Kentucky Derby. Is that Six-Shot Otto the Hound out in the car? He really is a nice dog.'

'He's seen life,' said Stigi, rather sourly. 'So have I. Have you ever been with a hooker, even? Some of these beauties do twenty a day. Twenty stinking rotten GI joes a day who pick their toes and piss in the sink. Imagine that?'

'To be perfectly honest, no,' I replied. Twenty a day sounded an awful lot.

Stigi winked and gave a broad smile.

'What you are about to see is how not to run a brothel. Dig?'

'Dig,' I said, with little or no idea of what to expect. The novelty of Midwinter's suggestion that I took an administrative post in the oldest profession, was beginning to wear off.

4

We went out of the front door of the bakery into the teeth of a cold wind and followed a cobblestone path that might have once been a street to the door of the adjacent building. We let ourselves in through a high front door and entered a marbled hallway where the smell of cheap disinfectant fought a losing battle with that of stale urine. In an old gold-painted birdcage lift with a broken cable was a shop-window dummy, naked except for a pair of stockings and a suspender belt. The dummy was male. The worn, gilded cage was strewn with contraceptives and a discarded syringe. A delicate plaster moulding on the staircase showed a bat catching a fly.

'After you,' gestured Stigi. 'You must fill me in on all those old Babylonian customs, kid. I'm not so old a dog I can't learn new tricks. I mean, how did the guy that invented the yo-yo get his inspiration? What about the hula hoop? We live in a world of golden opportunities. Creation is just waiting for me to have the right idea. Never be too proud to learn.'

On the first floor the largest man I had ever seen lay slumped on a food-stained couch behind a walnut dining-table. He was entirely dressed in black and his head was shaved, probably by a cut-throat razor, since the scalp had been nicked in several places; though the neat line of surgical stitches and the purple welts of savage bite-marks could not have been self inflicted. On the wall were wrestling posters with the legend 'Der Berserker' above a furious-looking individual with a glistening bald head. The man on the settee had a blond toupee nuzzling at his shoulder like an obedient pet animal. He was wearing rouge and one pearl droplet earring but there was no doubt he was the selfsame *Der Berserker*. In front of him was a disturbingly human pile of bones on a plate of rich gravy. When he snored the world held its breath.

Stigi put a finger to his lips and rang the electric bell by a sign which said Café Bok beside a nearby door. A postcard showed a goat having sex with a disinterested young woman in a PVC mac. The door opened. I was prepared for the worst.

'*Willkommen*,' said a pretty blonde teenager, who could not have been more than sixteen but had a haunting, empty stare. A look fixed firmly on the end of her life. The veins on her thin forearms stood out like trees in a winter landscape.

'Do you wish sex? I'm clean and cheap and my name is Cindy. I am your disposable. Tissues are extra,' declared the German girl, in heavily-accented English. Her eyelashes fluttered automatically.

'We are here to see *le patron*,' I said, looking down. The girl wore no bra. Her dress, if one could call it a dress, was a see-through version of a ballet dancer's tutu. Cindy had dyed her pubic hairs bright red and they shone through the thin material like a lamp. I felt very sorry for her. On a stool by a bamboo bar in what had been a ballroom, now crowded with dimly-lit tables, was a heap of clothes which turned out to be a small, fat man, crying bitterly. On the lapel of his jacket was a *Croix de Guerre*.

'I'm clean and cheap and my name is Cindy.'

'Her record's stuck,' said Stigi.

'Rubbers are free. Tissues are extra. My English is good. I am your disposable,' continued Cindy, bobbing in front of me and then twirling dreamily down an aisle between the tables to seats under heavily-curtained windows, where two older women sat with glasses of beer. They were both in their forties, I guessed; one had her knitting on the table while the other smoked a yellow and black pipe and began to stroke Cindy's hair defensively. The pipe smoker reminded me of a disturbed gardener we had when I was a boy. Near them was a small makeshift stage with a microphone. A film poster of Elvis in *GI Blues* had been fixed to a door marked 'Stage Door'. The leather-gloved hand of the lady with the knitting scuttled across the table like a crab and put a token in the juke box. 'Only the Lonely' drifted across the empty room. The women were frozen into a painfully exact tableau of inactivity, as though in a van Eyck painting, while the room was so crammed full of things it seemed to have a life of its own. I was looking at the detritus of more than a century of flesh peddling and the place might well have been a vast junkshop overhung by a fine crystal chandelier. By the nearest potted palm was a sabre and an abandoned croquet mallet. On the walls were photographs of stiff-backed officers saluting the Kaiser among beautiful girls outside what was unmistakably the building we were in. Other snapshots showed smiling fresh-faced boys who had once knocked eagerly at the doors. A long beer glass was full of what first looked like coloured marbles, but in fact were the mislaid glass eyes of forgotten glory-seekers. In a place of honour was a framed white piece of linen with a red stain on it bearing the legend: 'Proof Of Virginity, Queen Of Albania'. The establishment had seen far better times. On the bar itself, under a plastic palm tree, one wag had left an Iron Cross around a bottle of Bols Geldwasser. On another shelf was the peaked cap of an East German border guard, next to a Russian officer's red shoulder-board. The strangest item of all was a signed photograph of Mahatma Gandhi. In its time the place appeared to have catered for everybody; a sort of sexual United Nations. I felt the excitement of the totally new. I had never been anywhere like this before. My sensible shoes wanted to run.

'That's the little cunt,' said Stigi, pointing to the man on the bar-stool. Small feet dangled far above the ground. I was reminded of the little piggy in a nursery rhyme.

'*Monsieur?*' I asked, tapping him gently on the arm and taking the documents Colonel Midwinter had given me out of their folder. '*Monsieur?* Well, my name is Jubb,' I continued in English, a language which Stigi assured me *le patron* spoke. 'I represent the Government of Her Britannic Majesty Queen Elizabeth and am instructed to take over this building, formerly the territory of the Republic of France, forthwith and in accord with your Government's express wishes to renounce sovereignty over the said property and in strict concordance with the Four Power agreement of . . .' Quite suddenly the little man jumped off the stool and was clutching at my lapels. He had a sore just below his nose, and as he lunged in my direction I sincerely hoped the Frenchman was not going to kiss me.

'I do not care for your authorities. Take everything. Take the ruins of a poor Frenchman's life for it is the end for me. The dervish who lurks on the stairs has killed my best friend. He has murdered him because he says I am late with my wages. I cannot bear it. I cannot bear it. No one loves me. No one has ever loved me except Claude.'

'Who is Claude? Who's been murdered?' I began. 'Who is Claude?'

Le patron slumped against the bar and began to wail all the more. A giggle came from behind a large potted palm. A severely beautiful girl peered around a Polish plaster pillar. She had thick dark hair tinged with henna, and the dainty white face of a wanton Madonna; an earthiness which just stopped short of being hard. In her little black dress she looked like a favourite sister dressed up for the ball. She wore false eyelashes which appeared to give her a slight squint and smoked a cigarette in a long pearl holder as I had always imagined wicked women doing in Berlin. An amused dimple in her face showed a callous lack of concern for the homicide.

'Who was murdered?' I repeated, trying to sound in control. *Le patron* wept.

'I am clean and cheap and my name is Cindy,' trilled the flawed Cinderella, who skipped back to the bar. The sound of determined footsteps came from the stairs. Two tall men stood before us; one wore a fawn trenchcoat, the other a short raincoat, and was shivering. The first glanced round the room in disgust.

'Who is now in charge?' he demanded in French.

I nodded and was about to say '*oui*' when it struck me that it might not be entirely prudent to admit to being in charge of a brothel, in particular this one. Was it legal, after all? Did we really have any claim? Or was Midwinter just trying to get his paws on the gate? I felt a fraud.

'You are Mr Jubb?' he continued in English. I nodded again.

'We represent the Government of the Republic of France,' he said, walking across the floor gingerly as if it were about to open up. He too had come armed with papers in an expensive leather document-case. Both men had the reluctantly caged look of ex-paratroopers transferred from Algiers. 'Our Government would like to make it clear that it is with great reluctance that we hand over diplomatic territory and only do so under extreme protest and in lieu of the most generous reparations.' He laid down the documents on the bar as a gambler lays down a hand of cards. 'We will take *le patron* with us,' he added darkly, while his aide, who was recovering from the cold, produced a pair of dull black handcuffs. The Frenchmen were not amused by their surroundings. The handcuffs clicked around *le patron*'s wrists as I suppressed a desire to ask what General De Gaulle would receive in return for this corner of a foreign field. *Le patron* began to wail.

'Murder . . . !'

'Take care,' said the man in the trenchcoat adding something very abusive in Marseilles French. 'You are a wretched little man. You cannot even run a whorehouse. You are a disgrace to the Republic. A collaborator with the Nazis who now pretends he was in the resistance. Pah! So one of your whores was cut up. So what. Perhaps they will cut you up with the guillotine.'

'Murder,' whimpered *le patron* again in English, tears running down his fat cheeks. 'They have murdered my Claude. He was a better dancer than Fred Astaire. My, how he could dance. First poor Véronique. Now my Claude. *Il est mort.* Consumed by the dervish.'

The man in the trenchcoat sighed and flexed his large and very hard hands. The close-set eyes swivelled onto their target. The job was obviously beneath his dignity and he looked at *le patron* with undisguised loathing. However, for the moment he had to observe diplomatic niceties.

'Was the crime committed on French soil?' asked the other man.

'*Ici*,' replied *le patron*.

'By an Arab you say. Was Claude a citizen of France?'

'Not exactly.'

'Was this Claude a French citizen or was he not?'

'He had the head of Danton and the delicacy of Proust,' replied *le patron* through his sobs. 'Unfortunately he was born in Glasgow. But his soul was French. The man who killed him was a Turk, not an Arab.'

'Then the D G S E wash their hands of the affair. We do not become involved in other people's international incidents. Is there a body?'

'Only the hairy skin.'

'The hairy skin?'

'And his sweet little horns . . .'

Le patron did not have chance to finish the sentence before the

40

younger man, sensing the sudden murderous intent on the part of his superior, pulled the brothelkeeper off his bar stool and hurled him in the direction of the door. 'Sign here,' said the other Frenchman to me. 'We will question this creature further in the privacy of our headquarters. I am told there are some articles of archaeological interest here. I do not wish to see them now but you will make a full inventory.'

'Oh, they are nothing much,' I lied. 'Theatrical props by the look of it. Nothing very valuable. What is to happen to him?' The man in the shorter raincoat gave *le patron* a playful kick.

'That is the business of France, Monsieur Jubb. He has been in the habit of late of making imprudent statements about his betters and certain women. He seems to have lost his mind. You understand we will be reporting the matter of this Claude to the British authorities. Also, there is the murder of a prostitute to be investigated.' He drew himself up to his full height and I thought he was about to salute. 'Be sure to send me a full inventory,' he snapped. 'I declare this territory no longer French.' He left to the sound of his younger partner throwing *le patron* down the stairs.

'Little horns, eh . . . ?' floated up the stairs.

The painful sound of dull blows on fat body and the occasional yelp followed.

'. . . hairy skin . . . ?'

The front door slammed. Moments later a car accelerated away into the night.

'Poor man,' I said. 'He seems to have been very fond of this Claude.' I was concerned. Whatever *le patron* had done, he did not deserve to be beaten to death by two ex-legionnaire thugs.

The girl with the cigarette-holder giggled, which struck me as rather cruel under the circumstances. I had never met a prostitute before. Her teeth stuck out slightly, putting one in mind of a playground brace. She smiled at me.

'Are you fond of animals?' she asked.

'Fairly. Why?'

'Claude was a billy goat,' she sniggered, trying to master the muscles of her face and failing. Her breasts jutted at a gravity-defying angle and she wore gold high heels. She was as tall and rounded as a chorus girl. The soft accent had once been from the north of England.

'But *le patron* said Claude was from Glasgow?'

'He was. The lads from the Black Watch left him here one night. Claude was their regimental mascot, athough they didn't call him Claude. He really could dance. Honest, he could even do the twist. *Le patron* and he were very close. They used to waltz together. It wasn't very popular but they were lost in each other. The Turkish doorman, Twinkle Twinkle, got jealous. Last night he ate Claude and said it was on account of not being paid. Poor Claude didn't stand a chance. Twinkle Twinkle was jealous of anything which upstaged him and came between him and *le patron*. Affection can be a real drag in a brothel, and love is downright poison. My name's Betty. They call me Betty Bethlehem.'

'What's a nice girl like you doing in a dump like this, as if I didn't know?' quipped Stigi. She did not seem to mind the rather tactless question. Betty Bethlehem had a warm smile. She glided across the carpet and onto a bar-stool. She walked as if she owned the place.

'I was working in Regina Street in Nicosia. Lovely house. Then up comes these really nicely-spoken officers who offered to take me and Zela for a weekend trip to Palestine. I'd always wanted to go to the Holy Land and it was a sort of working holiday. Never trust an officer, present company excepted. They put us on this crummy cargo plane to come back and the next thing we know is that we wake up cold and in Berlin, me clutching this piece of the True Cross, bought on the Via Dolorosa. We came in marked "Dry Goods: Perishable". On top of that, we had to oblige the bloody pilot. I may not mind who I'm with but I like to know where I am. I'm pretty free, but one has to draw the line geographically.'

'Who was the girl who was stabbed?' asked Stigi, pouring us each a glass of chilled Apfelkorn proffered by Cindy. Betty lost her crooked smile. Her face was full of genuine concern. I began to like her.

'Christ, that was awful. Véronique was the one who introduced us to *le patron* after we nearly got ourselves knifed by this black pimp working the Stutti, I mean Stuttgarter Platz bus station, in broad daylight on a Sunday afternoon right outside that little cigarette kiosk. None of the bloody Germans gave a damn. *Le patron*, for all his faults, and they say he used to interpret for the Gestapo, gave us a room. Then one day they found Véronique on the wasteland by what was Gestapo headquarters. They said it was the border guards. But I don't think it could have been.'

'Why?' The question seemed natural. Betty's brown eyes fixed on the glass of Apfelkorn she was holding very tightly. 'No, I don't think it was soldiers,' she said quietly. 'It wasn't just someone strangled after a rape. Whoever did it used things those lads on the border wouldn't have to hand.' She drained the glass of the sweet liquid. 'It was horrible. Six of the girls buggered off the night she was found. If you don't mind, I don't want to talk about it.'

'Would you consider staying?' I asked, as she stared into space. Betty Bethlehem seemed surprised.

'Do you mean you are not going to close the place down? I thought at first you were the bluebottles. An old bastard called Midwinter came down and gave me the third degree. I thought he was going to arrest me. Then he told me to stick around, and that I might be useful. Well, here I am. I'm going nowhere, as Stigi has my passport, but then drifting is the story of my life. The headmistress at our approved school said I wasn't a bad girl. I just didn't have a moral map. Silly cow. I always try and speak my mind, though. But I recognise Stigi here from the newspapers, and not the court and social page.'

The thought did occur to me that Betty Bethlehem might be Colonel Midwinter's eyes and ears. I dismissed the idea. She would never have mentioned him.

'Glad to know you, Ma'am,' said Stigi, basking in dubious fame. 'Betty here can be our madam. You can't run a house without a madam. We'll turn this place around and give it a spring-clean and make it bigger than Babylon. We can put on spectaculars and shows. That should fit with old Midwinter's cultural cover, eh, Toby? He told me this was all meant to be run by that British Council of yours. Spread a little art, I say.'

'I've never been a madam,' mused Betty, pleased at being promoted. 'You don't suppose people will think I'm older than I am?'

'Not even a day,' I assured her. 'You will stay, won't you?'

Betty nodded, preening herself. 'Bigger than Babylon,' Stigi kept saying to himself. 'We'll be bigger than Babylon. We'll be famous . . .' I could imagine just how attractive a brothel would be as a base for Mr Weitz's multifarious rackets.

'But . . .'

Stigi's moneymaking ambitions appeared to be at odds with an intelligence operation.

'No buts in Berlin,' replied Stigi.

'So you will stay?' I asked Betty as the practical problems of the task Midwinter had set me began to dawn. 'Please, you are going to stay, aren't you?'

'I've nothing on,' she smiled, examining herself in her powder compact mirror. 'I've nothing on underneath either. All my knickers are in the washing machine. Don't worry. I'll look after you, Toby. Just like a mother. You're sleeping here tonight? Good. I'll make the arrangements. We'll all have a good laugh here, just you see. All we've got to do is run it proper. There are rules in this game just like everything else. Rules keep you safe, my mother used to say. If I hadn't broken the first rule and got in the club at fifteen, I wouldn't be here. Now, I must tell poor Zela.' In a flash she was gone. All that was left was the bright red lipstick on the Apfelkorn glass.

Stigi produced a bank roll from his pocket. 'I'm going to pay off those two witches by the window and drop them at a less choosy establishment. Shall we send Cindy along too? She's on the needle. A junkie.'

'She stays for the time being.' I felt sorry for the girl. 'Anyway, where are we going to get new staff? I mean we can't exactly advertise.'

'Oh, I wouldn't be too sure. Word will get around,' said Stigi as he walked over to the two women by the window. They accepted their fate stoically and without protest, carefully counting the money, knowing their worth exactly to the last cent. Cindy waved goodbye with a smile on her face like a toy doll. To send the women somewhere else, somewhere worse, although that was difficult to imagine, was a hard thing to do at Christmas. In the corner of the bar the lights of a tinsel tree winked on and off. I wondered how Véronique had died. What had been too painful for Betty Bethlehem to repeat?

All at once I was left alone in the old ballroom, quiet, except for the sound of Twinkle Twinkle snoring loudly on the landing. I walked over to the juke-box, which took my money and refused to work. Somehow I did not feel the lord of all I surveyed. Only last week I had been dealing with the lost passports and bruised egos of distressed businessmen, learning my trade as a diplomat in the commercial section of the British Embassy in Paris. Now I was about to run a brothel to solicit information from the Red Army so that my new boss, Colonel Midwinter, could have prior warning of the next global conflict; or anything else that was going to disturb the racing calendar. On top of that, I had in my possession a genuine Blue Gate of Babylon. I yearned for Smokey Robinson, but the record machine would not oblige however many marks I put in. I had my doubts about making anything work in that shabby Café. If anything went wrong I had no illusions that the good Colonel Midwinter would deny all knowledge of a large Englishman and an American with previous convictions running a bawdy-house in no-man's land. All the same, I felt childishly excited. Best foot forward, Jubb, I thought, as I picked up my glass of Apfelkorn. The stairs creaked. Betty Bethlehem stepped back into the room.

'I got your bed ready, Toby. It's just up the stairs on the right. There are clean sheets. I'd warm them for you myself . . . but I promised Zela I would look after her. Take Cindy, if you like?'

Betty's directness was alarming.

'I'm clean and cheap and my name is Cindy,' said the blonde, following Betty into the room. I shook my head and she came towards me with a frozen smile.

'Sorry, Cindy, not tonight. I'm a little tired from travelling.' Betty shrugged and took the teenager by her shoulders.

'Come along Miss Cinderella. You can come and sleep in my room and practice your English and have one of my camomile teas. You should start to look after yourself. All that coffee is not good for you. Say goodnight to Mr Toby.' But she didn't and began to cry. I left her sobbing in the arms of the brothel's new madam.

My room was plain and surprisingly spotless with a wardrobe, a washstand and a brass bedstead which had seen better days. The great house creaked and every time I fell asleep something woke me. But the heating worked and the sheets were perfumed with 4711 eau de Cologne, a bottle of which stood by the bed. Once I was roused by the unfamiliar sound of a two-tone police siren somewhere in the East, the sound magnified on the cold winter air. I thought of Betty Bethlehem's body and tried to imagine her breasts free of that sweater. The anticipation was almost painful under the heavy blankets.

The house I had lived in as a boy had creaked. When I was fourteen my father, with the money he had made from selling a junkyard of coronation memorabilia, had bought a mansion in the county of Oxfordshire. He was not a tall man (in fact small and round and I was already bigger than him) but would stand bolt upright by the white marble fireplace in the drawing-room toying with the gold and emerald fob of his grandfather's pocket-watch, as my mother hid her pale and amused face behind a copy of French *Vogue*. He had bought her a Jaguar Coupé that afternoon. She and I knew what he was about to say.

'Listen, Toby. Listen, boy. Did you hear that creak? That's the sound of history, my lad. Did you hear that? Many before you have heard that sound. The fellow I bought this house from told me the timbers came from a ship of the line. A man of war. A ship in Nelson's squadron. Listen to that, my boy. These timbers have witnessed our cannons engaging the French . . . powder monkeys no older than you would supply the shot and wadding . . . Nelson may have heard these timbers creaking. I often imagine I can hear a sea shanty as those jack tars heaved at the capstan. A Jubb knows history when he hears it . . .'

My mother would sigh.

'Do fix me a gin and it, dear.'

What my father could hear was the sound of an Edwardian house still settling on its foundation; and in my mother's sigh his marriage breaking to pieces. Even when the true age of the house was pointed out to him he clung determinedly to the idea that the framework was from an older house on the same spot. He read several popular histories on the Battle of Trafalgar. His windfall from the coronation had made him excessively patriotic.

'I know history when I hear it,' he told me, often wiping away a tear as he would when he had drunk too much whisky while reading his books and waiting for Mother to come home from the golf-club or wherever. Father was a great pretender.

He even pretended to be a catholic although he had not been brought up as one. Catholics are fashionable in the country, he would say. I remember holding my mother's hand tightly as I went with them both to Mass; my father nodding to business acquaintances, their faces the red-blue colour of jellyfish, and the rangy gentleman farmers who only had eyes for my mother. Yet they were the outward picture of wedded bliss. Yes, I held my mother's hand tightly, mortally afraid of the demons of embarrassment which seemed to laugh from behind the altar and up on the roof beam. I even watched jealously as my mother swallowed the body of Christ.

Afterwards she would stand outside with the priest and talk politely of her garden.

She was the most beautiful woman and had the best garden in the county. The fat priest, who had a face like a bread-and-butter pudding, often visited, and playfully accused her of witchcraft over the date and walnut cake.

'How can you make such bounty come from our poor soil. I suspect the black arts,' he would always say as tea was served.

'Only love, father. I only love my flowers. That is all.'

The house was white and floated like a ghost above emerald lawns, held down only, it seemed to me, by the clematis and vines which ran along the smooth cedar-floored balconies I loved walking on in my bare feet. It was as if the whole structure were floating on the scent of her flower beds, jungles of colour and fragrance which radiated out to a small wood. Everything grew there. In midsummer the profusion was almost obscene and the scent unbearable, especially around the summer-house, where sometimes my mother would sit, quite naked, playing her jazz records to the soft night. Sometimes my father's querulous voice would hover around her silence as he changed the records like a moth about a flame. Sometimes there were other deeper voices, laughter and the pop of champagne or the clink of glass.

Yes, the house I lived in as a boy creaked. At home the sheets had smelt of jasmine. One hot June night, when the scents of the garden were close and almost overwhelming, I had not been able to sleep. I was fourteen, you see, and a single sheet had been rubbing painfully against the fruit of my overheated imaginings. The garden was silent. The sheet had billowed over the bed, in places damp with sweat. Suddenly, as I rocked between waking and sleeping, I was not alone. Her perfume mixed with that of the night and made me shiver. I could see her silhouette framed in the doorway by the patterns of shifting moonlight streaming through the French windows. I opened my mouth to call to her, but something stopped me. She looked unfamiliar, small and vulnerable; a child, like me. I ached. She turned to close the doors and I caught a glimpse of a dark triangle against white flesh. I could not breathe, let alone utter a word, as she approached the bed with that swaying, dancer's walk of hers. She leant over and kissed my eyelids. She always did this at the end of a fairy story told in that husky voice. Playfully, she pulled the sheet above my eyes. The crisp linen slid from the bottom of the bed and, after meeting eager resistance for a second, finished up above my navel. My entire lower half was naked, my legs and my belly; totally and deliciously exposed to the cool night air. I did not know whether to feel embarrassed or ashamed. The night made my head spin and I almost cried out. But a delicate hand was reaching below the top of the sheets and stroking my hair. The sheet fell away. Her wet lips soothed my cheek and her long dark hair tickled the skin on my body. She murmured something, rocking me gently in her arms on a night I would never forget.

'My poor baby. It's all right. My poor big baby . . .'

The dark reaches of the garden seemed to overwhelm me and I do not remember her leaving. Had it been a dream? Or were, if I was truthful, there the more obvious signs of the succubus and her touch? I began to realise there are certain things every good boy should not know.

Two days later the summer-house burned down.

5

Snow was falling again in large flakes, a silent barrage which almost blocked out the looming grey of the sky and made the rubble mountains appear mysterious; a romantic winterland from the pages of the Brothers Grimm. A military bus skidded slightly as it negotiated the slippery corner on the main road, bypassing the cobbled street on which stood my new home and the bakery, icebergs in a sea of white. As I stood shivering in the doorway I could see the driver of the bus was laughing and a man who stood next to him waved a bottle. It was still Christmas and the snow was crisp and even. I caught a snowflake in my hand and let it melt with a tingle. Snow always made me feel ecstatic; a five-year-old again. A quite irrational attitude when the cold it represented would kill so many in the cardboard-thin refugee shacks on the border. But then I knew a chap at Oxford who said he came into cash every time he caught the clap, and that it was better than any money-spider. Naturally, he became a banker.

'Isn't it beautiful?' Stigi said, joining me on the doorstep. From the confines of his leather coat he too looked delighted with the day; as if the wasteland was Eden. I hadn't supposed he was interested in aesthetics.

'Yes, the snow is lovely.'

'No, dummy, not the fucking snowflakes. The Rio Grande. Out there. You can just see it. Bless their little hearts.' Stigi ran up and down on the spot as much from glee as a desire to keep warm. Less

49

than half-a-mile away were several wooden huts from which fluttered red flags. For me, politics seemed out-of-bounds on that morning. It was is if the epic landscape had never recovered from the last ice age, let alone the Second World War. The flags were like ever changing outlines of huge Santas in the snow. I had been staring at them without taking in what they signified.

'The Rio Grande. My border. Smell that . . .' Stigi inhaled. On the east wind there was a tang of woodsmoke. 'Do you know what that is?'

'No, Stigi. Please tell me.'

'That's another day, another dollar, my boy. That's my yo-yo, my hula hoop. In many ways I discovered that border. That is the smell of money. To put it another way, it is the scent of the Daughters of the Alamo soup kitchen near Checkpoint Charlie. It means refugees are still arriving. The border is still open. Until they close it again there is a pfennig or two to be made. Probably even after they close it. The world is a marvellous place, Toby Jubb.' A questionable enthusiasm positively steamed from the top of his head.

'It's chilly. Where does the border run? I expected barbed wire.'

'Don't say things like that,' he replied turning around and touching wood. 'The border comes within two hundred yards of us. It snakes by part of the Tiergarten. Sometimes in the summer they post a few sentries. I don't think anyone knows where the exact line is, believe me. But they cut us off at the time of the air lift and they could do it again.' He shook his head and smiled. 'Lots of kids over there want to come West. They want it bad. Silly things like watching the Lucy Show in German and drinking cold Coke and listening to Elvis the Pelvis. You'll see when we get some more girls. That's where the beauties come from. My scouts hang around the playgrounds.' He lit two Chesterfields and handed one of them to me. He smoked incessantly. A man mortally afraid of deprivation.

'More girls?'

Stigi smiled. He had a gold tooth at the left-hand side of his mouth.

'As you pointed out last night, Toby, we do need a few more to make ends meet.' Stigi was looking out into the snow. 'The girl Véronique, whatever her name was, the one they were talking about, bought it just out here. I had a medic friend at the checkpoint who attended. Grisly, believe me. A better class of murder. I've never heard of anything like that, not even in Chicago. See that building to the left of the flags? That building is the old Nazi Air Ministry. That's why Göring organised his private orgies in our bakery. It baked the cakes for the Third Reich and took care of their hot dogs too. The old sourpuss with the pipe who we jinxed last night could probably tell a tale. Out there was Potsdamer Platz. Hitler's bunker is behind those ruins to the left of Gestapo headquarters. So don't shed too many tears for the old staff. This cat house had many uncool clients.'

A car turned off the main road onto the hard snow of our cobbled street. A man stopped and hailed Stigi and then began to unload crates of whisky from the boot. 'Come on, let's have some coffee,' said the American, and we went to breakfast in the new Babylon while just under the blank covering of winter lay the twisted remnants of another Empire, threatening to burst forth again like the bulb of some terrible black crocus. The past cannot be shut out. Just under the surface were legions of eyeless clockwork soldiers clawing their way up to demand I return the glass one they left by their bed in the Residence; or kicking at the bakery door in a forest of jackboots and scars to demand a morning doughnut. In England we always buried the past as deep as possible, only examining it after a decent interval with our eyes closed and our finger in our ears to the sound of a military band. Here it went bump in the night.

'Do you want hot or cold milk with your coffee? There are croissants and rolls and I'm just cooking the egg and bacon. No rationing here. Dig in, duck. A big boy like you needs his strength.' Betty Bethlehem was wearing a Woolworths quilted dressing-gown and pink pom-pom slippers with beady little peepers and whiskers; yet she still oozed the kind of dark magnetism most mothers warn their sons against.

Breakfast was eaten at a large table in the ballroom. The room appeared much filthier in daylight. Thousands of cigarette burns holed the faded red velvet of the seats and chairs, as if the place were infested by some fiery worm. Above the drinks and mementos on the bamboo bar the upper part of the wall had been in shadow the night before. In the space between bar and ceiling hundreds of china dolls, some broken, others missing arms or legs, were fixed to the wall, looking at the world through perfect, sightless eyes. For me they did not smile. Their looks were accusing.

51

'Creepy, ain't they?' Stigi burnt his hand on a coffee-pot and winced. 'Betty tells me that Cinderella there amuses herself by digging them out of the rubble. They're always naked because their little clothes were often as not covered in the blood of their former owners, and eaten off by the rats. Nice hobby, huh?' Cindy was busy spreading a slice of rye bread with alternate layers of leberwurst and jam. Her expression was as enigmatic as that of her dolls.

Strangely, my impression of the brothel on that December morning was one of cosiness. I was reminded of my first day at school where, because of severe homesickness, I had breakfasted with matron and her Irish maids. The place now had that clean smell of carefully ironed linen. Betty Bethlehem reappeared with bowl-like cups of milky coffee followed by Twinkle Twinkle carrying a silver tray of bacon and eggs. What had sounded mere whimsy in Colonel Midwinter's study was now as disturbingly real as the Oxford marmalade.

The dolls stared down.

'Could you sign this?' said Stigi, putting a sheaf of forms on the table in front of me. 'Requisition forms for paint to make the place look brighter, and . . .' There was something in the sideways glance that made me look through them.

'Native levies?'

'Native levies,' he replied as if it was the most normal thing in the world.

'I don't understand.'

Twinkle Twinkle gave me an alarming wink as the American sighed.

'I found these forms in the Kindergarten and thought they would help with the girls' expenses until we get on our feet and they get off theirs,' he said. 'They are for recruiting local talent.' The form before me; a War Office P 7561/a (Oriental) was for the recruiting of native troops and divided into a list which included Sikhs, Parsees, Bhils and a few I had never heard of before.

'Put them down as Babylonions, Stigi. Herodotus says they make the best whores. Perhaps we should rename this place the Café Babylon . . .'

An hour later we were driving towards the centre of town. Twinkle Twinkle sat in the front, his shoulders blocking the view. He was in a playful mood and this morning had discarded his wig, rouge and eyeliner and apart from his little-boy smile was every inch *Der Berserker*. He yelled something in Turkish as we passed a wrestling poster. The car shook but everyone ignored him and he settled back into his private thoughts of Irish whips and forearm smashes with a smirk on his face. Stigi had confided that, dervish-wise, Twinkle Twinkle was more of a howler than a whirler. We cruised, in no particular hurry, in search of fallen women. I had the feeling Stigi was keeping me purposely in suspense, but I did not like to ask; it appeared somewhat immature for the person in charge not to know the tricks of the trade. He was not in any hurry to recruit our bedroom Babylonians.

In the manner of visiting royalty we made a stately progress through the shabby parts of town, where Stigi Weitz was an emperor, not a driver. Bundles of notes changed hands over sideways glances, or were offered for nameless wares in brown paper bags. Everywhere the energetic Stigi was patted on the back. A Turkish butcher offered us a whole sheep which Twinkle Twinkle placed in the boot. He gave Stigi a great deal of money and a firm handshake. When we got back into the car the American just turned and grinned. The street smelled of roasting coffee. No one bothered to explain the sly transactions, and I did my best to look adult and in control.

We ate lunch in the Café Florian, a restaurant where Twinkle Twinkle demolished incredible quantities of pork knuckle and sauerkraut, washed down with beer tinged blood-colour by raspberry cordial. We then drove to the Ka-De-We, the Kaufhaus des Westens department store, a polite version of Harrod's which was a cathedral to the new prosperity and the new prostitution, where Stigi was fascinated by the fish counter and ordered gefilte fish while Twinkle Twinkle ate a whole herring, including the head.

'Say, this is living. Twenty types of herring, boy. A few years ago there were only twenty types of the same potatoes. I love Berlin. I must be the only Jew who adores the place. Every cobblestone tells me, son, you shouldn't be here, fuck off. That's why I'll never go back stateside. I want to make a million on the dark side of the moon. I love screwing the old lady. I want to be Berlin's first postwar Jewish millionaire. It's my duty to my people. Do you hear that you kraut bastards? Now that would seriously piss off Adolph Hitler.' A floor manager watched us leave, his arms tightly folded. A woman cleaner was scraping chewing-gum off the carpet with her finger nails.

At four o'clock, a time so precise it must have been arranged, we parked outside the Kurly Wurly hairdressers in a grim part of Potsdamerstrasse where it runs through the Schöneberg district. The building was massive and self-satisfied and mostly full of squatter families who trailed their children's washing from the windows like sad bunting. Under the fluorescent lights in the salon on the ground floor a ridiculously fat lady was frowning at a sandwich she knew she was going to eat. I followed Stigi and Twinkle Twinkle through a door at the back of an overheated waiting room. A uniformed black American serviceman at a desk was picking his fingers. He nodded at us.

Stigi took my arm and looked up into my face. 'You stay here. Have a nose round. Enjoy. Examine the wares. I have business with an old acquaintance,' he said, handing me a moulded rubber penis from a display of sexual aids. He then hurried away with the Turk through a side-door at the end of the long and gloomy room. Apart from the black serviceman, who was taking off his army tunic and putting on a black polo-neck sweater, I was the only person in the entire place, which at first glance looked like the changing-rooms in a department store; except the walls were painted black and the shelves around the reception desk were decked with pornography. Cheap curtains, one torn, closed off the cubicles which squatted in the middle of the room. An ultraviolet light showed purple and red in the ceiling and illuminated a garish fluorescent sign which proclaimed a 'Beep Show'. Without warning the uncertain music of a flute broke the silence and the black serviceman nodded his head towards the curtains with a look which said, 'What's your problem?' I pulled back the drape to be confronted with a glass screen which had a tightly closed second curtain on the far side. A coin slot was marked '*Fünf Minuten*'. Dutifully I put in the money and the curtains parted in what seemed a mechanised parody of the confessional. At the other side of the glass, a chronically tired girl with black rings under her eyes, who was twisted into a yoga position, was disturbed into a practised smile. She was wearing white stockings and a suspender-belt and nothing else, except for a flowing bridal headdress. She stroked the blonde bushy hair between her legs with a blue-painted flute. She put the mouthpiece up to her fleshy vaginal lips and, furrowing her brow, played the first few notes of Beethoven's Fifth while reddening only slightly in the face. The girl stopped and wiped the instrument on a purple silk square. She beckoned me with a finger and spoke into a microphone.

'Let me play your bugle, soldier boy,' she began in English, with an accent doubtless perfected by listening to the American Forces Network.

'Press the button if you want me. Beep, Beep if you want me. We can be alone together. We can make music. I can play your tune.' From the expression of crushing fatigue on her pretty face it was the last thing she really wanted. I shook my head. In a flash she was gathering up the silk square and the flute and heading for a small door in that dark submarine.

'Please don't be offended. You play very well . . .'

'Thanks, *Arschloch*,' she replied, drowsily clutching a bathrobe as another girl pushed past her. I had not meant to offend. The new girl shed a silk robe. She was taller, much more graceful than the first, I thought as I pushed in more money. On the third coin I recognised her.

'My God, Magda.'

To see someone you regard as a goddess in the flesh can be quite confusing.

A sugary voice sang about 'Rudolph the Red-Nosed Reindeer' on a concealed sound system as before me my dream girl, so covered and gloved in the dimly-lit railway carriage, so in control, was now fully exposed for a few shillings. The suspenders and stockings and bridal headdress were the same but in black. Magda looked straight at me.

'Beep if you want me, soldier,' she cooed into the microphone, as she did the splits.

'Beep if you want to be alone with me. Beep, Beep if you want me.' She seemed delighted by her performance and I pressed and pressed until my finger hurt against the glowing red button just in case there was any other customer lurking behind the Kurly Wurly curtains.

'OK, lovers,' came the voice of the black doorman over the loud speaker. 'Room four. Ten minutes is fifty straight. More, you will be charged per trick.' English appeared to be the international

55

language of illicit sex, the stock market and air traffic control. As I left my booth Magda was already vacating the black tank and the serviceman pointed the way down a corridor off which there were several doors. Red lights were on outside two to show they were occupied. The uncertain sounds of a flute came from a third. In the fourth, at the other side of a bead curtain, Magda had taken off the funereal bridal headdress and was wearing a short kimono of damson-coloured silk. I did not know what to say. The walls were closing in. I rattled through the bead curtain and noticed the dragon on Magda's kimono had too many legs. On her ankle was a trickle of sticky wetness. The room was small and painted a dark shade of purple. The bed of clean white sheets was hardly creased. Perhaps the last client had specified his supplication on the orange carpet. I didn't care. A candle burned on the bedside table next to a half-eaten chocolate Santa, a yule log and three Christmas cards. My eyes were drawn to her lovely mouth. On the wall was a gnarled Bavarian crucifix.

'I never imagined you were . . .'

'A whore?'

'No, a Catholic.'

For a moment I thought she was going to lose her temper. I heard footsteps outside as she looked at a cheap watch.

'Kiss me, Toby. Kiss and moan.'

'Moan?'

'*Bitte*, moan. The man gets mad if he doesn't hear moaning after a few minutes. We're meant to do it to the customer as many times as we can. It's hard work. Please moan, Toby.' In her eyes was that look of ethereal panic I had noticed in the train. I opened my mouth and let out a sound which was more like a gargle. Magda grabbed me between the legs and kissed me fiercely, digging her nails into the base of my scrotum. I gave an animal yelp as the footsteps paced slowly away. I heard a low chuckle. Magda smiled and kissed me on the nose.

'Thank you, Toby. That was very diplomatic. But why didn't you call me? I have something of yours. I was a naughty girl.' She reached into the bedside cabinet and took something from inside.

'Here is your wallet, Toby Jubb. All your precious money is in there. Well, most of it. I thought you were brave. Were you going to telephone me? Is it good to come in here and gape like a schoolboy?

Do you get off on it, big boy? Why don't you count all that *geld*, Toby Jubb? Now what do you want for it? It's so easy now. You have the money. You can have me . . . for sure.'

Her mood had changed abruptly from the conspiratorial and friendly. She was mistress of her own domain; an unmistakable menace was telegraphed in the management's occasional footsteps in the corridor. Magda shook her honey-coloured hair and pulled open her kimono, examining herself like a little girl getting ready for a bath. There was an ugly purple bruise on her hips and a yellowish one on her ribs. I felt wretched. She lit a cigarette.

'Did you like being married to me, Toby Jubb? I bet you thought of me as a little excitement, but never as a whore, never as something bought and sold. A question of trade. That is awful, *ja*? You would rather I was hungry and lived in a coffee sack in Kreuzberg. You would rather I was beaten on the streets instead of having my own little room. My own place, away from the world. You would rather I slept on an U-Bahn platform. It is my karma to love people back into the world. Berlin is so cold. My God, if I want to be a Catholic or anything else I have the right. It is independence men find obscene . . .'

The footsteps returned.

'Trouble, Magda?' inquired the deep voice.

'Moan,' she whispered.

'Trouble?' the voice repeated.

We both moaned, myself more sympathetically this time as I now understood more about the order of service. Magda took out a packet of contraceptives and undid two, stretching them out. 'You have to drop these in a bin by the door when you go,' she said, looking away. 'They like proof of productivity. If we work hard the customers will come back and we will be paid more. In time Germany will be great again.'

She laughed. I sat marvelling at her. She was so completely beautiful. I wanted to take her with me. I put my hand on her shoulder and she reached up and took it immediately in hers. I thought there was a suggestion of a tear. Her eyes overwhelmed.

'My mother is a Catholic. She is very beautiful too. She has long dark hair, though.'

'Little boys always love their mothers,' she hissed angrily. 'Every soldier who goes to a brothel really wants his mama. It is pathetic.

I'm not going to be your mother, Toby. I am different. I require love. I need love. But I need to love everyone. You cannot understand and I cannot escape it. I know a saxophonist who is a Buddhist . . . I have to enjoy my fate piece by piece, nail by nail.' She was looking towards the crucifix.

'I am not good. I can never be good. But I am beautiful, and I must carry that cross . . .'

I didn't quite know what to say.

'Did the Frenchman promise to take you away? The man who gave you the bruises?'

Magda wound a lock of hair around a finger. 'All men promise such things. It makes them feel immortal. Men love to play at God. They adore to describe a heaven. They love the cruelty of leaving you even more, Toby Jubb. It's the next best thing to killing someone. They enjoy that too.'

The tear in her eye had fully formed now and dropped onto the back of my hand. I took her in my arms and she put her warm palms at either side of my face. My heart accelerated as she rolled me onto the bed. Her lips nuzzled the corner of my mouth and I pulled at the kimono. The overhead light caught her soft skin and small nipples. She picked up one of the condoms but I was determined not to be one of her procession of sheathed communicants; slaves to a guilt I could only guess at. My fingers reached for the damp springy curls between her legs. Before she could protest I had pushed her further up the bed and buried my tongue in her fragrant Styx, suppressing any desire to recognise the soft metallic taste of what might be the customer before me. She froze. I thought for a moment she would throw me out as I glanced up the curved horizon of her belly. Love was not on the menu at the Kurly Wurly; it took too long. Then in a deft frenzy she was undoing my belt and zip. Her lips hurriedly found the object of her search as her strong hips beat down. She did not let go until all the silent shuddering pleasure had subsided.

'My God,' I began, after moaning for real.

'He is on my side, Toby Jubb. I would have given you your money back.'

The footsteps echoed again outside. The experience was like making love in a prison.

'Regular for you, Magda. Is Moby Dick finished?'

'He's finished,' she shouted to the retreating boots, pulling me on top of her and joining us together with a slow, undulating motion. The coupling was over before I could say Merry Christmas. Here was a girl who made people happy to a tight schedule. She kissed me on the forehead. The greatest incongruity in the room was Magda's beauty.

'Please, Toby, do not promise me anything,' she pleaded as she licked the two dry condoms, tying them with a strand of pink wool into which she slotted a Flags-of-All-Nations cocktail stick from a box on the bed. We had countries beginning with the letter 'C'. The banners of our passion were China and Chad. Magda popped them on a towel.

'Put these in the bucket by the cash desk. They want to keep track of our tricks, so we don't pull the woollens over their eyes, if that is how you say it. We each have our own flags. Remember Toby, don't promise me anything. One can only be innocent in the present,' she said, disappearing through the bead curtain; no doubt to wash away the recent past.

In the front hall a fat German in an alpine hat was searching nervously about him as I dropped the used contraceptives into the half-full bucket. I wondered who had the job of counting up.

The black American glared at me.

'You made a lot of noise for just China and Chad, boy. What you after in there, boy? You some kind of loon? Nothing in there but wasted energy, spent money and broken dreams. Now fuck off and come again soon.'

The fat German snuffled a laugh. I tried not to imagine him with Magda. I reached for my wallet. Why did she have to love everyone? The man behind the desk shook his head.

'On the house, boy,' he growled. The notion seemed entirely against his principles and the laws of the universe judging from his expression as Stigi and Twinkle Twinkle reappeared through a door. Behind them someone sounded to be in pain. Twinkle Twinkle had a smile that only could be described as bashful.

'Have a good time?' asked Stigi, looking as if butter would not melt in his mouth.

'I think so,' I said, as we left the Kurly Wurly. In my mind were definite plans for my Café Babylon. The difference between Magda and Betty Bethlehem was extraordinary. Betty had drifted into the work, probably through an abortion and a pimp boyfriend. Magda was the kind who chose what she did . . . but why?

'Stigi, there's a girl who works there. I want you to get her. A splendid recruit for our native levies. She's really good. Believe me . . .'

He nodded and said he would try, but there had been a disagreement with the management of the Kurly Wurly, about which he did not elaborate. He was still muttering to himself in some mirrored hall of Byzantine gangland conspiracy when they dropped me on the Ku'damm on their way out to a regular poker game at the Mercedes factory. In the gathering darkness I went for a walk to clear my head of China and of Chad. Relatively pleased with myself, I strolled along the straight road that leads through the Tiergarten to the Brandenburg Gate and after a quarter of an hour stood where the statue of the winged victory turns her back on the West. Many cars waited pointing eastward for their papers to be checked before making a Christmas visit to relatives in the East, down Unter den Linden or what was left of it. The battered Ford Taunuses and Volkswagens with overflowing bags and boxes showed a touching decency and generosity of spirit that defied the Weitzes and Midwinters of this world. I turned north by the small sign which marked the border through newly-planted birch saplings towards the Reichstag; the ruins picked out by search-lights, like the bleached and twisted bones of a prehistoric victim on a lake bed in Arizona. A sudden movement made me turn.

Two large men came purposely out of the trees and mists towards me. A third stepped from behind them. The third man was Parr.

'You get a jolly sight better view near the river, old boy. Marvellous building. Hope we didn't make you jump.' The scrubbed face appeared as open as a Sunday school bible. His two companions, obviously military but also in civilian clothes, remained a few paces behind as we skirted the ruins and stopped to admire a gunboat in the River Spree, squat and deadly as old MacHeath's jackknife. A light flashed momentarily in our eyes as the boat's crew checked for smugglers. That haunted spot was not the sort of place where one ran into an old school chum.

'As a matter of fact I want a chinwag, Jubb. You always were damn clever, Jubb. Damn quick. Sure I didn't make you jump?' From behind came a rumbling chuckle. Parr's underlings lurked under a birch with the tight, muscled expectation of those who are waiting to throw someone into a river. The thick black water dotted with ice rolled by like oil and cotton wool.

'What's up?' For all the world I sounded like a third-former who has been caught smoking. Parr had that effect.

'Sorry to be so cloak-and-dagger, but you never know who's looking in town,' he said as border guards examined us through powerful binoculars by the well-lit building. 'I want you to do me a favour, Jubb.'

At first the request did not register. I recalled Parr once telling the astonished padre at school that he never prayed because he thought man should stand on his own two feet. My first guilty thought was that he had followed me to the Kurly Wurly.

'I want you to do me a favour, Jubb.'

'What sort of favour, Parr?' I fixed my gaze on the epaulette button of his grey British Warm. He frowned, an expression as contrived as when a child plays at being annoyed, and his black leather gloves squeaked with newness as he clenched and flexed his fists.

'You don't really want to stay in Berlin, do you, Jubb? It's not really your sort of place? I mean it might have been before the war. But not now.'

'Oh, I don't know, it could grow on you,' I replied as the patrol boat searchlight swept past us again and over the Reichstag to where armed parkkeepers had once shot Rosa Luxemburg's revolutionaries for ignoring 'Keep Off The Grass' signs. I appeared to be trapped on the set of a spy film.

'We always used to get off on the wrong foot at school,' he said, scratching his pointed nose. 'I suppose it was because of family. But now we're on the same side of the fence fighting a common enemy.'

'The cold?' I offered.

'Ha ha, very droll,' smiled Parr, almost ingenuously. 'Actually, I'm here with my official hat on, as well. French security think where Midwinter has sent you may have something to do with one of their nationals. A girl called Véronique and an individual named Claude. Hear anything about that?'

'Not a bleat.'

Parr looked at me closely. 'Now the girl wouldn't usually matter, except in the way she was killed. By all accounts it was a lesson to all such girls. I will send you a report. However, as I said, she was a streetwalker and probably got what was coming to her. But Claude. That's different.'

'It certainly is.'

'The way I look at it, and please don't take it personally, Jubb; you can't afford another disaster like your Paris fiasco. I know all about that, Jubb. No need to make excuses. Some French tart lured you into her bedroom. But you certainly can't afford a murder inquiry. It would be quite within my power to order an investigation, as the French have information that this man had served in the Black Watch and once met the Queen Mother. The Queen Mother is taken very seriously in military circles.' I did not even want to try to explain. 'I don't envy you your job, Jubb. Filthy creatures.'

'I'm cataloguing archaeological remains.'

'Call it what you like, old boy, but we both know you are trying to make contact with Hollmann. By the way, I would like to take a peek at your bric-à-brac sometime. Do tell me if you find anything remotely valuable. Please don't underestimate me, Jubb. I know the score. Turn Hollmann over to me before telling the Colonel and I can pull strings that will have you back in Paris before you know it. Father's old chums . . .'

At the mention of his father we both paused. I broke the silence.

'But I thought the whole point was to make Hollman come over of his own free will. To be sure of his information.' Suddenly Parr was angry.

'Midwinter is an old fool. Hollmann is dangerous, Jubb, very dangerous to all our plans and I want him. Personal reasons. Read his file. See how many villages he burnt. See how many war crimes he committed. Help me and I'll help you. Things are far more delicate here than they seem. I want you to help out, Jubb. Be a part of things. Do this for me and I'll see that you share in the spoils. I'm sure Midwinter has filled you in. If you even see this man, call me first. Not Midwinter. You understand? Good. I have to get Hollmann.' He turned, leaving me puzzled, and took a few paces before looking back.

'Merry Christmas, Jubb.'

The east wind swirled snow around us in the searchlights.

'Merry Christmas, Parr.'

6

Café Babylon
Berlin   December 31, 1960

Dear Mother,

Happy New Year. The girls have arrived, all thirteen of them, mostly from the frozen East and in clothes they appear to have knitted themselves. The prettiest is Helga, a sultry sizzler from the steppes of East Prussia who was a PT instructor and appeared on party recruitment posters until her boyfriend was arrested for robbing graves of personal jewellery. Helga has the most enormous breasts. Next, comes Lotte, who is six foot and will look fantastic in a leotard; Dorta Baang, who is Danish; three Brunhildes who are extremely svelte and chatter like mice; and two Gertas, one of whom could easily give Twinkle Twinkle a round or two. But my favourites of the new girls are Bernice, a shy little petal from Potsdam, and her sister, Ulrike. Both blush when you look at them and one almost feels compelled to take them back to the orphanage, except they would scream blue murder. They have never done this kind of work before but Mr Weitz, my assistant, has an approach which he says is almost foolproof, and that he has operated in his other leisure outlets. At the moment it is very easy for any would-be refugee merely to stroll across the border from East to West. The trouble is finding a decent job. So Mr Weitz puts an advert in the paper asking for attractive young couples. He offers the girl a job as a cocktail waitress in a night club, but leaves no one in any doubt as to what else will be expected. Then, when the couple are storming out, he promises a job for the husband or boyfriend in the new Mercedes factory. Apparently, Spartacus would sell his grandmother for such a treat and we have the girls for six months while Mr Weitz processes hubby's papers. Few turn him down. The amateurs, he says, quickly learn from the professionals. We also have three seasoned troopers Mr Weitz lured away from a surprising establishment called Kurly Wurly; which is a hairdresser's in front and a brothel in the back. From here came Heaven, an Amazon temptress from Zanzibar who looks as if she eats babies, and Kandy, who has a novel way of playing the flute. Last is Magda, darling Magda, whom I am in love with, though not as much as you, dear Mother,

All my love,
    Toby

The discussion in the bar was becoming strained.

'Love is the answer.'

'Please, Toby. Take my advice and don't mess around with love in one of these places. No close relationships. It only ends in tears. You've been talking to Magda. She means well, but if you ask me, she's right off her head.' Betty Bethlehem was annoyed. She thumped the table and her eyes were wide and staring. We were upstairs having a summit conference, Stigi, Betty and I, while downstairs, the conscript army of 'native levies' were transforming the Café Babylon, as the Café Bok had been rechristened, with brooms and paint and elbow-grease and a kind of energy one would expect from Hitler's children. Or perhaps some were relieved their initial duties were so banal.

'All I'm saying is that we should hold some girls in reserve. The professionals. They can form lasting relationships with the chaps from the East, as opposed to the ordinary customers. And what does it matter if someone does fall in love?'

'It would be wrong,' said Betty firmly. 'It would be wicked. We're not selling love.'

'We're not selling bagels,' said Stigi. Betty shook her head. She almost looked in pain.

'It would be disgusting. To lure young men to their deaths . . .'

'Who said anything about death, for God's sake? We're talking about love. About showing these chaps a bit of human warmth. About showing the girls a bit of consideration and stopping all this production-line twenty-times-on-Sunday rubbish. The soldiers from the East will want more then sex. They've been in prison camps. Brothel keepers in ancient Rome often encouraged girls to enter into serious relationships with influential clients.' I did not say so, but these men seemed no different from that Eyeless Clockwork Army who, in my dreams, came marching back to claim their glass peepers.

Betty was about to explode. She had her rules and we were breaking them. She didn't realize there were no rules here. Perhaps it was a Calvinist horror of giving away intimacy. Only the Devil gives such things freely; even if we always get a bill for them later. But we were not making a pact with the Devil. Betty pulled her housecoat close around her. She was as frightened of real emotion as a spinster is of sex.

'I like all this Classics stuff,' intervened Stigi, lighting a Chesterfield. 'It adds class to the act. In particular I like the Babylonian gimmick. Run the Babylonian gimmick past me again, Toby. Now that really has possibilities. We will be something out of Cecil B. DeMille. I love the bit about the seven veils.'

'You can fake sex, fake an orgasm. But if you start faking love it'll be bad luck. You mark my words, Toby. It's all a game to you. All we are is a box of toys . . .'

Stigi coughed.

'The only love these little beauties will have known is their sergeant's. Personally, I don't think Toby has a hope in hell of melting the hearts of former storm-troopers. But the Babylon thing is class. Tell me about Babylon, Toby.'

'Well, it's quite easy, really. We divide the girls up into amateurs and professionals. We follow Stigi's original idea to convert the bakery into a cabaret where the centre of attention is the Blue Gate of Babylon. We can build a stage around it. We can have the occasional show. The customer buys a token when he comes into the place and that takes care of everything. When he sees a girl he likes, he gives her the token and they leave the bakery and come across to one of the rooms here. He can then have the girl for the rest of the night. In a way we'll be celebrating the Ishtar ritual. Did you have any luck with the costumes?'

Stigi nodded. 'Yes, sir. The British Berlin Operatic and Dramatic Society were willing to lend us some fairy numbers from *Midsummer Night's Dream* and slave-girl togas from *Don Juan*. I did have to promise something in return, though.'

'What's that?'

'Well, they asked if they could use our stage if they had a really big company coming through on account of us being under the British Council. I thought there was no harm in saying yes. I also have to pick up more paint. It's Prussian Blue to match the gate. You were saying, Toby?' I cleared my throat. The idea of the British Council sending a Home Counties theatre company to Toby Jubb's brothel was not a happy one. I cleared my throat.

'Well, to me the plan is simple. Stigi gets in touch with the Baron's men who are already in the city and we offer them the services of Babylon. We hold the experienced girls in reserve for these men. The girls will attempt to make the Baron's men fall in love by kindness, understanding and a continual show of affection and loyalty. Love must be central to all this. We must show that we have more to offer than the usual quick soulless fuck. Love is what we will give them. Love is our weapon. The actual suggestion about defecting to the West must come from the men. To me it seems perfectly reasonable, but if you can think of another way, Betty, I would be glad to hear it. The girls involved will be well paid.'

Betty shrugged. 'Well, I say that's totally wrong. And what if the new girls don't want to stay?'

'If they're not in on the secret, they get their arses kicked back onto Karl Marx Strasse,' said Stigi, mildly. A half-smile played threateningly on the deeply-tanned face. 'I've also been distributing a little chemical kindness against the eventuality of a mutiny. The stuff came from our friends in the Pony Express.'

'The Pony what?'

'The black American soldiers who do the drug-pushing. The people who got my Zela hooked. I wondered when you would stoop to that.' Betty's words were bitter. Yet my mother had always approved of a little recreational morphine.

'I had to keep the Pony Express happy the other day by buying some dope along with their girls. The Kurly Wurly is theirs,' added Stigi. 'The purchase was just a matter of courtesy. I'm too hot to peddle it and hated to see it go to waste. Anyways, I should be getting my hands on more any time soon. What's wrong with spreading a little happiness?' With a peck on the cheek of a fuming Betty he was gone, off with dancing steps down a stairway fast being painted blue by my helpers from the East. I was alone with Betty Bethlehem. The moment did not seem to be right to explain that we intended to take pictures of the Baron and his men if Cupid's dart didn't find its mark. To me it was becoming an adult parlour game. Sin gives the delicious illusion of being so grown-up.

'Why do they call themselves the Pony Express?'

'They call heroin "horse". They distribute it all over Germany through the military bases. They're bastards. I'm shit scared of them. I'm shit scared of all this.' Betty's eyes were narrow and angry.

'You don't like what I'm doing, do you?'

She shook her head and her breasts quivered inside a tight purple sweater. Then she smiled.

'I know you have no choice, love. From what Stigi says I don't think any of us have a choice any more, it being Government work. Respectable people are the cruellest punters and educated men the worst pimps.' She pulled at a cheap silver filigree ring on the middle finger of her left hand.

'Did you ever fall in love with a punter, Betty?' The question itself sounded crass.

She smiled, shyly this time. She nodded her head but did not explain. For a second, there was a hint in her brown eyes of what it must have been like to work in the Blue Beret on Regina Street; to have soldier after soldier and more on Sundays; to have every kiss taste of brandy-sour and vomit. I had spoken to Zela. Love became important on such a barren landscape, important by its utter absence.

'At the best it can be a giggle. But mostly to us it's a mucky job. Some of the young lads would fall head-over-heels. Start hanging around with flowers but couldn't afford more than once. Soldiers all look the bloody same and on the game you don't remember faces. I once met Freddie Mills the boxer on a train and didn't clock him. We'd see the last customer to the door and find love's young dream out there, drunk and jealous. A ruck would start and the ambulances would come and the military police and you measure the love in broken glass and bloody footsteps. Oh yes, you're right, they do want love more than anything else. The trouble is they don't want any bugger else to have it.' She laughed. 'I only love my Zela. Start pissing around with love, Toby, especially in Berlin, and you might as well lie down at that crossroads and wait for the bus to run you over. Mark my words.' She sighed and her face thankfully regained its wicked smile. 'I'd better see what my little flock is doing. Can't have them getting into any mischief,' and then she was gone, leaving me empty and confused in the winter sunlight. Love does have a way of complicating things. But if I was to run a brothel, I was determined it should be done with a measure of compassion, with the emphasis on style rather than profit. I am a Catholic, after all.

I shivered. The sensitive-looking grey horse pawed at the icy rim of the Grunwaldsee as its rider patted it gently on the side of the mane. Steam rose from quivering flanks. The stallion smelled of the gallop. He looked around constantly to his master for reassurance. Colonel Midwinter had been transformed from the slightly blimpish minor college don, into an imposing equestrian statue of the kind one finds in northern municipalities. Twinkle Twinkle had delivered me to the lakeside and insisted on staying in the car. Among the beech trees I could see the Jagdschloss Grunewald, the old hunting-lodge of the Prince Elector of Brandenburg, which certain of the Kaiser's officers had used for transvestite orgies. The horse pawed on the beach of fine sand, only partially covered by snow. Like me, the animal seemed wary of treading on thin ice. Unbelievably, in the smoky light of a freezing winter afternoon a party of noisy locals was trying to chip a hole. At least the German sense of pantomime was not dead. They wanted to go for a swim.

'Makes you wonder how we beat them,' growled Midwinter as I approached.

'Well, we do have the Serpentine.'

I noticed he was wearing a monocle. He got down expertly and tethered the animal to a picnic table. The horse nuzzled his shoulder. Midwinter took refuge in what appeared to be a giant picnic basket with a settee inside, of which there were several along the beach. Ours was adorned with everlasting flowers. In the distance I could hear shouting, perhaps from the Devil's Hill. A small mountain had been made from the bombed-out buildings and children sledged down it. Magda had showed me the picture in the paper that morning. She wanted me to take her sledging.

'How goes it, then?' he asked, offering a hip-flask which I took. The peach brandy warmed all the way down.

'The Babylon's grand opening will be at the end of the month. If that's what you want.'

'That's exactly what I want, Jubb. The people in London want it, too. Remember that. I don't suppose for one moment that you have had a visit from our mutual friend Parr? Any visits from Mr Wolf, Jubb? These corn-dollies aren't made for someone of your size are they, old boy?'

I hesitated. 'Yes, Parr came to see me. I ran into him while I was walking. I was by the Reichstag and he suddenly appeared.'

'How apt. Like Mephistopheles, I presume, but without the sense of humour. Tell me all, Jubb. I do hope you are working hard. I think you now see where the ancient Persian comes in. I want you to get the Gate and other artefacts precisely catalogued. It will take your mind off your other problems. Getting that lot back home will be a feather in my cap, Jubb. And do tell me if there is anything . . . extraordinary. There is tell that old Koldewey who found the stuff also struck gold. But now I want to know about Mr Wolf.' I hated tales out of school, even about Parr. But I was very curious about what Parr had asked me to do, and why.

'He wanted me to tell him about von Hollmann, if I made contact, before I informed you, sir. As soon as I made contact. He didn't go into detail. I was going to let you know, sir. But we've been very busy.'

The Colonel smiled. 'Hollmann, eh? Well, I suppose he does have his reasons.'

I did not like the Colonel's tone.

'But how could they have ever met?'

'I suppose you know all about Parr's lunatic father, the General, and how he won the Victoria Cross, by blowing up a German munitions dump and capturing a column just before Monty's push on El Alamein. Didn't your family know him?' I nodded. I remembered the picture of him on the library wall at school doing the daring deed. The feat had been the start of a brilliantly indolent military career.

'Well, Jubb, a much younger Baron Rollo von Hollmann was meant to be part of the ill-fated column, except he wasn't. We now know from intelligence reports in my department's files that he was on a plane back to Germany to be questioned by the Gestapo on his Masonic involvements. We shall probably never know all the details, but it's clear that Parr senior and his men, in a bout of sheer keenness, became totally lost in the desert, went round in a large circle, and with a small band of commandos blew up one of our own fuel dumps. In the official accounts all survivors were tidily shot on the grounds they had been executing prisoners. We now have good reason to believe the unlucky victims were Australians. No one seemed to miss them, being colonials. Parr senior was decorated and promoted after the elation of El Alamein, and the raid led to the formation of the long-range desert group which of course became the SAS. One could see how young Selwyn would take it hard that a man who knows how his father really won the Victoria Cross is being wooed by us in a superannuated knocking-shop . . .'

'He intends to kill him, doesn't he?'

The Colonel turned and looked at me quizzically.

'Parr is what we term a headhunter. Things can get terribly bogged down in red tape between the four powers, so if someone is causing too much upset we call in Parr's unit and the problem is removed. I'm telling you this, my boy, because you're a Classics scholar and will understand. You may have noticed a predilection for extreme violence in Parr's schooldays. I shouldn't imagine he was a good little lamb.'

The thought brought back unwanted memories. 'He was very serious. He had a picture of his father with Winston Churchill. Can't you stop him?'

The Colonel shook his head. 'Parr's unit is very hush-hush indeed. Their purpose is to dispose of top Eastie Beasties and their friends over here. The idea is to put them on the defensive, ho ho. He answers directly to Whitehall and it would do no good for me to order him to lay off the Baron. After all, you are my creation, Jubb. I mean, his father was a senior member of the General Staff even though he couldn't read a bloody map and reckoned up on his fingers. The Parrs are damn difficult territory. If you get in his way he's likely to kill you too, you know. I'm not meant to know about Parr killing people. A picture of Winston you say? At school? How depressing. The idea almost has a whiff of paedophilia. I've wondered about him for some time.'

'So what do I do, sir?'

'Go after the good Baron von Hollmann, my boy. Use your considerable charm and your girls before Parr uses his garrotte. I want him. He can tell me so much. But he's no good to me dead in a ditch. If Parr should succeed in his murderous little plans the future would look bleak for you, Jubb. So go after the Baron with the forces of love and your pretty ladies. If Parr gets too close I would rather Hollmann escape in one piece so we can try again another day. I have my reasons. And look after those Babylonian bits and bobs. Don't lose sight of the fact they are important too. I fear from what you tell me that Parr has plans for those as well.'

As he spoke one of the would-be bathers, a portly lady in her fifties, casting care to the wind suddenly revealed she was a nudist. She skipped like a pink hippo across the ice with a smile on her face and a determined spiritual abandonment to the forces of nature, and fell through with a loud shriek that sent a huddle of wild geese clattering into flight.

'Take note, Jubb.'

'Of what, sir?'

'To tread very carefully indeed, my boy.'

The old bakery was cosy and warm as I rummaged later that day through the books on the Ishtar Gate and Babylon I had been able to borrow from the British Council, the American Library and, most strangely, the Society for the Propagation of the Gospel. Twinkle Twinkle and the sinister little caretaker had started up the bread-oven. Everywhere the girls were cleaning and scrubbing, scouring and polishing. The smell of new bread won a battle against the damp. On top of the pile of books was the Histories of the old liar Herodotus, which fell open at the point where he claimed the Babylonians buried their dead in honey. He also said that certain Indians employed giant ants which sniffed gold for them in the manner of truffle-hounds, and were nearly the same size. 'There is found in this desert a kind of ant of great size; bigger than a fox, though not as big as a dog.' Further on he mentions the perils of flying snakes of this remote land with every hope his more boorish countrymen would take him seriously. But if I were to write about my present situation, would I be believed?

A more important source, if I was to catalogue this alternative Gate of Ishtar, even prove its partial authenticity, and save my sanity, was the German archaeologist Richard Koldewey's *Excavations in Babylon*; a rare English edition. My bundle also contained another Herodotus in the Greek and a selection of publications from the German Oriental Society, *Die Tempel von Babylon* and *Borsippa* and *Babylonische Miscellen*. Out of one book fell a page of what seemed to be acknowledgements from Koldewey, whose diggings were carried out under the auspices of the government in Berlin at the turn of the century. I was seeking any reference to the great golden statue of Bel Marduk. At the top of the list was the President of the Deutschen Orient-Gesellschaft, his Excellency Baron von Hollmann, whom I took to be Rollo's uncle, if not his father. In a peculiar way I felt already related to the Baron.

Playful teeth bit my ear.

'*Liebling*.'

'Magda.' The fur collar on her coat smelt of perfume and winter. Cindy trailed behind her. She was sucking hard on a cheap golliwog lollipop.

Magda handed me fifty marks.

Despite my brave words in the last few days, I could not stop my hand shaking.

'Look how clever we are, Toby. We have been working the cemetery. When men put flowers on the graves of their wives it makes them so sentimental. They need comforting. We have been angels of mercy, have we not?'

Her eyes smiled dreamily into mine. To Magda prostitution was a crusade. 'What are these? More stories? Oh, how lovely. They are about the Gate? Can I read one, my dear husband? Can I bring them to our room? So the Babylonians were interested in astrology . . . ?' I stood there looking down at her, my hand shaking slightly. I was still not sure how I felt about being in love with a girl with such a vocation. She had accepted her change in circumstances from the Kurly Wurly without surprise or thanks; rather like an obedient Jesuit who is sent from his own Pyreanean village to a mission in

Java. She had moved in with me, with her clothes, crucifix and a large bottle of Dulbosan patent disinfectant which she used along with 4711 in every bath, and she took three baths a day.

'Tell me about Babylon, Toby. Did they ever have B-girls in Babylon, Toby? Did they have girls like Cindy and me?'

I read the passage from Herodotus which described how everyone had to sell their love as a sacred act on at least one day of their lives, traditionally on the night before their marriage. Once a woman had taken her seat in the temple precincts she was not allowed to go home again until a man had thrown a silver shekel into her lap, and taken her outside and made love to her. 'Tall, handsome women soon manage to get home again, but the ugly ones stay a long time before they can fulfil the condition the law demands, some of those, indeed, as much as three or four years . . .' Magda's face lit up.

'What beautiful, sensible people. How I love them,' she exclaimed, caressing the top of the book and kissing me on the chin. I began to tell her of my plans to use the Ishtar ritual and the Gate when we opened, though I left out Betty Bethlehem's opposition.

'Clever boy, Toby. You must let me read all about it. I must be the high priestess. You are very young for this work, Toby Jubb. You are still a mother's boy.'

'Thank you for moving in with me.'

'We are married. Please promise me you will look after me, Toby. But do not promise me too much. I am afraid I do not have the fabled heart of pure gold. I think dear Betty's trouble is that she has. She thinks she cannot give in this work without destroying herself. It is so sad to reduce it all to lucrative athletics. But I like her, darling. Really I do. Forgive me if I ever hurt you. I will always forgive you. But I must be what I am, Toby. We have killed all the gods. We have no commandments any more, so I have to make my own. Tell me of your mother, Toby. In the photograph by our bed she is so serene. A little like you. Your father is not like you at all. I think you are a child of love.' She sat down next to me, gently, on the hindquarters of a winged Hittite horseman.

'She is very good-looking. I wrote to her this morning.'

'And good? Is she good also? Is she good to your father? He looked a sad man in a shiny suit. Can you do the twist, Toby? I do not like the twist.'

'Mother's good to me, but not usually to my father. She leads him a dance. She is frightened of getting old.'

'Your mother betrays him?' Magda was interested.

'Yes, I think she does. I mean I know she does. Often. Quite often. It's a thing with her.'

'But that is the only weapon women have,' she said shrugging off her black fur coat. Stigi had provided the fur. Cindy had found a dead bird and was poking at it with the lollipop stick. As I stood below the portals of Ishtar, discussing my mother's infidelities with a lady who sold herself in cemeteries, her particular trade seemed to have nothing prurient about it at all. I put my hand on Magda's hair and stroked the tumbling curls.

'My mother never needed any kind of a weapon with father. He always did everything for her. I remember he once ran her to an appointment with a man because it was raining.'

Magda smiled knowingly. 'Oh *ja*, *Liebling*. I know the good and kind man who marries a beautiful woman. The pillar of the community, the centre of the family; the great king who can forgive everything and often has to. His wife can join in his fantasy. She can kiss his feet and worship him and be his slave. Or she can be bad. She can be free. I'm glad you are bad like your mother. Only a little bad perhaps. A little dirt on your angel wings. But if you were truly bad, you couldn't . . .' Suddenly she stopped. A door opened to the snow at the other end of the building and even at this distance there was a blast of cold air. Men, under the direction of Stigi, were bringing in boxes and placing them in high stacks which soon began to rival the monuments of Babylon. Black market structures of everything from whisky to Carnation milk. Magda did not drink and she was trying to give up smoking.

'Yes, if your mother could see you now, my big *Berliner*.'

'You remember I explained how I want the professional girls to entertain the Baron and his men?'

'Yes, *Liebling*.'

She was staring at me. I turned the pages of a book. The silence was an awkward one. I only wanted to protect her.

'If you want, that can mean you don't have to go with anyone else.' She looked up angrily from a faded copy of the *Wissenschaftliche Veröffentlichungen der Deutschen Orient Gesellschaft*. 'You don't have to do what the other girls do, Magda. I can decide that.'

'I'm clean and cheap and my name is Cindy.' Tired of playing with carrion, Cindy stroked my shoulder.

'How dare you decide anything for me,' began Magda. She picked up a fragment of fifth century BC pottery and hurled it at the bakery wall, where it shattered to fragments.

'We will not be happy, you and I, if you do not understand me. Be a proper man, Toby. Allow me to breathe. After all, that is what your mother would want. Now I must have my bath.'

'Rubbers are free. Tissues are extra,' added Cindy, with a determined seriousness, mirroring Magda's mood. One wondered at the frost that had arrested the girl's development. What those empty eyes had seen.

Magda, still fuming, scooped up an armful of papers and books.

'I will read these. If I am to be your priestess, Toby. Come up in a while.' Cindy followed in her wake with an overplayed professional wink. She pulled up her dress as she passed Stigi who was walking towards us. Six-Shot Otto the Hound trotted at his heels. The American looked a content and prosperous man with a contented and prosperous dog. Six-Shot was wearing a little tartan coat. Stigi was telling one of the girls in German that before the grand opening the clientele would be by invitation only, while two other girls began to paint the green, peeling walls of the bakery a light blue in black-market paint. I interrupted his enthusing.

'One question, Stigi. Everyone pays for a girl with the shekels they get from Twinkle Twinkle. But will the Eastie Beasties have enough cash? If we give them rates lower than your smugglers and GIs they will suspect. How will they afford this garden of delights?' Tables were being brought in. Babylon was taking shape. I was beginning to get nervous. As in any close relationship, the brothel was acquiring a life of its own. If I were not careful it soon would be running me.

Stigi looked down at his shoes. From his inside pocket he took a cigarette-case from which he extracted a fat reefer. He had already introduced me to the habit, which I had to admit was very pleasant.

'Amphetamine sulphate,' he said, after lighting up, taking a drag and handing the cigarette to me. I coughed.

'What?'

'Not this, stupid. Speed. A stimulant. The raw material for the purple hearts all the kids are taking, or soon will be. That's the future, Toby. Ask Six-Shot, there is too much back-seat promiscuity about to make an honest living as a pimp these days.'

'But how does that affect the Baron and his friends?'

Stigi sighed. 'The Soviets give them the speed, right? Pure sulphate which the Baron's men claim keeps getting rain-damaged. They've tons of it. There must be pure amphetamine sulphate mines in Siberia or somewhere with lots of over-happy workers manically chipping the stuff out to the tune of the balalaika. The Eastie Beasties' idea is that when they invade, all the tank crews swallow a dose and they roll into St Nazaire by lunchtime. Unfortunately, the Baron's right-hand man, a wide boy called Wolfgang, realised they had a gold-mine in every tank's glove-compartment. It's how I made contact. Wolfgang and his boss were interested in a little rest and recuperation and had the drugs to pay for it. They doubt their good luck can last.' His eyes shone as a gentle winter sunlight slanted through the skylights, now being cleaned of their cobwebs.

'Mr Toby, is it okay if we paint outside?' asked one of the Helgas with an American accent.

'Fine,' I answered without thinking, taking another drag on the reefer. Blue was suddenly my favourite colour. I turned back to Stigi. 'Isn't it a trifle dangerous to keep narcotics on the premises? What if we are raided by the *Polizei*?'

'Do you think I would be so dumb?'

'You keep it in your secret apartment?' He seemed annoyed I had mentioned his flat in an ordinary middle-class house on the fringes of the Grunewald.

'No, it's in a very safe place guarded by a mean lady.'

'By your mistress?' The file didn't mention a mistress.

He laughed. 'In the zoo, Toby.'

'I beg your pardon?'

'In Berlin Zoo, Toby.'

'It's a big zoo, Stigi.'

'In the new polar bear pit at the Zoological Gardens. They have a real mean polar bear called Lulu who used to have two swimming-pools in her pen. Now the lady only has one and the other is full of my assorted goodies. The keeper is the bakery's old caretaker. We will use some of the stuff to pay off the Pony Express, or we end up with our throats slit. The bear is extremely neurotic with reference to loud bangs. She survived the Allied Bombing and

76

the Red Army assault and in consequence is easily upset. The word is, she lived on corpses for several heady weeks. I booby-trapped my stash with some thunder-flashes, so anyone trying to help themselves will have to deal with a very angry bear.' As I looked up at the shining blue, enamelled Gate I thought Paris now seemed tame. My life was becoming too exotic and running a mite too fast on fated rails. I had a deep need for a piece of *Schokoladentorte*.

'Oh, a man told me to give you this. I think it must be from our friend Parr.' I opened a buff envelope. Inside was an incident report from the Special Investigations Branch of the Military Police on Véronique, the girl who had been murdered. The envelope contained black-and-white photographs of what I eventually recognised as a horribly disfigured corpse. At first the shapes and shades of grey did not make human sense.

'How on earth could anyone . . . ?'

'I told you it was horrible. And different.'

'But what are . . . ?'

'He does that. Leaves them like that. It's his trademark . . .'

Stigi put his hand on my shoulder. At the bottom of the report was written a few words in a rounded childish hand. 'No hard feelings.'

The script was the painstakingly exact writing of Anthony Selwyn Parr. A cloud had passed over the winter sun and I took another pull on Stigi's reefer. As far as I could remember, Parr's feelings had never been anything else. He knew I had been to see Midwinter. The letter was a threat. Parr wanted to destroy my bright new Babylon. In some ways I could hardly blame him. Did he know I had confided in Midwinter?

I turned back to the tortured white flesh and thought of Magda.

7

As I sat in the back of Baron Roland von Hollmann's car outside the Café Babylon, the man was not at all what I expected. Moreover, he was not what I wanted him to be. I had quickly learned that it was not the client who had the power in my new business. Many of the American servicemen who came to the Café Babylon politely took their hats off as they entered the bakery, as if going into a church. They talked in low, breathless whispers. Snatched litanies of excitement as they smoked too many Lucky Strikes and drank nervously, looking about them all the time. We soothed the boys with bourbon, marijuana and Buddy Holly played over a sound-system Stigi had stolen from the foreign correspondents' club. After many failures we had hired a Brazilian salsa combo. The earthy music seemed right. But the boys, often in uniform with the flashes of the Airborne and Tactical Missile groups on their shoulders, were always subdued until they purchased their token from Twinkle Twinkle (which I called the Queen's shilling, and Stigi dubbed the magic shekel). The sweet-natured Turk was treated with even more respect than usual due to the fact Betty Bethlehem had dressed him in a long black robe with a monk's cowl, under which he could hide his grinning face with mascara-heavy eyelashes and vermilion lips. The faces of the soldiers were disturbingly similar to the photos behind the bar in the Residence. To the boys Stigi brought over, Twinkle Twinkle was the genuine article; the high priest of decadence they had never even imagined in Denver, Buffalo, or Victorville, California. The young soldiers treasured their tokens, dancing with the girls in their flowing costumes of lapis-lazuli or amber silk; frowning over choosing the right love from the start, with more heart-searching than most marriages. All the while we assured them they were in a safe place. They smiled. They were then led quietly through the Gate of Ishtar to the rooms of the Residence and, afterwards, if they came back onto the dance-floor, it was to smooch with their partner like high-school sweethearts. Betty did not approve. The cigarette and egg smugglers were more to her liking. Shifty men who were used to defining their pleasure in deutschmarks and minutes and were too furtive and suspicious for my creation. They were quickly in and out and seldom came back. Love to them smelt of a trap. However, the Baron was far beyond the merely cynical. His weary brown eyes had seen it all before. Yet he had not become old. The frost of the labour camp had preserved his features without breaking his spirit.

'Why is your brothel painted blue?'

'A mistake.'

'A mistake?'

'I told the girls to paint everything blue. Once they'd done a little they said it was a shame not to do the rest, even though Gerta caught a chill, and we suspected frostbite. She's all right now, though.' We sat warm in his old Mercedes and looked at the ridiculous blue building looming out of the snow, surrounded by nearly half a mile of open ground in every direction. The Café Babylon blended into the background with the same ease I did. The Baron appeared amused.

'Do your girls do everything they are told? I have never known such girls.'

'I hardly tell them anything. The place has a life of its own.'

'Why blue?'

'Well, we were able to come across blue paint. Also, it's the colour of Babylon. We call it the Café Babylon.'

'Herr Weitz has informed me of your Grand Gate of Ishtar.'

'Has he now?'

'Did you know my family was involved in the Koldewey excavations?'

'No . . .'

'I would like to see your version of the Gate. My family were involved in the excavations at Babylon. My father was attached to the embassy in Baghdad at the time. However, Herr Weitz will also have told you I have to be discreet. From here your operation does not look terribly discreet. Why does a young Englishman come to Berlin to start such a place? Was the interest sexual, criminal or literary?'

I had my answer. 'Bad back, really. I was here with the army and fell off a horse in a charity point-to-point. The sensible choice was going back to dreary old England to manage a farm for my family. Berlin is a city of opportunities, so I stayed. I've had more fun here than anywhere else. Damn good times. I ran into Stigi in a bar . . .'

The Baron was looking at me closely, the thin, sensitive face suddenly unbelievably sad, as if I had mentioned a much-loved relative recently deceased. The face surely was not that of the tank commander who had won the Knights Cross twice. How on earth did Midwinter expect me to trap such a man with sexual amateur dramatics? Babylon beamed blue on the horizon.

'Politics do not concern you?' he said, at last.

'I am a businessman, Baron. It is the only thing to be in our new Europe.'

We were just on my side of the border. The Baron wore a cashmere coat with a black Persian lamb collar. He sat perfectly relaxed and even his shoe-laces fell in an orderly pattern, as if governed by some timeless aristocratic protocol. His eyes smiled out at you in a childlike way, with a complete conviction that nothing in the world was amiss or mattered that much. He had all the patrician ease and easy manners of the *Junker* class. The Baron's file placed his age at about thirty-seven, but he still looked in his late twenties. The only lines were from laughter. His hair was as fine as a girl's, light brown and curly, which together with his high cheekbones gave him a delicacy that was almost effeminate. I wondered what he was like when he had joined up in 1941. The lid of one eye occasionally twitched ever so slightly and if you looked closely there was a pinched cadaverous look to the sides of the face. More than that there was a sweet smell. At first I thought it was the eau de Cologne drunk by the Soviet forces when they could not get vodka. But it was something else; the subtle hen-house smell of a relative visited in hospital for the last time. A smell of decay. Here was a man who did not care any more. However the only major indication of times past was that he drank brandy constantly. A bottle of Delmain cognac by his side, thoughtfully provided by Stigi.

'Why do you want to take the risk?' I asked.

'I promised my men . . . I hear the authorities are investigating a murder. The murder of one of your girls.'

'Oh, not exactly one of ours. The inquiries are just routine. You will love the club. We're running it along the lines of the sacred temple brothel of Babylon. The girls are to be in costume so it won't be out of place to put some favoured customers in disguise.'

'So . . . we used to have masked balls in the old days.'

The Baron slapped his thigh and his eyes lit up. Two of his men were in front of us in an almost identical car. He appeared delighted. Yet I could not forget that here was a man who had reduced a Russian general to tears and to a self-inflicted bullet through the brain after an officially forgotten battle in some nightmare salient to the East, where young Rollo would not give up his colours and fought on. A willing member of that Eyeless Clockwork Army which lived under Potsdamer Platz. In the file there were numerous stories of his social daring. Of how he once attended the Berlin Opera with the Führer's party in his sister's full-length evening gown. Of how when dining with a fawning Gestapo officer he palmed a human finger out of the soup (collected by him on the battlefield the day before), and winked at his horrified hostess, saying, 'You really must stop Willi bringing his work home with him.'

He patted me on the knee.

'I am sure Herr Weitz has told you all about me, Toby Jubb. He has told me all about you.' I felt uneasy. 'You must understand we have been in the camps. Then we have been confined to barracks. In our time we have seen and done many things. My men have not had a good time. I do not think they will keep us in Berlin long. The Russians do not trust us. I wonder why?' He grinned. 'Why shouldn't we have a bit of fun?'

'How many of you want a bit of fun?' I asked, a little concerned.

'Oh, don't worry. On a single night we will probably be six persons. Forty people will be involved in all in these pleasure excursions. Of these only three are enlisted men. The rest are officers. There will be no trouble. You will not need to set up soup-kitchens and dressing-stations. Herr Weitz has forged us papers saying we are official military observers if there are any questions. I love my men. I hope I have learned something about men. I think I know you, Toby Jubb, but no matter. Our poet Goethe says we only have three weeks of happiness in this life and some of my boys have had none. Absolute zero.'

Suddenly he looked much older. He took another drink of brandy and looked up at me. 'Remember, Toby Jubb, if you think of double-crossing me, that I have nothing to lose. I am completely at your mercy as, I suppose, you are at whatever is left of mine.'

It was not a threat. Without a goodbye he leant over and pressed down my door-handle. I got out and his car sped quickly away, back to his beloved men. No doubt as many before me, I had already begun to like the Baron.

In Kindergarten Number Nine Colonel Midwinter had his back towards me, looking out of his window. A cat had climbed to the top of a pinnacle of stone on a bomb-site, to escape from two barking dogs. The Colonel turned around and faced me.

'Ugly word, blackmail, don't you think, Jubb? You've only been in the hush-hush business two minutes and now you're proposing blackmail; a bad manners operation. Splendid. The credit is all yours. I only suggested the man be lured over to our side.'

I had not even mentioned blackmail. Midwinter had generously added it to my growing portfolio of sin.

'Oh, Stigi is taking care of the photographs and things of that sort. But I don't think we will be needing them somehow. I have a feeling about the Baron. I have met him. Nice chap. He and his men have been denied any sort of comfort and warmth for so long we will have them bringing each other over in wheelbarrows. They will beg to defect. True love will be the reason, sir, not Mr Weitz's snaps. However, if they backslide it may be we have to remind them with our bad manners. There is just one thing.'

'What?'

'Parr.'

'I thought I explained to you, Jubb, that he is not under my control.'

'But he could ruin everything.'

'Not quite at the moment,' said the Colonel trying to light his

Senior Service with a taper torn from *Berliner Zeitung*. 'One of the aspects of young Selwyn's work is to create even more fear and distrust than usual among the Berlin underworld. Especially those trading with the East. Chaos is his function. But it so happens for the next few weeks there are to be secret talks by the Four Powers at the conference centre on the banks of the Spree. Chaos has been cancelled for a while. But you do not have that much time. And remember, Jubb, no slip-ups. Everything quite, quite steady. These talks are important. But we mustn't be caught with our pants down. Don't be a faller at the first fence, Jubb. I don't want any scandals.'

'No, sir.'

'Parr won't be in a good mood, Jubb.'

'I know, sir.'

On the bomb-site outside, the black cat had disappeared and the hungry dogs were searching for something else to kill and eat.

Beneath the balloons and bunting around the bar, ready for the opening night of the Café Babylon Stigi Weitz looked even more worried than his beagle. The place had been transformed from its former squalor. The juke-box was gone, along with the bamboo, and the ballroom had regained some of its faded dignity. Stigi Weitz was fast losing his.

'Please tell me what it is, Stigi.'

For a few moments he strode around with his hands deep in his pockets and a painful expression on his face, the very imitation of a dramatic role by Frank Sinatra.

'Disaster of disasters, Toby. You know I told you I stashed the speed I got from the Baron's tank crews in the polar bear pen? Well, they sacked the keeper. They sacked the fucking keeper on the grounds he's too short. They fear a visit from Kennedy himself if the Peace Talks go well. Some Nazi public relations man has decided my keeper is too short to be pictured with our new American President, good old pearly teeth Kennedy and his beanstalk wife. Give an impression of stunted, undernourished West Berliners and be used as propaganda by the Russians. The Pony Express is breathing down my neck and the Zoo are going to flood Lulu's swimming-pool. We got to get the stuff out, Toby. Those tiny crystals down there are the bricks and mortar of Stigi's fame and fortune. They are my Marshall Plan. I promised a quarter of it to the Pony Express for the girls and a quiet life. They can be very mean if they don't get paid. They might even ask for Magda back.'

Moments later we were driving to a rendezvous with a man too short to be pictured with a US President.

The keeper of Lulu the polar bear was a small, awkward man who politely took off his cap as he came over to the window of our car. We were parked behind an ice-cream stand closed for the night by the Zoological Gardens' main entrance. In front of us were the lights of Berlin and the Kurfürstendamm. Behind was the dark of the Tiergarten and the East. Berliners had always adored their Zoo; it satisfied a passion for carnival on Sunday afternoons. The pinched man got into the car. I recognised him as having helped start the bread-oven at our bakery. There was a sharp smell that was both familiar and exotic.

'Polar bear shit,' said Stigi grumpily.

'I'm sorry,' replied the man in English. His voice was deep and melodious and trembled slightly.

'Polar bear shit,' repeated Stigi.

'So sorry . . . I'm so sorry . . .'

'You're sorry,' retorted Stigi, in German. 'You're fucking sorry. We stand to lose thousands of dollars because I can't get my merchandise out from under your polar bear shit and you are sorry. Explain to my friend how you got fired. We are not sure we believe you.' Hunted and resentful, the sad eyes turned to me. The man hung his head and began to shake it from side to side.

'I have already been given the sack today, mister. I no longer work at the Zoological Gardens,' he continued in English. 'Ever since before the war I work there. I know all the bears. I know all the big cats. They are my friends. They are my good friends. Now I cannot even afford to go in and see them unless I get another job. I remember the night in 1943 when a thousand animals dies and the birds flew on fire into the sky screaming for God. I led my friends to safety while even the peacocks burned. Thousands of birds on fire in the sky, like the lost souls of the damned. Where do I go after such a profession? I am not a young man, but I am innocent of no major crime and have always been humble . . .' Stigi drummed on the steering-wheel with impatience.

'So why did they sack you?'

'Steady on, Stigi,' I interrupted. The man's agitation seemed to make the smell in the car worse.

'Why did they sack you?'

'They sack me because I was too small,' said the keeper. 'They sacked me because I was too small.'

'Too small,' echoed Stigi. 'I don't believe you.'

'The thing is quite simple,' said the man, on the verge of tears. 'My bear, my Lulu, is adopted by Mrs Eisenhower, the wife of the great Allied commander.' The man's voice was an eerily beautiful tenor. 'Mrs Eisenhower is the personal sponsor of Lulu. My Lulu is named after one of Mrs Eisenhower's coloured maids in the White House. When the plaque was put up Mrs Eisenhower sent me a signed photograph. The new President and his young wife will come and see Lulu, soon perhaps. But the *Bürgermeister* said I did not reflect the new spirit of Berlin. They want a young man with blonde hair to shake hands with Frau Kennedy. They always want young men with blonde hair. But what do they know of polar bears?'

'That's terrible,' I said.

'Do they know about polar bears?'

'What's more to the fucking point,' began Stigi. 'What's more to the fucking point is, can we get at what's in Lulu's plunge-pool? You'd better have some way to go back in unless you want to find out there are worse things than unemployment.' Stigi switched on the overhead light and the man actually managed a smile, showing a row of bad teeth.

'Once I was young and strong . . .' He fumbled in his pocket and pulled out a bunch of keys.

'Now you are talking, Pop. Are those the keys to the whole place?' The bunch must have weighed several pounds.

'Every cage. Yes, once I was young and strong and knew my own mind. Of course, it was wrong for me to allow you to store whatever it is in my Lulu's pen. But it seemed harmless. Since she killed her mate Bobo, she has not been very interested in swimming, though I have caught her sniffing around the manhole cover. I did not tell the head keeper that Lulu killed Bobo. I said he must have escaped. They were very worried and feared for their own jobs. They would not have understood a lover's passion. I had to be very careful. What she did not eat I took home in a lunch-pail.'

A silence filled the front of the car.

'Lulu is very dangerous then?' I asked.

'Dangerous? No, well not to me, sir. To me she is a *Liebling*. She lets me kiss her nose. I scratch her back.' His face shone with pride. 'But if she rushes at you, remember to sing. Lulu does not like bad noises and sudden movements. I do not like them either. What do they know of polar bears?'

'Great, Pop. How do we get in? Do you think you could lock your little Lulu in her sleeping quarters? Me and Toby don't want to leave here in a lunch-bucket.' In the Zoo something howled as the keeper began to mumble again.

'. . . When I was a boy I dreamed I could go and fly to the moon. I thought I could stand unharmed in the way of a speeding truck. But I suppose everyone does. We have to be content with much smaller accomplishments. But what do they know about polar bears? It is a question I will make them think seriously about.'

'Please cool it, Pop. Here's the money we talked about. Take it, and shut up.' We all got out of the car.

The man reluctantly took it and shambled in front of us as we skirted the perimeter wall and came to a small entrance. A sign stated the gate was reserved for members of the Berlin Zoological Society. The keys jangled and caught the light of the moon. We slipped into the zoo through a turnstile which clanked unbearably loudly, like an anchor chain running out on an ocean liner. What if Parr had followed us?

Once inside his domain the little man changed; a creature of the underworld returning to his Hades. He skipped along while Stigi and I fell over ourselves, edging around the enclosures. By one cage the sudden explosive roar of a tiger made us collide into an untidy heap. The tinkling laughter of the keeper came out of the blackness by a cage, where another cat paced, thrashing a long tail against the bars in the pearl-grey light. Monkeys began to chatter. The night was very cold and my knee started to ache.

'Well, it seemed like a good place to hide it at the time,' said Stigi, almost apologetically. The tiger roared again and we followed meekly in the footsteps of the keeper. The night was full of growling wildness. Eyes, mainly green, gleamed out of enclosures surrounded by bars or pits. Our every move was on something's menu.

The new polar bear pit was an immense, sunken oval, at the centre of which a raised granite tundra sparkled in the moonlight.

Below, the flatter living areas were divided by unclimbable cliffs of rubble and girdled with a moat. At the far end of one of these sections was a menacing black hole with what looked like bars on the door. I hoped Lulu was sleeping soundly.

'How much is down there?' I inquired.

'Oh, about half a ton. Some of it's mixed with glucose, so it's not all pure. Yes, about half a ton, with some new pills from Switzerland. Play our cards right and we'll be up there with the Gettys.'

The little man slipped away through metal doors to make sure that Lulu's portcullis, which prevented her from roaming the slippery frozen granite of her pen, was firmly down. He returned with a ladder and gingerly I followed Stigi across the moat. The old wooden ladder creaked under my weight as I thought about the frozen water beneath. The blood thumped in my ears as Stigi took a small crowbar from his pocket and prized open a grating by Lulu's plunge-pool, before carefully removing a small bundle attached to copper wire of what I took to be explosive. At our backs was the cave in the rock where Lulu lived. With Stigi's help I pulled back the heavy steel cover to the pool. We lowered ourselves down into the black hole. Stigi stripped back layers of tarpaulins and polythene and eventually, in the thin beam of a pencil-torch, we saw a sack which had burst open. Thousands of sachets of powder, many of them leaking, were exposed.

'Use these bags,' said Stigi holding out some sacks he had brought from the car. 'First, put them over the rim of the plunge-pool. Then you get out and take them to the side of the moat. Tie them to the rope I'll have ready, and I will haul them up,' he whispered, and before I could protest he was back over the moat. The little man had left us. Down in the pit was the unmistakable odour of *Ursus Maximus*.

I began to work, slowly and quietly transferring the plastic bags to the hessian coal sacks, always conscious of the bear's den only twenty yards behind me. I remembered a cheerful nature study master at school relating how polar bears, the 'white death of the arctic', often kill Eskimos for fun. I was finding it hard to keep my mind on the job. I dropped one bag and then another. I bumped my head on the metal pool-cover which had not been pulled back far enough. In the beam of the torch, which I had rested on a sack, the air was dancing with powder, like motes in a sunbeam. My hands had started to shake. My nose began to run. Try as I might, my fingers kept going through the plastic bags and before long a covering of narcotic snow lay both in and around the rim of Lulu's plunge-pool where I heaved up the sacks. Suddenly I began to feel much happier. I heard Stigi shouting. He seemed to be calling from the bottom of a well. But I was thinking of Magda, her eyes, her face, her breasts. We must not let the Pony Express take Magda. Unaccountably, I began to weep and sat down on the hillock of amphetamine. Tears ran down my cheeks. Magda was so beautiful, so very beautiful. I felt bags bursting under me and heard Stigi yelling again. He appeared concerned. I started to whistle to stop my mouth drying up completely. Stigi was shouting louder. But when I glanced up the stars were gone. Who had stolen the stars? Had Mr Weitz sold them? Had I betrayed them? Had Parr murdered them? Had Magda seduced them? Had the Pony Express done things not recorded in the Bible? Yes, the stars had gone. Just a twinkle around the edges of the night. I felt as if I was looking into a black pit instead of up from one. All at once the fathomless universe shifted with a low grunt. Oh my God.

'Stigi, help. Help me, Stigi!' I was screaming.

The moon came from behind the clouds to confirm my worst fears. Before me, in increasingly hideous detail, I saw the spectral awfulness of Lulu, standing on her hind legs, as pitiless as an iceberg. She towered fifteen feet into the air, but it could easily have been a mile. I could make out the currant eyes and soot-black nose on that blunt instrument of a head as she capered about. Her keeper spoke quietly and stroked her clawed paws with a long pole. The bear dropped back onto her four feet with a thud which jolted the steel pool-covers and then she began to lick at the loose amphetamine around the rim. I watched in fascinated horror. The keeper spoke.

'You were whistling. Do not stop whistling,' he said in a voice both friendly and concerned. So calm in fact it nearly made me vomit. 'Better still, sing. Lulu loves to dance. When she stops dancing she can get real mad. She might gobble you up. Ha ha . . .'

'Stigi, for God's sake!'

'Your friend has run away. I have let the other animals out of their prisons. Please sing, there is no choice unless you want to be her supper.' The bear snuffled closer to the edge of the hole. Her nose was the size of a cricket ball and her movements were becoming as frenzied and jerky as my own. I began to sing. A croak came from my lips. As the words spilled out I began to laugh and sneeze. In the circumstances I could only think of one song.

> 'If you go down to the woods today
> You're sure of a big surprise.
> For every bear that ever there was . . .'

Lulu's great white head raised itself up. She stood again and cavorted from side to side, moving away from the hole. I could see the little man dancing round her faster and faster. I felt giddy. I sent up a silent prayer to the Almighty that if he let me out I would endeavour to be better.

> 'Will gather there for certain
> Because, today's the day
> The teddy bears have their picnic . . .'

The song had a strange effect on the bear. She actually seemed to enjoy it; twirling and twirling towards her sleeping-quarters, guided by the keeper with his little stick, which he banged occasionally on what sounded like an old tin kettle. Lulu then dropped down onto her front paws and disappeared into the den with the keeper following behind. Now I had stopped singing, he was crooning a German lullaby. I scrambled out of the pit. I thought of Daniel in the lions' den. I fled across the ladder over the moat, clutching several sacks of narcotic. On the path surrounding the enclosure there were torn sacks Stigi had dropped and something had been licking up the cocktail of glucose and amphetamine and God knows what else. A shadowy creature, large and fierce (and suffering from nervous overdrive), growled hyperactively. I ran like a man possessed with the low bushes beside the path snarling and hissing as I passed. In front of me was a wooden fence over which was a canal which connected to the River Spree. A gate was open. Without a second thought I burst through and clattered onto a makeshift plank bridge across the small canal. I turned and kicked four planks into the water in time to see a large cat – it may have been a panther – hesitate for a second in front of the bridge and then lope after a friend along the bank into the Tiergarten. I sighed with such complete relief it took me seconds to get my breath back. Gingerly I climbed a bank following an ostrich which then walked through a side gate with a small giraffe. In two minutes I was back at the car. But as soon as I tapped on the window the headlights of two other cars blinded me.

A megaphone crackled into life.

'Put those bags down, sir. Hands on top of the car. You are under arrest . . .'

'Get in, dummy,' yelled Stigi. 'It's fucking Parr.'

Immediately, we were spinning round and accelerating up towards the Siegessäule victory column where the great golden angel looks down on a wicked city. Stigi drove around the Grosser Stern with the determination of a man who knows exactly what is pursuing him. Parr was close behind when a car in front swerved violently and we slewed into the oncoming lane. If Parr caught us with the drugs and handed us over to the ordinary police, it would be no use bleating about intelligence matters. Midwinter would wash his hands of us. As we hurtled down the wrong side of the road towards the roundabout I suddenly saw what had made the car in front change lanes. Out of the woods bounded several kangaroos jumping higher and further than I had ever seen. The sound of automatic fire came from the border. Bison rumbled by, overtaken by leaping Thomson's gazelle. Zebras ran onto the road, at least ten of them, followed by a gnu only a paw's length ahead of an enormous lioness who was sprinting with her tail held as erect as a radio aerial on an American jeep. Monkeys tumbled out of the treetops of the Mark von Hohenzollern and, as we skidded past a baboon, searchlights from the border were turned on a whole ark-load of animals heading towards the Brandenburg Gate in an amphetamine hurry.

The little man had been busy.

'The conference centre,' Stigi was shrieking. 'We must get to the conference centre. Parr cannot cause a scene there. Not even Parr is allowed to wreck Peace Talks. We'll use your diplomatic pass.' The decision was hardly a sober one, but in our accelerated dementia the conference centre represented a haven of peace and solace in a world overrun by baboon and hyena. A herd of dik-dik ran across the road in front. Parr was gaining as Stigi slid the big car through the gateway to an inner security barrier. I leant out of the window with my nose and eyes streaming and showed my diplomatic passport. 'Emergency,' was all I said to the French guard who was already waving me through with a bored expression which immediately vanished.

He had probably never seen a leopard before.

We ran inside. People were clapping inside the foyer of what might have been a solemn, utilitarian hotel. The audience spilled out from the conference hall. The leader of the East German delegation, whom I recognised from the newspapers, was winding up his speech.

'Comrades, I have proof that headhunters and kidnappers and arsonists from, or in the pay of, foreign intelligence services, have been making cynical attempts to damage my country's glorious progress and in turn threatening world peace . . .' But all at once he faltered, glancing towards the plate-glass windows. 'Comrade Taubmann is feeling slightly unwell. He asks your indulgence for a few moments. He has to take medication for a thyroid complaint,' interrupted a flat American voice in needless detail. We pushed forward into the crowd. Parr had entered the hall behind us looking furious. Another East German speaker continued, this time in English, on the theme of cross-border sabotage. Parr had seen us. His expression changed into the relaxed smile of a cricket team captain about to claim victory. He stopped and watched me, his lank hair falling over his forehead. He was now in no rush. But screams from the rest-room behind the podium fractured his moment of triumph. A door opened and a man staggered through it torn and bleeding. Several men from the Russian delegation surrounded him and began weeping uncontrollably. For a second a shot silenced everyone, as did the sight of the hindquarters of a lion disappearing through an open window. A volley of pistol fire followed, and the words: 'Courage, comrades. The second secretary has been eaten by a lion.' I caught sight of Parr retreating from the hall. He was not smiling.

In the debriefing that followed, I could not understand why Colonel Midwinter was so philosophical, or why the subject of the drugs (which we had given to a fierce man called Moses from the Pony Express) were never mentioned.

'I suppose you don't know this, no reason why you should,' reflected Midwinter, polishing his glasses and shaking his head over a collection of papers and telex reports two days later as I sat in his study in Kindergarten Number Nine. 'But I was Anthony Eden's private secretary for a while. We used to feel it was our duty to keep the worst consequences of his mistakes from him. He was a very sensitive man much given to drumming on the floor with his fists and biting the carpet. Yes, we used to hide the morning papers. I'll never forgive his wife for telling him about the Suez crisis. He ruined a Persian rug. However, looking at this, I can understand how he felt. Thank God the *Kommandatura* has powers of complete censorship.' He paused. There was no denying the hint of malicious glee in his eyes. He appeared to be on our side.

'Now, there is only one copy of this Allied digest,' he said, putting on his glasses. 'So I shall read it out loud. The Eastie Beasties are more than a little excited about this, I can tell you. Try to put yourself in their shoes, Jubb. You send a high-ranking officer in the Communist Party over to Peace Talks, claiming we have been trying all along to wreck any negotiations by arson, kidnapping, assassination and white slavery. So what happens to this man? What filthy tricks do the West have up their silken sleeve? Is he cleverly killed by the CIA in a road accident? Is he blackmailed into defecting? No, he is eaten by a lion.'

We both stayed silent for a moment. I was staring hard at a pair of new suede shoes Stigi had provided.

'Eaten by a lion,' he repeated, pausing to let the words sink in.

'To quote this report from our American friends. "There was a scream from the men's room at the back of the hall. When I and CIA agent Berkowitz on Four Power security duty in the conference centre gained access to the room where the second secretary of the East German Communist Party had been recovering after medication, we fired at a crazed and fast-moving mammal we believe to have been a male African lion, that leapt back through an open window by which he must have gained access. The window is some thirty feet from the ground and thought to be far too high for this sort of hazard; though we were obviously not planning security around a possible termination with extreme prejudice by a wild beast from the Kenyan savannahs. Sadly, both the second secretary and his assistant perished from their wounds, but only the second secretary was partly eaten; the lion escaping with the majority of his body. The Agency has expressed regret through the proper channels and will be sending Class Alpha floral tributes to the interment . . ."'

The Colonel looked up. 'Interesting phrase that, Jubb. Only one was eaten. Can you imagine how delighted the East Germans will be? I know politics isn't your forte, Jubb, but try to imagine it in terms of the Medes or Persians or some such . . . Only lost one senior party member. The silly sausage shouldn't have left the window open. Man-eating lions are a bit of a nuisance in Berlin at this time of year . . .'

The silence had a courtroom finality. I felt a cell had already been reserved for me in Spandau military prison. Midwinter went back to the report.

'We were rather lucky that the single serious civilian incident was when a troupe of baboons boarded a bus bringing back elderly stroke victims from a weekend trip to a spa town in the East. We are officially saying the whole sorry incident was due to hallucinations caused by food poisoning, although this does not quite explain the teeth-marks on the patients.' He turned a page. 'You don't have anything personal against the Allied Intelligence services do you, Jubb? You aren't a Dadaist by any chance? Some sort of anarchist perhaps? A Communist would never have your imagination for disasters . . .'

'No, sir.'

'*Eaten* by a lion, Jubb!'

'Yes, sir.'

'Then let me read you this. "A border guard reported that opposite K sector a man who appeared to be riding on a polar bear crossed into the East. The creature was heading for the Berthold Brecht theatre where it went to sleep. The East Germans are hailing the bear's defection as a propaganda triumph and say it ran away because it was being mistreated in the West. The whole thing is rather embarrassing diplomatically, as the animal was given to the zoo by Mrs Eisenhower and named after her coloured maid . . ."'

He paused, as if trying to gain some perspective on the events. He shook his head.

'"A few hours later, at the town of Wittel fifty miles inside East Germany, hysterical villagers reported they were being attacked by Martians. Units of the 26th 'Friedrich Engels' Soviet tank infantry were sent into the town to investigate. In the shooting that followed, most of the town was destroyed although only one invader was slightly wounded. The creatures were found to be *macropus giganteus*, the big red kangaroo. The villagers, never having seen kangaroos before, thought they were being tormented by devils or beings from outer space. The East Germans are treating this as an unprovoked assault and are demanding compensation. They are also complaining about the use of specially trained marsupials in modern warfare, which they claim is expressly forbidden under the Geneva Convention and by the Catholic Church. Of course, there are other incidents, Jubb. I particularly like the one about the black panther driving away in the staff car. Anyone can get into a staff car these days and tap on the partition window for the driver to pull away. Not often you find your passenger is from the Paraguayan jungle, has black fur, green eyes and whiskers and is suffering from post-narcotic depression.'

The Colonel took a riding-crop from his desk and stood up. I thought he was going to lash out. Instead, he flicked it at a picture on the wall. An upside-down one with a horse falling at the first fence.

'You are very lucky indeed, my boy, that this incident, for which I am convinced you and Mr Weitz are responsible, is so bizarre that in the end the Eastie Beasties cannot make too much of it. But if I were you, I would deliver the Red Baron as quickly as possible now the Peace Talks have prematurely ended. *Quam celerrime*, as you scholars say. Do try to be a little steadier, Jubb. You're a jolly big chap. Do try and act like one.'

'Yes, sir.'

The riding-crop came down on the table with a crack. 'Or I will personally feed you to the lions.'

8

The mornings were the very best with Magda. I would have given anything for it to remain that chill, sharp time of the day because, and it was a thing I had in common with all my fellow harlots in the building, it was mine. If they had a man in their bed, they disappeared quietly without a goodbye and padded in soft slippers down to breakfast in the Residence to talk and knit and make plans for meeting Mr Clean. Betty Bethlehem said it was a time to rebuild one's dreams. Dawn was not negotiable.

I woke first that morning, a week before our planned grand opening, and watched her as the light from a gap in the heavy curtains cut a golden path across our bed. We had been together last night. She snuggled into my shoulder and had the sheets pulled up around her like a little girl except for the traces of mascara on the pillow. I touched her hair and a lock fell down across her forehead. She half opened an eye.

'Darling . . .'

'I love you, Magda. You're so beautiful.'

She looked at me wickedly.

'I think I have heard that somewhere before. Oh Toby, you are such a big sugar bear. Perhaps not a bear. A bear is too grumpy. No, you are a panda. You like things black and white. An adorable, cuddly panda.'

'What?'

'Yes, you are a panda with a ringmaster's whip. You make us all jump . . .'

95

Magda yawned and stretched and the covers fell back from her breasts. She smiled.

'Is it really morning?'

'Yes, it's morning.'

'Has it snowed?'

'Snowed?'

As I reached for her suddenly she was awake and at the window. The room we shared above the ballroom on the second floor of the Residence was large, though almost theatrically shabby. The impression was of sleeping in the bedroom of a grand house in Louis XVI's time, after it had been looted by the Committee For Public Safety. On one wall were two ancient armoires and an ornate but tank-like dressing table in whose impregnable oak bottom drawer I kept my strong box. In places the walls were bare to the plaster. In others were glimpses of the Chinese silks that once had covered them. I would not allow the decorators to paint in here; it seemed a sacrilege to tamper with such decadence. By the window was a vast wooden harem screen which some enthusiastic officer had some-how brought back from the tiled halls of the Middle East, for the girl he called his mistress.

'Toby, look. Look! It is so *schön*. Again it has snowed, Toby. You promised. Oh, you promised. You must take me sledging. I adore to go sledging.'

'In Berlin?'

'*Ja*. Very good sledging. An American airman took me. Up on the Devil's Hill. It is really high now and they have made the slides smooth with dirt. I want to go sledging, Toby. Please take me sledging. Please.' She jumped back on the bed and began to bounce up and down and laugh.

'The Devil's Hill? Are you sure?'

'Why not?'

The Devil's Hill, as she was fond of telling me, was the artificial hill, more of a tor or tumulus, by the Grunewald, from where you could look down on the city. I had recently seen it in a picture in *Life* magazine. The hill was made with the rubble from a million homes.

'Well . . . I am meant to be meeting the Baron.'

'Bring him along. We can introduce him to Betty.'

'I don't know. He may be a bit old for sledging.'

'Then we will let him make a snowman.'

She put her strong arms around me. I really should have argued with Magda that morning. But seconds later we were making love. I liked sledging, too.

When I went to explain our plans (it is not every day that you attempt to take a tank commander who has won the Iron Cross sledging, though, as Magda pointed out, what could be more disarming,) Betty was not over-enthusiastic. As I sat on her bed in her newly-painted room she seemed determined to extract sweaters and an old overcoat from the wardrobe she shared with Helga, clothes that made her look like a vagrant or one of the frightening underclass that still roamed bombed-out buildings with all the instincts and ferocity of rats. I had not seen this side of her.

'I am not sure of what I am getting into, Toby, love. I don't think you know. Are you sure this Midwinter is being straight with you? Are you sure, Toby? What are they really after? That's the question you have to ask yourself.'

'Don't worry, Betty. The Baron's not that old. Well, he doesn't look that old, anyway. Just think of it as, er . . .'

'Another trick?'

'Something like that.'

'I don't like it, Toby. If he wants to get out and he can walk across the border, why doesn't he?' She took my hand, tenderly but firmly. 'These men want something from you, Toby. Mark my words. Don't just drift with their plans. The worst thing you can do in this life is drift. I should know. A woman should know. I got here by drifting.'

We looked at each other sadly for a moment. She was genuinely scared. Was I being duped? Had I missed something, like the time Magda's slim fingers removed the wallet from my pocket? No, Betty was just a softy. A lovely softy all the same. Suddenly we laughed and I kissed her on the cheek.

'I bet this is the first time you have had to go sledging with a melancholic Major-General. But I am certain you will come to like him, Betty.'

'Oh, I am sure I will, Toby love. I'm sure I will. I always do . . .'

At twelve noon exactly, by the Grunewald on a small avenue of quaint middle-class houses with Italian-tiled roofs that had survived the war, Baron Rollo von Hollmann's old Mercedes diesel clattered its way into the parking space beside us. The Baron got out. He was alone as Stigi had promised. His car drew away almost immediately and left him standing there, smiling, vulnerable and alone and puffing on the inevitable cigarette in its amber and ivory holder. I could never work out whether this was an affectation or he had always smoked like that. He slapped kid-gloved hands at the sides of his old overcoat. I got out and walked over. For the moment the girls stayed put in the car, listening to Eddie Cochrane on the American Forces Network radio station. The car smelled of perfume and face powder. Outside the woods had that peppermint cold tang of snow which hung on the silver birch saplings. The Baron was smiling. He looked younger and more animated than when I had last seen him.

'A lonely spot.'

'Not for long, Baron. I have brought along some of my girls in the car.'

'We agreed to have lunch alone, Mr Toby Jubb . . .' But he was smiling. 'You have disobeyed orders. I will definitely have you shot.' He was looking towards my car. I had come in Stigi's black Cadillac.

'Just the sort of car to go unnoticed,' he said.

'I'm sorry,' I replied. 'You see, we couldn't get the toboggans in the other car's boot.'

'Toboggans?'

'Absolutely.'

'For why?'

'Well, one of the girls, Magda, thought it would be an idea if we all went sledging. Up on Devil's Hill or one of those mountains of rubble. I said yes, and I didn't think you would mind. I brought along Betty. You will like Betty.'

The Baron examined my eyes for a long time. The harsh lines of his thin face slowly transformed into the sweetest of smiles. He then threw back his head and laughed. So loud that an old lady came out of the front door of her house and looked at us. The Baron patted me gently on the back.

'Bring on the sleighs, Toby Jubb. But I must warn you, I am so very good at this game . . .'

From the very start the two of them were attracted to each other. The fact they were both German had little to do with it. We all talked in

English as again and again we dragged the small sleighs up the hill among mothers and sons and daughters enjoying the snow, toiling up and then whizzing briefly down the steep slope to the woods below. A small black dog ran beside one sledge and barked, pretending to savage its laughing rider. When the Baron walked beside Magda at the top of the hill they were out of step. They grew closer. Hips naturally brushed together and they smiled. His hand went around her waist.

'He is old,' said Betty.

'He's seen a lot.'

'So have I. Magda fancies him.'

'They . . . they've only just met . . .'

'You wouldn't think that to look at them. Believe me, Toby, I've seen little bobby-dazzlers like the Baron before, all over you with charm. He's after more than getting inside a few girls' knickers. Look at them. You'd think they had grown up together. He's all over her. Or is this part of your plan, Toby?'

For a moment I paused, carrying the small toboggan under my arm. My lips were frozen and shaking slightly, but not from cold, as I saw her take a cigarette from him and hand it back. She saw I was looking at her and said something to the Baron, who took her arm and led her over.

'What a wonderful surprise you have given me, Toby. I expected something . . . I never expected to be a little boy again. And surrounded by such beauty. I can understand why you did not want to go back to England and the family business. Betty, will you ride with me this time? Down the Devil's Hill of broken dreams?'

'Yeah . . . sure. Broken what?'

'Oh, it is so wicked! With all the other children we take our few moments of pleasure built up at the expense of so many good German families. Is that not true, Toby? If we dig down like archaeologists beneath this snow we will be in the impacted living room of the Schmidts, or perhaps the kitchen of the Muellers, or where the Sichels were holding a party for their daughter's twenty-first birthday until it was interrupted by two hundred kilos of high-explosive. Much of old Berlin is beneath us. Bulldozed into a fine hill, all for our enjoyment. Let's slide down the Devil's Hill together. What a beautiful way to use the bad luck of others.'

'That is so horrible,' said Betty. She turned her back.

'Oh, don't take me seriously, please. I have a rotten sense of humour. Please, I am not being disrespectful. One of my family's houses is down there somewhere. Many of my friends were killed in the raids. It just seemed so absurd that the rubble of a city which my family were a part of and helped to build should now serve as a slippery slope that gives the child Hollmann so much pleasure. *Danke*, Frau Schmidt, and you, Frau Mueller, and you, Frau Sichel. Come on with me, Betty. Please smile.'

Before she knew it he had swept her up and was hurtling down the steepest part of the slope which the mothers tried to make their offspring avoid. Magda was laughing.

'He's so much fun. Not like a soldier at all. He is so alive. Don't you like him, Toby?'

'Oh, yes. He . . . he seems very jolly. What does he talk about?'

'Nothing much. He has confided in me of course how he and his tanks will invade the West tomorrow. Do you ever wonder if there will be another war, Toby?' She was staring dreamily in the direction of the Tiergarten and the Brandenburg Gate. 'If there was there would be an even bigger Devil's Hill.'

'And no one left to sledge on it.'

'Except us.'

'And Betty?'

'And Baron von Hollmann. If not for his sense of humour, for his hip flask full of plum brandy.'

'I wondered what the attraction was.'

'Come on, let's catch the others . . .'

Head first, with Magda's legs astride my back, we flew down the Devil's Hill, towards the man on whose failings depended my immediate future. Did he realise the danger he might be in? From what he had said, I think he was past caring fifteen years ago in some dreadful part of Poland or Russia. Yet he was so gentle. So polite. So unlike someone of Anthony Selwyn Parr's mould, who for me typified the universal soldier. Was the smiling Baron really part of that Eyeless Clockwork Army that still lurked just under the surface of the city?

'Toby . . . *Scheisse*!'

Before I could blink we closed at giddy speed on the root of a dead tree and flew off into the snow. I picked Magda up and kissed her before she could complain.

'You big idiot, Toby Jubb. You should look where you are going . . .'

'I love you, Magda,' I said. 'Whatever happens.'

We lunched in rooms which Stigi had acquired in a spacious old house just north of the Kurfürstendamm. At first the Baron appeared reluctant to get into the gleaming black Cadillac. He ran a kid-gloved hand along one of the tail fins. He did not trust us.

'You could walk to the S-Bahn station, if you'd rather. I can give you the address.'

'Yes. It may be better. You understand?'

'I understand.'

'I'll come with you,' said Betty, rather surprising me, and they had walked off hand-in-hand. Tactfully, I parked the Cadillac a block away from the apartment. The Baron and Betty were already standing outside. He was whispering something in her ear. She was giggling. When we rang the door opened to reveal the familiar face of Twinkle Twinkle.

'Stigi thought it would be best if we got to know each other first on neutral ground so to speak. Oh, don't worry about him. He's very good-natured really.'

'Will Herr Weitz be joining us?' said the Baron as Twinkle Twinkle took his coat.

'Stigi? No,' said Magda, leading the way up a gloomy staircase to a surprisingly pleasant room on the first floor. 'Stigi is playing in a poker game at the Mercedes factory.'

'Part of the economic miracle?' asked the Baron.

'When Stigi is playing every card game has a note of the miraculous.'

'He cheats?'

'Doesn't everyone?' said Betty Bethlehem.

'Shall I open the champagne?' offered the Baron. 'It is quite some time since I had some.'

The meal was superb. We sat around an oval deal table in the room with sweeping red curtains Twinkle Twinkle insisted on drawing even though the sun had not set. Candles were lit and a small broken-looking man in a waiter's tails kept the glasses constantly charged. On the table was an enormous pot of Seruga caviar.

Twinkle Twinkle brought in hot toast and sour cream and chopped onion. Tiny glasses were produced and filled with ice-cold Wolfschmidt vodka. The Baron smiled.

'Here's to Toby for giving us a nice day on the Devil's Hill,' he said, tossing the vodka down his throat, and a tiny drop ran onto his chin. He reached over with a silver spoon and scooped up the precious sturgeon's eggs. He had noticed that Betty seemed unsure quite what to do.

'For me, it is better without trimmings,' he said, popping it between her red lips.

'Do you like it?'

'I think so,' said Betty Bethlehem, and she gave the Baron a huge kiss, mapped in lipstick on his scarred cheek. We toasted each other again, this time in champagne.

'Do you know, Toby Jubb, I think I am beginning to enjoy myself?' The waiter brought in a heavy silver salver under which was a whole *filet* of beef. The meat had been slashed down the centre, an inch deep, showing that it was very red, oozing blood and decorated with sliced truffles, watercress, and at both ends there were little piles of rock salt.

'So!' exclaimed the Baron. 'Here is the sacrifice of Toby Jubb to the gods of our friendship. No! Take away the vegetables. There is a special way of eating such meat. But we must not spoil our clothes. First we must strip to the waist.'

No one moved. In a second the Baron was taking off his shirt and pulling it from his trousers. His skin was almost disturbingly white. Betty watched in tipsy wonder and Magda in a kind of silent admiration as the half-naked man seized the meat, dowsed it in spirit and set fire to it, blowing the flames out almost immediately. He then took a luxurious bite and the juices ran down his chest. He grinned and swayed slightly.

'Here is the proper way to eat the *filet*. This is the way the Russians do it. Please try it, Betty?'

She laughed. In one movement her sweater was over her head and the waiter watched with ever-widening eyes as the fat snake of meat was held between her breasts and white teeth bit into the red meat. Gravy ran down on to her stomach and a morsel of truffle lodged in her cleavage. Her nipples shook. She chewed and swallowed.

'Bloody hell, it's gone all down me slacks . . .' She looked at me for approval, her hesitance earlier in the day seemingly forgotten. 'May as well take them off, I suppose.' Betty had not got the black slacks past her waist when a large hand on the shoulder of the waiter propelled him towards the door. Twinkle Twinkle followed him as the Baron's full lips fastened around Betty Bethlehem's nipple and he sucked away the gravy. I watched, quite breathless with surprise at the Baron's extraordinary behaviour.

'Our turn next, Toby,' cried Magda, pulling at my shirt. She scooped up a stray truffle from the table and, putting it in her mouth, then pressed it into mine with a musky sweet kiss. Suddenly she too was naked and, clutching the meat to her body, wiped it across her belly and down past the line of pubic hair before proffering it to her mouth.

'Eat me, Toby!'

A shout from the Baron indicated that his chair had fallen over backwards as I bit into the pungent meat, into which Magda, too, had sunk her teeth. The warm juices ran across my stomach as she tugged at my belt. As we slipped, kissing, to the floor I heard the Baron's voice.

'. . . And we are not even in Babylon yet, Toby Jubb.'

Several hours later we sat smoking cigars and drinking cognac on a sofa in the window alcove of the room. We both wore trousers but were still stripped to the waist and disgracefully sticky. I had never done anything quite like that before in my life. I was trying hard now to feel at ease. The Baron had taken command. Yet a spent camaraderie had naturally emerged between us.

'I went to school in England for a year,' he said, tipping up the brandy-glass.

'Where was that?' I wondered if it was there that he had learned his table manners.

'St Paul's. My father was a military attaché at the London Embassy. It played havoc with my English. Everyone thought it very clever to speak cockney. They had a Latin master who was interested in archaeology who used to take us for digs. He came round to the house sometimes.'

'So you are very interested?'

'Oh, yes. All the stories my father used to tell me. The stories of fabulous gold and treasure. He said that if you made a wish under the Blue Gate at the time of the new moon it always came true. He told me that in the material found with the Gate was indication of a great golden statue.'

Everyone, it seemed, was interested in gold.

'The statue of Bel. Herodotus mentions it. I think that must have been lost at the time of the second Darian invasion of Babylon . . .'

'Don't you dream of finding gold, Toby? Wouldn't you wish for it under the Blue Gate of Babylon?'

I took a long pull on the Davidoff cigar.

'To be honest, Rollo, I have not thought much about it. But to find that statue. Gosh, that would be something. But you have to be careful what you wish for under the Blue Gate. If the Blue Gate represents the dark side of the moon, of the goddess, I would be very careful what I wished for. Anyway, what would you do with such riches?'

He looked down into his brandy-glass, as if seeing the sun rise.

'Have a jolly good time . . .'

'Oh, I think we can do that without having to find golden statues. But you must come and see my Gate, even if it is a fake.'

'I will give you my inexpert opinion, Toby Jubb. Now I'm afraid I will have to clean up and go. My employers might wonder where I am . . .'

He kissed Betty as he got out of the car in the dark lane near the Grunewald, where we had first met him that day. A dreamy hand waved as he got into his waiting car, which started and pulled away. Twinkle Twinkle drove after, with the girls asleep on each other in the back. I sat in the front and examined the family signet ring my mother had given me. The evening whirled before me like a dream. The headlights pierced the fog. The Baron was a remarkable man. Even Betty had seemed to melt before him. A man capable of anything. We now reached the bright lights of the Kurfürstendamm, where a group of lanky G.I.s were discussing the price with two ladies of the night. All being well, Rollo would be safely back in the East with his tanks and men and the smell of engine oil. The contrast would make the evening all the more delicious.

Perhaps one day he would find his golden statue. For his sake, I hoped so. Part of me, a large part, wished we did not have to entrap the man. But it was not a wish I would make under the Blue Gate of Babylon.

9

Café Babylon   January 26, 1961
Berlin

Dear Mother,

Excuse me for not writing to you, dear Mother. We have
been so busy and are about to open tonight. Perhaps I am being
totally naive but I do not think Berlin will have seen the like. To
add further spice, Baron von Hollmann and three of his men
are visiting us. We have to lure him to our lair, Mother, and I
was going to use Betty Bethlehem, but she says she has the 'flu.
Magda is insisting on taking her place. I love Magda and I
think she loves me. Magda says our friends from the East are
the kind of Germans she wants to love back into the world; to
free from the past. I have met the Baron, Mother, and have to
admit he is a very nice chap. All would be so much easier if he
were an utter cad. To me he appears honourable, brave and a
lot of fun, but keeping his principles in the direst circumstances. In fact, everything we all try to be. The problem is,
Mother, I fear he is of heroic proportions and I am just big.
Until this moment it's been a playful fantasy. Oh, Mother, at
times I am so frightened. If what I do is wrong, it is a sin
committed in innocence. But so many have said that before.
Berlin is a wicked place and in my dreams a bony hand is trying
to break through curtains of flayed skin to point the way home.

I have been cataloguing the Koldewey ruins, Mother. They seem to harbour a personal warning and I am not as tough as King Darius and his invading Persians who took and retook Babylon. I scrape at the surface of things with care for fear that bony nightmare hand will be at my throat. I am now sure I love Magda, Mother. Parr, the man I told you about from school, is making things difficult for me. But then, he would. I don't like to worry you, dear Mother. Please give me some indication of what to do.

Your ever loving son,
Toby

The girls were all being especially nice to me today. They kept putting their heads round the door with a shining, scrubbed look. The queues outside the bathrooms reminded me of school on Speech Day; everywhere was so spick and span. Ulrike, the former bicycling champion, knocked gently and brought in a camomile tisane for Magda. Ulrike then brushed Magda's hair and when she was finished gave me a child's kiss on the cheek. She was dressed in a flowing short gown of lapis blue. 'Betty says you must come and find me later,' she whispered, leaving with a smile. I glanced back into the room where Magda was sitting up in bed.

'She is a pleasant girl. Very healthy,' observed Magda.

'But I love you.'

'What is that?' she asked, throwing back the covers, shrugging off her robe and striding naked to the dressing-table. It was loaded with perfume bottles and a pair of curling-tongs and many furry animals and dolls collected from past customers. She had such long, smooth legs. Today, I was working on some of the more valuable Babylonian relics from the bakery. 'Why have you brought those toys into our bedroom, you bad boy? Have you stolen them? Look, I stubbed my toe on one of your tiles this morning. Do you understand what is written on them? Are they valuable?' She kept curling a strand of hair around a finger.

'No, I haven't stolen them,' I replied, as Magda began to rub a silver spoon on a love-bite at the base of her neck to take the red welt out. I had not given her the mark. 'This one, the scroll of the Temple of the Unknown God, is priceless . . . But I am not sure if this other inscription is a joke. It is too well-known.' Before me in the corner of the room, propped against a case of Johnny Walker whisky, was a section of crude bitumen-bound bricks with a simple yet terrifying message burnt into them. I had been thinking about that message.

'What does it say?'

'Something nasty.'

'Tell me.'

'*Mene, Mene, Tekel, Peres.*'

'Do not make a joke with me, Toby darling. I can see you are worried. What does it mean, big boy?'

Her hair fell in a voluptuous cascade down the fleshy arch of her back, which she always held very straight like a ballet dancer. Sometimes I had to keep touching her to make sure she was real. The bedclothes were still in a damp, tumbled chaos. I did not know quite what to say.

'The words are mentioned in the Bible. In the Book of Daniel. The message is to Belshazzar, son of Nebuchadnezzar, the builder of the Blue Gate and the famous ziggurat of Babylon. When Belshazzar gave a feast for a thousand lords using silver and gold stolen from the Temple in Jerusalem, a ghostly finger appeared and wrote the words on the wall. *Mene*, means God has numbered thy kingdom and finished it. *Tekel* means, thou art weighed in the balance and found wanting. *Peres* means the kingdom is given to the Persians. I said it wasn't cheerful. After the prophet Daniel read the message when all the soothsayers and astrologers had tried and failed to interpret it, Darius and his Persians entered the city. Babylon fell.' If I was right about Daniel, he would have been pissed out of his mind.

'But who wrote it?'

I laughed. 'God.'

'Oh, *ja*,' Magda shivered deliciously, as if it were a ghost story. 'Toby, you are so clever. You tell such a good tale. When will our Babylon fall? Do the little marks tell you that?'

'I think it's a joke,' I repeated. 'A clever fake. For the entertainment of Mr Göring and his friends.'

'God numbered their kingdom,' said Magda simply, turning back to a hand-mirror to pluck at her eyebrows. 'God finished it as well. Do I look beautiful?'

108

'Yes.'

'Was Darius like the Baron?'

'A bit. Really Darius was only happy when he was conquering something. He wasn't good at living with himself, or his ambitions. He was a bit like the Devil in all of us. What does Milton say, 'Only in destroying do I find ease, to my relentless thoughts . . .' Darius came to the throne by a clever pretence. The trouble was, when he got there he was terrified another pretender was going to snatch it from him. He must have killed Smerdis the Magus, the great pretender of Babylon, a hundred times over . . .'

'Kiss me, Toby. You are so clever.'

An hour later she was almost ready. Her beauty was enough to make one weep. My initial plan had been for Betty Bethlehem to be the goddess of the New Moon, in a white dress with a slit up the side and a simple gold metal and blue stone collar around her neck. She would have been wonderful; but now Magda had taken her place. Her eyes, made up to be more elaborately Egyptian than Babylonian or Persian, had grown darker. She put the headdress on and tied the plaited braid of blue and gold. I felt her softness. I could imagine her as the goddess herself. The Venus of Babylon. Magda looked at me suddenly dropping that ethereal veil, with a smile capable of giving St Francis trouble in tight trousers.

I coughed and felt nervous. I wished I had the courage of a King Darius to carry her off.

'Marry me,' I said simply. 'You don't have to take Betty's place tonight. You don't have to do this any more. You don't have to sell yourself. Marry me . . .' She came over and kissed me tenderly on the lips. She tasted of the violet-scented cachous she kept in a pill box by the bed.

Magda laughed. 'Perhaps I will. But you forget I have already been once in that particular institution. I don't want to be a *Hausfrau* again, just yet. *Kinder, Küche, Kirche* does not feel right for me. I must have my dreams, Toby. My own dreams. If one does not dream properly, madness can sneak up and ambush you. In a second. I saw it happen to my mother. Once she was a neat and proper woman who would have dusted the ghost of Siegfried if she had found him on the stairs . . .'

Magda's eyes were suddenly full of tears but she did not cry. I cupped her small face in my clumsy-looking hands. 'Oh, please don't cry. You have never really told me about your family, Magda.' She sniffed.

'My mother was very beautiful. More beautiful than me. She worked as a waitress in a café, the Dobrin Konditorei. My father was a driver of trams on two days a week. The rest of the time he worked for a tailor on Chauseestrasse. The tailor was called Gluck. I was born on *Kristallnacht*, on November 9, 1938, Toby. I have never told you that, have I? My mother tried to warn the Glucks. She overheard things in the café. She knew what was going to happen. She was often invited out by Nazi Party members. She used to go and bring food home for Papa, who didn't like it one bit at first. Gluck wouldn't listen to her. He could not believe anything would happen to him. He said he had connections. He imagined he had friends. They came and smashed his shop. They smashed every shop that was owned by Jews. My mother was so worried that night it brought on my birth. So you see, Toby, I came into the world to the sound of breaking glass.'

I cleared my throat. 'They were very bad times, old girl. Come on, cheer up.'

'How dare you tell me to cheer up!' she snapped angrily. 'You have no idea what it was like for them. How people were drawn in. Ordinary folk like my parents. They knocked on my papa's door and smiled. They gave him the handle of a pickaxe. They didn't say a thing. They knocked on other doors along the street. One man protested and they said if he didn't help them he would be reported. The street was full of men. Papa told my mother it started slowly. Some were reluctant. But then the S.A. guards and Hitler Youth started to hurl bricks at a shop window. My father cut his hand. When he came back from hospital, Mother said the stitching in the shoulders of his jacket had split from swinging the big stick. Blood was on his coat. She never saw Herr Gluck again. His shop became our shop from then on and my father made bad suits, badly, for bad men. I wonder if anyone told Herr Gluck and his family to cheer up?'

The electric light flickered. Magda was staring straight in front of her. She seemed almost in a trance now, her body limp. The warm smell of perfume was overpowering. Her cheek, down which rolled a single tear, was to me the most perfect thing in the world. The shattered edges of existence are often well disguised.

110

'What happened to your parents? You told me you were an orphan.'

'Aren't we all, eventually? My mother was invited to more and more parties and I was looked after by an aunt. I still have a picture of my mother somewhere. She knew many high ranking people. She met Göring. She may have come here. She was very much in demand and my father conquered his jealousy, ate meat and joined the Party. Soon Party members would call at the house. But when she was at home she would cry and cry and often pray by her bed underneath the crucifix which I still have. She took it out for her prayers and put it back into a secret drawer in case anyone saw it. She told me she had to do that because the man on the cross was a Jew. I misunderstood. I thought she was praying for all the Jews to die on crosses and crying because some were still alive. Our teachers said Jews carried disease. I reasoned that was why they nailed them all to pieces of wood. The more men would come and take her out, the more she would pray. I thought she was stupid. The bed would creak in the afternoons and later she would weep and pray. When I become big, I said to myself, I'll have a good time. I will not pray. I will make people happy. If I deny what is in myself . . . and in my mother . . . she will go straight to hell.' Another tear ran down Magda's cheek and onto my sleeve. I hugged her to me. 'As soon as the war broke out they sent for my papa. He did exactly as he was told. They said he died instantly from some exploding ammunition at the barracks.'

'What became of your mother?'

Magda lit a cigarette.

'She became the mistress of a Party official and then another and another. Each one in turn went away. She told me when I grew up I would be a great actress. One day a bomb fell near our house as she was praying to her Christ of the Bottom Drawer and the blast ripped her dress off. She was naked and ran into the street screaming. Her hair was smouldering. It was a horrible smell. Everywhere was panic. They took her away in a van. Someone said she was mad. She shouted to me through the bars that I must love everyone. You must love everyone, little Magda. Don't let them make you scared. Just love everyone. More bombs fell and the van drove off. I saw her hand waving from the small window. I think that is why I behave as I do. In those days mad people were taken to

111

the camps, like Herr Gluck before them. I know it is no justification, but loving a stranger makes me feel cleaner. I think it is better than sobbing to Christ in a drawer. We destroyed all. You cannot return to the old ways when everything has been blown to atoms. We must find new ways. But I don't think you understand. All you do is look at me with those big eyes . . .'

The sounds of laughter drifted up from downstairs. The band started to play a slow tango. Outside in the street someone smashed a beer-bottle. The time had come for the goddess of the New Moon to be incarnate. I felt like crying. I looked at the crucifix on the wall. I wanted to take hold of Magda. To prevent her going. But in a deft movement she danced out of my grasp and closed the door between us. The words written by the moving finger hissed in my head; *Mene, Mene, Tekel, Peres* . . .

The grand opening of the Café Babylon was perfect.

The air was perfumed with incense and sandalwood chips smouldering at the base of large candles. Men bought a silver token from the Rasputin-like figure of Twinkle Twinkle, and went to sit and look and drink. Stigi began greeting and shaking hands. He was expectant and eager. I had never seen him quite like this. In the background the band began to drum as the girls took to the stage under the towering Blue Gate, lit by two powerful spotlights at opposite corners of the vast bakery. These were the new girls from the East, the chorus as I called then, who seemed either happy with their life or at least narcotically reconciled. Betty Bethlehem came down from her sickbed. I helped her to one of the small tables on the walkway in front of the Gate. Stigi beamed at me.

'You sure learn quick, kid.'

'I have a good tutor.' Our nervous words meant nothing.

The girls wore short skirts in silky blue, which were longer in front, touching just above teenage knees. But at the back much of the material was raised and tucked under the braided belt to expose the first hint of the cheeks of the girl's bare bottom. I had the idea from a description of the courtesans of Belshazzar I had read about one hot, airless afternoon in the Bodleian. On top the dresses were prim, buttoning to the neck with long full sleeves. Of course, nothing was worn underneath. A gasp of delight rose from the tables as the girls started to turn and pick up lighted candles from the stage. The spots dimmed. The chorus whirled around and around, the candlelight spilling onto smiling faces and catching for an intant the line of a thigh or curve of a buttock. The drumming grew louder. The girls began to chant the ritual of Ishtar, the Babylonian Venus. The hymn to the goddess of fertility and battle. The drawing down of the new moon. I felt strange. Transported back to Babylon as on the first day. The time of the sacrifice, I felt, was at hand. All at once framed in the Gate was a shimmering white figure. The priestess of the new moon. Magda was standing there in a spectral white dress with her arms outstretched holding two small ceremonial daggers. The drumming stopped. The tables had filled but one couldn't hear a sound. Magda had not said a word. But beneath the lions and bulls and dragons of those twenty-five-century-old reliefs she held us in the palm of her hand. The drumming began again, now softer, as Magda spoke.

'*Willkommen. Willkommen* to all. Welcome to the feast of the new moon. Welcome citizens of our new Babylon,' she announced, speaking in English. 'You must help me, men of the city. You must take the coin in your hands. You must take the bright silver shekel and drop it into the lap of one of my followers. One of these beautiful girls. Her duty is to please you, in order to please the goddess. Come, men of the city. You must choose. You must enjoy my girls so we may please the goddess.'

'Is this for real?' said an American.

'Sure is better than a prayer meeting,' said another.

The drumming grew more insistent. Two silvery figures joined Magda. Their dresses were hitched up well beyond the customs post of decency. Kandy clutched her blue flute and Cindy, who was slowly gyrating her hips and stroking her smooth thighs, began to point at the audience.

'Meet my special priestesses, men of Babylon. We three can pick our own man for the night. Choose, choose, choose any girl as they pass among you. Please choose and do the will of the goddess. Then we will choose for ourselves.'

The band suddenly exploded into life. The sound of trumpets was deafening after Magda's quiet, husky voice. The chorus rushed out with their candles, darting this way and that in the pathway of lions, stroking a man's hair here and tweaking an ear at another table. Then they were gone, running back to the stage. They sat beneath

113

the Gate. An American airman got to his feet. He was holding the silver token. The coin glistened in the lights. He took a step towards the stage. I recognised him as one of Stigi's friends. He was a big man but he tenderly put a finger under the chin of a tiny girl called Helga, before dropping the silver coin into her lap. She stood and her hands clutched at the back of his collar, the long finger nails rasping up through the prickles of his crew cut. He put his arms round her waist and lifted her clear of the ground. With a smile she kissed him on the nose and, after he lowered her gently to the floor, led him off in the direction of the back door, to the Residence and her bedroom.

'True love?' I whispered in Betty's ear. The soldier had chosen the girl before.

'Is dangerous,' she replied, taking another sip of hot whisky. 'Believe me, Toby. All this is very dangerous.'

However, it did not appear to be so at that moment under the awesome blue cliff of the Gate. Here was not a trace of the Kurly Wurly club or the Turkish houses in Kreuzberg which stank of babies and boiling cabbage; where the sordid background of the transaction built an unscalable wall between the seeker and the found. The barrier was built long before she opened her legs on a dirty mattress and he rolled on the *R3 Naturcontact* condom, a contradiction in terms; '*elektronisch geprüft*', it said on the blue and yellow packet, and 'for your security' in English. We always put up high walls out of fear of loving, really loving.

Yet part of me knew Babylon was something I could no longer control.

Stigi tapped me on the shoulder, nodding towards the door. The Baron was here. He was taking off his heavy overcoat and accepting a token from Twinkle Twinkle. Two men were with him and a girl showed them to our table. As they sat down a bottle of champagne arrived in an ice-bucket. The Baron was sitting beside me watching Magda, entranced.

'My good God,' he said at last, screwing a cigarette into his short amber holder. 'You have brought me to the halls of Venus, Toby. The Venusberg is here. I'll bet these are the gorgeous creatures who dine only on the ejaculations of unicorns.'

Stigi looked puzzled. 'We used to have a goat,' he offered helpfully, to no one in particular. He took out his cigarette-case and began to hand round reefers. I reached for the bottle which had already been opened.

'A glass of bubbly, Baron?'

'Yes,' he nodded, holding his cigarette delicately between thumb and forefinger. A gesture of slightly foppish, calculated decadence I found attractive.

'You really do have the Gate. Or something that looks like it. As a child on the floor of my father's study I used to play with pieces of Babylon. Here is my friend Wolfgang, and . . .'

I did not catch the name of the other man, blonde and taut as a clenched fist. Wolfgang was small and soft-faced with a figure which seemed too ample for tanks. His dark hair was receding. Except for his eye-patch he looked more like the jovial owner of a coffee shop. He wore mirror-polished shoes which looked almost laughably small. His insistent and attractive laugh was virtually continual. In fact the life and soul of the party, as his collar-stud burst and his carefully combed hair fell forward across his forehead. Yet there was a fixed and darker star which refused to twinkle in those teddy bear brown eyes. A trait he shared with his friend the Baron.

'You should have come sledging with us, Wolfie. Toby here is an expert. To say nothing of the lovely Magda . . .'

I felt embarrassed, and a little angry. But the Baron did not linger on our winter sports.

'Yes, I congratulate you. Wonderful! The Blue Gate of Babylon. My, I wish she were mine . . .'

'Some of the Gate is real,' I said, as the Baron peered at one of the lions. He turned back to Wolfgang.

'My God. This is insane.'

'We have always been insane, Rollo,' said Wolfgang. He grabbed me and pulled me to him in an absurd tango position, his head resting on my chest. 'I think that is why we are still alive, Rollo. We amuse the Gods. War, like syphilis, only comes as a surprise to the dull and innocent pedestrian. You see, Toby, our madness separates us from the common herd. We are not, as you say, the good sports. We are the goats. But we Germans' fanatic ability not to see the consequences of such inspiration puts us among the immortals. In the great Café Babylon in the sky, Toby, they know we are already *gefallen*. You are privileged to dance with a dead man, Toby Jubb.'

He looked deep into my eyes, and I shuddered.

Wolfgang let me go.

'A drunken philosopher. Toby, you must let me examine your Gate better in the light. It is fantastic.'

The drumming stopped.

'I want you.' Magda was pointing directly in front of her. A spotlight from the side of the stage lit up the Baron. She came slowly down the steps, dancing towards us along the processional street until she was level with the table. Slowly pushing back a chair with her sandal, she prodded the Baron gently with one of the ceremonial knives. Baron Rollo von Hollmann glanced towards me as if for reassurance and then back to Magda. There was no mistaking the look in his eyes.

'The Goddess claims you,' announced Magda, her voice shaking. The lights went out. When they came on again the Baron was gone. Gone to our bed.

'You're not jealous?' asked Stigi, as Ulrike came over and stroked my hair.

I clenched my fist under the table. How could I be jealous? I had staged the show.

'You're a cold fish, Toby Jubb,' said Stigi. 'What really matters to you . . . ?'

Later when I awoke I wanted to say I was sorry to Ulrike. We had been playing a game in her room. She liked to be slapped on her bottom. She told me how her father took her knickers down if she wet them.

'Slap me hard, Toby. No, harder. Otherwise there is no point.' She giggled.

Now the space in the bed next to me was cold. Ulrike's poster of James Dean gazed down from the wall at me, cold and ambivalent.

'Didn't see her,' replied Betty Bethlehem when I had dressed and gone downstairs. Champagne bottles littered the landing but the bodies were gone. 'Get this order for me from the butchers, love. Go on, lazybones. You look as if you could do with some fresh air. Don't worry . . . The Baron's gone. Best leave Magda for a while though. Leave her be. Trust your Auntie Betty. Are you all right, love?'

I nodded. She kissed me on the cheek. She looked much better and seemed to be giving thanks we had survived the night. My ideas on introducing love into the Café Babylon were still an abomination to her. But we had all managed to avoid bringing down some dreadful curse on our heads for misusing the Olympian laws of hospitality. I went down the stairs to the street door where my overcoat hung unmolested on a peg. The entrance to the Residence was now as neat and carpeted as any middle-class block of flats. Outside the air was crisp as I set off in the direction of the far line of buildings which made up Kreuzberg. A man was putting up a poster on which a girl in long, white evening-gloves was advertising a champagne substitute. Dieter was the nearest butcher this side of the border and because of the lax crossing restrictions still had as many clients from the East as the West. I hadn't realised how early it was and luckily there wasn't a queue. The butcher had just arrived on his pushbike. An amiable florid man with a nose the colour of one of his own *bratwürst*s. He was often starting work as I was going to bed.

'*Guten Tag.*'

'Good morning, Englishman,' said the butcher cheerfully. 'How is the trade in more profitable flesh?' We both smiled at his regular joke and the sun came from behind a cloud. Two doors away a Turkish grocer was opening for business. Excited children ran out of the doorway and came laughing down the ramshackle street on the frontiers of nowhere. The street had no name but most of the buildings were engaged in trade of some kind. Dieter was a good butcher who scrubbed out his old fridge once a month and told you so. He did not like the Turks. But I never heard him say a harsh word to them. It was implicit. He bent down to unlock the shutters of his shop, secured by a padlock.

'*Scheisse.*'

The butcher detached the smashed lock from the eyelets which held the shutters in place. He was breathing quickly, muttering something under his breath and looking over his shoulder at the grinning Turkish children. 'My shop's been broken into,' he said simply, in German. His hands were criss-crossed with disfiguring scar tissue. The nervous slip of the knife when boning meat. A knife, he explained to me, had to be sharp to cut through the muscle and sinew of animals. Dieter was often off work, nursing his cuts. He did not wear them bravely, as the duelling scars of his trade. When he rode his heavy black bicycle home to his wife he wobbled under the gaze of a thousand phantoms. He worried, he told me quite seriously, not so much about the future as that the present was but a dream and he would wake again, among the furies of the recent past.

Dieter pushed up the shutters with a resigned flourish. His sausages and hams still hung from their hooks and racks in the tall, gloomy room. He stepped inside. He appeared to be counting. The noise of the ghetto, the playing children, the whine of the Ottoman music mixed with the tang of garlic and cured meats from the shop. A boy passed wheeling a brand new Mercedes tyre, no doubt stolen from one of my richer customers. I looked back. Dieter was standing very still. I took a step inside the door.

'Are you all right? Is anything missing?'

'*Jesus Maria.*'

'What?'

'They have come again. As I told you. They have come again. The swine, they cannot be content. They do not rest.' His voice was high-pitched and very excited.

'What is it, Dieter?'

In front of us was a white marble slab across which marched legions of fake parsley. Above this, suspended from the roof by a pulley was a series of parallel rails on which the butcher hung the preserved meats for which his shop was famous, even in the Soviet sector. He locked the fresh meat in his immaculate fridge at night, as he always informed his customers. Now, up in that stalactite roof of sausage something else was trussed and dangling from those hooks. Dieter could not take his eyes off it. He picked up a cleaver from a wooden butchering table, as if for protection.

'They have done this. It is unclean. I run a clean shop!' His blue eyes were wide. His cap fell from his bald head. A horrible event had taken place, something every deep line on his face recognised as a sacrilege.

'Who are they, Dieter?'

'They are who they always are,' he said, not very helpfully.

Dieter crossed himself. Small, barely perceptible movements, another kind of washing; as if some almighty scrubbing, a little divine elbow-grease could erase whatever it was he saw, or imagined he saw. I took another step.

'What is it, Dieter?'

Once the children who lived in the ruin next door had put a dead dog in the shop. Dieter had been distraught. I took another step, and froze.

Trickles of red, the same bright colour as the border flags, had spotted and dropped between the parsley lines, and a reservoir of blood had built up around a drain hole. The droplets blew across the marble, as if the butcher's Catholic magic had started to work. The droplets were joined by another shade of red. The red of petals, flower petals. The wind sent red rose petals fluttering down from high above. On the slab, too, was a single, bloody cobblestone, two inches by two inches by two inches, the raw material of Berlin, covered in a darker red and the petals . . .

I looked up.

I looked away.

'Murder!' shouted Dieter, almost before my watering eyes could focus.

'Murder! She is so young. So beautiful. The lovely hair. The fair skin . . . My God, they do this. Out, out of my shop. My shop is a good shop. A clean shop.' The cleaver narrowly missed my left arm.

'Dieter! Stop!'

I held up my hands. I was outside the shop now. A dark-eyed line of boys was watching the scene with a frighteningly detached interest. They formed a circle in the street as we came out.

'Murder!' shouted Dieter.

'They have come back. They will kill, kill, kill, kill.' He began to slash at the air with his cleaver in wide arcs.

'Get the cops. The old fool's finally gone loony,' said a man behind me. 'What's this about murder . . .'

'In the shop . . . a girl,' I said.

'The butcher has murdered a girl,' cried a Turkish mechanic I recognised. 'The butcher's murdered a girl.'

'He is selling human meat?'

'The swine has made a girl, a human girl into *bratwürst* . . .'

But Dieter was unaware that he had been judged and sentenced by the Turks on that bitter street. Things were moving too fast. My head spun.

'We must stop them,' said Dieter. 'Stop them before they can trick us again. They are everywhere.'

'He's off his rocker.'

Dieter slashed again with his cleaver as I took a step towards him. There was nothing I could do. As they waited for the police, like

119

terriers baiting a bear, I staggered onto a bombsite and towards home.

The butcher was still yelling as a larger squad of Turkish mechanics arrived on the scene brandishing spanners and tried to disarm him.

'My shop is a clean shop . . .'

I tripped over a pile of loose cobblestones, the same uniform two-inch cubes of grey granite as the bloodstained intrument of torture which had dropped from the girl's body. I was shaking. I began to run. In the middle of that wasteland I was sick under an unforgiving sky, which seemed to have no time for the little things squirming below. Who could do such a thing? Who were the 'they' Dieter talked of? Were the soldiers of my Eyeless Clockwork Army clawing their way up and breaking through the thin skin of the past, through the caked make-up of those present; intent on making lampshades again. My, the Eyeless Clockwork Army certainly had its hobbies . . .

How else but sacrifice to guarantee the crops of a wicked city . . .

Not for the first time I realised that consciousness has its own censor. My mind would not reveal to me all that my eyes had seen in the butcher's shop. A soft, pink body bent back on itself, hanging like a trapeze artist. And roses . . . roses forced into her body, the thorns piercing. A mouth opened very wide and eyes closed at the horror of her own crucifixion. The grimace of a child taking bitter medicine. Suddenly, I stopped. In the distance the shouting had died away and there was only the two banal tones of the police siren. A realisation dawned.

Was that Ulrike hanging there?

Had I just seen the girl I had slept with brutally murdered and not bothered to get close enough to find out, to look into that face for more than a second? Now I could only see the smile of Ulrike, the girl I had spent the night with. Had I gone so far through the Blue Gate of my Café Babylon not to care any more? Is there really a road to the furnace that begins with the charming and the banal? Why would anyone hurt poor sweet Ulrike? Was it Ulrike? If someone could do that to any girl they could do it to Magda. I had to make sure. Now I saw Magda's face among those wicked roses. I stumbled again and this time fell full length in the slush, grazing myself on the half bricks just beneath the surface of the snow. A green and white police car came from the direction of the Tiergarten and stopped on the road. I caught the reflection of field glasses behind the windscreen. They were searching. They were on a murder call. I picked myself up, dusting my overcoat. As slowly as I could manage I made my way to the road, and back to the Babylon; all the time trying not to look towards the police car or even think of the murder, or what it could mean for me. Had Midwinter's Mr Fox started to murder Jubb's chickens?

As I walked along the road which snaked past the south side of what had been Potsdamer Platz, whose very emptiness seemed to float up like a vast question mark over humanity, another police car nosed into view, examining every brick and blowing piece of newspaper. In front of me the metal door of a road gritting bin opened with a clang and a piece of wood began to bang on the edge. German obscenities came from within. The thick wooden stick waved around. The police car stopped. Two Berlin *Polizei* in ridiculously large peaked caps and short leather coats got out, almost casually. One grabbed the piece of wood and hauled. A man was on the other end, short, bearded and clutching a bottle. The stick was the wooden leg of a drunk who had been sleeping it off. One of the policemen bent down and with kind words appeared to be adjusting the limb. Then in a quick movement the leg was off and the policeman was beating the drunk with it; blows rained on the drunk's head. He put his hands up and I remembered Herodotus's dictum that people from cold climates always have dangerously thin skulls ... The man was bundled into the police car; wide-eyed and legless. As they drove away another nearer bin opened. I blinked.

For an instant I saw the unmistakable grin of the tipsy prophet Daniel. He was speaking to me.

'What do you expect, fool? Roses? History is whatever you make of it. Everyone pretends. But Babylon will always fall.'

When I got to the bin there was nothing inside but a small pile of excrement. Perhaps I imagined it all. I ran upstairs when I got to the Residence.

'Ulrike ... my God, I mean, thank God. You are still alive? Did we have an argument? My God, you are still alive. It doesn't hurt? I thought you were in the butchers, among the sausages and hams. I ...'

I had gone straight into the old ballroom of the Residence which used to be the bar and where the girls now had breakfast. I was met by brightly-coloured dressing-gowns, the smell of hyacinth-perfumed soap and hair-setting lotion. Here and there was a head full of plastic caterpillar curlers. The girls returned to their breakfast of eggs and cheese and black bread in an embarrassed silence. I pressed Ulrike to me. Magda, talking to Betty at the other end of the room, was frowning. I wanted to hug them all.

'I thought . . . I thought you had been . . .'

'Silly Toby. You have your nightmares again,' said Ulrike prettily.

'Dr-e-e-eam, Dream, Dream, Dream,' sing the Everly Brothers. Had I dreamt it all?

I ran straight up to my room and sat, breathless on the bed. The Baron's gold cigarette-case was on the dressing-table. At that moment it seemed an obscene intrusion. I felt a twinge of resentment against him but then opened the bottom drawer and took out the strong-box containing my papers and the inventory of the Babylon artefacts. In a buff envelope was the Special Investigations Branch report on the earlier murder which Parr had sent me.

Downstairs the juke-box was already playing the first record of the day, Wooden Heart. I could not focus on the words. The murder at the butcher's and the murder of the French girl were exactly the same.

'. . . severe beating . . . concurrent with the suspected manner of . . . massive internal bleeding . . . two cobblestones of the type used all over the city . . . anus and vagina . . . a known prostitute . . . long-stemmed red roses . . . exactly similar . . . resources do not permit . . . piercings . . . a known prostitute.'

A known prostitute? Whatever did they mean? Known by whom?

'But I don't have a wooden heart,' sang the juke-box. I had tears in my eyes. Someone knocked at the door.

'Yes.'

Betty came in. She too was crying. She held on tight to the padded lapels of her robe.

'I'm sorry, Toby. I didn't believe you just now. I thought you were just joking or something. You have been a bit strange recently. But . . . there has been a murder.'

'Who . . . one of our girls?'

'Yes . . . the other Ulrike. Ulrike Lenz. She only came the other night. How did you know it was a girl named Ulrike?'

I did not know what to say.

'The two of them look alike,' said Betty. 'They had started to pretend to be each other . . . as a game.'

'A game?'

(What are you doing, Toby Jubb? What are you doing to these girls and yourself, I thought, hunched on the bed.)

'Come on, love. Come on, Toby. You couldn't help it. Come on now. The police are downstairs.'

10

'I think you should make a contribution to our expenses,' said the enormous, Buddha-like figure of the Chief of Detectives. 'A place of the Café Babylon's type causes problems when there is an upset. Paperwork, you understand. At times, I think I'm being buried in paper. A small contribution for all our extra work. You will hear no more. I promise. These young farm-girls from the East always meet bad ends.' He laughed and examined his carefully manicured nails. A companion brought in a cup of scalding coffee. I had been in the cell all that day and by now it was getting dark outside.

'You . . . you're not going to investigate?'

The fat man looked hurt. 'All we require is a token payment, Herr Jubb. Believe me, this matter, even though the details are so horrible, so fresh in our minds, will soon fade.' His voice was soft and concerned. The cell was hot and airless. 'I am sure it is for the best. If we start to investigate, who knows what work we would make for ourselves. As I'm always saying to Michael here, how can we be expected to run a police force if we are always out investigating crimes? I see you agree.'

I nodded.

He stood up. 'My Sergeant will make the arrangements with your excellent Herr Weitz. You must tell your girls to be more careful in the future. Or is someone trying to threaten you, Mr Jubb? Have you got into deep water? But that is your affair . . .'

I took a step towards the cell door.

'Oh, and Herr Jubb.'

'Yes.'

'We would like to visit your club sometime. Off-duty, of course. Will you keep us a table? Such a pity about the girl. I wish there were more love in the world. Do remember to keep us a table, Herr Jubb. A table near your wonderful Blue Gate. Oh yes, we know about that too . . .'

The days got warmer and the snow melted but my slide down the Devil's Hill was as inexorable as it was gradual.

In the early days of April the wind rattled the loose panes of the bakery skylights as I tried to make an exact drawing of the Blue Gate of Babylon. I stopped to remove a discarded button of bubble-gum which had been pressed into the eye of one of the lions in the processional street. I was trying to keep busy. Under the Blue Gate the Baron sat on the edge of the stage and held Magda's hand, exploring each of the long nails in turn. She watched him and occasionally toyed with the hair at the back of his neck which was starting to spill over his collar. They were in love and didn't care who saw them. The wind whistled. My plans were out of control, and were taking the woman I loved away from me. The Café Babylon had taken me over. I could not escape the laughter of the goddess. I was at the mercy of a huge joke invented by Colonel Midwinter. The Baron brought Magda flowers. Hot-house daffodils. After the murder red roses were out of fashion. Two of our girls were missing. The butcher had closed his shop and sold it to a Turk who repaired Mercedes taxis and was unconcerned about the building's past. Everyone presumed the worst about Gerta and Helga. But the *Stadtpolizei* showed even less interest than in the murder of Ulrike. They appeared to have the attitude that if a girl sold her body the customer could also take her life, if he so desired. They called inactivity discretion, and made me pay for it, even popping in from time to time for a glass of champagne. Suspects were not considered. Fingerprints were not taken. Eventually the detectives had to pass the files to the British authorities and an ageing Wolseley was now parked a safe distance from the Café Babylon. I had no doubt the occupants were Parr's men. He had obviously shown the fat Chief of Detectives with the carefully manicured fingernails a little financial consideration. The Baron kissed Magda tenderly on the cheek.

125

'We are becoming too successful,' said Stigi, dodging from behind a pillar with a wedge of dollar bills in his hand. 'My God, if we could only expand. Get more girls. Set up new places. Advertise, even. Say, that's really good, Toby. I didn't know you could draw. I didn't know you were an artist.'

Stigi never looked back; someone was usually chasing him.

'I don't think Midwinter would like it if we advertised. We seem to be doing far too well without. Frankly, I think it's time we put our case to the Baron and shut up shop.'

I poured some water into the palette of my old watercolour set to give the drawing a blue wash. Magda was now kissing the Baron's lower lip and chin. Every night men queued outside the door, yelling for sweethearts who might be with someone else. A knife fight had started over one girl. When the local uniformed *Polizei* had gone, I had taken an old army torch and with Betty followed the bloodstains through the snow. We skirted the wire where a family were welcoming relatives ducking underneath the single strand. The border soldiers' brazier was only a hundred yards away. They completely ignored the exodus. The lovelorn American soldier had fallen into a ditch, formerly the basement of a building, strewn with broken yellow tiles the colour of rotten teeth. The exact opposite to the blue tiles of my gate.

The man was dead. He was in his early twenties. His grave was all that was left of Gestapo headquarters. We left the body to the cold and the dawn patrol.

'Mark my words, I told you there would be trouble,' said Betty Bethlehem.

Today, she sat with six of the other girls by the old bakery oven to the right-hand side of the Gate. One of Twinkle Twinkle's Turkish friends who could speak English had shown me documents, or rather scraps of paper, emblazoned with the Nazi Swastika which he had discovered while cleaning the place for *le patron*. He showed me teeth and bones and a misshapen ingot made from gold fillings. A more abstract question had begun to nag. Where does the naughtiness of children, the naughtiness of the Café Babylon, stop and true evil begin? The little ingot was heavy in my hand.

Betty Bethlehem sat in the centre of an adoring group. The girls were all addicted to their horoscope books and had developed a surprising appreciation of the Babylonian occult. Cindy had even

learned the hymn of the Goddess. She waltzed up to the makeshift
desk on which I rested my books and kissed me on the nose.

> 'Wash him with pure water
> Anoint him with sweet oil
> Clothe him with a red garment
> Let him play sweet music
> On a flute of lapis-lazuli
> Let courtesans turn his mood
> I'm clean and cheap and . . .'

Betty Bethlehem was a few steps behind her and grabbed Cindy.
The girl did not protest. She was smiling at me. She had the dead
blue eyes of her foundling dolls. 'Come along, Cinderella. Go back
and join your friends. Toby will come and play later.'

'She's really into that witches' brew stuff,' remarked Stigi, taking
a puff of a reefer. It was ten in the morning.

'They all are. But it's Magda who is the real enthusiast,' said
Betty, turning back to us. 'I think it's time to do what you plan. I've
been with that little fat one, Wolfgang. Now, he's a greedy man. A
nice man though. I think he would come over like a shot. Look at
that bloody Baron. I thought you loved Magda, Toby?'

'I do.' But while she was with him I had not been entirely a monk.
From pillow talk, I knew the gossip of several small East German
farming towns. Betty Bethlehem spoke again.

'Do you know what the Baron is saying?'

'No,' I said.

'He is asking her to marry him. He's in love, Toby. Con-
gratulations, big boy. Your plan has worked. The fish is hooked.'

If I had truly hated women (as I was coming to realise the owner
of a brothel must) things would not have started to get so out-of-
hand. I kept trying to make myself more jealous, or at least jealous,
just as, when one is young and drunk for the first time and the
wardrobe is spinning around the bedroom, one tries to be sick.
Jealousy would lead to anger and anger to some purgative action.
The pangs I had felt at the beginning when Magda had first seen the
Baron had magically vanished, as if I too were under the spell of

Ishtar. More than anything else, I was frightened now of loving Magda, for fear of what might happen to her.

My thoughts were interrupted by a frenzied banging at the door of the bakery. Shouts followed. Stigi carefully put out the reefer and we went over. It sounded as if someone were rolling around among the dustbins. I was about to go out, but Stigi, who was looking through the spy-hole, held up his hand.

'Pony Express,' he hissed. 'I don't think they like us taking their trade. Especially as we're getting all the big shots. I know three congressmen and a British MP who want to visit. The brothers are jealous. They think we're going to cut in on their act. They get murderous if anyone threatens their monopoly in comfort and joy.' Footsteps retreated back up the alley, followed by a groaning sound. 'They've beaten up some customer,' Stigi added, as I slid back the bolt and opened the door. A man was lying among the dustbins covered in kitchen rubbish.

'I am assailed on all sides by Nubians,' he began. 'They mistook me for someone called Toby or Tony. I'm from the Shakespeare festival. We have to find somewhere else for our *Midsummer Night's Dream*. The place we have has been taken over by the Daughters of the Alamo to become a refugee centre. I said we were refugees but you cannot argue with a Daughter of the Alamo. It just didn't wash. So here I am. I was about to knock, and then I was set on. The ringleader would have made a brilliant Othello. He had such presence. They also had a baseball bat and I feel somewhat bruised. They demanded money and beat me. I say. That's a spiffing stage.' A man of Oscar Wilde proportions and fragility, he pushed past us to gaze at the Gate of Ishtar, under which stood Magda and the Baron.

'Now that is wonderful, absolutely darling. We even have Pyramus and Thisbe already in residence. You'd probably make a good Bottom. Bottoms need big shoulders. I can hardly believe this is British Council.' The theatrical affectation failed at times to disguise flat northern vowels. His eyebrows shot up further as he caught sight of Cindy and the rest of the girls. Cindy came rushing up.

'Where thou lookest in pity, the dead man lives again
The sick are healed . . .'

'I say, she speaks English, the little dazzler,' said the newcomer. 'I always love to hear the Bard on the lips of a foreigner. Don't tell me. I know. *Love's Labour's Lost.*'

'Not quite. The trouble is we're putting on our own show, old boy,' I said, patting him on the shoulder. After all the scene in front of me was now a stage. 'I wouldn't have thought you would want to come down here again. Not with a top-notch company. The chaps who beat you up think I'm running a brothel. But I do see what you mean about Pyramus and Thisbe. We must get round to it some day. Berlin is just the spot for a bit of lamentable comedy.'

The chap looked at me, pale and bruised and unconvinced. Twenty minutes later he was gone with the instinct of a man who has wandered into a world more precarious than his own. Yet he had eyes for everything. In particular the Gate. He had even asked if it might be possible to take the Gate back to England. It made me suspicious: he had been acting the actor. But then they all do. Twinkle Twinkle escorted him into town. I returned to my desk and opened the ledger that contained our bookings. We were solid until August. Demand might start making it necessary for the chorus to see more than one person a night. Clearly, something drastic had to be done.

Later that evening I was playing chess with the Baron.

'Check.'

'You are almost too good for me, Baron.'

'My father taught me.'

'Did he beat you a lot? Does he still beat you?'

The Baron looked at me quizzically. I was not meant to be party to his family details.

'My father used to beat me all the time. He beat me at chess too. To lose was not in his nature. He had a bad temper. He could become a bear. But it did not stop him winning. He taught me that was the point of all games. He learnt it from Bismarck . . .'

'The labour camp must have been pretty terrible.'

'Oh, not so bad. Better than the military academy.'

I felt a shortness of breath. We were alone at a table in the old ballroom of the Residence. If I made a mistake now it would all be for nothing. Smoke curled up from the Baron's Havana cigar. We were waiting for Wolfgang and Betty to return. He had taken her to the Berlin Opera and then dinner at a restaurant on the Kurfürsten-damm. It made my heart beat faster to think of Parr following Stigi in the decoy car which had left just before them. The Baron saw me looking at my watch.

'Don't worry my friend, she will be safe with Wolfgang. Like me, he loves beautiful things.' He sighed. 'The murders have made Magda ill. She is lying down with a fever. How could anyone do such a thing, *ja*? You are good to let us still come. I for one have never felt such kindness. We did not expect such . . .' He took a sip of cognac as he searched for the right word.

'Yes, the murders have upset everyone. All Kreuzberg is jumpy and we are vulnerable here on our small blue island. We may have to close down. Who knows? Already we've had to stop some of our more important clients coming. To save embarrassment with the police,' I lied. 'Your move, Rollo.'

'Surely you would not close down?' The sad brown eyes were alarmed.

'The military authorities can do what they like. Things go all right in Berlin provided no one notices officially. One greases the right palms and knows the right people. But if the murders continue . . .' I shrugged. 'Perhaps we will move to Munich. Have you ever thought of living in the West, Baron?'

He did not reply immediately but made his move, taking a long pull of his cigar and sending the smoke up among the crystals of the chandelier. I had made my move. It was up to the Baron now. On the chessboard he appeared to be throwing the game away after all. Suddenly, he stripped off his jacket and, placing it on the back of the chair, unhooked a simple gold cufflink. He rolled up the right sleeve of his blue cotton shirt. From his elbow to his knuckles the skin was white and hairless and I had noticed before a nervous habit of pulling the sleeve of his jacket down over his right hand.

'The skin here is the skin of Wolfgang.' He smiled. 'Ripped off the man without an anaesthetic to save his commander. Any of us would have done the same for the other.' A pulse throbbed in his jaw line. He was making things difficult for me.

'I know this is going to sound like bad manners and the abuse of hospitality and everything crass like that, but if you wanted to come over, to the West I mean, it could be arranged. Wolfgang, too. You

130

might have to tell a few tales. Not secrets exactly, but the odd military detail. You see, I would be taking a risk on your behalf if I contacted the authorities. You appreciate the delicacy of someone in my position. Perhaps the odd detail of coming manoeuvres? Any plans to close the border again? You know the sort of thing.' I tried to make it sound matter-of-fact. He was watching me closely. I felt like the local dignitary accused of rifling the poor-box. Then he laughed and slapped his thigh.

'Look, I am free again. I have escaped.'

'What do you mean?'

'My king has escaped check.'

'You have no interest in coming to the West?'

The Baron sighed. 'They would shoot my men, Toby. They know we sneak over. So they keep tabs on a few of us. A handful of my best friends are always on night duty when I am in the West. They would be shot. I cannot betray them. Also, I cannot betray the love I have been shown here. Yes, love. Anyway I am much too old and ugly to sell myself to President Kennedy. I feel sure you are only thinking for the best, Toby. I would like nothing better than to go and move to Lugano with Magda and live a normal life. To have children and a little house. Believe me, Toby, love and friendship are all that matter in the end. There, now I have you in check. The match is going to be a draw. How depressing.' The smile was set hard in that boyish face and I had an intimation of the stubbornness that had made one Russian tank commander lose his mind.

'But you are fond of Magda?' I could not say the words without almost choking.

The Baron glanced up from the board. His play was fast and based on hit-and-run. When he spoke he made it sound as if he were trying to spare my feelings.

'We have become friends, Toby? Yes? I know that is true. But we have only known each other over a few drinks and a few nights of chess in three months. All my men I have known since 1941. But I knew many of them before as boys on my father's estate. We love each other. You could almost say we were married. We think up a plan to have fun and some women and we find your place and a lot more. We found love. Please do not ask me to betray such a precious thing by betraying my men. Do not betray yourself,

Toby. You have something here very special indeed . . .' The Baron turned back to the chessboard and shook his head.

'So you have no plans . . . ?'

'No. Please do not ask Wolfgang or the rest of my men. They are all very grateful to you for bringing a little happiness.'

I squeezed a pawn in my hand. My diplomatic career was evaporating in a volatile mixture of sweet reason and moral sentiment. My plans, it seemed, had worked too well.

'But Rollo . . .'

'Check.'

'I mean, you're not a Communist.'

He laughed out loud.

'No, I'm not a good Communist. But then, I was not a good Nazi. Check. One has to keep one's mind on the game.'

'None of us can help being called up.' The game had turned in the Baron's favour. He puzzled for a minute over his next move.

'Check.'

He surveyed the pieces with satisfaction.

'I think that is checkmate. Yes, Toby, no one can help being conscripted. But, please do not be shocked, Wolfgang and I were Nazi party members. We destroyed. I can see that. Now we find ourselves on the other side precisely because of a talent for destruction, and you want me to betray my friends and change around again. My poor head spins. Do you know, I still wake up in the night and smell my flesh on fire? It's true. No, I will not betray my friends, Toby. Anyway, the Americans know exactly how many tanks we have just the other side of the border. My unit is there only to provide the fiction of a reborn, socialist German army. Ha. In fact the Soviets do not trust me an inch. How could I know what will happen? Of course there are rumours of a blockade which never comes. I have listened to speculations about it on the BBC. For sure, I would like to duck under the wire and disappear on a tram down the Ku'damm. But not if it means the death of my comrades. Yes, I think that is checkmate. Now tell me something, Toby Jubb.'

It was all too much. My schemes were beginning to unravel like an old sweater.

'Anything,' I said, setting up the pieces again for another ritual slaughter. I could not imagine the sensitive man before me sacking towns in Poland; lining men, women and children up by hayricks

132

and machine-gunning them. At that moment he was making me feel dishonourable.

'Who spoke to you of this business of my defecting? Are you involved in intelligence matters?' He seemed to look straight through me.

'Oh, a few diplomatic types were shooting their mouths off. They were talking large sums of money.'

'And you are so interested in money? Ha! Even to a good Communist like me I do not think you are a good businessman. You are not interested in profit like your friend Herr Weitz. You are more concerned with archaeology. You are fond of Magda. Yet you would let her go off with me. Have you found something you value more? The clue to the great golden statue, perhaps? Many things about you I do not understand.' He took a gulp of brandy. 'Are you my good friend, Toby Jubb?'

'Of course I am.'

'Then please, Toby, give me fair warning to get back across my side of the wire if you hear they are coming for us. Please, Toby. We would do the same for you. Do not get involved in stupid games. Leave the bad men alone, Toby, whatever they promise, whatever they call themselves. They are always Gestapo.' In a flash he was up and walking to the door, no doubt to see how Magda was recovering. What made me feel so unclean? My mother deceived people all the time with a smile on her perfect face. Perhaps I was more like Father after all.

Two hours later I wandered down from my room, where I had been working on a particularly difficult piece of cuneiform script to take my mind off things, and went over into the bakery. A covered walkway now connected the two buildings. The band had gone home. A couple sat drinking and ignored me as I walked towards the Gate of Ishtar down the processional street. Another couple stood by the warm oven talking in low voices. No record played. Little endearments fluttered on the night like so many moths. The Venus of the East appeared to be exercising her power over everyone. I looked up at the Gate and shivered. I touched the tiles themselves and imagined a slight vibration. A force appeared to mock the precise history and measurements I had catalogued in my books. I had translated the accounts of rituals for the amusement of the girls, and so it was with a certain amount of horror I found I had reinvented a very attractive religion. But where was the harm in that? Most of the girls from the East were Catholics. They warmed to the idea of a Goddess replacing a Virgin who had ceased to work miracles for their parents. They followed Magda, who was hungry for the new. And after all, chaste goddesses are not popular in a brothel.

I heard whispering.

'Are you sure, my darling? Are you sure?'

'Yes, of course I'm sure.'

'And it is mine?'

'Of course.'

'How do you know?'

'A woman knows. Trust me, my darling.' Below me, at the other side of the Gate, two figures were intertwined on a couch. I heard a snatched and unmistakable gasp of pleasure.

'Hold me, Rollo.'

'You would come to the East? You will be mine? I wish you were mine. I wish it with all my heart under the Blue Gate. Truly mine.'

'Truly yours? Don't make promises you cannot keep, Rollo.'

'Mine.'

A strong hand grabbed me from behind and Cindy led me away. Later, as I lay awake, there was a scream in the night, then another. They came from the wasteland.

11

A skylark was soaring high over the farmland where the northernmost tip of Berlin becomes the German Democratic Republic. Higher and higher the bird flew, singing and singing as it looked down on the gentle landscape on the edge of spring. On the outskirts of a small village within the limits of the city one could sense the ache and anticipation of the changing season and smell the May blossom in the hedgerow as winter stepped over the precipice into summer. Changes came quickly here. I shaded my eyes to catch another glimpse of the lark, and began to cough. We were parked on a small track that ran from a collection of traditional high-gabled houses and an inn. It was late afternoon and, because it was Saturday, overloaded Volkswagens were disgorging blinking, dough-faced *Berliners* who made a weekly sceptical pilgrimage to the pockets of countryside around the city, to worship Mother Nature. It was not that the flattish fields were of any devastating beauty, or that many of the visitors craved the healthy outdoors. But like the prisoner who grows mustard and cress on his face flannel or keeps canaries, they wanted to reassure themselves that they too were part of the eternal cycle; that not everything was as manufactured and restricting as the steel and glass buildings of their booming city. Very fat men and their wives came to stride about in an innocent and natural world of which they, alone among Germans in their capacity for mischief, had never been part; a land of myth and epic legend and rather earnest fairies. The lark soared higher. The Baron adored the countryside, probably because his family had once owned so much of it. Perhaps that was why Parr had brought me here. His family had started stealing other people's back-gardens in the stone age. He was busy doing bunny-jumps dressed in a white rugby shirt and baggy blue shorts and running pumps. Two military policemen stood by, sweating slightly in their immaculately pressed woolly British Battle Dress; boots polished, belt and anklets blancoed snow-white. The belt-brasses glistened in the sunlight and the red band on the regulation caps stood out like a warning, the peak bending abruptly down over the nose and hiding the eyes. The skylark's song was now out of earshot and I was anticipating betrayal. I began to cough again.

'Glad you've come to your senses, old boy,' gasped Parr. 'Some of these bunny-jumps would do you good. How many can you do, eh? I bet I can do more. Never see an unfit bunny.'

With his bony hands in front of him on the short grass, he began to hop back and forth, his face reddening. I kept telling myself I was there out of loyalty to the Café Babylon. A kind of public school house-spirit. I did feel a strong bond to the girls. I had to end the murders. Zela had been gone three whole days and Betty Bethlehem was beside herself with worry. It was not just because I wanted the Baron with all his damaged charm and delicate manners safely out of Magda's way. There were the murders to consider. Why had Parr sent me the report on Véronique? He was capable of anything. Parr had sent for me, but even more, I wanted to see him.

'Come on, Jubb, a few bunny-hops.'

'No, thank you, Parr.'

'Press-ups, then?'

'Don't mind me, Parr. Go right ahead.'

'I knew you would see reason in the end, old boy. Running that sort of place must be sheer hell for a swot like you. I suppose you give those harpies of yours a wide berth? Don't touch them with a barge pole?' he said, as he did his press-ups.

'Actually, I'm rather fond of them.'

'Those women!'

'Mostly girls, Parr. Somebody has been murdering them. I'd like it to stop.' He turned and looked at me in mid-press-up.

'You always were fond of girls,' he observed. The statement was not a compliment; more akin to a kind of medical admonition, as if I were deficient in zinc or copper or had an overactive thyroid. Englishmen aren't really meant to like girls.

'I don't suppose you go out with any of them?'

'Go out with them?'

'You know quite well what I mean, Jubb.'

'Well, they often come and tell me their problems. For some reason they're all very kind to me.'

'How many, Jubb?'

Parr had stopped doing press-ups.

'How many what?'

'How many have you "been out" with?'

'Oh, that. Well, a few, I suppose. They're affectionate, normal girls and I feel responsible for them. To you it may sound silly but I've always tried not to hurt their feelings. We respect each other at the Café Babylon.' Parr could never understand. The trouble was, when you were alone with one of them she looked at you in that particular way. Your lips quivered. And as you felt a total inability to speak it was quite natural she started to touch you. After all, touching was her job.

'And I suppose all this respect is why squaddies are queueing around the block and sticking knives into each other to get in? Come off it, old boy.'

'We try to offer love as well as sex, Parr.' The one they called Mother Redcap, an ancient nickname for a senior military police sergeant, suppressed a chuckle.

'My God, idealism in Berlin. A prostitute is worse than a slave.' Parr seemed angry. His mother had run off with a man in the vegetable trade . . . who knew my father. For a whole term at school he had refused to eat his greens and had broken out in the most fascinating rainbows of adolescent spots. I shrugged.

'As the poet says, Parr, only the dead are not slaves.'

'You're very fond of the girl called Magda, I'm told. The Baron's woman. That's really why you wanted to see me, isn't it? Not all this tripe about love, old boy. Spare us that. I don't think you care tuppence about these murders. I know you, Jubb. I care far more than you do, Jubb. I want order. I believe in a decent future. Always have.' I didn't answer. 'The thing is, it's impossible to love everyone. We have to shut some people out, Jubb. I told you that at school. We have to exclude those who would take our loved ones from us. I think that's why you've sought me out. Glad to see you've come to your senses. You're a good egg really, aren't you, Jubb? We like good eggs, don't we, Sergeant?'

The sergeant wisely said nothing at all.

'But you can be sure of protection from myself and Mother Redcap here,' said Parr, nodding towards the large and dangerous-looking military policeman. 'Mother Redcap knows how to deal with problems in your part of town. I'll bet you can tell me where and when I can pick up the Baron, if you think about it, Jubb. All I need is a telephone call. A prearranged signal to one of our cars. I'm sure you've seen my cars waiting outside. But we never seem to net that damned Nazi. How about a spot of leapfrog, Jubb? Remember the cross-country runs at school? British Bulldog on a crisp morning? Not to mention the wall game. Don't say you've forgotten, Jubb?'

For me it would be easier forgetting one's first toothache or visit to the dentist. Parr was grinning at me as if I really was a long-lost friend from his schooldays. A boy could die playing games. We had a plaque at the end of the chapel to commemorate one unfortunate's demise. He had been hit with a hockey ball, just above the heart. Parr's grin vanished. Mother Redcap took a step towards me. It appeared I was about to play leapfrog.

'Come on, Jubb, bend over. Don't be such a big girl. And you, Sergeant. Don't smirk at me, Corporal. Bend.'

The word had a sinister ring coming from Parr. He had beaten me often in my pyjamas, cold and shivering in his study. He had even beaten me for being too tall for the cricket team. He had beaten me because of Mother. He had torn up my only photograph of her. Yet here I was playing leapfrog and asking the man for help. Why do we English always regard ourselves as so completely normal?

'Bend.'

If anything, the corporal and the sergeant were more embarrassed than I. Under my raincoat I was wearing a sweater and slightly baggy jeans, as I had lost more than a stone in my time at the Café Babylon. With my long legs I effortlessly cleared Parr's hard-muscled back but had to jump higher to get over Mother Redcap and the corporal. If you are going to make a fool of yourself, you might as well do it properly. Best foot forward, Jubb, I said to myself. As I bent down and looked back I saw Parr coming towards me. His eyes were staring and far too wide. Parr was over in an easy vault. The two heavy military policemen nearly pushed me into the ditch. Parr was laughing. Was it too far-fetched to believe he could have a hand in killing my girls?

'Come along, let's go round again.'

A small crowd of weekend strollers had begun to take an interest in us. Children who had been dancing in circles were drawn from their mothers and picnic baskets. A group of men with gipsy faces dressed in the fashion of medieval mummers were propping up a man wearing a fierce dog head on a pair of extremely long stilts, which were proving difficult to control on the slippery grass. The children seemed to prefer our cabaret.

'*Kommen Sie her*,' commanded Parr. In minutes there was a parallel junior chain of leapfrog in progress.

'All one needs is a bit of leadership to enjoy oneself healthily. Just look at them.'

'I don't think they've ever been wanting for leadership. But the last man to play "Simon Says" was a bit of a disaster. If I were them, I'd be reluctant about playing anyone's game for a while.'

'You'll play my game, Jubb, if you're sensible.'

I nodded. As he held up his hand we abandoned the leapfrog, now being played in a sexually ironic fashion by the Berlin children.

'So you're worried about your doxies? You want to stop them being murdered?'

'Yes, Parr.'

'Well, I'd say we have to have a suspect. Wouldn't you say so, Mother Redcap? I mean, these are brutal murders. Sounds to me like the work of a local. One of those Nazi chappies left over from the war, eh, Jubb? I wouldn't be at all surprised if it wasn't this Baron of yours. I hear his war record is far from unblemished. Atrocities, Jubb. A military fact of life. His lies have also blackened the characters of many brave men. I'd say we should nab him. What do you say, Mother Redcap, in your considered opinion?'

'Let's hook him, sir. Pick him up. I'd say it was him doing these horrible murders, sir. Regular Jack the Ripper. Shouldn't be allowed. It stands to reason. I shouldn't think we will bring him down without a struggle though. Not that we mind a struggle.'

'We don't mind a struggle at all,' said Parr, taking a towel out of the Landrover and wiping the sweat from his brow. 'Not for us the easy pathway, eh, Jubb?' He wound the towel around him. 'Hold this, will you?' Parr then removed his baggy blue shorts and slipped on a pair of cavalry twills. My mother always said the Devil wore immaculate trousers.

'I'll give you a call when we want to pick him up. Don't worry, old Midwinter will forgive you.'

As I got into the vehicle I listened for the skylark. But there was nothing, just the suspicious faces of the daytrippers around me. Perhaps for me the skylark's song was forever out of reach.

It was a pleasant evening when I finally got back to the Café Babylon. I had walked slowly from the centre through the Tiergarten, where couples were necking on the grass, the boys in drainpipes and the girls in bobbysocks, always a few years behind the fashion. My blue brothel was now fringed with purple willow-herb which swayed in a gentle wind on that warm Saturday night. At first I put my foreboding down to a bad conscience. Of course, I told myself, I did not intend to deliver Rollo to Parr. I would warn the Baron to stay on his side of the fence and then, blaming everything on Anthony Selwyn before Colonel Midwinter, ask to be sent back to Paris. Even if they exiled me to the Passport Office in Birmingham, I would take Magda. Strangely, I did not harbour any animosity towards the Baron. I did not feel beaten and cuckolded as my father had been when he had retreated weeping into his garden and built his miniature Pyramids and Great Wall of China. In a way I could understand him better. He was as overpowered by Mother as I was by Magda. I stopped. Yes, something was definitely amiss. On a Saturday night the bumping, brawling line of soldiers should have been stretching round the block; dissolving into fights as the night wore on and they realised they were not going to see Dorta or Kandy, the flute player. Stigi had kindly given me a small beretta pistol in case of emergencies with the Pony Express. The gun fascinated me like a Dinky Toy. But I always left it safely in my desk. The line scared me. They would call out my name and grab me as I went in past Twinkle Twinkle, as if I were a rock-and-roll star. One boy, crying for his beloved, had punched me on my already bent nose. Today the queue had vanished. Knots of contented-looking men were sitting down and playing cards. As I came closer I saw bottles of whisky being passed around accompanied by fat reefer cigarettes. Even Stigi was outside marvelling at a scene of peace and tranquillity.

'Hi, Toby! Come in. Come in. My God, where have you been. I looked for you everywhere. Come in, the world's gone mad.'

'So I see.'

I followed him around to the front door. Unusually, no one was banging against it and screaming the name of his chosen one. No one was trying to blow the twelve-foot portals off with gun cotton as they had last week, or take a pneumatic drill to the hinges as they had the month before. A smiling red-haired French paratrooper, of whom we had made an exception by ejecting—owing to his insisting on practices that not even the most hardened professionals could stomach—offered me a whisky bottle.

'*Bonjour, mon Capitaine*,' he said in a slurred voice. He made no attempt to come inside, but banged his head against the wood to whatever jolly tune was playing between his ears. I stood with Stigi in the cool hallway.

'It's the Baron.'

'What's the Baron?'

'It's immoral.'

'What's immoral?'

The world had to be turning in a very peculiar way for Stigi Weitz to be talking of morality.

'What's immoral?'

'Anything that's moral. That's just the point. To the Baron at the moment nothing seems to be off-limits. He's gone a bit crazy. He went into town and drew some money out of an account he had in Switzerland. He bought presents for all the girls. Then he comes out here and starts giving out booze and telling these men to love each other . . .'

'They seem to have believed him. What started it? Had he been drinking?'

'No. But he was with Magda. Well, you were out when Betty Bethlehem woke everyone up and said another girl had been murdered. It's Zela. Roses in the mouth, the whole works. They found her in an old cellar. She'd been chained up for a while before they iced her. Betty just cried and cried. The others went to the Gate and started chanting. Then it happened. I think I saw it with my own eyes. But there has to be some other explanation.'

'Explanation of what, for God's sake?' Stigi leant against the cage of the lift and took a deep breath.

'Spooks, Toby. A lady spook. The girls were chanting to the goddess and Pow! Suddenly everyone claims they have seen the lady. I do admit that everything did go a bit silvery around the edges. Everyone saw that and the place started to hum as if someone was trying to start a generator in the basement. I know there *is* a generator in the basement and it could have been the sun catching the roof glass at the wrong angle, but that's not the point. Everyone believed, Toby. I thought I was wrong in the head or something and went for a walk. When I came back it was much worse. Everyone was kissing and hugging and crying. All for free, god damn it. Magda was up there with this strange look in her eyes saying the Holy Mother had made herself known and that there was to be a New Age. An era of peace and love. The Baron started crying. All his men were crying. That was when he waltzed off into town and got money out of some account and started buying everyone presents. He then handed out my Scotch to these punks outside. He says no one has to pay any more. I know there is an angle in here somewhere but I can't figure it. Believe me, my friend, I saw this silvery figure. At first I thought it was poor Zela. I mean it couldn't be true, could it?'

In the bakery they were still chanting beneath the Gate of Ishtar. Cindy was leading them, discarding an item of clothing or jewellery as the ritual demanded.

'Hail Mother Ishtar, daughter of light,
In seven forfeits, take away night . . .'

Her seven forfeits were blue and silver bracelets tied with scarves, two anklets, two rings and a heavy necklace of Berber silver. She looked wonderful with her straight blonde hair and unsmiling face. Her pubic hairs shone like the burning bush as she removed an anklet and rubbed it over her milky white body. She was in a trance. Suddenly the top of the battlements was bathed in evening sunlight. Everyone looked up. One of the girls moaned. There was a babble

142

of voices. I thought I saw something too. The incense made me sneeze.

'Toby, my love. Did you see her?' asked Magda.

I was looking at Cindy.

'Not her, my darling, Ishtar, the Great Mother. She has been appearing to us. Did you see the light?'

'I saw something.' The tops of several of the turrets were studded with crystal. We could have been talking of a spectacular deception of the setting sun. But Magda's face was flushed. Her eyes were glowing. So were the Baron's.

'You saw the goddess.' He had decided for me.

'Well, it was the shape of a woman. I couldn't really tell. The effect didn't last long enough.'

'You didn't see because you doubted.'

'She is the morning and the evening star.'

'She has the power to heal my people. Magda says she has the power to heal Germany,' said the Baron, grabbing my arm. He gripped so hard it hurt. The same look was in the eyes of all those who clustered around Cindy below the Gate. Two of the other girls started to caress her legs. She was beckoning me. I turned back to the Baron. The last thing I needed was religious mania. But Rollo would not shut up.

'I have been bad to you, Toby,' he began. 'I did not know that you and my Magda were so deeply in love. Often it is hard to be sympathetic when one has always been a soldier. Now we can all be friends. We can all be friends and worship the Goddess.'

'Absolutely,' I replied, as Stigi joined us. The sheer guilelessness of the scene was overwhelming. In the shadows under the Gate I blinked as I saw men dressed in short amber robes. They had flowers in their hair, as the ritual had called for. Exactly the way I had imagined on the first day. They kissed and caressed their partners. They kissed and caressed each other. My dream of love had come true. Mother would be proud of me. The only fly in the ointment was that at the other end of the city, at the British Army Barracks, Anthony Selwyn Parr was vigorously rubbing his own private parts with pungent NAAFI carbolic, singing the Eton Boat Song and wondering which of his beloved pistols (he had always worshipped guns at school) to take with him to 'arrest' the Baron. I was not exactly sure what my old head-of-house would make of the

New Age. God, to Parr, was a stiff-backed Englishman. Parr regarded Edith Piaf as the ultimate in worldliness. I could not begin to imagine the expression on his face if he came through those doors. However much I resented the Baron, I knew I could not hand him over to Parr.

'We must all love each other,' repeated Magda, adjusting her eyeliner in a tiny mirror she kept concealed in her skimpy blue costume. Lately, from her puzzled expression, the ritual was not so much to correct her appearance as to make sure she was still there.

'I am coming to sit on your lap, Toby. I am going to kiss you. Look, Rollo does not mind a bit,' she said, reaching out and touching a small scar on the Baron's chin.

'Hail Mother Ishtar, daughter of light,
In seven forfeits take away the night . . .'

Cindy began the chant again and was pulled down onto a convenient couch by one of the Baron's men, who was entering into the spirit of the occasion as well as the flesh. Bodies squirmed beneath the Blue Gate. I wondered, fleetingly, if Herodotus had ever witnessed such an orgy. Perversely, it was the tongues that fascinated me. Magda pulled her dress over her head and was now sitting on my knee, naked except for her votive jewellery. She put the palms of her hands on both sides of my face and pulled me towards her. But then she sneezed.

'You will be my divine lovers. You and the Baron. I will sacrifice both of your loves to the Goddess. Atishoo.'

The Baron and I both sat very still as Magda had a sneezing fit. Her exquisite face grew quite red. Her upturned breasts shook. Stigi poured out a drink. Betty Bethlehem came out of the shadows. She and Stigi were the only ones apart from myself wearing modern dress. 'Atishoo.' She reached for me. 'Atishoo.'

'Where is my mirror?' Lipstick had smudged on her face. She could not find her precious glass. I had a mirror on my desk at the back of the bakery. 'We must all make love. We must all serve the Goddess. It is the only way we can lose our guilt,' said Magda.

The Baron nodded enthusiastically. I got up to fetch the mirror. Despite my reservations concerning the imminent arrival of Parr I

144

found walking difficult. Part of me at least was looking forward to Magda's suggestions.

'Atishoo . . .' she sneezed.

'Hail Mother Atishoo . . .' said Cindy.

'Don't worry, Magda, I have a mirror on my desk. Can you help me move something, Stigi?' I wanted to get the Baron to the working-area I had screened off at the side of the bakery. I had the glimmerings of a plan. If he would not go peaceably, I would have to use force. After all, my neck was at stake as well as his.

'Not a chance,' smiled Stigi. He had already started to unbutton his shirt in anticipation. I winked at him as he lit another joint and he took an offended step back, misunderstanding entirely.

'The Baron will help me. Won't you, Rollo? There's a heavy frieze of tiles propped across my roll-top desk behind those screens and I can't move it on my own.

Rollo looked almost relieved. Even after spiritual visitation, the prospect of a mass public orgy, especially with people you know and with whom you are likely to have breakfast and play the odd game of chess, is ticklish, to say the least. His bare chest looked painfully thin, almost emaciated. Even Stigi had become quieter, almost subdued, as the heaving mass writhed like snakes under the Gate of Ishtar. At times there was a glow over the battlements.

'Come along, you two. Only take a minute. Please come and help me, Stigi. They've already started without you.'

Magda smiled and opened a tiny locket-bottle of perfume which she began to sprinkle over her breasts. She stretched, closing her eyes and pointing her toes. 'Hurry back,' she called after us.

The frieze of tiles was resting against the front of the roll-top desk. They weighed about a hundredweight and had been propped there so I could draw them. I could easily have moved them on my own. They were the plain ochre mud tiles with the dire warning the moving finger of God had delivered to Belshazzar. *Mene, Mene, Tekel, Peres* . . . My little kingdom was being numbered and finished as well and if I wasn't careful the Persians, in the form of Parr, would be crashing through the bakery door in their armoured Landrovers.

'Is this piece important?' asked the Baron. 'What does it say?'

'It predicts the fall of Babylon. But it's a fake.'

'How do you know?' he demanded. The Baron was interested in

every fragment. I had seen him climb up onto the battlements of the gate and examine the tiles.

'The workmanship is too good,' I remarked without thinking. For it would be a crafty forger indeed who could better the hand of God. We picked up the heavy slab of tiled wall and moved it to behind one of the towering basalt griffons. Here, in a glass case, was laid the heavy stone scroll of the Unknown Temple 'Z' of the Koldewey excavations. The cylinder was covered in cuneiform script and I had wrapped it in cloth and tied it up with string. There were spots of gold on the scroll. I had been working on it for days, and was convinced it contained the key to the existence, or not, of the great golden statue. But first it would serve another purpose.

'Hey, you guys. I'm taking all the weight.'

Stigi was affronted by any pleasureless exercise.

'Right you are, Stigi.'

'Fuck right you are, Stigi. There's an orgy going on. A spontaneous one, and this son of Satan is missing out.' I left the Baron holding one end and picked up the stone scroll of the Unknown Temple 'Z'. It was about the size and diameter of a baseball bat, but much heavier.

'Put your end down first, Rollo,' I said softly. 'Now be gentle with those tiles, even if they are a fake.'

Dutifully and carefully, as one would expect from a military man, even one with the flamboyant predilections of the Baron, he lowered the frieze of tiles, wedging it with a loose piece of brick from the floor. As he bent over I stepped quickly behind him.

I swung the scroll of the Unknown Temple 'Z' like a scythe and it caught the Baron just behind the ear. He went out like a light. Blood trickled from his ear. Perhaps I had hit him too hard. But it would have been no use reasoning with him.

'Hey, what are you playing at?' snarled Stigi, dropping his end of the frieze with a small crash. Tiles shattered. 'That's not fair.'

'Fair?'

'Just because you're jealous of him and Magda, it don't mean you should try and kill him. He's got as much right as anyone else. Orgies are democratic. I fought for democracy.'

'Look, Stigi,' I said, taking hold of his shirt. 'Parr is probably on his way. Yes, Parr. I've had a tip-off from Midwinter's staff. Parr has a warrant out for the Baron's arrest. He wants to blame Rollo for the murders. I think he intends to kill him. If I really hated Rollo I might just let it happen, but I have the feeling that we would end up sorry too. Can we get him past the duty-guard outside?'

The mention of the magic word 'Parr' had almost captured Stigi's entire attention.

'Shit. No. But what about . . . the drains . . . I can take him down the sewers. Say, have I really got to miss . . . ?'

'Stigi, for God's sake! You live in a brothel. Whatever you want is available eight days a week.' We were hissing at each other.

'But it's different when everyone wants to do it. I mean, of their own free will.' The goddess had affected even Stigi. Wearily, I now understood perfectly the inscription Darius had ordered carved on his tomb. 'Forsake not the straight way. Sin not.' If I got out of this mess I would strive to be better. I would. I smiled at the eager American.

'Try not to think about it, old boy. I'll get Twinkle Twinkle to help you with the body. Where's the nearest sewer, by the way?'

When I returned to the festivities beneath the Blue Gate of Babylon Magda's knuckles were white, gripping the back of a chair. But she was more aroused than angry at my absence. She was looking longingly at a couple who were engaged in a dangerous form of tango on the dance floor. Hips moved in unison with a fluidity and control one would never have thought possible under the circumstances. Fear gave me a certain aesthetic detachment. Marked contrasts emerged between the taut bodies of the soldiers, with their tans ending abruptly at their necks and wrists; the bloated bodies of the smugglers who were mostly watching, swigging beer; and the soft bodies of the girls . . . a sherry trifle of flesh. I had come a long way since I first walked through these doors with Stigi. Why had it all seemed so harmless? I had pretended to myself. Now the chariots of Darius were coming for me. All I could discern of Cindy was her blue painted toe-nails under a scrum of bodies.

'Where is Rollo? Where is Stigi?'

'They had to go out. Twinkle Twinkle went too.'

'Is anything wrong?' Magda looked concerned.

'Of course not. One of Stigi's friends has called at the Residence. You know, the existentialist druggy with the black polo neck. He's brought a new kind of potion.'

'Wonderful . . .' she said, without conviction. 'Kiss me, Toby. All of a sudden I feel very lonely.'

'Toby, come here. Come and join us,' gasped a voice from the floor.

'Toby, please kiss me. You are so distant. Is anything wrong, Toby?' There was nothing wrong, except that everything was so incredibly public. Orgies have always struck me as rather continental. They must happen in England, but probably only among the type of person who learns Esperanto. An Englishman prefers a sit-down dinner to a buffet any day. I had a rather wicked idea.

'Oh nothing's wrong really,' I said, a little too loud. 'It's nothing. Only rats. We found some really big ones in here the other day. Must have come out of the sewers. You can imagine the things that must have been put down those sewers in the war . . .'

'Oh please, Toby, don't. I have smoked many reefers. Oh, Toby, I can feel them. They are under my feet.' Her eyes were wide. I believed her. Stigi's dope was very strong.

'Yes . . . and they carry fleas too. Big, itchy, bloodsucking fleas.'

'Rats?' said someone from under the pile of bodies.

'Who said rats?' asked a smuggler.

'Where are they?'

'I see it! I see one!' shouted a bleary GI.

The low moans and subtle liquid sounds that send a pleasurable tingle down one's spine came to an abrupt halt. The rustle of disengaging pubic hair in retreat could be heard throughout the bakery, as everyone made sure that what was running up or down his or her leg was not beady-eyed with whiskers and a tail. Lovers of a moment before blinked accusingly at the furry triangles surrounding them. Narcotic panic was abroad . . .

'Rats? Rats? Did he say rats?'

'Let's go.'

'To the Residence . . .'

In ten minutes and a stampede of fleeing white bottoms Magda and I found ourselves alone, except for Cindy, who was busy trying to spot one of the rats. Cindy liked rats. Magda came up and put her arms around me, pulling up my shirt, and pressing her warm, lithe body against mine. She smiled.

'Clever Toby. Now you have got me all to yourself and I you. Now let us sacrifice to Mother Ishtar in the way the goddess intended. Do you see her getting brighter at the top of the Gate?'

The really unnerving thing was that for once all Magda said was true. The goddess had come for me too. I could only give in. At least to Magda.

'Clever Toby . . .'

12

My dearest Mother,

I hold my breath, but things may have taken a turn for the better. Since, that is, I had to depart from my childish idea that it is possible for two men to love the same woman and remain friends. When the Baron was here I was not sleeping, Mother. I was not eating. In short, I was at my wits' end. Now the old tiger is gnawing his paws with jealousy in a cold T 54 Soviet battle-tank, or whatever, only half a mile from where I sit. With any luck he will be learning Russian and eating kasha, an awful porridge oats with boiled cabbage. He will be drinking himself to death on eau de Cologne and being poetically miserable. I keep telling myself I don't feel good about it, but I do. His going is a relief. Of course, it has not stopped Magda having other lovers; but at least she is not deeply in love with any of them and likely to disappear to a freezing billet in the East. She is pursuing her crusade to breathe a little love into the German (and any other nation's) soul with the missionary energy of a suffragette.

Rollo has written pleading letters but I have managed, I think, to convince him that seeing her would be suicide. My old head-of-house Anthony Selwyn Parr has been a great help. His

150

unmistakable unmarked cars lurk among the rubble mountains like sharks on a reef. The day I bopped the Baron on the head (probably offending all Jove's laws of hospitality to my certain doom) Parr and his men thundered in to the Residence only minutes after I managed to sweep the last telltale signs of pagan orgy under the carpet. Betty Bethlehem had her knitting out. I told Parr that he had just missed the Baron and that Rollo was to be sent on a special course in anticipation of being promoted to major-general. I told Parr I was just about to telephone him and offered tea and Danish pastries. Parr was so mad he bit his swagger-stick and lost a filling.

The poor Baron once said the gods only grant us three weeks of happiness, and checking our records I'd say he has had his quota many times over. He must be feeling pretty scratchy in his tank. Perhaps I should put him out of his misery and allow him to come back. Parr would then take him away in a jam jar and pull his wings off. Good Colonel Midwinter appears to be otherwise engaged with his horses in Hampshire. As it is, my flock is very friendly and serene, mainly due to an outbreak of amateur goddess-worship which seems to have caught on like the yo-yo. Everyone is so sweet to each other. All except Betty, that is, who feels responsible for the murdered girls. Also, she has just recovered from an infection. You always said we must have the courage to enjoy ourselves despite the consequences; it is what distinguishes us from animals. I am in Eden, Mother; that is, if it wasn't Babylon.

Love and kisses,
Toby

I lay on Magda's bed, glad that things were under control. I turned the pages of my inventory of the Gate of Ishtar and the other relics in the bakery. The book had a reassuring Victorian quality. I had now made pen-and-ink and wash drawings of each piece, instead of photographs. The snaps taken of our more important customers had devalued that medium for me. Even the paper in the old ledgers I used felt wonderful. An entry caught my eye.

Item: 56. The foundation scroll of the Temple of the

Unknown God. In length exactly a metre, allowing for slight damage and covered in cuneiform, calling down a curse on anyone who disturbs the stone scroll. Can find no evidence to suggest this is a forgery. Koldewey, on the other hand . . .'

Perhaps I could use the work towards a doctorate. What did intrigue me was that I kept finding traces of gold. Fine gold-dust, especially on the relief tiles of the Gate. A knock on the door aroused me from my archaeological daydreams. The door opened and the untidy room I shared with Magda was filled with the scent of bath salts.

'Hello, Betty.'

She had been crying. The flesh under her eyes was puffed out into dark rings. She had been crying a lot since they found Zela. At first she had tried to hide it for the sake of the other girls, but was finding it more and more difficult.

'Magda is going hysterical, Toby. She got another letter from the Baron. What is more, the Goddess will not appear.'

'Magda is hysterical?'

'On account of the place being surrounded. Did you know?'

'I know.'

'It's terrible. Everything's falling apart. Everything's bloody rotten. How could that happen to Zela . . . I have never had the clap before. Never. It's a curse.' She began to weep. A whimper at first, then a wail.

'Oh, please Betty. Please don't. Come over here for a bit of love. For a hug and a kiss.' She looked at me, her lower lip still pushed out and quivering, and stepped over to the bed.

'Hold me, Toby. I feel so fucking scared.'

'Please don't cry, Betty.'

'I've got a confession to make.'

'What's that?'

'I've been phoning Midwinter . . .'

'What about?'

'He asked me to keep an eye on you. He asked about Parr. He asked about all the old stuff down by the Gate. If I didn't tell him it was prison . . . I didn't mean to, Toby. I had no choice.'

In a way it didn't come as a total surprise. Betty was a clever girl. She had had to protect herself.

'Don't worry, Betty, love. It's all going to be all right now.'

'Is it, Toby? Please tell me it is.'

I was hardly the one to grant anyone absolution.

She did not bother to take off her short, padded nylon house-coat as she climbed onto the bed and hugged me fiercely, her body shaking with sobs. To me it felt like comforting a sister after she had had a bad nightmare. The disasters Betty Bethlehem had prophesied had come to pass. Yet, the Café Babylon, like Berlin itself, still hummed with a strange indestructible energy. Betty and I had grown closer of late while Magda seemed more concerned with bothering Eternal Forces. Betty snuggled down beside me as I stroked her auburn hair. I kissed her forehead as we lay there. I recalled the first night I had met her; cool and assured, with a smile as sharp as a stiletto. I felt so sorry, so very sorry she had lost poor, plump Zela. Betty Bethlehem had become my closest confidante and I hoped now she would go back home to England. Any day I expected orders to come from Midwinter to close down the operation. After all, whatever Parr might hope, the Baron was gone for good. I wanted to take some of the relics, and in particular this version of the Blue Gate of Babylon, back to the British Museum, if that could be diplomatically arranged. I prayed Magda would come with me. I wanted to be free of Berlin and hear skylarks again.

The knocking at my door this time was loud and urgent. We hardly had the time to pull the covers around us where we had fallen into a shallow sleep.

'Good God! Wolfgang! Stigi! What the hell? We were just taking a nap.' The bed was damp and Betty Bethlehem's mascara had run onto the pillow. I opened my mouth to explain. Then I stopped.

I had never seen the urbane Wolfgang so worried.

'Rollo intends to come back.'

'How did you get here? Parr's men ring the place.'

'Stigi brought me through your tunnel.'

'A tunnel strictly for emergencies.'

'We have an emergency.'

The two men fidgeted at the end of the double bed. Stigi took an occasional breath between incessant pulls on his cigarette. I laughed.

'Well, I hope the Baron doesn't come visiting today. Parr himself is out there.'

Wolfgang shook his head and held up his hands as if I had said something completely absurd.

'If Rollo comes back, they'll kill him . . .' I continued.

'I don't think so,' said Wolfgang, with a smile I did not care for. 'Not the way he intends to return. You know how the Baron likes to make entrances.'

I was watching Stigi. 'Have you made some kind of deal, Stigi? What form is this second coming due to take? I don't care what he promises. I don't care what he will pay. At present he can't come back. In fact, we may have to close entirely.'

Stigi walked over to a chaise-longue stubbing out a cigarette butt and sat down, taking out a fresh packet of Chesterfields.

'He intends to come back whether we like it or not.'

'But . . .'

'He has started the engines of our tank squadron,' said Wolfgang.

'Rollo is going to roll back in his tank,' added Stigi. 'Man, will that be bad for business.'

'He will be ready to attack in four hours.'

'Look, I had no choice. I was only doing what Midwinter told me to do . . .'

'He will bring the end of the world. They will drop the H-bomb,' began a stunned Betty Bethlehem, getting out of bed and pulling her house-coat around her. 'I must get Magda. They'll drop the bloody H-bomb, mark my words. First my Zela, now this. They'll drop the bloody H-bomb.'

'But he only has a dozen tanks in East Berlin,' I said, trying to keep calm. 'He told me he only has a handful of tanks.'

Wolfgang shook his head.

'A column of armoured vehicles fifteen miles long is on the road from Potsdam. The Baron requested them. He claims the number of tanks he has under the Four Powers agreement are not sufficient to stop the present border incursions by Western saboteurs and kidnappers. Believe me, Toby, he has become a crazy man. He started the engines and put the men on alert a few days ago. He was drunk, but of course the men were still prepared to follow him. So several of us senior officers tied him to the tracks of his own tank as he was about to mount up. We told the men it was a joke. They laughed and thought it was just their beloved commander clowning around as usual. He howled at the moon all night. It was a full moon. He has not spoken to me since. I have not seen him in such a temper since Russia. He says her name to himself all the time, under his breath, Magda, Magda, Magda. You have to help us, Toby.' Behind Wolfgang, Cindy stepped into the room dragging a suspicious and obese smuggler in a yellow towel. He was bundled unceremoniously out again by Stigi. Cindy was wearing nothing except for a silver anklet and her Egyptian style make-up.

'He will be ready to attack in four hours. In four hours. In four hours. They will drop the H-bomb.' She had been listening to Betty Bethlehem.

Cindy sat happily on the end of the bed. The marks of a cane were on her bottom.

'What can I do?' I said.

'Give him Magda.'

'Absolutely not. He can't go around threatening folk. He can't.'

'He will be ready to attack in four hours. They will drop the H-bomb,' smiled Cindy ecstatically, sitting down beside me. More of my customers wandered unannounced into the room. I felt naked and alone. The faces had the self-satisfied but curious expression of those around a death-bed.

'You are asking me to give her up to a madman. Parr will follow them.'

'I think that's a risk we will have to take,' mused Wolfgang. 'I have seen the Baron like this before, my friend. He is capable of any sort of foolishness if he gets it into his head. He is a child, and part of the problem is, he thinks Magda is carrying his. He has been drinking cognac and saying he's being deprived of a son and heir by a deceitful English pimp.'

I very nearly retorted that it was absolutely not my choice to be a pimp. Luckily, Cindy pinched me peevishly on the bottom.

'I am not a bloody pimp and as far as I know Magda's not pregnant.' She had told me as much.

'How dare you?' said the woman we were talking about. She swept regally into the room in a dress made out of seven flimsy light blue veils. Magda had specially devised it for the Ishtar ceremony after Cindy refused to give up the seven pieces of ritual jewellery and threatened to bite anyone who took them from her. Magda checked her make-up in the bedside mirror. 'How dare you talk of my intimate possibilities in such a manner in front of all these people?

155

You swine,' she stormed in English. 'I can do whatever I wish with my body. My future is entirely my own . . .' She was barefoot.

'It's the absence of a future we are concerned with,' growled Stigi. 'I don't want to wake up and find I'm not here.'

'They will drop the H-bomb. He will be ready to attack in four hours. He has started the engines. They will drop the H-bomb. I'm clean and cheap and my name is Cindy.' At the back of the room someone began to cry.

'You don't think he's serious, do you, Stigi?'

The American nodded.

'I think he is seriously crazy when it comes to Magda here. All tank commanders have an insane desire to crawl back into the womb and will murder anyone who stops them. That's why they climb into tanks in the first place. My old employer General Patton was the same. Fortunately, he was just in love with himself.'

'You fought with Patton?' said Wolfgang, with a professional interest.

Magda let out a scream of rage. The mirror-backed hair-brush cartwheeled through the air, narrowly missing Stigi and shattering into fragments against an unmoved-looking griffon.

'You silly *Mensch*. You silly *Bocks*. Rollo is hurting so much he could kill us all. Send us up like a firework and you talk of tanks and boyish games. Pa! . . . Pa! Pa! Pa! I hate you. I think men will never learn to live together. What kind of world will it be for me and my baby?'

'I say, old girl, so you *are* pregnant? I mean you should have . . .'

The large bottle of eau de Cologne which had a stopper topped with a miniature replica of St Sophia's Cathedral in Istanbul smashed and scattered glass all over the bed. A piece cut my shoulder. Cindy licked the blood which fell in red spots onto the sheets.

'They will drop the H-bomb,' Cindy said simply, returning us to the subject in hand. 'He has started the engines.' Magda, failing to find something more damaging to hurl, sat down on the fur-covered stool by the dressing-table and began to sob. Wolfgang put his arm around her.

'Perhaps if Magda could go and talk to the Baron? Or he could try to come here the way I have. But it would be very dangerous. There might be an agent within the Café. It would make such a difference if Magda could speak to him. At heart he's a good man.'

156

'A good man who doesn't mind fucking the world for a piece of pussy.' Stigi was already holding up his hands as Magda's eyes met his.

'*Scheisse* . . .' In an instant Wolfgang was in between Magda and her target. She had grabbed a ferocious-looking pair of curling-tongs from the dresser. 'Take that little worm out of my sight. I could kill him.'

'Your mob are always trying to kill someone,' I heard Stigi mumble, as he moved strategically to the other side of the bed with Six-Shot Otto the Hound following him in retreat.

'I think you should let Magda go over and talk to Rollo, Toby.' Betty Bethlehem had come back into the room. I still wanted to ask Magda about the baby. 'Come on, Toby, you can't afford to be jealous. Magda will be able to talk some sense into him. Will you go and see him, Magda? Spare a thought for the poor man. At the very least he could be getting himself into a lot of trouble. He and Wolfgang could find themselves back in the camps. At best. At worst . . . I thought you and he were friends, Toby?'

Magda clapped her hands.

'I will go and see Baron Rollo von Hollmann.' She sat with her back very straight and her head held high, sneaking only the briefest sideways glance at herself in the dressing-table mirror.

'The face which launched a thousand tanks,' quipped Stigi.

'They will drop the H-bomb.'

At that precise moment I don't think I would have cared very much if they had. Magda got up and left the room. Wolfgang nodded to me.

'We must go immediately,' he said, as I pulled the clothes over my head. 'Immediately, now, there is no time.'

'The Baron has started the engines,' began Cindy, then switched suddenly into her prayers for Ishtar.

> 'The emperors of the night will assail her,
> But she will triumph seven times seven times,
> The bright lady will claim her promised lover
> – From everlasting night . . . He has started the engines.'

'He certainly has, old girl,' I said. 'Do you think you could pass my trousers?' If I had misjudged Rollo, and I hoped to God, any god or goddess, that I was wrong; we needed all the luck in the world.

13

As a small boy I had a fondness for tunnels. They seemed dark, safe and secret places. The troglodyte life was much more secure than existence above ground for an only child who was a size bigger than everyone else in the playground and whose parents did not always appear keen to play Mummies and Daddies. I dug tunnels in a sandy bank, anxious to befriend Cerberus, hound of the underworld, and set him on my shitty father. All went well until one rainy day when, just as I had slithered into the entrance, my entire underworld collapsed with a terrifying rumble, as if the Devil had slammed a door in Hell. Only my legs were free and I kicked them until they hurt. A cloudy, blue whirlpool was sucking me in when someone took hold of one ankle. After a furtive fumble my rescuer pulled me clear and I blinked into the bad-toothed grin of the under-gardener. 'Don't worry, I won't tell, Master Toby.' We had got him from the County Asylum.

So it was not without a certain act of will that I inched after Magda in that Stygian place.

'Please, Toby. If you cannot go faster you should stay behind,' Stigi Weitz hissed ten yards ahead.

We were in the cavernous main sewer which led by a circuitous route under Potsdamer Platz to a second tunnel which went under the border wire. At the time of the Berlin airlift, Stigi assisted American Intelligence and had been involved in a lunatic venture called Operation Gold. A conduit had been dug along which

American *Geld* was meant to be passed in the form of dollar bills to fuel the outbreaks of sabotage and arson much complained of on East German radio. A blockage in the pipes had subsequently been discovered in the vicinity of Stigi's pockets.

'Enjoy yourself, Toby,' shouted back Wolfgang. 'We are treading in the shit of the old Reich ministries. Not everyone has such a privilege. Some of these turds may even have belonged to our glorious Führer.'

The sewer certainly smelt as if it had not been flushed out since the war. The stench was of an age-old corruption rather than the hearty manure-heap smell of the usual German public convenience. The torch and the candles carried by Magda, who was essential, and Cindy, whom we could not get rid of, illuminated the curve of small oblong bricks, that made the arch of the tunnel, as I placed my feet carefully on either side of the midden. Rats rustled. The bricks were very similar to the ones which had formed the foundations of Babylon.

'Oh, the stupid thing.'

'What is it?'

'My dress.'

A sharp piece of metal, perhaps an old nail, had torn away two of the silken veils of Magda's costume and they now lay in the channel. She had only had time to put on a thin raincoat which she insisted on wearing around her shoulders like a cloak. It had already fallen into the mire.

'Good thing it's not cold.'

'*Schmierfink*,' she hissed, half playfully, stumbling against a rock-fall. I reached for her arm and realised I loved her all the more. If I hadn't felt so giddy I might have seen the funny side. However, it was not the imminent immolation of mankind that had made her keep that flimsy dress on; it was the bother of finding something else to wear. Cindy was not helping matters. She was wearing one of the short blue dresses. When I shone my torch at her, she held up by the tail a dead rat she had found.

> 'To the land of no return,
> Further to the realm of darkness,
> Ishtar the daughter of Sin,
> Set her mind . . .'

'For God's sake, shut up, Cindy,' I snapped, knocking the rat out of her hand. She was misquoting part of the old Persian poem which describes how the Goddess Ishtar journeys into the Underworld to bring back her lover Tammuz, descending through seven gates and shedding garments or jewellery at each one. I recalled a line from the splendid L.W. King translation in 1902 of the Ishtar Hymn. 'Thou lookest with mercy on the violent man, and thou settest right the unruly every morning.' As we scrambled around more rock-falls I prayed Magda would be able to set right the unruly Baron. A torch flashed ahead and I envisaged being caught by the border police with a known smuggler, a deserter and two partially naked women.

'What's that?'

'Relax, Toby, it's only Twinkle Twinkle. I sent him ahead so we would not miss our way.'

'Are we under the border?'

'We are just about to go under. The sewer here had been sealed up in front by the *Polizei*. You see that man-hole cover that Twinkle Twinkle is pulling up? Well, under there is the biggest bucket of shit you are likely to come across. A virtual swimming-pool and no one knows how deep it is. All the nastiness from miles around has drained in there for half a century. The police patrols take off that cover and have a peek and a sniff inside and drop it again. If you think the pong is bad now, you just wait.' Stigi took a long drag on his cigarette. 'But even the most disgusting things have their uses. Mustapha, a good friend of Twinkle Twinkle, who used to run the smuggling around here, helped me dig a passage up from the old CIA tunnel underneath. The passage comes up around the lip of the tank, almost to the man-hole. I'm afraid it's a tight squeeze. When you go in at the man-hole, you have to pull yourself along the first bit over the lip of the tank using steel handles set into the roof. But once you are down into the old Operation Gold tunnel, it's a clear dry run under the border. Twinkle Twinkle will hold your legs while you twist around and get hold of those hand-holds. Remember, the shit is just two feet below. Whatever you do, don't slip. We are under Kreuzberg at the moment. Have a stretch while you can, Toby. Ladies and gentlemen, in a minute or so we will be in the other tunnel and crossing my Rio Grande.'

'What happened to Mustapha?'

Stigi shrugged.

'No one knows exactly. I think he may have had one cherry vodka too many in the East before trying to climb around the tank. It's like quicksand. It sucks you down. What a way to go . . .'

I shone my torch up at the ceiling. We were in a great chamber. I could feel a pulse beating in my fingertips from the fear of that dark, dripping place. The torchbeam picked out a swastika. On the wall was a plaque with the date June 7, 1939. Not far away was the coat-of-arms of the last Kaiser. Other sections of brickwork betrayed ruined buttresses and the skill of earlier and more painstaking hands. Many rulers had had far more fiendishly elaborate plans for their subjects' excrement than they ever had for the people themselves. I began to think of Parr.

'You won't get down there wearing that wet coat. You'll get stuck. Magda, for Christ's sake. Take it off.'

The love of my life threw the coat at Stigi, enveloping him. Three more of the scarves which formed the flimsy skirt had come away from their moorings, and had been lost somewhere back in the tunnel. A pert left breast threatened to escape from the sheer blue silk as she tried to adjust her tatters. Twinkle Twinkle was already lowering Cindy into the very small hole. Best foot forward, Jubb.

'I say, that's rather cramped, isn't it?'

'No problem, Toby. Look, Cindy's managed it.'

'I'm a little bigger than she is.'

'Now do what I say, Toby, or you could be in for a terminal surprise. As you're lowered head first, Toby, you have to reach forward and grab one of the rings in the roof and haul yourself along the couple of feet to the lip of the tank to mad Mustapha's little hole. It's as easy as limbo-dancing. I could do it in my sleep, and often have. It's easy. But whatever you do, don't let go. One false move and you're really in the shit for ever. If they found you, you'd be a fossil.'

I watched with mounting horror as Cindy, whose body was almost double-jointed, struggled giggling to wiggle her frame past the nauseating obstacle. All the most horrible putrefactions from a tramp's sock to the venereal odour of rotting lobster rolled from the pit and caused a gagging sensation in the back of my throat. Twinkle Twinkle grinned as he was left holding several pieces of Cindy's dress. Wolfgang went next, with a nimbleness I had hardly expected. Magda planted an affectionate kiss on my cheek before it was her turn. She then walked over to the Turk who grabbed her ankles and in the torchbeam I saw her bare legs being held at waist-height by a hideous genie who appeared to be drowning her in a puddle. The roof glistened and something fell with a disturbing plop into the sump. After Magda had negotiated the bend, Stigi followed with the agility of a rat. My turn had come. Twinkle Twinkle was beside himself with anticipation.

I sat down by the man-hole. Twinkle Twinkle grabbed my legs with a fierce passion which brought back memories of our disturbed under-gardener. With careful hands I probed into the blackness, touching, then instinctively pulling away from the bubbling pool of greenish-brown excrement. I held a pencil-torch in my mouth and accidentally put my hand into the mire. I wondered how deep the sump was. Panic seized me but it was too late. Twinkle Twinkle held my legs in the air and I slid within an inch of the slimy surface, a lock of my hair slipping forward into the foulness. I saw the face of the prophet Daniel sneering at me from the gloom. At least he was pleased. I reached out and gripped the hand-holds, which seemed very sharp. Ahead of me was another faint torchbeam. With my legs in the air at right angles to my body I tried to inch forward, only to become wedged tight at the start of the late Mustapha's tunnel as it disappeared over the rim of the tank.

'Help,' I gasped.

'What is it now?'

'Stigi, I'm stuck. I'm stuck fast.'

'Yeah, I always said you were halfway round the bend. I thought this would happen. Twinkle Twinkle? You hear me?'

A Gothic grunt came from above.

'Plan B.'

As I wondered what was going to happen, Twinkle Twinkle wrapped one arm around my legs. Then I heard something which sounded like a cigarette-lighter. Once, twice, three times I distinctly heard what sounded like a ratchet on an old-fashioned lighter. Suddenly, everything was very quiet. All I could hear was the water dripping. I felt a glowing warmth on my left ankle.

'Arghh! The bastard. The bastard's set fire to my fucking trousers!'

I pulled myself forward from the pain with all my might and shot like a champagne cork from where I was wedged. My heels splashed into the sump releasing new and noxious gases. I fell with a bone-juddering crash onto a pile of rubble, much to the amusement of the girls.

Magda had completely lost her top.

'You did it, darling. How clever. I tore my dress again.'

'He has started the engines,' said Cindy.

'You really didn't have to do that,' I began, brushing myself down, but Stigi only laughed. The old CIA tunnel below Mustapha's little burrow was a more functional affair. The American construction was a luxurious five feet high and for all the world like a concrete waterpipe and was sealed behind us to the West. Wolfgang patted me on the back.

'By the way,' I asked, 'is there anything to stop the Baron if this doesn't work? Would the other officers restrain him?'

Wolfgang shook his head.

'I do not think so. No, I do not think so,' he said, pausing for a moment. 'A few months ago some Ukrainians and Poles from the camps were brought up as forced labour. It was said they were there to erect an anti-Fascist barrier. It was just after we were embarrassingly invaded by crack imperialist kangaroos. But for months our glorious new construction workers have done nothing except complain and eat everything that moves. However, the barrier is partly composed of a series of prefabricated tank-traps which could be in place in an hour or so, and which Rollo couldn't get round in a hurry. I told them there were orders to start work at a certain time. I also invited the Young Communist League to come and inspect our tanks.' His lip curled in a wicked smile. 'Rollo hates speeches. They will insist on making speeches, so he will be further delayed.'

'By the way, what happens if we're found down here?'

'By the Eastie Beasties? What do you think? In a tunnel built by a foreign intelligence service?' Stigi did not elaborate further but drew a finger across his throat and Magda shrugged. If she failed to convince our mutual friend he was still her Tufti-Wufti, or whatever pet name she called him, it could all be over.

'I love you, Toby,' she said. 'Please remember that. Remember it always.' Before I could answer and beg her to turn around and come back with me, Wolfgang was leading the way into the pipe. Every movement to me seemed to herald collapse, a panic which now was inseparable from the fear of losing Magda. If only I had been better to her. I should have acted sooner.

'No talking,' whispered Magda, who was ahead of me. 'Pass it on.' I caught a glimpse of the outline of her breasts in the torchlight and her long legs. I wanted to reach out for her, even here. Her perfume was overwhelming. My mother says the ultimate art of being a woman is to cheer unmentionable places.

The abandoned CIA tunnel ended in a dark chamber and our torches lit up a spiral staircase. I could hardly stop myself running for it and breathing fresh air once more.

'Stay here,' whispered Wolfgang. The floor was damp as we slouched against the walls. Above us I could hear voices. It sounded like a football match. Footsteps echoed on stone stairs. Would a border guard believe his eyes if he found us?'

Magda had her head between her hands.

'Do you really love him?' I asked. She did not answer. Even in the sewer, even after all my conspiracies, I was under her spell.

'You have always been out for yourself. You never intended to take me with you. In a year I will be the little German girl you once had. You never intended to take me with you and if you remember, I did not expect it.'

Before I could reply, Wolfgang who had reconnoitred ahead came back breathless and concerned.

'It's a rally. The Young Communist Party I invited. The platform backs onto the building above us.'

'You mean we can't get out?'

'Toby, I am not in uniform and the girls are wearing almost nothing.'

'We could cast a spell and draw him here,' said Magda, I thought a little unhelpfully, as Cindy examined her nipples.

'We just have to wait,' I offered.

'Come up to the level above,' suggested Wolfgang, pursing his lips. 'There may be another way to slip out. It is lighter and drier up there.' We followed him up the winding staircase. We came first into a cellar caked in soot and then up again into the dark basement of an old industrial building. Around the walls, at a height well above my head were small windows, some of which were broken. I went to look. I had to climb onto an old crate to see out. The sound of chanting and stamping made the bomb-damaged shell of the former factory shake. I could hear the speeches.

'We must build a barrier against the Fascist arsonists, headhunters and murderers from the West. The men who kill. The men who slip into our homes in the night and take our women and children to sell them into prostitution and the mink-lined trap of the bourgeois family. We must build an anti-Fascist barrier . . .' I glanced at Stigi, who looked away.

'That is the leader of the construction workers,' whispered Wolfgang in my ear. 'As he and his men have been sitting doing nothing for months, he would do anything to make himself appear more important.' Another speaker took the rostrum. The crowd roared as if Caesar had entered the Colosseum.

'Comrades, may I join you in saluting Comrade Hollmann who has been re-educated from his Fascist ways as a mercenary under Hitler. Now he is a vigilant member of our new Red Army. Did he not bravely start the engines of his tanks only hours ago, prepared to defend our mother-land to the death? Salute him, Comrades.'

I could not see the face of the speaker but one of the men in military uniform turned away from the applause. Rollo was both embarrassed and very angry. His hands were clenched. The crowd cheered louder.

'Thank you, Comrades . . .' the young speaker went on, riding the Baron's acclaim. He paused. When he spoke again his voice was quieter. 'There are those amongst you, especially those in the construction battalions, who beg us never to forgive those who fought with the Fascists. All I can say, Comrades, is that many in Germany prostituted themselves. I am a former prostitute . . .'

'I am a former prostitute,' chimed in Cindy behind me. 'I am clean and cheap and my name is Cindy.' Magda was leaning by what looked like a coal-chute. Only shreds of her dress remained. She appeared to be chanting to herself.

'Darling? Are you cold? Do you want my jacket?'

Magda ignored me.

There was a snuffling at the windows. An Alsatian guard dog snarled down at us. The dog's head was replaced by that of a soldier. A moment later the Baron appeared at the top of the coal-chute. He had gratefully torn himself away from the adulation.

Magda called to him.

'Rollo! Rollo! Thank you, Holy Mother, for answering my prayers. Darling Tufti, you look so wonderful in your uniform.'

166

'Magda! It's you!'

The frown on the Baron's face melted. His brown eyes were tender. He stretched out his hand and Magda took a step onto the coal-chute. At the sides of the slide were makeshift foot-holds for workmen to climb up.

'No!' I shouted.

I ran over. But far faster than any of us was Cindy. With the speed and agility of a wild animal she shot up the coal-chute, what remained of her dress snagging against a protruding piece of metal. Now, quite naked, she squeezed through the astonished Baron's arms, disappearing behind him as the dog began to bark. He turned back towards Magda.

'Darling, I love you,' the Baron kept repeating in German. 'You have come back to me.' He seemed completely stunned.

'Please, Rollo, promise me you will not do anything stupid . . . with your tanks. I would never speak to you again.'

'Nothing so certain,' added Stigi.

The Baron was peering down into the basement, stretching towards Magda who had taken another step up the coal-chute. What remained of her veils was held in place more by luck than design. Cheers, shouts and wolf-whistles erupted from above.

'Trouble,' said Stigi. 'We have to vamoose.'

'Get out of here, please,' Wolfgang pleaded.

A new voice took the microphone. The words were delivered in a familiar nursery rhyme sing-song. The speaker was Cindy.

'I am a prostitute,' she declared to the audience of several hundred construction workers who had been away from home for many months. 'I'm clean and cheap and my name is Cindy. I'm from Babylon. The Baron has started the engines. I am a prostitute. They are stealing our women and children. Build the anti-Fascist barrier.'

There was a startled silence. I turned again scrambled on top of some boxes to look through a small barred window at the platform. Dignitaries and speakers had fled to the right and left of the shapely and quite naked form of Cindy before an awe-struck mass. No one said a word.

'Build the anti-Fascist barrier,' she shouted again enthusiastically.

The response was immediate and thunderous. The vocal approval for the other speakers had possibly in most cases been born of political necessity. Now every man in the audience seized on the anti-Fascist barrier as a deeply personal quest. Cindy's buttocks shuddered with heartfelt attention. She took a slow pace forward. The opportunist speaker we had heard before fell in behind her.

'Here is proof, Comrades, of how they use your womenfolk in the West . . .' But his words were drowned. There was a movement to the right of me. The Baron was reaching down.

'Magda, give me your hand. I love you. You will be shot if you are found in there. I love you. You know we are meant for each other.' Magda stretched towards the Baron's hand. She was halfway up the chute before I grabbed her. I had hold of a slippery leg and my other hand clutched at the last remnant of her dress. She pulled away. I blinked back the tears.

'Come to me, my love. Come up here, Magda. I have been heartbroken. I do not mind if you see Toby also. I am sorry if I alarmed you . . .'

'Magda, no!'

I tugged back harder and was left holding a rag of blue silk. The white, mud-splashed body of Magda slipped out of my grasp, completely naked, scraping against rough chips of coal. I tried to follow. I scrambled to the top of the chute but could not get my shoulders through the hole. I slipped and tumbled back.

I heard a gasp from the microphone.

'Here is another new Comrade the brave soldier Hollmann has saved from the Babylon of Western decadence . . .'

'I said we'd be bigger than Babylon,' murmured Stigi, grabbing my arm. A guard was peering down at us. At the other end of the basement someone was trying to open a door. Wolfgang was very agitated. He helped me stand up. Above us the speech continued.

'Before you are two Comrades the Baron has snatched from the jaws of shame and degradation. We must protect our womenfolk. We must protect our children. We must protect our household animals,' continued the opportunist speaker. The door at the end of the cellar was now being battered down. I pulled myself up to the bars of a window. Magda was looking back at me. Tears were in her blue eyes. The Baron was putting his jacket around her body.

'You must go! Go now! We will send them back tonight,' urged Wolfgang.

I was frozen to the spot.

'Let her calm him down, Toby. You will have her back in the morning. Sure as eggs. It's better than World War Three. If we don't get out of here we'll be shot.' I hesitated. Stigi was pushing me back down the stairs to the tunnel as Wolfgang made for the coal-chute. Above us I heard a crash as the iron door broke away from its hinges under the battering. One word echoing through the cellar made us fly along the concrete piping.

'Saboteurs!'

'Saboteurs!'

'Saboteurs!'

In the present state of hysteria I did not want to stop and explain my visit to the GDR in terms of love and friendship. We were just negotiating the sump as the first shot rang out behind me.

'Faster,' gasped Stigi, now in front. This time there was nothing else for it but to dangle my legs in the tank of excrement as I pulled myself up into the welcoming cavern of the main sewer. Twinkle Twinkle had gone. I turned and was about to shut the steel cover when a voice made me drop it with a crash.

'You really have soiled yourself this time, Jubb.'

I went cold. It was the voice of Anthony Selwyn Parr coming out of the darkness. A British soldier prodded me with a sub-machine gun and other hands propelled me along the larger tunnel for twenty yards. Shouts and shots came from behind. A tremendous explosion flattened me and my captors and sent a rain of filth and roof-bricks down on us. A wave of choking dust broke over us. I panicked and tried to get up.

'Don't fucking flap,' were the last words I heard as someone hit me very hard. They were the last words I ever expected to hear as I journeyed down a blue, black whirlpool of oblivion. My world had collapsed.

14

When I awoke I knew immediately where I was, even though my head buzzed and there was a strange taste of onions in my mouth. Parr's men must have pumped me full of some restraining drug after knocking me senseless. I was handcuffed to a camp-bed in the classroom of Kindergarten Number Nine. Someone had taken off my watch but the room was warm and full of sunlight, playing on a map of the world on which the dominant colour was an anachronistic Imperial pink. Snarling at me from the bottom of the bed was the hardboard cut-out of Mrs Big Bunny. Her dreadful pale blue eyes were enough to disturb the most balanced child. They disturbed me. Their manic stare bore a nasty resemblance to that of Captain Anthony Selwyn Parr. The door clicked open. A military policeman, made to look even more enormous by the tiny varnished wood chairs of the infant's classroom, came in and grinned down at me. The man was the sergeant they called Mother Redcap whose expression of cheerful enthusiasm had me searching for a means of escape. Where was Stigi? I must get Magda back. With a great effort I tried to sit up.

'So, sleeping beauty's awake, is she? You'd better come in and guard the young gentleman, corporal. We don't want him harming himself now, do we? That would be a shame. Jump to it, corporal. I'll go and get Mr Parr.' The sound of steel-shod army boots echoed along the stone corridor of the little school. Even Mrs Big Bunny seemed to shiver at the noise.

'I want to see Colonel Midwinter,' I said to the military police corporal who appeared to be dressed in his best kit. A sallow youth, he had scars from terrible acne. He was armed with a sten gun.

'They're going to hang you, chum. Touch of the old last waltz, without the dance floor.'

'But they can't . . .'

'If it was down to me, I'd string you up myself, matey.'

'I say, hold on. I'm attached to this Kindergarten . . . I mean this intelligence unit with the rank of captain. I won't stand . . .'

'No you won't. They could shoot you, I suppose. What with you being a traitor. And if you won't stand for the firing-squad they'll tie you to a chair and you'll die a coward's death. Then they bury your body in quicklime so there's no trace left even of your bones to affront decent people.'

He made a whistling noise through the gap in his front teeth. I could not help thinking that as a youth he deserved his acne. 'I think it must be horrible to be shot,' he added. 'Imagine a bullet hitting you smack in the nose. Of course it would kill you. But it would really hurt first. Hurt more than burning, my dad says.'

Along the corridor came the rhythmic crashing which warned of the return of Mother Redcap. In his large hands was a Dansette portable radio.

'Listen with Mother,' he said, laughing until his shoulders shook. The corporal laughed too.

'I want to see Colonel Midwinter.'

'You'll see Mr Parr in a moment. He requires us all to listen to the radio. A very fair man, Mr Parr. He needs you to be fully aware of what you have done. Of all your wickedness. You've had your hands down the trousers of history, Mr Jubb, and what you have brought out is an erection.'

'I want to see Colonel Midwinter.'

'If I were you, lad, I wouldn't ask for that gentleman. You can only make things worse . . .' Mother Redcap turned and stopped speaking as he saw Parr was standing in the doorway, the lank quiff of hair falling over his forehead. He was in uniform, in shirtsleeves. Between the bony fingers of one hand he held several of the crushed silk scarves that had made up the bulk of Magda's dress. The cloth, brilliant against the dull, chalk-dusted tones of

171

the classroom, was covered in dark red stains. They were blood-stains.

'Colonel Midwinter . . .' I began.

'Is no longer with us,' snapped Parr. The voice was cold. The room itself actually began to darken and feel chilly. The white faces of the two regular soldiers betrayed a growing wariness. Parr brushed his straight hair back over his forehead, as uncreased as mine. Parr's deeds inspired fear, not his looks. These men had obviously witnessed him about his business.

'Begging your pardon, sir,' said Mother Redcap. 'Shall I switch the radio on? It's nearly time. They'll have another bulletin.' They turned as my foot touched Mrs Big Bunny causing the creature to rock forward. For a moment she seemed to be going for my throat.

'Carry on, Sergeant.'

'Thank you, sir.'

Snapping smartly to attention Mother Redcap switched on the BBC World Service.

'Good morning, this is London. The East German authorities last night erected barbed wire and tank-traps around the whole of Berlin's western sector for a hundred miles. The East Germans have dubbed the construction the *antifaschistischen Schutzwall* or Anti-Fascist Rampart. Seventeen people were shot attempting to flee to the West, though many hundreds escaped. President Kennedy . . .'

My mind would not focus. Then, strangely, from the lips of Mrs Big Bunny seemed to come the words of Herodotus. 'Babylon lies in a wide plain . . . The great wall I have described is the chief armour of the City.' I could not believe my ears about the *antifaschistischen Schutzwall*. But then many scholars did not believe poor Herodotus and he said the wall around Babylon only stretched for fifty-six miles and had taken years, while one had been put around one hundred miles of Berlin in a night. My head hurt. Something came back to me.

'Oh, my God. Build the anti-Fascist barrier.'

'What did you say?' snapped Parr.

'Cindy must have picked up the phrase. She's disturbed. She just parrots phrases like that. It's her only way of communicating. It's all a dreadful misunderstanding . . .'

Parr's face had gone a greyish-purple colour. He stuck out his jaw. Despite the apprehension, I felt I had a distinct desire to punch him on the chin as I had done once when he put a small silk orchid my mother had given me in the school incinerator. Parr had said it was cissy. Mother was having an affair with his father. He lost face after being struck by Jubb, the third former. My life had been hell after that. Now he had something else to blame me for.

'Come on, Parr. It's all a mistake. How could I be responsible? The Easties have been planning something for months.'

'You knew about this, didn't you? You had something to do with it,' he stated quietly.

'Treason, Mr Parr, if you ask me,' pronounced Mother Redcap, shifting his great weight from foot to foot.

'I want to see Colonel Midwinter.'

'Midwinter has defected.'

'Pull the other one, Parr. He's a member of the Jockey Club.'

'He slipped over on an S-Bahn train just before the wall went up. He never uses the S-Bahn. It was the first thing they blocked from East to West. He must have known all along. Just like you, Jubb. Midwinter was in serious financial trouble, Jubb, from backing his own horses. Now, no doubt, he will be allowed to spend the rest of his life breeding donkeys in Georgia or somewhere. The Russians always trap people by their weaknesses and hold them through their hobbies. Your weakness is women, Jubb, and your hobby seems to be falling in love with them.'

'I don't believe you.'

Parr shook his head. 'I've been suspicious of Midwinter for some time and especially of your squalid little operation. All you seem to have achieved is to provide evidence that we abduct East German citizens and use them for purposes of prostitution. You let the one man who could have told us about this wall slip through your hands. We've been talking to your Mr Weitz. He admitted you let the Baron go. He said it was your idea. You are a Soviet spy. Your love for this Magda is all pretence. You'll never see her again. She may be dead.' He held up the bloodstained material and examined me closely.

'I do love her,' I said. 'Is she all right?'

'Then why did you give her to the Baron?'

All three of them listened intently.

'Why didn't you let us take care of this man when we offered? He's nothing to you.'

I did not expect them to understand. 'He was in love with Magda

173

and she cared for him. We had a message that if he couldn't see his Magda he would come with his tanks. We went over to try to talk him out of it. But there's been gossip about building this wall for weeks. You can't blame us for it. Ask any one of the girls. Ask Magda when she comes back.'

'She won't be coming back,' said Parr, with a great deal of pleasure. 'She is stuck forever on the other side of that wall you helped create, Jubb. We have taken away your girls' false papers, Jubb, and I think we'll dump the little sluts back in the East. Soon we'll be blowing your little pleasure palace to bits. Tell me it's absurd now, Jubb. Tell me it's all a joke. The Baron has been sent to Moscow, I'm informed, where he has been promoted and will be spreading all sorts of lies. I'll bet the Baron managed to get away with quite a few of your artefacts. Tell me about the Gate, Toby. Did you make a deal with the Baron as well as Midwinter? Your girls will be sent to camps, you know. To work on their hands and knees at another sort of scrubbing. Sluts like your bloody mother. You really have shown your true colours this time, Jubb.'

I managed to get up on one elbow.

'Fuck off, Parr. Leave my mother out of this, unless you want a discussion about your father. You don't understand anything. The Baron is a very honourable man. He wouldn't come over to our side because of what they would have done to his men.' Somewhere in the city an air-raid siren sounded. Even Parr stiffened.

'Did you consider the Baron's "honourable" war record?' he replied simply. 'Why did you not give him to me? Midwinter told you to let him go, didn't he?'

'No. It was more than that.'

'More?'

'We started something at the Babylon we couldn't control. Everyone was in love. Betty Bethlehem warned me about it.'

'You're not asking me to believe your actions were motivated by love, Jubb? For your information, someone answering the description of Betty Bethlehem made her escape on the Bonn rail link with a bald-headed Turk. When we raided your headquarters we did not find much evidence of love. We did find evidence of drug-dealing, white slavery and devil worship. However, I think espionage will put you safely behind bars. You will have a long time to contemplate this little wall game, Jubb. Weitz has admitted you were personally trying to ruin my career. That's why you tried to make that deal with me.'

'I wanted to stop my girls being killed.'

'Have any girls been killed since your precious Baron went back to the East?'

I sighed. There is absolutely no point on insisting on the truth when you are manacled to a bed. An orderly brought something in covered by a napkin.

'Do you know what I think, Jubb? I mean, just glancing through what we have now? I believe what we have here is one of the most serious and devious acts of sabotage the free world has seen. I always knew you were bright. With a series of cleverly devised events you have brought the great Powers to the brink of war. I wonder if a court-martial would consider seriously your defence that it was all in the cause of true love? Your family were great engineers once, Jubb. You told me so. Now you've built something horrible. Do you know what you are, Jubb?'

'Please don't send those girls back. I only wanted to stop them being killed, Parr. I'm sure you know what I mean.'

He ignored me.

'You're a filthy Communist. Weitz agrees. He says the girls were encouraged to give their services for free.' Parr paused. 'I can't believe you were in my house at school. You know far more than you let on. You and Midwinter were as thick as thieves. We have found traces of gold. We have found gold rings and small ingots in Midwinter's safe. What do these mean, Jubb? Do be a good chap and tell me . . . now!' he finally added, stalking out and off down the corridor. Mother Redcap pulled the cover back off what I thought was my lunch to reveal a kidney-shaped surgical tray and the largest hypodermic needle I had ever seen. He pressed the plunger and a jet of liquid squirted up in the air.

'Do you think he's one of them?' he asked the corporal.

'Like Burgess and Maclean?'

'Yes, like that.' Mother Redcap advanced towards the bed. Rough fingers pulled down the waistband of my trousers.

'I'm not a Communist,' I protested.

'They was queers,' corrected the corporal.

'Well, I'm not a homosexual, either.'

A finger probed my bottom. A titter followed as the needle jabbed into my arm.

'No, but I am,' said Mother Redcap, as I heard the door being locked and felt my limbs begin to numb. 'A free-thinking gentleman like yourself should not put up barriers to experience, sir. Really, it's no good building walls. We don't want to hurt you, sir. But you is in our hands, so to speak, just like those poor girlies was in yours. Now fair's fair. What says we have a bit of a lark while Mr Parr is out blowing up your Café Babylon? They say too much of this medicine damages the old brain-box. We'll have to be careful, won't we, sir? We'll not have to fucking struggle . . .'

'Dr-e-e-eam, Dream, Dream, Dream,' sing the Everly Brothers. I often dreamt myself into Babylon in the Bodleian. I could dream standing up, wide awake. In one bound my mind was free.

The procession is passing through the Blue Gate of Babylon and soldiers lead me away from the priestesses of Ishtar. They then bind me and carry me to the Temple of Bel Marduk. To the huge ziggurat; the great tower. They drag me towards the fire, the fiery furnace where Shadrak, Meshak and Abednego were saved by an angel because they were righteous, and the flowers are torn from my hair as I am pushed through the final doorway to the inner sanctum.

I scream.

Out of the holy fire the priestess of Marduk draws out a butchering knife and as she strikes I feel the temple walls explode. Everything is pain . . . I'm running . . . running blindly. I must get back through the Blue Gate. I must . . .

'Hey, Sarge, I think you've given him too much of that gizmo . . .'

15

The battle chariots of King Darius's regiment of the Immortals were searching for Toby Jubb. I could see them clearly as I stood by the white-painted bed in the Strictly Locked Ward of The Firs; a discreet government sanatorium with high walls for the mentally wayward former employees of Her Majesty. Today I could make out Darius himself at the head of his mighty armies in a splendid chryselephantine helmet of Parsee gold and boars' tusks, arranged in ascending circles. He often stood in his fighting chariot looking up at me. I shivered in that dark and dignified gaze; it was only a matter of time before Babylon fell. A bandage was wound across his face. The monarch of all the East still had toothache. The time was before breakfast and I was scouring the leafy hedges as they dipped away from the carefully manicured and well-patrolled lawns which always looked too antiseptic for worms. In a field to the west a lone cow was chewing her cud. Every morning I performed my visual patrol to push my mind into remembering. It was not exactly that I had completely forgotten everything that had happened in Berlin; some memories and faces were fleetingly vivid, nestling between the lines of hazel hedges like prematurely fading snapshots bought from an unscrupulous beach photographer for a battered family album. But Babylon had become my reality.

Everything had been much worse. I could recall a time without hope. I had been kept alone and naked in complete darkness for what seemed like weeks until I was forced to seek refuge in my dreams and walk through the Blue Gate of Babylon and smell the sandalwood, burning dung and rotting dates. I had recited the details of the Koldewey Excavations and the rituals of the city as something familiar and warm to hang on to in my freezing cell. The doctor had encouraged me. One day I found myself looking down from a window in the forbidden southern citadel onto a garden of palms on a warm summer evening, listening to the hymns from the choirs of Bel. But that was long ago, far beyond last Christmas and possibly several more.

The interwoven hedges of rural Oxfordshire now were the desert wilderness beyond the Blue Gate. The hospital walls, the ramparts of the great city of Nebuchadnezzar. Nearer still the thin white face of a cruel and angry man with lank brown hair falling across his forehead appeared within the walls, wearing the rich silks of a Magus. He was Smerdus of Babylon, enemy of Darius, powerful and very dangerous. Pain and blank spots crowded my recent past as the muddy dewponds lay dank and slimy in the watermeadows. I must have been admitted to The Firs for a reason. The why and the wherefore of the undefined crimes they said I had committed eluded me. But beyond last Christmas and possibly several before they had strapped me to a low bed in a white-tiled room and forced a thick piece of rubber between my teeth, as helpless as any temple sacrifice. A doctor had then placed two steel electrodes with thick black wires trailing from them at either side of my head. The current made my body jerk. Most of all I hated the sweet burning smell somewhere between that of fresh bread and seared meat of the temple sacrifice.

'Mr Jubb! Stop! We shall cut it off!'

My semen hit the window, rather higher up than usual. The patient in the next bed did not look around. I called him Stigi and it helped that he was a hopeless catatonic. My ejaculation was now trickling down the glass in droopy strands, like melting candyfloss. I had managed to reach the third pane up. My best shot yet. One day I would fly the horizon. I would be free.

'Mr Jubb! You will clean that filthy mess up at once. You'll clean it all up or no breakfast. All up, you understand? Christ, do you think they understand anything?'

I was never sure who were the doctors and who were the policemen at The Firs. In the psychiatric hospital in Germany where they had first taken me the two were exactly the same. The fact of having virtually wiped that period from my memory frightened me. Persian cavalry, in full armour, pennants trailing from their bamboo lances, wheeled to the right and galloped off as the sun came out from behind a cloud. A newspaper in the white coat pocket of a male nurse stated that it was a time of peace and love and there was to be a war in the Middle East, which seemed rather silly as any fool could see the hospital was surrounded.

'Mr Jubb, will you please wipe that mess up? You wouldn't do this at home, you know.' I didn't like this nurse. She was nothing like Gwendolen. I was walking out with Gwen, or anyway that was how she put it. She was not pretty, but at least she smiled.

I took the cloth from the nurse's hand and wiped the window. Her attention was now turned to the man I called Stigi who was also deeply engaged in masturbation. His penis stood out furiously rigid and purple against the stark whiteness of the ward. Everything was white, even the nurses' shoes, as big as teapots and viciously scrubbed. For the first time in my life I began to associate cleanliness with evil; they were trying to erase our spirits and mask the crime with Dettol. Stigi's stubby fingers could not be prised from his cock.

The doctor was making his rounds. Lately he had been escorted by several lesser priests of the Temple of Bel, who stood solemnly by in their blue robes, except when they made insulting remarks and tittered behind their hands.

The ritual of the rounds started as a klaxon sounded out in the corridor at the end of the long ward, which ran the entire top storey of a wing at The Firs, built in Victorian times as a minor country house in honey-coloured brick and surrounded by a depressing collection of the world's pines. After the klaxon came an uncivilised bell of the type employed in fire-alarms. It signified that the Doctor had come through the outer door and was in the cubicle where an armed military policeman sat. The Redcap then unlocked an iron-barred door. Another bell was pressed at a second door. This had a slightly less insistent ring. The Doctor was now through into the nurses' area which was shielded by unbreakable glass (many patients had tried to smash it with cast-iron government chamber-pots and failed, drenching fellow inmates and leading to violent arguments). From here the sane could watch the insane and occasionally venture through a door marked 'No Admittance' on our side.

When I asked them questions they never admitted to anything.

'Feeling better, Jubb?'

'Of course, sir.' I had pulled up my striped pyjama trousers in time.

'Of course, eh? You don't feel you're about to be attacked by the raiding hordes of Darius the Persian today?' he sneered. 'No moving fingers writing warnings?' The priests of the Temple of Bel looked on with cruel smiles. In the circumstances it seemed absurd to answer.

The Doctor moved on. He was a very erect little man who wore chocolate-brown suits beneath his white coats. He smelled of pipe tobacco, had studied in Switzerland and did not seem to notice that most of the ward's twenty male patients had joined in the morning chorus of masturbation.

'Shoot the ringleaders,' boomed my friend, the Major.

'Major, will you please not stand on that bed? Put your bottoms back on this minute or it's Solitary for you.'

Solitary confinement hardly seemed a sane solution to masturbation. But this was The Firs.

'Shoot the ringleaders. Damned Communists, every one of them, even the snotty-nosed kids. We used to shoot the kids as well. World's a better place without them, isn't it? I mean, we didn't make a mistake, did we? It would be awful, awful . . .'

The Major got back into bed, pulled the blue and white covers over his head and wept. His sobbing was ignored. He usually masturbated over a picture of his favourite labrador.

'Splendid animal, good bones, chest as big as a cathedral.'

But he didn't seem to have the snap this morning. Gwen said many of us had done terrible things under the covers of the Official Secrets Act.

'Shoot the ringleaders,' echoed a stocky man who was forever doing press-ups and tapping the side of his nose as if he knew something we didn't. 'We never wasted bullets. Not even on a white man.' The stocky man who did press-ups always covered his prick with a sheet. The organ was very small, bright red and button-like and reminded me of an angry camellia.

'Shoot the ringleaders.'

The Doctor went from bed to bed spending (they had given me back my watch) exactly two minutes and forty-five seconds with each patient. The only deviation from this norm was a new arrival. A man who sobbed behind screens. A very young man who was wounded in the leg. He screamed at night, sometimes in German.

'Report any change to me,' snapped the Doctor at a nurse as he tried to prise the young man's pleading hands from his white coat. 'We will start treatment in a couple of days, when his leg has been removed.' He gave the insistent fingers a painful twist. The priests nodded approval.

'Shoot the ringleaders,' shouted the Major from under the sheets.

Gwen had nicknamed us The Ringleaders. Suddenly everything stopped at the sound of the drugs trolley's squeaky front wheels. Today, I was not going to take my dose. The temptation was to swallow because the pills made you feel so damn good, but I held them under my tongue and then slipped them into the man I called Stigi's bottle of orange squash. I had to find out who the person in this large body was. Anyway, what's a little oblivion among friends?

'Open wide now, Mr Jubb. Let's see if my big teddy bear has taken his medicine? That's a good boy,' said the teenage nurse without a glimmer of a smile in her eyes. She had a purple love-bite on her neck. 'Oh, and Mr Jubb, you have a counselling board at eleven, so best not to go off to bye-byes now. Can you hear me?'

I nodded. The counselling boards were new and sometimes they let information slip about the past. They were charming and polite but one always had the distinct impression of being on trial. They were seeing how much we could remember and how successful their treatments had been. They always told me I was very sick. I caught a glimpse of Gwen, pert and dark, through the glass screen. She lifted a small, work-worn hand and smiled in acknowledgement.

'Hello, Gwen.'

Gwen told me to keep calm and not worry about the past and they would let me out. What made them free people was a mystery and nothing to do with mental health. Two of the sanest unfortunates were still in the ward after twenty years. The overheated room hummed with the familiar smells of urine and soiled sheets. I had to break free. Gwen was an angel. I was frightened that someone might have seen us in my exercise period last week dodging between the heating oil tank and the safety wall. For the first time I had put my hand on her black silk panties as we stood next to a sign which warned 'Extreme Danger: No Naked Lights'. Now the horizon where the green of the fields turned into an indistinct blue had lost its early morning haziness. In the sky freedom was a space too big for even the seagulls to encompass in their majestic arcs. Like it or not, I could smell the camp-fires of King Darius. Babylon was falling.

'Ready for the counselling board, are we, son?' said a Redcap, though he was only a lance-corporal and younger than me. But there is no such thing as rank and respect when the other man has a uniform, heavy shining boots and a revolver and you have a dressing-gown, pyjamas and ridiculous knitted woollen slippers donated by the Women's Institute. They probably made them to a government patent to make lunatics easier to catch on the well-polished parquet floors.

The military policeman talked to the nurse as if I wasn't there.

'You coming to the dance on Friday?'

'Who's asking?' She had thin lips and the corporal was a small man with large hands. I imagined them groping at the girl's lard-white body in some rain-soaked lane, the clumsy dance-steps of passion that inevitably slid in the same direction. The corporal would have the pungent scent of her vaginal juices and Rimmel Beauty-On-A-Budget on his fingers as he went back to barracks, to remind him of his night of fun. To him I was a loony, a person to be kept outside the walls of the castles of love.

One could never have the disturbed engaged in something so disturbing.

'Well, are you coming?'

'Who's asking?'

'I'm asking.'

'Pick me up at seven at the nurses' home and watch out for matron.' We were now past the security doors in a long corridor where the windows high up on one side were still painted a black-out pea-green from the last war. On sunny days it gave the impression of being beneath a tranquil sea of turtle soup.

'Wait there,' said the nurse coldly indicating a chair. She turned to her escort. 'He'll be all right. He's harmless. Fancy a coffee?'

'I'd better wait. Just in case.'

'Saturday, then.'

'Saturday.'

The mutual gaze lingered for a second. The day of the week was an unspoken sexual contract. The corporal would not pay for her with a silver temple shekel but in vodka and lime. The nurse rustled away in her starched linen and I was left looking into the man's eyes.

'You don't give me no trouble, Mr Jubb,' he said, propping himself against the wall. The door opened and it was time to go in. The military police corporal waited outside. In a minute or so he would be having sly drags on a half-smoked roll-up he habitually kept in his pocket. The room I stepped into was a disused ward from which the beds had been shifted. Behind a trestle table sat the Doctor who had done the morning rounds and three other men, one in an officer's uniform. On the table was a vase of daffodils and a copy of the Revised Standard Version. The other two could have been civil servants. A bowler rested on a hat stand in the corner. A rotund chap impatiently waved me towards a chair as if I were late. The chair was always too small and too hard and enhanced the feeling of nakedness and vulnerability I had in my dressing-gown, as if I had stayed up with the grown-ups long past my bed time.

At that moment I noticed her. Indistinct at first in the corner of the room, seated on a stool made of human skulls, was a priestess dressed in the blue and gold robes of the Babylonian Venus. Her dark eyes, thick with make-up, watched me without pity, though with a certain amusement. She had a gap between her two front teeth. I could hardly bear to look at her.

'Now, we are your friends, Toby,' said the fat man I had never seen before. I was always prepared to believe the best in anyone, except when they told you about it themselves.

'Yes.'

'What would you do if you got out of here?'

The priestess smiled and nodded at me. My hands were sweating.

'Oh, a bit of teaching. I recall I studied Classics. Perhaps a bit of writing . . .' The tubby man looked up. He had great bushy eyebrows like false moustaches. His assistant was much smaller, occasionally attempting a reassuring smile made lopsided by an unfortunate lump on his chin, just one of the twists and bumps meted out to his body by polio, or some dreadful birth deformity. He slobbered slightly and his briefcase on the table in front of him bore the name Quibell-Smith. The military man was in his fifties with greying hair and the mild-mannered, faded look of an old

Officers' Mess sofa left too long in the Punjab sun. But when he opened his mouth to speak his teeth bared in a nervous twitch at which he closed his blank blue eyes and brought his jaws together like a steel trap, and then looked around surprised. The sight of those lantern jaws imitating the feeding behaviour of the Great White Shark was hardly reassuring.

Even the Doctor looked embarrassed that my future was in the hands of men who could easily have been his patients.

'What sort of damn fool writing did you have in mind?' began Eyebrows, placing his chipolata fingers together one by one. 'You don't intend any memoirs . . . ?'

As I began to speak I tried not to look at the priestess who was now floating a foot above the ground.

'I haven't the slightest intention of writing things to embarrass. My subject, as I've pointed out, was the Classics. I would like to pen something on Herodotus' account of Babylon, of King Darius and the Persian wars. I would like to create something of my own for posterity. It's pride, I know, but I think I can make a contribution in that field. I feel I do know it quite well . . .' My words were written down with Eyebrows' rolled-gold Parker propelling pencil.

'So he does remember his schooling, Doctor,' said Eyebrows accusingly before turning back to me. 'Now, Mr Jubb, you must accept you have been ill. You were part of things which are, shall we say, best forgotten. By that I'm not implying they are of any great significance. Any memories which may float to the surface are most unlikely to be what actually happened. I mean, you are looking at the past as if through a glass darkly, aren't you?' He turned to his aide and laughed. It was not a very nice noise. 'And as every schoolboy knows, Herodotus was a fibber. Wickedly so.'

The Faint White Shark opened his mouth to say something, his jaws twitched involuntarily, and he bit the end off his indelible pencil which turned his lips purple. But his face cleared like a spring morning.

'A bit of a wag and a rotter, this Greek chappie.'

'Just so,' agreed Eyebrows, passing the man a glass of water. 'You don't want to be a wag and a rotter where your country is concerned do you, Jubb? That would be unthinkable.'

'Unthinkable,' echoed his aide.

'It's not that we want to censor. Heavens, no. Totally the wrong word.'

'Prune.'

'Yes, prune.'

'Prune's a better word.'

'We need to prune the vines of State occasionally if they are to continue to bear fruit,' concluded Eyebrows. 'Snip, snip, snip. All quite painless really.'

The priestess watching us burst into silent laughter.

'One sometimes has to be cruel to be kind,' observed the Faint White Shark, controlling his jaws with difficulty. 'But I'm rather partial to prunes, old boy. You can write all you like about those little blighters. Keep you regular.'

Eyebrows pursed his full red lips. 'Freedom always means responsibility, Jubb.'

'Responsibility,' echoed Quibell-Smith.

'That's why we want an agreement. A binding agreement that anything you wanted to publish or utter publicly would first have to be vetted by us.'

'Binding.'

'But not censorship,' added the Faint White Shark quietly. 'A dose of prunes, old chap. Always does the trick.' The jaws snapped shut again and another pencil lay decapitated on the desk.

'I cannot recall being involved in anything . . .' I answered truthfully.

'That's just the point,' whispered Eyebrows. 'You have hit the nail fairly and squarely on the nose. But please don't tell anyone you have forgotten what you might remember. There is an awful lot of tomfoolery about these days. A lot of beatnik chaps about that don't even know the meaning of the words "Desert Rats". Now, it wouldn't help if you told all these nancy boys and peace-merchants you had something on your mind. They'd encourage you to make up some damn fool thing. It really wouldn't be to anyone's advantage if you told that cock-and-bull story you mentioned to the chaps in Wiesbaden before your anti-depression therapy . . .'

'I can't remember exactly.'

My knees felt suddenly very weak. I could see the priestess clearly now and was distracted by the striking resemblance she had to my mother. To make matters worse she started to take off her clothes.

'I can't remember.'

'Good, good,' beamed the Doctor, who obviously had a great deal to do with my amnesia. 'In my profession one realises painful memories are often the cause of so much unhappiness. Like tonsils, adenoids, the appendix, even the spleen and certain fingers, one does not miss them and in some cases is far better without them. Mr Jubb has been sick since early childhood. His writings show it. We were just in time.'

The priestess had slipped out of her jewel-encrusted tunic and was now unlacing a complicated bodice holding in milk-white breasts.

'We were just in time,' echoed Quibell-Smith, staining his blotter with spittle.

'Or perhaps not,' interjected Eyebrows sharply. 'I wish to try something. We cannot take the Doctor's word that he has forgotten everything. Now listen to me, Jubb. No one knows the full extent of your hideous crimes in Berlin and, what is more, your file tells me you have also been suffering from paranoid delusions. You told our medical staff at Wiesbaden that King Darius and his Persian army were at the gates of Babylon because the great king was hopelessly in love with a Jewish harlot of the sacred temple brothel run by Her Majesty the Queen and the British taxpayer. All against the background of the indecent and brutal murder of a dozen or so women and the disappearance of many more. Do any of these things ring a bell? What does it mean to you now when I say the word "Wall", Jubb?'

I was not following him as closely as I should have been. The woman undoing the beribboned blue silk bodice was quite clearly my mother, even with her hair piled up in a rather fetching Assyrian fashion. One could not mistake her sharp nose or the slightly carnivorous grin. She pouted slightly at me as the garment fell away. The priestess in the corner by the radiator bore no resemblance to another bright, blue-eyed madonna of my dreams. A hypnotic darkness seemed to flow from the priestess's eyes as she began to undo the cords that held up the long blue skirt. There was no denying her beauty.

'What does it mean when I say the word "Wall" to you, Jubb?' repeated Eyebrows impatiently. Mother held the waistband of the dress teasingly.

'Please, Mother, don't do that . . .'

186

But with a smile she had let the flimsy garment fall to the floor and, quite naked, walked over to me and kissed me on the cheek while rubbing herself against me like a cat. She stood on tiptoe and her tongue explored my ear.

'Did you hear him talking to his mother?' said the Doctor triumphantly. 'His mother is very significant,' he added as she continued to caress my thigh.

'Jubb, are you all right? You have gone quite red in the face. Tell me what you remember of Colonel Midwinter?'

For a moment I felt a jolt not unlike the electrical current of the ECT machine, at the mention of the name Midwinter. But my mother planted another soothing but less than maternal kiss on my lips, touching my nose with a gold-leaf covered fingernail and pointing at the blackboard on the far wall. I could see the foyer of somewhere called Kindergarten Number Nine; the name was on a large notice next to an unnerving giant cut-out rabbit with fanatical blue eyes. Mother pointed to the legend underneath the rabbit's basket. The words 'read, Toby' hissed around my brain like air spilling from a puncture. I obeyed as a dutiful son should.

'Midwinter?' repeated Eyebrows.

'Mrs Big Bunny Loves Good Children,' I said, to Mother's delight. Mother's hands had started to wander inside my dressing-gown. The Faint White Shark seemed pleased, although Eyebrows appeared rather irritated.

'Colonel Midwinter was head of British Military Intelligence in Berlin . . .'

'Please,' protested the Doctor. 'Take care, it could be dangerous for the patient to have such information.' The fat man ignored him.

'Colonel Midwinter defected just before the Wall was built. He must have known what was going to happen. Now think, Toby. What did you say to Colonel Midwinter? What do you know about the Wall, Jubb? You want to help us, don't you?' The three supposedly wise men stared at me as the Doctor shuffled his notes in annoyance. Mother stroked my shoulder and I thought how strange it was that she was naked, I only in my dressing-gown, and they fully clothed. Again she prompted my answer.

'The walls of Babylon are two hundred cubits high. But they have been numbered by the Lord and finished. The Persians will overwhelm them. Babylon is falling.' Mother gave me another much sloppier kiss. I turned and looked at her impish face. There was so much I wanted to catch up on with her. She certainly looked extremely well. Her breasts were firmer than I remembered, with large prominent nipples. Her stomach and legs were as smooth and muscled as in the photographs of when she had been a dancer in Paris. I touched her young bottom just to make sure it was real and she held my hand there. On the left cheek was the tattoo of a tiny serpent and the words *Aude Vide Tace* which she had put on after a liquid lunch party with Cyril Connolly in Brighton. She told me the gipsy in the next tent on from the tattooist had given her three cowrie shells and said one day she would be a goddess. Her skin shone with a strange blue luminosity beneath the white.

'Mrs Big Bunny Loves Good Children,' I added for good measure, getting into the spirit of things.

'Splendid,' said the Doctor. 'You will agree, gentlemen, my technique has worked.

'Completely cuckoo,' offered the Faint White Shark, immediately succumbing to a biting attack and sending daffodil petals fluttering in several directions. Mother seemed entirely pleased and held her fingers to her lips as I was about to interrupt. Everything about her was so much more pronounced. Her hair was a darker black than when I remembered it falling across the pale pink silken pillows of a bed my father hardly slept in.

'Are we sure he's not just being clever? Very sneaky indeed?' mused Eyebrows, ever the sceptic.

'Absolutely sure,' replied the Doctor in a manner much more mellow than the vinegary one he reserved for the wards. He turned to me. 'Mr Jubb? Can you hear me? Can you hear what I am saying?' Mother put her fingers to her lips and I gazed straight in front of me with my arms rigidly at my sides.

'As I thought,' continued the Doctor. 'We can say anything we like now. He has gone into a trance-like state due to the trauma of the questions you asked and cannot hear us. One thing we knew about Toby from the start is that he is passionately in love with his mother. Isn't any boy, you may say, but not like Jubb. He wrote to his mother all the time he was in Berlin, though she was in no position to reply. He still writes from time to time. A forbidden love, gentlemen, early buried under a precocious interest in the Classics. Even before the Wall we're talking about, Jubb had an obsession with the ramparts and barriers of the ancient world in order to keep his own thoughts safely penned in.' The last sentence he delivered in a whisper with a nervous glance at me. Mother dug me in the ribs with her elbow.

'Babylon will fall,' I said, and she looked delighted. I bent down and kissed her forehead.

'So you see,' remarked the Doctor, 'using techniques pioneered by myself, coupled with methods recently learned in Korea, we have successfully interred the details of the Wall under the passions and complexes of a man's childhood, which in turn are buried beneath the sands of Persia. I have seldom seen a more tortured mind, even in my native Switzerland, so we cannot expect such a result in every case. I can certainly guarantee that this fine fellow is safely off his rocker and has a memory hopelessly compromised by ancient history. You see how he kisses the air? My guess is he's kissing his mother! You may wince, gentlemen, but for our purposes we should be glad. We should also allow him more freedom immediately to see if greater opportunity to stroll in the village brings back any dangerous recollections. Naturally these rambles will be strictly confined to the daytime. In a few months we can release him back into society.'

'Is that wise? Won't he stand out like a sore thumb?'

'Oh, not in rural Oxfordshire,' said the Doctor. 'Are we agreed on his possible release in several months?' They all nodded and Mother was ecstatic, but as I reached for her she disappeared.

The Redcap marched me back by a slightly different route which, as he stopped to talk to one of his soldier mates, afforded a view of the front drive. They day was cold and only a few tulips were out. I was in something of a daze. I was trying to concentrate on what the Doctor had said. Gwen was talking to someone, arguing with them. She was very upset. Suddenly she ran up the drive back to The Firs. A man stood by a car with military markings. He stood very straight. His face was flushed with anger and lank hair fell over his forehead. It was the face I had seen by the wall in the grounds. Smerdus the Magus, the great pretender, the enemy of King Darius. A man I felt instinctively frightened of . . .

'Anthony Selwyn Parr,' hissed my mother's voice in my ear. 'Anthony Selwyn Parr.' The name did not sound very nice. I was sure I had heard it before. I turned round to see Mother again under

189

an almond tree already in blossom. The smile on her face was as wicked as it was knowing.

The Doctor, it seemed, was not the only one who had plans for Toby Jubb.

16

As the moon came from behind a small cloud, that all-seeing light caught me playing with a purple head of lilac blossom, behind a tree rather too small for someone of my bulk and dimensions. The air itself appeared to glow and I could make out every shade of the flowers. Immediately I suspected Mother of being around and playing tricks again. However, look over my shoulder as I did from time to time, she was not hovering delectable and mischievous on that hypnotic night. The scents of the summer were overpowering. They thankfully blotted out the Old Spice after shave I had borrowed from the Major's spongebag. What I hoped were stiletto heels clicked against the drive. I listened carefully because at a distance they sounded not dissimilar to the spiked, iron-clad wheels of a Persian battle chariot. But I had been seeing the armed host of King Darius less and less in the past month and for the moment he appeared to have withdrawn behind the low hills towards the new Swindon industrial park; although I could still discern the glimmer of his camp fires from my window at dusk. My memory was getting better by the day and it slightly worried me, as I might soon be able to remember what the authorities at The Firs wanted me to forget. Clack, clack, clack, the heels came nearer. The Major and I had been transferred to a less secure ward several weeks ago, and before I had slipped out he had pulled me close to him, tears running down that wreck of a face and said above all I must love my country. He appeared annoyed when I confided that I didn't know where I stood with Babylon yet, let alone perfidious Albion. At least I felt part of the former; it is hard to love a country where the status quo relies on denying horrors past and, with a narcotic draft of myths and lies, soon has heads sufficiently numbed to repeat any atrocity. The heels drew level. I would give Gwen a couple of minutes and then follow her slowly. I crushed the lilac and made my way along the tangled tree-lined drive as innocuously as my size and the moon would allow. It crossed my mind that the management at The Firs might know of my midnight strolls, scrunching underfoot every dried twig. Bright stars mingled from the early summer sky and there was a spark from Gwen's high heels as they scraped on the metal weighbridge. The guard at the gatehouse would hear that sound.

'Evening, Gwen. Come in here and play with my gun,' jeered a soldier whose torch preceded him in the doorway. Inside under a harsh light a radio was on. A dance band was playing 'Red Sails in the Sunset'. I wriggled through an elderberry bush in order to slip around the back of the building while Gwen talked to the soldier, but found myself stuck. I could not see where I was caught.

'Come and play with my gun, Gwen.'

'You should clean that rifle, Mr Tonks, and your mouth out with soap. I shall tell your poor wife . . .'

I raised a hand to my corduroy jacket where something was preventing me going further. I froze. My fingers pricked against barbed wire. I had a sudden impulse to bolt. My attempts to break loose appeared to move every bush and tree in what was a cross between a tidy avenue and a wild spinney as if a portion of the garden had been affected by a sudden hurricane.

'What's that?'

'Oh, it must be the wind,' said Gwen.

'There's no wind tonight. No wind at all. We chucked some barbed wire into that coppice in the hope of snaring a deer . . . or a loony. Maybe I should take a look.' As I tried to take my jacket off I heard him step out onto the weighbridge.

Gwen called him back. Her voice had changed. Her lilting Welsh voice was soft and seductive.

'Show me your radio first, Mr Tonks. I've always admired the tone. Is it by any chance a transistor?'

'The very latest model. My brother's in the trade.'

'In the trade, is he?'

'Yes . . .'

'You must be very proud . . .'

I saw the flash of moonlight on Gwen's PVC raincoat as she stepped inside. The radio was turned up and switched to a popular station which was playing a Beatles song and I managed to shuffle free from the barbs. The radio was still blaring as I tiptoed from the covers and onto the drive, crouching as I went past the gatehouse inside which Tonks appeared to be pursuing Gwen around the table. But I am not the jealous type and anyway Gwen is Welsh Chapel and only permitted things to go so far. In ten minutes she caught me up at the wooden bus shelter on the outskirts of the village where a seat faced a conifer plantation and one could be quite private. The road was seldom used though on my daytime walks I had seen the battle chariots of King Darius rushing by, horses at full stretch in their endless hunt for rivals and pretenders to the realm.

She kissed me primly on the cheek and, taking a Kit-Kat chocolate bar from her pocket, offered me a piece. She had large brown eyes with huge lashes but her face was a little too round to be thought pretty and prone to spots as well as the puppy fat which had followed her into her twenties. Gwen was a martyr to chocolate.

'Is it better in the new ward?' she said, munching.

'Oh, much,' I replied sliding my hand onto her bare knee. The right one had a dimple. I could feel her fear.

'I hope you're not going to be trouble . . .' she began but then sat bolt upright. In the moonlight I could see her lips quiver. She seemed very upset. At first I thought she was ritually spurning my advances or trying to get them in puritan perspective from the start. Usually we kissed and she allowed me to fondle her breasts and touch the outside of her panties but no further. Now she began to make a gurgling noise.

'Are you all right, old girl?' I asked putting my hand around the back of her head. 'Are you all right? Gwen? I say what are you doing?'

Her hand was on the fly buttons of my trousers, positively ripping them open and burrowing through my Y-Fronts to grab the member she previously regarded as the devil incarnate, and who was still at ease and quite unprepared for the frontal assault.

'Gwen, I had no idea . . .'

193

But her mouth was on mine and she clawed at my hair with her other hand banging my head against the wooden wall of the shelter. I hoped there was no one waiting for a bus the other side. Strong fingers caressed, while an extremely practised tongue probed inside my mouth. Now she was unbuttoning my belt and tugging down my trousers and underpants.

'I love you, Toby . . .'

Deftly kneeling down she took me unprotesting into her hot mouth. She pulled up her blouse and still sucking so hard it hurt managed to unclip her own bra and then taking my wet erection in her hand pressed it between her breasts, before fastening her mouth around it again. I gasped for breath.

'Gosh, Gwen, you're jolly passionate tonight.'

Last week she had brought her scrapbook of the Royal Family, which was not my idea of a diverting evening, although bursting into tears over a picture of Princess Anne possibly showed the same facility of compassion as it took to give way to the amorous advances of a loony. Also, soft sentimental Gwen was an awful snob and the first thing she had told me in the draughty village church was that she only went out with officers. She was now tearing off her own mini-skirt. My teeth began to chatter, although it was certainly not cold. As a nurse she was used to lifting men and had the strength of a thousand blanket-baths, but the immense power that held me down was something quite different. With her two puny arms she pushed me back against the shelter, standing for a second, her large breasts and thin hips indistinct in the strange light, and then she tackled me again and the world was spinning. We rolled onto the floor and I was on top of her, aware of something delicious sliding under the surface of my mind. I saw the inside of a temple and as we pounded on the concrete I was in the arms of a priestess on an exquisite couch in the Temple of Bel. The face below me appeared to change. The hair grew darker and the eyes larger and took on a hypnotic beauty. We climaxed with a shout fit to wake the dead.

'Mother!'

My hands were around Gwen's throat, fingers pressing.

We lay there for perhaps a minute before she suddenly froze. All at once she started to pick up her clothes in a frenzy of putting on, buttoning up and smoothing down.

194

'I'm sorry, Toby. I'm not like that. Really I'm not. I don't know what came over me. My mum . . . she always brought me up chapel. You didn't even use a rubber. You must think I'm awful. A right tart. A bloody scrubber. I just don't know what got into me. I've been out with people before, but never like that. I don't . . .' She burst into tears. I stood up and put my arms around her. She was shaking. I heard laughter somewhere in the night.

'Why did you call me your mother?'

'Did I?' A sudden coldness made me shiver.

'It's because you love me isn't it, you big effort. I knew you loved me. I love you too, curlytop. There isn't anyone else, honest. There was one man but I've finished with him. He was peculiar. There's no one waiting for you, is there, Toby? On the outside?'

'I hope not,' I said as I scanned the bushes. I looked back at Gwen half expecting to see someone quite different. But she was sitting there with her Cardiff dance-hall allure intact again.

'Who's the unlucky man?' I asked, for something to say as I sat feeling violated and pulling on my trousers.

'Captain Anthony Selwyn Parr,' said Gwen almost proudly, reaching in her bag for her lipstick. 'He's a strange one. But he's got a lovely car. But strange. You must think me wicked, Toby. A harlot. Toby, what's wrong?'

A tinkling laughter floated through the night like the water splashing into the fountains of Babylon, or the blood onto the temple floor. How could I begin to explain?

'We should have used a rubber,' added Gwen.

Three days later I was in the Doctor's study watching him gaping at his goldfish. The man and the fish both had bulging eyes. The habit of randomly opening and closing a large round mouth was also the same, although in the case of the fish it was understandable and quite necessary to extract oxygen from the crystal clear water. With the Doctor it merely contributed to a patient's despair that he could not help them. The Doctor had several other props to make his patients feel awful and not really worth his expensive attention. He would suddenly take his shoes and socks off and go and sit on the leather couch which he never allowed his patients near, as he believed it had once belonged to the great Sigmund. One day he intended to sell it at Sotheby's. On the couch he would proceed to

195

cut his toenails. On other occasions he would poke out his contact lenses, or, most revolting, probe between his stained teeth with a piece of dental floss. The latter had caused one Irishman to become so incensed he had unzipped his fly and urinated in the goldfish bowl, or so Gwen had told me. The Irishman had been taken away in an Everfresh Flowers van, never to be seen again. The Doctor was a man of power. One trod the gardens of his dignity with great care.

'Feeling better?' he asked the fish in his squeaky voice. The hand holding the container of ant eggs was shaking slightly. One had to be so alert. At The Firs rigorously sane behaviour was diagnosed as an ungrateful attempt to deceive the authorities and was rewarded by Electro-Convulsive Therapy. On the Doctor's desk was a picture of him and his wife with Sir Anthony Eden. After my last ECT session it had taken me weeks to realise what cricket was, even though I had stared at it for several days on television. At The Firs the psychiatrists built walls and if one did not cross them using the appointed gates things could be painful. I had the permanent option of retreating back through the Blue Gate of Babylon. The Doctor had the option of the Everfresh Flowers van.

'Feeling better?' The muddy brown eyes were now looking at me. 'Having trouble sleeping?'

'A little.' The doctor liked his patients tired.

'Nightmares, I suppose,' he said, suddenly interested and rubbing his hands together. 'Creepy-crawly things oozing from under the bed, eh? Bad dreams can seem so real when one does not have a future. Are you encouraged by our progress, Mr Jubb?'

'I like to take things slowly, Doctor.'

'Would you like to take things slowly on the outside, Mr Jubb?'

'If you felt I was ready,' I replied, a little breathless. I had not expected release so soon. For a multitude of reasons I was frightened of the kingdoms beyond the gates. 'I do like the walks in the village, Doctor . . .' The Doctor made a whinnying noise. It was laughter.

'Oh yes, quite. Gives you an impression of freedom, eh? Well it should. The village is on military land. All part of a big Yank base really. But we must be allowed our little white lies. Believe me, there is no running away from The Firs. Fishy want some ant eggs?' I kept quiet and looked down at my new brown leather shoes.

'I like you, Jubb. You're very intelligent. Your amazing file says

196

so.' He stabbed at a buff folder in front of him on the desk. I noticed he bit his fingernails. 'Some of us can be too clever, Jubb. Some men can think they know best. It's my job to make my patients face up to the hideous ghouls of the past. But in your case, Jubb, as with many men who come in here, there is a time best left deep within your unconscious. Remember what curiosity did to the poor kitty? Now I have some questions, Jubb.'

'Yes, Doctor.'

'You used to write letters to your mother, Jubb. You wrote her letters, Jubb, but you did not send them. Can you enlighten me as to why?'

'Not a sausage, Doctor. Is Mother well?'

'You are still very close to her, aren't you, Jubb?' He smiled knowingly at me. I hesitated. At times I did want to tell him about the things I witnessed, even though I had not actually seen the Babylonian priestess who resembled my mother for some weeks. But the Doctor cut me off. A short, wiry figure, whom I recognised as Daniel the satrap of Babylon, the prophet with the drinking problem, was now sitting at the Doctor's desk pulling faces at me. The Doctor was looking at my file. Daniel came across and whispered in my ear.

'The lions were too appalled to eat me. History is so often a question of taste.'

I did not doubt it. The Doctor looked up.

'. . . Excellent, Jubb. Do you know you wrote letters to your mother in a very familiar way, almost as if she were a lover? In fact, the letters were more passionate than most men can ever manage. You write almost as if you had shared something forbidden.' The Doctor was breathing harder now and the prophet was sticking out his tongue. 'Do you remember, Jubb? Do you remember?' I could smell my mother's perfume and see her silhouette against the moonlight.

'Do you recall writing this?' The Doctor's manner was almost friendly, as if we had been at college together. 'Do you know any of those names? You wouldn't be trying to deceive me now, would you, Jubb?'

'No, Doctor.'

'Liar,' hissed Daniel the prophet, taking a swig from a bottle. 'Beware all pretenders, Jubb.' He then disappeared.

I was much more interested in the letter and took the paper greedily. It was written in a meandering hand I did not recognise as mine and was dated March 18, 1961.

Café Babylon
Berlin

Dear Mother,
Magda flew into a rage again this morning. I had gone into the bathroom which adjoins our bedroom and lifted the cover of the bidet to find a gimlet-eyed grey and red parrot, who bit my finger when I touched him. He flew back into our room screeching horribly, and all at once Magda was hitting me from behind, telling me not to be so cruel while the parrot sat on a light-fitting and swore at us in German. His name is Mungo. I knew you would not let me keep Mungo . . . I knew you would not let me keep him, she kept saying. The bird growled continually, just like a dog. Why had she put the poor thing in the bidet? There was nowhere else at the time, she said, as she had another customer. Was I accusing her of being thoughtless? Why had I tried to hurt the poor bird? Apparently Mungo had had a very disturbed childhood on a succession of East African tramp steamers, all of which had sunk. Not surprisingly, he is not in great demand as a ship's parrot. Magda began to hurl things from her dressing-table as the parrot flew around the room. Both the parrot and Magda competed for who could shout the loudest. A moment later her rage vanished and she came and kissed me and said I always understood. I was such a nice person. She would give the parrot to a friend who had a bar on the Ku'damm. She suspected it of being possessed by an evil spirit anyway. What is more the Baron did not like it. Magda gave me a kiss on the cheek. Such is our life together here, Mother. One minute Magda is the kindest, most wonderful person in the world and the next she is a wild thing who keeps parrots called Mungo in the bidet and loves everyone she possibly can. We have made a pact not to be jealous, which in the circumstances would be absurd. You would like her, Mother. At times she reminds me so much of

you. I dearly love her. Almost as much as I love you, my mother.

Please, Mother, I still feel I let you down with the Paris business, which after all is why I am here as an absurd shopkeeper, peddling flesh for lies. What I am trying to provide is a little love also. I know it is a dream. It cannot be so wrong. But Betty Bethlehem says I am playing with fire . . .

The letter was obliterated further in harsh black pen marks and a whole section had been cut away at the end.

'I wrote this?'

'You were very disturbed at the time, Toby. In Freudian terms the letter is very revealing. Especially the parrot in the bidet. Trust me. I think you were trying to shock your mother, poor soul. In other letters you are very candid about your life in Berlin. It appears a series of brutal murders of young girls, of quite extraordinary bestiality, rather as if they were to do with some cult, took place at the time. Do you remember?' Outside it had started to rain. On another sheet which he handed to me, was the hurried, uncorrected draft of a poem.

'Read the lines I have marked, please.'

'In the sweet tension of every sucked breath,
My hands clutch the throat, offered and white
Her smile spreading as my strong thumbs seek life
Cutting away feeling, plucking the red flower . . .'

The doctor waited for my reaction, smiling to himself.

'Not exactly Lord Byron,' I said, after a minute or two. I truly could not remember writing those lines.

'We have twenty-four others on the same sort of tack. Some are even more violent; others just revolting.' He crouched down level with the fish tank and his face was magnified to frightening proportions.

'Are you saying I'm some kind of killer, Doctor?' I blurted out, forgetting to be careful. 'A schizophrenic? Dangerous in some way? Is that why I am here? I could understand that, Doctor.'

199

'Could you? The mind is a very sensitive, fragile thing, Jubb. Very fragile, especially yours. Now let's return to the matter in hand. Do you remember Magda?' A shudder overtook my body and in a mirror behind the Doctor's head I could see the familiar Blue Gate of Babylon. It was time to watch what I said.

'I know the name. But there is something else, Doctor.'

'What is it, Jubb?'

'It's trivial really, but you told me in our other sessions to tell you everything . . .'

'Yes, yes . . .'

'Well, I still can't remember what cricket is, Doctor.'

The Doctor looked ecstatic. The family photograph on his desk appeared to reflect his joy.

'Splendid, Jubb. I confess myself delighted. Our treatment has been a success, Mr Fishy. Have some more ant eggs. Mr Jubb cannot remember what cricket is. Now let's be clear, Toby. It's not just the rules you cannot remember. Not some arcane fiddly bit about the positioning of leg slip.' I shook my head.

'No, I mean I can't remember what cricket is in the same was as I can't remember Berlin. I feel I used to be quite good but at times it's as if I had never seen the game. It frightens me like airplanes terrify Amazonian Indians because flying machines are totally outside their experience. When the plane has gone they can't even draw the thing. Cricket, I'm sure, should be familiar, but all I see are strange white shapes. I have to switch the television off or leave the room. When I think about it my mind won't focus and I start to shake. I have nightmares. Magda and Berlin are . . . I know I must have done something awful. I'm like a jigsaw puzzle or an archaeological dig . . . A city in pieces. A ruin. Smashed like the Blue Gate of Babylon. I feel as if I have been smashed to pieces and don't know how the pieces fit.' In the mirror the Blue Gate began to disintegrate. Had I been pretending?

'Good, very good,' said the Doctor with a smug expression as if his mouth was full of butter fudge. 'I am going to recommend that you be released. I must call a colleague. You're a case in a thousand, Jubb. A case in a thousand.' His fat fingers drummed on the table.

'So you think I am sane?'

'You can't remember cricket? Splendid.' He picked up the telephone and began to dial. 'Do show yourself out, Jubb. Dr

Clotworthy? Is that you? I'm sorry to wake you up. I forgot the time your side of the pond. I have the most amazing news. My technique does appear to be working . . .' I left wondering quite why Daniel the prophet had appeared and what the Blue Gate meant. But my imminent release suddenly hit me and I began to smile. The guard outside was immediately suspicious. They did not approve of happiness at The Firs.

17

The Firs Psychiatric Hospital
Oxfordshire

June 18, 1965

Dear Mother,

I know you are out there, Mother. Why won't you appear to me again? I must say you look absolutely stunning. You took me a little by surprise. One does not expect to find one's mother dressed as a Babylonian priestess and taking off her clothes. But really, Mother, I wasn't offended, and often feel you are close. Gwendolen says she is pregnant, Mother, so I am to be a father. At times she is so passionate and then so utterly prim. How does one explain it? I am sorry this letter is so short but I have only a piece of toilet paper to write on,

All my fondest love,
Toby

On a warm night in June the Major died. As I had been becoming stronger and more confident, he had been wasting away and one morning I found him crying in the washroom in a pool of urine, unable to get up. He made me promise not to say anything in case they took him to the infirmary. Nobody ever came back from the infirmary. In return he said he would tell me many secrets. That night he sat bolt upright staring straight in front of him. His voice was steady and dignified. The tone made me shiver because I was sure I was listening to a man already dead. The voice came from a long way away. From the bottom of a deep well. The Major did not go quietly.

'Toby, dear boy, I'm dying. Dying, you understand. The last walk without Nanny. You must hear my confession. I've heard you talk in your sleep about Berlin, my boy. I used to light fires and blow things up. Five fires a night either side of the wire. I used to light five fires a night with devotional candles I bought from the Catholic mission . . . my little joke. I would go to the Ka-De-We and buy cotton wool, the kind you get for babies which comes in coils exactly an inch in diameter. I would wrap these around the candles about three inches down. I'm dying, dear boy, I'm dying. I was a craftsman. When I lit my candle I always said a little prayer to ask God to forgive me. I was best in basements. Berlin is such a dry place, dry as a mummy, a dehydrated husk like a syphilitic's prick. When they killed people I would burn the bodies. One time it went wrong, very wrong. My superiors wanted me to demolish a building near the Turkish area. I remember women, lots of beautiful women, and touching the face of one who was dead. Some of the women died in that fire. They were screaming. I hear them screaming when I go for my morning walks. They screamed from my cornflakes. So they sent me here. They made me blow up a lovely blue gate. Shatter it to pieces. The Blue Gate of Babylon. You've talked about it in your sleep, dear boy . . .'

'Please, Major, hold on, I will get a doctor.'

'No time, dear boy, no time. Beware of those evil men at Kindergarten Number Nine. I'm dying, dear boy, I'm dying. Shoot the ringleaders. Shoot the ringleaders, that's what I say. I am going to burn in all the fires of hell.' He went heavy in my arms and the life in him seemed to rush out through the bottom of the bed. A nurse had switched on the lights.

'Did he say anything before he went?' demanded the young woman accusingly.

'Not really, nurse. I think he just wanted me to light a candle for him.'

The next day everyone was especially nice, in a nervous sort of way. 'Doctor wants you to go for a walk in the grounds. He says you can call at his house for a chat afterwards,' said a new nurse with a pretty face and a sulky mouth. As I looked down out of my window I saw the Everfresh Flowers van had come to take the Major's body away. I would miss him. He was a kind old thing whatever he had done. There must be some forgiveness, or we end up with no one to blame but ourselves. Yes, I would miss him. But the day could not have been better. A misty summer morning promised a clear blue sky by noon; it was a morning which quickened my pulse and made me glad I was alive. Today they let me put on a shirt and trousers but pedantically they still insisted on a dressing-gown so I could easily be spotted as insane. The exact details of what the Major had said were fading but that something very wrong had occurred, for which we were not entirely responsible, was as painful and clear as the hole in my second-best shoes. All I could think of was The Blue Gate of Babylon, lying in a thousand fragments.

Outside I smiled at a guard, skirted the front of the hospital and aimlessly walked towards the sound of construction work. The throb of a compressor had burbled to a halt and there was a scrape of picks and spades breaking ground. Workmen were building an extension to The Firs. But between me and them was the thin figure of one of the priests of Bel dressed in a flowing blue robe, who pointed beyond the wall. I stood very still. Blood thudded in my ears. I could see the hosts of Darius lined up, thousands upon thousands of them, ready to fall on Babylon. The sunlight glittered on their spears and helmets and there was complete silence except for the occasional tinkling of a harness and sighing of chariot horses. I was so completely lost in this vision of impending disaster that as I took a step forward I tripped headlong into the workmen's ditch.

'Cup of tea?'

Two men, one with a pick and the other with a shovel, were excavating a long drainage trench while a third watched them, resting on a shovel. He had a spotted handkerchief around his neck and his trousers were held up by a thick leather belt. His dark hair and eyes made him look Persian.

'Cup of tea? What you staring at?'

'Do you see anything out there? The other side of the wall?'

'No, mate.'

'Then I'd like a cup of tea. Yes please.' But the man made no move to get me one.

'You're not digging that trench to build some kind of rampart, I mean, wall? I'm very interested in building. All my family have been builders. It must be very hard work.'

The man with the spotted handkerchief winked at his mates. One of them rummaged in a bag.

'I wouldn't say we were exactly builders. Certainly, we aren't builders at the moment. We're diggers at best. At worst we're the wickedest kind of hooligans known to mortal man. Do you know what lies under your feet? Well, I'll tell you. You're standing on the cemetery of the asylum before they built this present college of the damned.' One of the men whipped something out of a sack with the speed and precision of a conjurer plucking a rabbit from a hat. An irregular off-white globe tumbled through the air and landed at my feet. The object was a skull. The top half of a human skull. The priest of Bel motioned I should pick it up.

'I'll have that tea now.'

'You what?'

'I was offered tea. I'll get it myself,' I said, striding over to where a workman's billy-can lay brimming full of tea on the grass. I poured some of the tea into the surprisingly clean plate and helped myself to two large spoonfuls of sugar from a bag of Tate and Lyle nearby.

'Chin chin.'

In one quick motion I drained the last drop. The action impressed the diggers, if not the Persians. The priest of Bel merely looked on and smiled.

'We were bagging bones for the Colonel's garden,' said the man with the pick, uneasily. 'I didn't mean anything, no offence.'

'Colonel who?'

'Colonel Parr, Colonel Sir Anthony Parr.'

'He digs it into his rhododendrons.'

'And his roses.'

'Always wins the prizes.'

'At the shows. He was a hero.'

'Very fond of his garden. Tortured by somebody or other . . .'

Without a word I walked back towards the part of the hospital grounds where the Doctor had a grand and comfortable house. I knew I would probably find him in the garden reading in his striped deck-chair. The name Parr had come up again. What sort of man fed his flowers with the dry bones of lunatics? As I turned my back on both the diggers and the Persians this Parr seemed so powerful that the entire sky became his face. I saw the shattered gate. If I could only make all the pieces fit.

The warm sun was on the daisies as I stepped around them. I picked up a stone and bowled an off-break. Now I knew I could beat them.

The Doctor's house was surrounded by a copper beech hedge. As I approached the hedge Mother stepped out of the purply green leaves. She was wearing the same blue dress I had seen in the classroom. A long finger heavy with rings beckoned me to follow. Her feet were bare and made no impression in the morning dew.

'Mother, I have many things I want to ask you. Am I out of my mind, Mother?'

But all she did was put a gold fingernail to her lips. As I looked into her dark eyes I realised the most important thing, indeed the only consideration, was to get out of The Firs; to escape from my present Babylon. The trouble was, it was the only place that felt in any way familiar. We rounded the corner of the hedge and paused for a moment by a wicket gate. Mother was close. We could hear the voices of the Doctor and the counselling board, but they could not see us. A pheasant flew in squawking confusion from the covers.

'You say he's forgotten how to play cricket?' asked the Faint White Shark, in a puzzled voice as he tried with mixed results to eat a cucumber sandwich and not his fingers. Mother stroked my hair. I could actually feel her hand.

'I don't think you quite understand,' said the Doctor patiently. 'Jubb has forgotten cricket itself. The game makes absolutely no sense to him. As with some Hottentot who did not know our customs, Jubb would probably stroll right through a game he once played and loved. The point is, if this is true for cricket it's true for other things, including Berlin. His interrogators say cricket was the last thing he clung to except for his passion for Babylon. We have used that. When things become too hard to bear he retreats back to the time of the Persian conquests and his beloved Herodotus. The Classics were a world he often fled to in an unhappy childhood. As I tried to explain before, whenever he thinks of Berlin he finds himself back in Babylon. Now do you understand?'

'How did you do this?' asked Eyebrows.

'Oh, a combination of things . . .' mused the Doctor. 'Mainly we kept him in isolation, in the dark. His imagination had to work on something. It was a pity really. We had to numb parts of his considerable mind. Despite his childhood he was, judging from this file, brave, honourable and kind to his friends. His devotion to his friends seems to have been his undoing.' Eyebrows coughed. 'Jubb's future will hardly be exciting, but at least from your point of view he'll be safe.'

'I hope he hasn't forgotten the National Anthem,' added Eyebrows sarcastically. 'Shame if he did.'

'Shame,' echoed Quibell-Smith.

'All our patients know the National Anthem,' assured the Doctor. 'Singing it is one of the rules of the institution. Where would the mentally ill be without tradition? The unfortunates who do not know the words howl respectfully.'

Mother pushed me gently and I opened the gate and stepped into the Doctor's garden.

'Ah, Jubb,' began the Doctor with a smile. 'You've cut yourself.' I hadn't noticed.

'We can't entirely trust your mumbo jumbo, Doctor,' interrupted Eyebrows. 'With all his letters and poetry Jubb shows a depressing tendency to jot things down. He must sign this declaration never to publish anything without our permission, or else suffer the gravest consequences.' He produced a piece of paper from a black briefcase and a Parker pen. 'He can still write, I suppose?'

I went over to the table and picked up the pen but it did not work, and blood from my arm dripped onto the document which was headed 'Ministry of Defence'.

'No ink? Well, he can sign it in his own blood if he likes,' chuckled the fat man. So I dipped the nib of the pen into the spot of blood and signed my name with a flourish. Mother was pleased. The Faint White Shark looked sadly away.

'You understand that you will not utter, write or broadcast anything for profit without first going through the proper channels,' droned Quibell-Smith, very much like a country vicar at a wedding ceremony. 'Do you understand and agree?' I nodded my head and grinned in the way lunatics are meant to; Mother did a little pirouette on the lawn. All the men appeared satisfied.

'I can release him?' said the Doctor.

'Yes,' said Eyebrows. 'I understand accommodation has been found?' With that they left me and when I turned around Mother was gone too and the hordes of Darius. Only her perfume remained. I heard laughter at the front of the house. The counselling board could dine out on that story of an outsize idiot who had signed a deposition within the meaning of the Official Secrets Act in his own blood and had forgotten cricket; as long as they only told it to themselves, of course.

18

English funerals are painfully awkward occasions. While no one would ever expect them to be happy we are at a double disadvantage because few of us believe any more that the deceased has popped off to a more comfortable armchair in the sky, where his glass of Warre's Nimrod port is eternally refilled by a Windmill girl dressed only in mauve ostrich feathers. The only pleasure for the mourners is to look into the damp ditch and be thankful one is not there. As I drove North to Shropshire I could not help wondering if, as Herodotus noted, the Massegetae had got it right, and elderly relatives should be included in a general sacrifice and then joyfully eaten by those left behind. In his declining years my father would probably have not disagreed with the theory. The only difference being, after a life spent in commerce, he would have insisted the participants be charged an admission fee. The church was far from full and I tried to conceal myself behind a pillar near the door. A middle-aged man shuffled towards me.

'Family, are you?'

I felt like telling him I had come for the sheer fun of things. What better than to drive to a freezing church, unfrequented even by bats, in what was now an agricultural desert of enormous fields, where farmers dined on fish fingers from the freezer, and poppies and cornflowers are weeds. At least in here the sharp airless smell was real and one could only recognize one's once beloved country in the vicar's steps on the echoing vaults below. A beam creaked and I remembered my father. Water leaked from a chipped font. My father had become Church of England, after all the fuss. I don't know why he bothered.

'Family, are you?' the man repeated.

'Yes,' I said.

'Close?'

'Close . . .' The last time I had seen Father was at my graduation. I don't think he cared. The trouble was, you see, I was a walking reminder of the past, and her. Instead he buried himself in something that never hurt him, money. The church was more full of business cronies than friends.

'He led a tragic life,' said my pew partner, a travelling salesman type in an ill-fitting charcoal lounge suit, shiny from too many car journeys.

'Really?'

'His son was taken away to a loony bin. His wife . . . well, everyone knew about her. But it was terrible the way she died. Some say it was murder. He never recovered from the fire. She burned to death in the summer-house. They couldn't find anything to bury even though she's on his gravestone. She led him a dog's life. Some say he lit the . . .' He stopped -- I think it was the way I was looking at him -- and shuffled crab-like down the pew, glancing at me sideways from time to time. He hurried away afterwards, thankfully, and was not present at the reception where we ate gloriously inept prawn vol-au-vents and asparagus rolls, which, in their turn, looked and smelt of corpse. I did not know a soul. Father had no friends when he died, only acquaintances of the kind he had been making steadily all his life.

'He's left you everything,' said Mr Harmsworth, the kindly solicitor, as if he were surprised. The reception was in a hotel in the nearest town. 'Will you be opening up the house again?'

'No, I'd be grateful if you would sell it.'

'But no instructions were left . . .'

'Sell it, please. It's mine and I don't want to live there. If you'll give me the keys I'll go and take one last look. It's ages, you know.'

When I arrived at the house I was glad Gwen had had the 'flu and not come with me. She loved the idea of my father's money but hated the fact he had not come to our wedding, a rather barren affair in a registry office. It was best that I came alone. The gravel drive was overgrown with weeds and although Harmsworth had given me the keys I did not want to go into the house, which would probably now become some stockbroker retreat. Instead I walked around to the back and after pausing for a moment under what had been my room I strode across the lawn, which had turned into an anarchic tide of rye grass. However, the profusion of the garden had not been entirely stilled. The remains of the summer's flowers, delphiniums and sweet william, were showing colour, sheltered by the great copper beech and oak. To me it was still an enchanted garden. I stopped and stood in what had been the summer house. All that remained now was a fairy ring of pink autumn cyclamen. Mother would have loved that. A tear made its way down my cheek. To me she would never die.

Due to the sudden manner of my father's death, trustees had been appointed to run his estate. I had the rent from several farms and a small but adequate allowance from a trust. After I eventually managed to sell our old family house (the memories were too painful) in the spring of 1967 we bought the lease to Selwyn Hall, which I found out much later had once belonged to a branch of the Parr family. Parr seemed fated to haunt me and at least in this small way I could haunt him. I had my marriage to Gwen blessed in the draughty wooden church. An old lady had come to watch. Men in plain suits from unmarked cars had confiscated her confetti.

Even the rooks were silent.

For me, the best thing, the very best thing, was that Maria had been born eighteen months before, like an express train on the dining-room floor. She was a truly lovable child. A laughing baby, who did not look like Mr Khrushchev or a being from outer space, she quickly became a toddler and would sit on my knee twirling my hair in her little fingers as I marked books from the tutorials I gave, to keep my brain alive rather than body and soul together. I felt if I kept mentally fit one day I would be allowed an insight into my past. And I now had someone to live for again. Maria was such a sensual child with her fingers always gouging at the plasticine or burrowing delightedly into the mud. She would munch handfuls of rose petals and laugh and laugh as I played old 78s of 'The Good Ship Lollipop' on the wind-up gramophone out in the garden. Gwendolen would complain about the noise. After Maria had toddled beyond babyhood, Gwendolen changed. As Maria grew up and the years rolled by, Gwen became quite sour. She nagged me to make something of myself. Beds to her were now for sleeping in, alone.

'Babies are lovely things. But it's disgusting to think what makes them. Disgusting,' she would say. Gwen would hardly let me touch her any more. My wife became more respectable than most Mother Superiors and gave tea parties for the vicar with York ham and fairy cakes but nothing so messy and vulgar as Maria's favourite chocolate eclairs. These days she would never dream of kissing anyone in a bus shelter, or smoking Woodbines, or sucking bright red gobstoppers she bought at the hospital shop in The Firs. I knew I had truly lost her when she went to a British Legion meeting and brought home a nasty-looking uniform. Everything would have been very bleak, except for my writing and Maria.

'No one in my family has ever been called Maria,' my wife had said stiffly. The birth had been difficult. Early on it was to have been twins. But one child, a boy, had died and been absorbed by the other. Gwen would not talk about such things. Even when Maria was walking she still, perversely, complained of the name we had both agreed to. On nights when things had gone badly at the British Legion or the Women's Institute she would steer the conversation round to what she considered to be my family's history of insanity, as she failed to do the *Times* crossword with a grim determination.

'No one in our family has ever been called Maria. I don't know how you ever got me to accept the idea. People will think we are foreign.'

'My mother's middle name was Maria.'

'But do you think that is wise, Toby?'

'Her parents did.'

'Your mother had troubles. Things we don't want to be reminded of. Do we, my little Loopy Loo?'

'What on earth do you mean?'

'She had problems with her nerves. Serious problems.'

'Don't we all?'

'I wasn't going to mention your problems, dear. We all know about those. All I want is the best for my daughter. I want her educated. How can she be properly educated if people say she's not right in the head?'

'No one is going to say that.'

'They will if our child is called after a mad woman. A stupid foreign-sounding name, if you ask me.'

'I loved my mother.'

'More than you've ever loved me these past years. My God, if I'd known I'd never have agreed. Yes, you love your mother. I've seen you mumbling to that memorial urn in the church. It's a wonder they allowed her to be buried in a respectable cemetery. I've heard what she was really like. People say she was a slut . . .'

'Stop it, Gwen.'

'I think you loved her much too well, if you ask me. If you ask me, it was unhealthy.' My little daughter smiled as Gwen turned away to go back into the kitchen. She was baking for the village harvest festival party. I thought I heard her grumble the word 'disgusting'. I was never quite sure of how much she knew about my parents. But she was more sensitive to scandal than a duchess and had heard whispers in the cake shops of Faringdon. Perhaps that is what killed her. In the ten years that followed we did not drift apart. Visibly we were a couple. We could be seen in the garden together, or at the village fête. But when Gwen was at home, instead of out doing good works, we communicated more and more through the emotional sounding-board of Maria, who Gwen doggedly insisted on calling Loopy Loo, because she abhorred the name I had chosen. Our marriage was serviceable if rotten, like the guttering on Selwyn Hall. But just as I was getting my bearings, someone turned the world topsy-turvy again.

I sat at my writing-desk, trying to marshal my thoughts. At times such as these there was only one person I could turn to.

Selwyn Hall   May 9, 1980
Nr. Faringdon,
Berkshire

Dearest Mother,

I saw you again at the village fête. I only wish it could have been in much happier circumstances, Mother. Excuse me for standing and staring like a complete idiot, but the vicar had organised a beauty contest and at first I thought some lovely newcomer to the village had stumbled upon the costume of a

213

priestess of Babylon. Honestly, Mother, I am not just being flattering. You looked stunning, but why did you run away? I followed you down into the old deer park and sat by the lake for ages hoping you would reappear. That was where the vicar's wife found me. She said I had nodded off to sleep. I am prone to that these days. I thought Gwen was fussing. She had been nagging me so. It was then that they told me she was dead. Stone dead under the table of the white elephant stall she had organised single-handed. Absolutely stone dead.

I went back and at first everyone stood around getting in each other's way. Her eyes were wide open and had a most frightened expression. She had a cut on her chin, a thin deep cut, presumably from where she had fallen. A boy said he had heard her arguing with someone. But lately that has been a normal occurrence. Her stall was right at the edge of the fête, by the path that leads to the deer park. She was quite stiff. The vicar said the proper thing to do would be to get her home. We put her in the back of my old Daimler. Mrs Podbury from the village shop took care of Maria who was very upset. She is such a beautiful child, Mother, but I am sure you know.

When we got home the vicar could not help me carry Gwen into the house owing, he said, to having put his shoulder out playing cricket. He was very upset and kept repeating that she was a credit to the locality. Our doctor, who had been running the tombola, helped me instead while the vicar held his bag. He said this was the first time a parishioner had ever died at any of his fêtes. We took poor Gwen upstairs for the doctor to examine and I gave the vicar a Scotch. By that time several ladies from the Women's Institute had arrived, one of whom insisted on humming 'Jerusalem' to herself. Another asked me if foul play was suspected. I told her the doctor said it must have been her heart, which was a lie as Gwen was as strong as a bull.

Well, it was ages before the doctor finally came downstairs. He did not look at all well. Moreover, he was very embarrassed. Oh yes, it was probably her heart in the long run, he said as I offered him a cup of tea, but he seemed lost in his own private thoughts. The vicar and the ladies stayed for ages and the village policeman called but went away again after the doctor signed heart failure on the death certificate. When you come to think of it 'heart failure' must cover just about everything. Poor Gwen. After the others had gone the doctor hung around and poured himself a whisky. I had not known he was so attached to my wife. Then he said he had something to tell me. He coughed a lot and reached into his pocket and took out several pebbles of the type found in the brook and four extremely fine, tiny ivory elephants about an inch long. Do you know where I got these, he asked. Were they in my wife's pockets, I inquired. He shook his head. Was she clutching them in her hands when she died? He shook his head again. Surely she could not have swallowed them? Again he shook his head. Then he put his lips to my right ear and in the lowest of whispers told me exactly where he had found the elephants and stones. I could hardly believe it. All he said was that while we think we know people we cannot even guess at all their secret ways, even if we are married to them. He added she was not wearing any underwear and he hoped this had not shocked me as he had long respected my family. He would not mention what he had told me to another soul. The first person to find her collapsed had been young Mrs Mills and she was convinced she had heard Gwen's last words which were for the Colonel, who she had met again through her voluntary work and who has a dose of the summer 'flu at the moment. It was typical of her to think of someone else. Her very last words were, 'Anthony Selwyn Parr'. Personally, the name makes me shiver. Do please help me to understand all of this, my mother. My dear mother,

All my love,
  Toby

I buried Gwen in what was now the Jubb plot of land beside the weatherboard church. I made a joke to the undertaker about boiling her in vinegar and water like the Massegetae, but the undertaker said he preferred lily-of-the-valley and formalin for embalming.

'You have been working too hard, Mr Jubb,' he added, suddenly realising what I had been saying. 'Too much time spent with those big books . . .'

215

The village turned out for the occasion and the vicar praised Gwen for everything from her stand against abortion to her quince conserve. I looked around for the figure of Parr. He was not there. Instead he had sent a bouquet of roses. Maria was there, beautiful and blonde with her pert nose peeping from beneath a turban-style hat, which would have been ridiculous on anyone else but made her look like a Polish countess. She had dreamy blue eyes which could persuade you of anything. I loved her. More than that, I was determined to be good to her in a way I had not been to the others. Part of me felt I had let the side down. I had not done enough. I had not cared enough. But perhaps we always get into these knots at funerals. The fog of her breath condensed on her red lips.

'Don't cry, Papa.'

But I wasn't crying. Really, it was the November wind in my eyes.

'I'm all right, darling.'

'Mother's . . .'

'I'm sure she is, darling.'

Maria had brought her boyfriend, who had a shiny mop of black hair and sniggered uncontrollably as we threw dirt into the grave. I could not be angry. His was one of the few honest responses. He, at least, was not pretending like the rest of us. While I tried to persuade the vicar that I did not want to dedicate the Hall's chapel to my wife, secular saint though she was, over cold sausage-rolls, and have it run by himself and the diocese, as, among other things, I was a lapsed member of the Roman Church, the boy with the shiny quiff made love to my daughter in her bedroom upstairs. We could hear my Buddy Holly records through the floor.

A year after that the murders of the young women began.

19

A dark wedge of cake stood at a sun-dial angle on the plate in front of an empty chair. Above it on a mantelpiece crowded with archaeological layers of dust and trinkets, between a dried seahorse from Capri and a rosary of questionable emeralds blessed by Pope Pius X, was the silver-framed photograph of Maria, playing on the sands at Budleigh Salterton. It wasn't like her to be late, at least not this late. She had not telephoned. Her favourite grandfather clock ticked accusingly as a soft sunlight played upon my garden. The roses did not seem to realise summer had gone, while clouds cast racing shadows over distant hills warning of December and the night. She had never let me down before, not in her twenty-two years, and momentarily I feared she had driven her little car off a twisting Oxfordshire lane and lay helpless and in pain in a field of winter wheat. But I should try and ignore such morbid imaginings now (the Doctor had said so) and anyway, Maria was a good driver. In practical things she took after her mother, who squinted disapprovingly down from a portrait painted badly and on the cheap. I did not miss my late wife. My teatime ritual always was to cut the butter-soft Dundee cake and place it on Maria's plate, the nursery one with the picture of Mr Rabbit, hoping it would conjure the girl and her greedy blue eyes (she took after me in the appetites) into my untidy sitting-room, where, wearing in her honour a clean white linen shirt and red bow tie with white spots, I had abandoned marking Latin Common Entrance Papers (Summer 1988, Oxford

Board). The endless mistranslations of the obvious Julius's pitiless war against the Gauls had been particularly perverse today: one could joy in the decay of ridiculous empires and the demise of pompous men and pretenders, but never in the death of rational thought itself between the ears of the vandal adolescent. Yet, I was one to talk. A log slipped on the fire threatening to ignite a pile of Kennedy's Latin Primers. But the ember came to rest and hissed on a crumpet by a brass toasting-fork; the burning odour redolent of secrets I was at last remembering, but wanted to forget. Of a time I had rendered unto Caesar.

At that moment I heard the first gunshot.

As is usual in the country, where things always seem to have to die in pairs, the shot was followed by another and shortly after that by a delicate, though determined, knocking at the front door. The caller did not wait for me to get up but tumbled into the hall, her face white with abject panic. The girl was not Maria. Instead, Tracey Podbury, the daughter of the couple who ran the village shop, scampered past me and flinched at the next bang, putting her fingers, one of them inky, into her ears. Her auburn hair quivered. By a freckled schoolgirl nose there was a suspicion of a tear. I could feel her heart beating. But I could never take hold of my feelings when it came to women, any women. She was wearing her mother's perfume.

'Please, Toby, I mean Mr Jubb, it's the vicar. Please go out and stop him. He's shooting again. He says the church is being consumed by vermin and he's going to shoot them all. Oh, please don't let him shoot the woodpeckers. Mind your head on that beam, love . . .'

Immediately, she was handing me my tweed jacket, which would soon have to be thrown away as the leather patches on the elbows were almost worn through. A shadow, made enormous by the powerful reading-lamp on my desk, enveloped the corner of the room now the sun had started to set. My left knee was stiff and painful. However, it would be a sorry day if a man did not gird himself up at the request of a pretty lady in defence of the Green Woodpecker, *picus viridis*, the latest and most determined creature to attack St Thomas's. (After all, Hermes had disguised himself as a woodpecker to free Hera when she had been turned into a sacred cow, and my old friend Herodotus's name means 'gift of Hera'.) I ran my hand through hair turning strangely red instead of grey. I caught my reflection in the glass of the clock. The whites around my blue eyes were clear. A bit of a wreck perhaps, but I didn't look too decrepit. Best foot forward, Jubb.

'You'd better stay here, my dear,' I said, putting my hands on her shoulders and steering the girl towards the tea table. She did not pull away. 'Never crowd a man of God with the means to resolve arguments on the afterlife. Now you sit down and listen for the telephone. My scallywag daughter may ring . . .' The girl was looking at me in the most beguiling way. All at once the room seemed too small.

For a second she hesitated, a cheap coat hanging around her blue and white cotton dress like a chaperon. Her parish councillor father did not like her walking over to see me, bringing apples and comfort and the promise of more. She had turned up once and baked me a cake, and I later learned he had flown into a rage at the idea of my size eleven footprints in her spilt icing sugar on the warm kitchen flagstones. However, since the murders it had ceased to be a joke.

'Don't eat all the cake, mind,' I added, suddenly embarrassed, picking up a weighty Greek lexicon to stop my hands from shaking. 'It will spoil your figure, my dear . . .'

'Yes, Mr Jubb. You be careful,' she said opening the door, but not so wide that I did not have to brush past her young body. Despite the vicar, her playfulness had returned. She pivoted on a stiletto heel, too thin and high for country lanes, and went back into the gatehouse cottage. Leaves were flying on the wind and I walked out into a country that had never lived up to my own youthful expectations. I hurried towards the sound of gunfire. The vicar was the kind of cleric who never let Christianity get in the way of impressing hostesses on the sherry circuit. He already had a church, but for complex reasons to do with the snakepit of diocesan politics, wanted another and really hated the fact St Thomas's was mine; a private chapel, in a manner of speaking. The place came with Selwyn Hall, the dilapidated country house where I now chose not to live and could hardly afford to keep up. Gwen had done a stiff little jig when I told her I had bought the lease on the pile and she would not have to suffer my classically educated forehead thumping against the beams of our former rented cottage, a sound which annoyed her far more than my occasional adultery. The white weatherboard church was falling down in a much more spectacular manner than the Hall. To me its accelerating disintegration underlined the folly of man and telegraphed the glory of the gods to anyone who could smell the fust of violet ground-beetle in the broken organ. I wanted it to rot. To me that was a joyful idea. Part of me wanted everything to rot. The very thought made my knee feel much better. I did not want to destroy, you see, only not to be disappointed any more.

Decay is the only thing man can celebrate with any certainty.

My wife had never liked a fuss and had taken the authorities' side when they forbade publication of my book, written after the business in Berlin. The work had been about Herodotus' view of Darius and the Persian wars against Babylon, a lamentation on the chameleon nature of truth and the relativity of honour. The story of a monarch who hated pretenders, told by a wonderful old fibber and now examined by a middle-aged part-time Classics master whose mind was considered far from sound. But the powers-that-be had recognised themselves across twenty-five centuries and were not amused. They confiscated the book and ordered me not to write another line, except with their express permission. Several years ago a man called Runge had dropped in at the Hall unannounced and ticked me off for contributing a series of letters to *Gardening News* about making compost from old copies of *The Times*.

'Consider your country, Mr Jubb. I do hope you see. We trust you will be more sensible now you are so happy and well these days. Just give us a tinkle. You know where we are. Better safe than sorry . . .'

I hardly dared wonder if my present revised scribblings would be as controversial as compost. When I had given them 'a tinkle' there had been a sigh at the other end of the line. But they would see me. They were always polite. They had been infuriatingly charming about King Darius and the Persians and had taken me for lunch at the Mirabelle and congratulated me on how I had made the period come to life. I was about to explain a few things when they pointed out official generosity did not include returning the manuscript.

'I think we had best hang on to it . . . and if you could send us any other copies you have. I think you know why, Mr Jubb. And if you are going to ask me about those letters to your mother, I think you will have to play the white man with those too. Don't want them falling into the wrong hands under the circumstances. It's the principle, Jubb, the principle.'

Another shot sent the rooks wheeling again as I walked along the edge of a ploughed field parallel to the lane that leads past the village and St Thomas's. A hunched couple in a red Ford Cortina were drinking coffee from a thermos and glaring suspiciously at the countryside with the doors tightly shut, as if they expected Persian battle chariots with bowmen and spear-throwers to explode from the nearest coppice. But the driver's window was open several inches and the radio on. I caught a snatch of a bulletin. The wind blew the bad news towards me.

'A mutilated body has been found at a farm near Cumnor. Police are linking the killing with a series of brutal murders in the locality and appeal to women not to . . .'

I prayed Maria would call.

In order to take my mind off my daughter I tried to turn my attention to other things. I concentrated on every mole-hill. My heavy Greek lexicon was still tucked under my arm. The white weatherboard church, covered in lichen and peeling paint, was hidden by a screen of ragged yews on the edge of the village. The trees had once been part of a considerable topiary which had been responsible for the immolation of the previous Victorian place of worship. At the start of the last war the family of pop bottle magnates who had bought the Old Hall from the Selwyn Parrs (on account of Grandad Parr's eccentric rubber investments) had been enthusiastic appeasers. They had, with the unwitting help of the local Home Guard, sculpted the delicate Jacobean topiary into an immense Swastika only discernible from the air, as a precaution against German raids. On one moonlit night a tired and war-soured Luftwaffe captain had dumped his Heinkel's entire load of bombs and incendiaries on his Führer's beloved emblem, incinerating St Thomas's in the process. Not that it was the first time this particular house of God had been bothered. A church on or near the site had been sacked by various Normans, Henry VII, both Cromwells and a party of Hock-crazed devil worshippers said to include Lord Byron. The present disgraceful effort had been erected at the end of the war by the Wing Commander of a nearby RAF base in return for some rough shooting. A lop-sided rabbit-hutch of a bell tower at one end and a cross at the other was the military's nod to two millennia of divine architecture. These adornments did not compensate for the stencilled lettering which betrayed that most of the holy portals had once been intended as a Field Latrine Mk V (prefab). I could only agree with the vicar when he preached that St Thomas's was a symbol of Britain's rich heritage and the moral values and stability of the English country house. The point we differed on was his plan to repair it. I hated plans. Men with indelible blueprints for the future cause chaos and misery.

I wanted my church to rot.

I peered over the stone wall of the churchyard which was much lower than the field I was standing in. Sycamore spinners blew on the wind. I could see the rotund Vicar's remaining strands of wispy hair flying about the dome of his bald head less than four yards away. He was reloading as his eyes searched the gables for pagan green woodpeckers; the latest and most determined creatures to attack the church. Mrs Podbury at the sub-post-office said they were the children of Satan. Personally, my money was on the snails munching away at the flimsy foundations. The vicar eased two cartridges into the chambers. He stepped backwards and raised the gun to his shoulder, taking aim at a brilliant flash of green.

But he never fired.

My Greek lexicon (given to me as a confirmation present) hit his pate with a thud, and he crumpled senseless onto the couchgrass as I shinned over the wall. My knee was really hurting now. The man before me groaned and rubbed his head.

'Hello, vicar, is that really you? I thought I'd bagged a poacher.'

The expression in those amontillado-muddied eyes was one of barely controlled fury. For a moment he could not speak. But then country vicars never expect the miraculous. I picked up his shot gun. He snatched at the weapon but was too slow.

'Jubb!'

'Yes, vicar?'

'Give me back my shotgun, Jubb.'

'I'll hang on to it, vicar, if it's all right with you. We have to protect the wildlife . . .'

'Damn it, Jubb. I was not poaching. Your late wife gave me permission to use St Thomas's. I spoke to her the day of her unfortunate death. Where is the sense of letting rats gnaw at the altar and woodpeckers demolish the rood-beam? With a bit of hard work it could rise again. The Bishop agrees.' He faltered, noticing the gun was pointing at him.

'Rise again?'

'Repair would not be costly.'

'Much better to let it fall.'

'Fall? I don't understand.'

'Crumble to dust. The Lord has numbered thy possessions and finished them. Look in the Book of Daniel.'

'You're mad,' he said, backing away and tripping over a child's grave. 'Quite mad.'

'I know. But then Daniel was a bit dippy. He was an alcoholic, you know. Told the odd whopper. Otherwise, in prophet terms he is one hundred per cent. Up there with the best of them, is Dan.'

'How on earth . . .'

'How do I know? Daniel told me.'

The vicar looked at me with a mixture of loathing and real fear.

'You've not heard the last of this. Lunatics are not allowed firearms,' he cried with shrill and sad inaccuracy as he ran to his Volvo in the lane. 'I shall have words with the hospital.' The sound of the engine quickly disappeared and the woodpeckers began to drum again on the rotten weatherboard. Babylon was falling, and I wandered slowly home.

The fire had gone out when I awoke and Maria was still not there. The girl from the village shop had eaten her cake and left before I returned. I had been dreaming of Berlin, but it made no sense to me. Every time I started to think of it when I was awake I found myself back in Babylon, standing beneath the Blue Gate, or watching King Darius's battle chariots hunting endlessly for their prey. Were they searching for me for straying from the straight and narrow? The awful roaring noise a battle chariot makes is enough to make anyone examine their soul, held up before the cruel mirror of their own terror. The sound of being chased by all the Furies under Mount Olympus. I wanted to flee. But most of all I wanted to understand who I was and why I was being pursued. I wanted to unlock the secrets of my mind and had once contemplated breaking into The Firs. But even if I could manage such a thing, how could I be sure the files I read were correct? To be suspicious of the written word was the lesson learned from studying the imaginative

Herodotus. But increasingly, I felt the answer to my puzzles lay with the old liar. Perhaps he could tell me what or whom the chariots of Darius were looking for. Maria was such a consolation. I loved her deep blue eyes and her blonde hair tumbling down her back. She was such a good and generous girl and possessed an effortless sensuality. Maria filled the gap left by the name of Magda. Maria believed in art and love and couldn't care a fig for politics and the alchemy of power. These days she was always in love.

I went into the kitchen and plugged in the kettle. On the table was the local paper. True to form they had relegated to the bottom of the front page a report on the string of five exceedingly brutal murders in the past year. A picture story at the top announced that Sir Anthony Selwyn Parr had won the end-of-year Faringdon and District gardening competition. Especially commended was a purple clematis called Xerxes. 'The wonderful display from this gallant old soldier stole the hearts of the judges. But he refuses to give away his secret . . .' Just as well. At that moment the phone rang.

'Mr Jubb? Mr Toby Jubb?'

'Yes.'

'You are Mr Toby Jubb?'

'I'm quite sure.'

'Well, I'll put you through then. Putting you through. You're through.'

'Hello, Mr Jubb?'

'Hello.'

'My name's Quibell-Smith. We met once. I sat on the board that approved your release. Shall we say, from a certain place. Mum's the word.'

'It certainly is. How can I be of help?' Surely they could not have heard about the incident with the shotgun already?

'We would like to see you, Jubb.'

'Look, if it's about the vicar, I can explain.'

'Explain what?'

'Why I threw the book at him.'

'Threw the book at him?'

'In the churchyard. He was trying to pot poor old *picus viridis*. There's absolutely no need to shoot them. I read of a lady in California who lures them away from wooden buildings with peanut butter . . .'

224

There was a long pause on the other end of the telephone.

'You are well enough to see me, aren't you, Jubb?'

'My knee's giving me gyp, but otherwise I'm as right as ninepence.'

'No problems with the nerves?'

'I feel fine. Is it about my book?'

'In a way.'

'You still have the manuscript.'

'Yes, I know. I've been re-reading it. I've been mugging up on the Service's own ancient history too, Jubb. We have a bit of a security flap on at the moment. There are a few things I want to clear up. I believe you can help us. Why should you, I hear you saying? Well, I can't explain on the telephone. Hush-hush, you know.'

'Mum's the word.' I couldn't resist it.

'Mum's the word,' repeated Quibell-Smith automatically.

'Where do you want to see me? Shall I come up to London?'

'Not necessary,' he replied, the tone a shade cooler. 'I'm a big wheel these days, and I fancy a spin in the country. Do you know the Red Lion at Depton? You must. If you could see your way clear to meeting me in the Red Lion car park at seven o'clock tomorrow night? I will be in the white Rover with the diplomatic plate. You know the Red Lion? Just outside the village. We'll go somewhere else actually to talk. Oh, and one small thing.'

'Yes?'

'Give my love to your charming daughter.'

'What?'

My hand tightened on the receiver.

'Give my love to your charming daughter. I trust she is well?' A certain knowing inflection made me very fearful indeed. Maria was more precious to me than anything.

Quibell-Smith was not in the car park of the pub I thought he meant; a posh road-house which sold bland game pie to trippers and left them feeling fleeced and grumbly on the hot drive home. I was too worried about Maria to recall his directions. The Red Lion which the secret civil servant mentioned was in a council-built hamlet a little further down the road. The pub was frequented by farm-boys, with shove halfpenny, fights on Saturday nights and an encrusting of old vomit on the urinal pipes in the outside gents. The place had achieved a brief celebrity in the tabloid press when one of the regulars had bitten the head off a chick on Easter Day in the tap room. Behind the pub, banger races took place in a field which was now given over to a travelling funfair. I knew about this other Red Lion only because I had once taken a lady in there by mistake. The children of the showmen from the rides looked longingly at the hub caps on Quibell-Smith's Rover. The little man appeared to have come alone. There was a cushion on the driving-seat. It occurred to me that a more violent parent might beat the truth out of a man he suspected of knowing what had happened to a missing daughter. Yet I could not even pretend such a course. We British will make anything (war, high tea and awkward adulterous love) but never a fuss. Herodotus would have been fascinated.

'Jolly good of you to come, old boy.'

I looked down at the delicate hand. Quibell-Smith had been eating a pastry. There was a hint of cream and crumbs at the corner of his mouth.

'Meeting me cannot be easy,' he said.

'Oh, I'm sorry,' I replied, taking his small hand in my large one and shaking it politely. Another of the things I always find surprising is how the British are unfailingly polite to adversaries. Was Quibell-Smith my adversary? Was night dark? Do bullets kill?

'Yes, meeting me can't be easy,' he repeated. He looked up, unblinkingly, into my eyes.

'And I am not referring to my good looks,' grinned the small man. 'I meant . . . I meant, I know you better than you know yourself, Jubb. About your time in the hospital and your adventures before. I have the files. I have the pictures. I know of your affection for your mother. But the past is a greasy pole for you, isn't it, Jubb? The minute you start really to understand anything you find yourself back in Babylon. Your shrink told me all about it. No, I don't care if you're courteous to me at all. I can do anything I want, Jubb. I can send you back to The Firs, or worse. So please don't worry about hurting my feelings. That clear?'

'I'm sorry I'm late. I thought you meant the other Red Lion,' I found myself apologising, trying to collect my thoughts. 'It's a damn sight nicer than this place.'

'Yes, I know. But we don't want to run into your old chum Parr, now, do we? I understand he wants to buy your country house. Of course, it used to belong to his family, didn't it? Before his father squandered all the money? A bad business ... Yes, there's a meeting of the horticultural society at the other Red Lion tonight. One must find something to do when one has to take early retirement. The devil finds work for idle hands, what?'

'You keep an eye on Parr?'

'We keep an eye on everyone. In particular chaps who were once deputy head of the security services. Especially just now, old boy. I've been asked to tie up a few loose ends. I don't believe some of the things that I read in the files, you see. I'm a suspicious man, Jubb. You, as a student of Herodotus, must know how the truth can be embroidered and downright altered. Well, we're concerned with hunting traitors. I have read the files on Berlin and feel depressed and disturbed that some things do not jell. But I don't yet want to cause a fuss and change the official version of events. A bit of a head-scratcher. By the way, did Parr like women?'

'I ... I can't remember exactly. Not much. Why do you ask?'

'We're concerned about the habits of all our old boys. We have to look into every rumour. Every bit of gossip. Yes, we heard he doesn't like women. He may even have some quite nasty habits.' The man looked directly at me. He had a twinkle in his eye. The game had started. He had stopped being polite, stopped pretending.

'Isn't it strange? You're the only chap who can throw light on what actually happened in Berlin and it's impossible for you to do so. Let's go for a ride on a roundabout. I love fairgrounds, don't you, Jubb?'

We set off for the funfair. Quibell-Smith had a very bad limp. He was hardly tall enough to come up to my watch chain and his walk was in crab-like jerks.

'Had polio when I was a boy,' he explained, breathing hard. 'Yes, I must have been one of the last children in leg-irons. But one thing I loved was the fairground. For tuppence a ride I could have the same thrills as everyone else. I would take any dare. Stay on longer. Close my eyes. There I was, anyone's equal. Until the music stopped, of course.'

I did not say anything as I walked with him across the muddy grass.

'Look, could we get to the point?' I began, as he scuttled in front of me. 'I really should be at home. I am waiting for a call from my daughter.'

'Ah, yes, the anxious father. What a strain with all these murders. But do come for a ride with me on the 'Orrible Octopus. I really don't get much chance these days. Berlin used to have a nice funfair. I've seen pictures. Did you take Magda?'

'I . . . I may have. I can't even remember her face clearly, so how do you expect me to know a thing like that?' At times I could picture fleeting faces, like friends glimpsed between the painted horses on a roundabout. I recalled the starched sheets on an old brass bedstead and a collection of French perfume bottles. One face was more beautiful than the rest. I knew her name was Magda.

'Ride, sir? You look like you need cheering up. Only half a quid. Safe as houses. I'd let my mother-in-law ride on it. We all need cheering up, sir. Only half a quid. If you dare.'

Quibell-Smith paid the man and we took our places, the giant and the senior intelligence officer who was not quite a cripple. I did not like the way he had traded on my sympathy. There was not much one could teach such a man about fear and pain. But it made his mention of Maria all the more ominous.

'I'll wager you can recall more than you let on. In my experience these shrinks are never one hundred per cent. Your function was to get someone to defect and blackmail them if they didn't want to. Am I right? Do you remember the term "bad manners"?'

'I think it rings a bell. Do you know anything about my daughter? Please tell me.'

'If she's lost we'll help you find her. If you help us, that is. I'm afraid no one does anything for love these days.'

'I'll help you. Just give me time to think.' We sat in the half-moon-shaped seats waiting for the ride to start. The fair was not busy. Only a handful of listless youths mooched about the booths and rides. Two girls with dyed blonde hair and identical leather mini-skirts fought over a bright pink teddy bear. The big dipper, covered in many-coloured lights, stood out incongruously against the village church, as if a stained glass window had rebelled and assumed an adolescent life of its own. I caught sight of two large, over-smart but casually dressed men by the rifle range. So Quibell-Smith did not trust me enough after all to come alone. He did not regard me as a totally harmless, if mildly eccentric, Latin master.

228

'Bad manners, Jubb?' he repeated.

'Off we go, gents. Pull in that safety bar, my son. We don't want any nasty accidents, do we?' The man in charge of the ride bent over us. He smelt of stale beer.

'Tell me about bad manners, Jubb. Tell me about the blackmail operations to make people defect.'

The wooden-planked floor underneath us started to undulate and turn.

A courting couple in front of us were kissing each other's ears.

'I'll help you.'

'Who else knew what you were doing, Jubb?'

We began to turn faster.

'You will have to give me time. I find it hard.'

'Hard to go through the Blue Gate? What do you know about the Blue Gate of Babylon, Toby Jubb?' Quibell-Smith moved nearer to me. The little round chariot we were seated in was now revolving. Loudspeakers crackled into life.

'Pretty, pretty, pretty, pretty, Peggy Sue,' sang Buddy Holly.

As we spun faster I felt sick. A youth leapt onto the uncertain floor and gave us a shove. Our little seat spun on its own axis while the roundabout picked up speed. Coloured lights flashed past. Purple, green and white lights swirled and eddied. Then all I could see was blue.

'The Blue Gate, Toby?'

'Pretty, pretty, pretty, pretty Peggy Sue.'

As we whirled around I tried to hold the picture of the girl I supposed to be Magda in my mind. She was in a silver dress and beckoning me through the Blue Gate. My legs felt weak. I followed her down the Street of Lions inside a building like an aircraft hangar. She leant against the Gate and blew me a kiss. She disappeared to the other side. I pursued her, and suddenly was under a wide blue sky and a man with a dark curly beard was hauling me into a chariot which rushed back through the Gate and out of the city. Beyond the great walls we galloped, alone into the desert, as I held on for all I was worth to the throwing spears in a quiver by the reins. The man next to me was whipping the horses. We hurtled on in a mile-wide circle across the sand. He did not know where to go. A horse stumbled and we slowed. I looked at the man. He was dressed as a king. A Persian king. But there was no mistaking the face. The blue eyes and the slightly crooked nose. I was looking at myself. I screamed at the top of my voice and shut my eyes. Someone grabbed hold of me from behind.

'You shouldn't bring anyone on who's had a few. It stands to fucking reason. Do you want me to lose my license? Are you pig-ignorant or what? Look at me when I'm talking to you, you little cunt. If you ask me, your friend is off his fucking cakestand.'

The music had stopped and I was seated next to Quibell-Smith. He ignored the owner of the ride and patted my hand. One of the casually dressed men pulled up the safety bar. The other went over and gave a ten-pound note to the owner of the ride, putting his finger to his lips as he did so. The showman said nothing more.

'I used to go on faster rides when I was five,' sniffed Quibell-Smith.

'I'm sorry,' I said.

'Oh, don't worry, old boy. Tonight has served its purpose. Let the gods lead us. I hope you are not upset. Here is a friend of yours. I hope you remember him without hysterics. Forgive me, old boy. My little joke.'

I was still giddy. A slightly stooping figure with greying hair was bending over the rail of the ride. At first I thought it was the drunken prophet Daniel returned from under the Blue Gate and out of my dreams. The face was attempting a smile.

'Hi, Toby,' he said, giving a mock salute. 'Stigi Weitz, remember me?'

'It's such a disappointment, isn't it, when the music stops. I do so adore whizzing round and round in circles. You two must be pleased to see each other. We must do it again soon. Yes, by George, quite soon. I do so hate it when the music stops.'

I would have liked a long chat with Stigi. His indestructible face had remained with me over the years. But he looked a shadow of his former self. However, we drove in separate cars towards Oxford. Quibell-Smith came with me. I had no choice, it seemed. Stigi went in the Rover with the two men. He was careworn and resigned.

'Does he work for you these days?' I asked, as Quibell-Smith took a packet of liquorice allsorts from his bulging pockets and selected a yellow and black one. He looked longingly at it before popping it in his mouth.

'My heavens, no. Mr Weitz would find it hard to secure a place in the modern world of intelligence. My Lord, no. Anyway, after Berlin he didn't even have the stomach for it. We let him go. In our business the truly corrupt are often the most trustworthy. We can always claw them back, if we want to.'

'What did he do?'

'What didn't he do, the rascal. But there was a change. His schemes lacked nothing in ingenuity. However, after Berlin the joy went out of it for him. Do you know what he does now? Runs a pet cemetery on the North Circular Road. He sells the skins to whoever will take them. Not an edifying profession. Here we are, on the right. Park behind my boys. I'm afraid I can only promise you more disagreeable surprises. Personally, I think Parr has a lot to answer for.' With that he was scrabbling for the door handle and struggling out of my car.

The house was one of those self-confident piles built by Victorian nonconformist dons which have endless rooms and smell of mothballs and ancient adulteries. Quibell-Smith led the way into what had once been the billiard room. A projector was set up. Stigi was already seated in an armchair gratefully sipping a Scotch. He smiled weakly at me.

'Lights. Run the film, please. I'm sorry to be so old-fashioned but we have not transferred this one to video. I unearthed it in my recent investigations. I'm sure you'll both enjoy the experience.'

A moment's pause was too long for Quibell-Smith.

'Run the film.'

Instantly the countdown numbers to a black-and-white film appeared on the screen. Next came a hand-held card which said 'Top Secret'. A soundtrack crackled into life. A scene showed Berlin in the late 1970s. Everyone was striding purposefully around their economic miracle.

'In the past ten years the West German government has been extensively compromised by what have come to be called honeytrap or bad manners operations. Only recently, and too late, have we realised the sophistication of the East German intelligence service, the GRP . . .' The film was terse and to the point. Pretty secretaries had been introduced into key business and government posts in West Germany. No one had suspected. NATO countries had thought East Germany did not have access to the kind of person who could organise such a delicate operation. MI6 and the rest were wrong. The screen filled with pictures of middle-aged men and the beautiful women who had unzipped their careers on king-sized beds in anonymous hotels as microphones listened and cameras turned and recorded the damp incidents for a questionable posterity.

'We believe the woman behind grooming these agents is the wife of the East German General, Roland von Hollmann. The woman, Magda von Hollmann, is a former prostitute who once worked for Western intelligence services and defected immediately prior to the building of the Berlin Wall.'

A sequence of film showed a smartly dressed, stiff-backed but still very attractive middle-aged woman getting into a Zil limousine. With her was a younger, severe-looking blonde who had her hair tied back.

'My Christ, Magda. Did she marry him? That's Cindy.'

'Stop the film.'

The projectionist managed to wind back to the required shot.

'Those ladies are Mrs Magda von Hollmann and Lisa Holtz. The latter girl is responsible for a department in the Ministry of Propaganda.'

Stigi made a sniggering noise.

'Are you all right, Toby?' Quibell-Smith asked.

'Yes, thank you. I seem to be coping.'

The film was re-started. 'In the past three years Frau Hollmann has retired. The operation has, however, passed on to her son who showed no desire to follow his father into the army. Here is a recent picture.' Quibell-Smith touched my arm. On the screen was a very tall young man who towered over his admiring mother. He seemed almost too big for the shot and the concealed camera had difficulty getting him into the frame.

'It's Toby,' said Stigi.

'It's not.'

No one spoke for a few moments. The likeness was obvious. The lights were switched on again. Quibell-Smith patted my hand and smiled.

'He does look like you, doesn't he? Well, I suppose it is to be expected.'

'Why didn't anyone tell me?'

The question was ignored.

'He's in England. I wonder why he's in England?'

Quibell-Smith paused and examined the cathedral he was making with his fingers. One of his men refilled Stigi's glass.

'Do you think he wants to set up the same operation in our green and pleasant land? Or perhaps it's to look for you, Toby? He hasn't paid you a call, has he?' I hardly heard him. One doesn't discover every day that one has a grown-up son.

'No,' I said. 'Have you lost your reason? I don't know what you're trying to do. This is brutal.' Quibell-Smith was relentless.

'I suppose he could have come to take revenge on Parr. Betty whatsername has never been the same. Several of the other girls had a very bad time, quite apart from those murders. But do you know what really intrigues me, Jubb?'

'What's that?'

The little man suddenly looked very excited.

'That there could be a fourth reason for his presence. Something that we have all missed in the files. I do so love puzzles. Almost as much as roundabouts. Another thing fascinates me. Slides now, please. Lights.' A slide-projector whirred into life.

We were in darkness again.

'Observe a picture of your lovely daughter.'

The slide changed.

'And here is one of your late wife, Gwendolen. Here are separate pictures of several of her boyfriends before you came on the scene. Oh, and here is a photograph of a document showing a copy of a statement she made to the security officer at The Firs in line with the terms of her employment contract and within the meaning of the Official Secrets Act. You had only just met in the village church the week before. She states that she believes she is pregnant.'

The slide changed again. The picture was of Gwendolen in an MG sports car. The man with her was Anthony Selwyn Parr.

On the next frame the face of Parr filled the entire screen.

'All the big boys at the top of the Service have their peccadillos, but Parr takes some beating – although there was old Tetlow out on the Hong Kong listening station who couldn't do without rotting fish somewhere in the room. Oily, pelagic fish like herring were just the ticket but he always kept a pot of gentlemen's relish for emergencies, he told me. Yes, Parr is a man of many parts beneath that respectable exterior. I want to know why he was interested in the Blue Gate of Babylon. We are only beginning to find out some of the things he was up to in Berlin. I want to know more. He has been becoming more eccentric as he grows older. He never married, of course. He must be lonely.'

I did not answer. My mind was filled with confusion and a great golden statue . . . I was beginning to see things more clearly. My glass was refilled. Even the tips of my fingers felt numb. Quibell-Smith coughed.

'Now what can I do for you, Toby? I wonder where your Maria can be? Such a delightful child. I think you two characters had better stay the night.'

On the screen the face of Parr, the great pretender, smiled out at me.

20

The murder was on my own doorstep. A mile and a half from Selwyn Hall at a crossroads where they hanged the penultimate highwayman.

After his cruel slide show Quibell-Smith had been charm itself. He had given us a supper, exquisitely prepared by a resident housekeeper, of cold salmon and roast duck and told us amusing stories about the yet unexcavated sexual scandals of the Macmillan era, and of the good and the great betting on dildo races across the Persian carpets at Number 10, Downing Street. Our rooms had already been prepared. But he had no objection when I asked Stigi if he wanted to drive out next day and see where I lived. We were not prisoners. All Quibell-Smith said was: 'Don't fail me, old boy.'

Stigi sat beside me, uncharacteristically silent, even as we had to slow and negotiate red traffic cones in the road. White tape was twisted around metal stakes pushed into the hard earth. It had not rained for a week. Four police cars clustered around each other as if for reassurance in a violent world. A caravan stood next to a translucent plastic sheet strung on a rope between two trees to form a makeshift tent. As we drew level two middle-aged men emerged from within. Their faces were white as they conferred. Such are the tell-tales clues to an English roadside murder.

I thought of Berlin and remembered that witches and evil things always haunt crossroads.

My car radio furnished the details.

'Police believe the body found today beside the A40 to be that of Jeanette Murphy, a secretary and mother of two from Swindon. She had been sexually assaulted and police have reason to think that this murder is linked to others in the area. Mrs Murphy, a keen member of a local light operatic society, was last seen on her way to a production of *The Mikado* in London . . .'

Stigi spoke.

'I heard Q-Smith's goons talking. The murderer leaves a flower just like in Berlin.'

'He does?'

'The other shit, too.'

'What other . . .'

'Inside the body. You know . . . pushed inside. In Berlin it was cobblestones, remember?'

'My God.'

The cottage came into view and I felt huge relief. I glimpsed the Hall through the trees. But as I glanced towards the church, I saw them. A line of chariots were drawn up. One of them was empty. Were they waiting for me? I felt wretched. I had gained a son and lost a daughter and a monster was now stalking the hedgerows of Oxfordshire. The bony hands of the Eyeless Clockwork Army were breaking through, and the black crocus was growing again. Now the battle chariots of King Darius's Immortal Guard were in my crab-apple orchard. They wanted me to lead them.

'Look out, Toby!'

My old Daimler narrowly missed a gate post.

'The car knows its way. It's all been a bit of a shock. Seeing you. What that little bastard said. Would you like a scotch? I think I need one.'

'Now you're talking.'

We went inside. The cottage had an abandoned and strangely violated quality. But the cleaning lady from the village had not been. The pots were still dirty in the sink. I rescued two tumblers and poured the drinks.

'Christ, Stigi. It's all so bloody filthy . . .'

He stood looking up at me. As he held out his hand falteringly I took it. All of a sudden I was hugging the little man to me. His long grey hair was greasy under my hands. His whole body was shaking

236

with emotion in an old sheepskin coat which had not only seen better days but probably other owners.

'My God, Toby, I'm sorry. They worked on me. You've got to believe that. They kept me in a little cell and Selwyn Parr kept coming in and saying he would cut my balls off. They wanted the Baron. In the end Parr dumped all the girls in the East and went after Rollo. Parr got Wolfgang, but Rollo was safely in Moscow. They broke Betty Bethlehem's pelvis when they caught her. She's in a wheelchair still. She runs a boarding house near Brighton. The bastards won. I'm living proof.'

The garden was bathed in sunshine. Poor Wolfgang. So war did affect the less than innocent bystander. Betty would have put up such a fight. I would like to think they had not broken Betty.

'I wonder if Magda has been happy with Rollo?'

Stigi shrugged.

'Rudi looks a lot like you.'

'They put me in a loony bin. They chased her out of my memory. They chased me out of my mind.'

'You had a harder time than any of us, Toby.'

'Now they try and tell me Maria's not my daughter.'

'After a while I just didn't want to play any more. If I was a religious man I'd have committed suicide. Q-Smith told me Parr's father did the decent thing. He said that was one of the reasons Parr hated you and your family. Parr's a bastard. What happened with Papa Parr and your mother?'

'I'd rather not talk about it, Stigi, if it's all the same. I'd rather not talk about it. How can they say Maria isn't my little girl? She's all I have.'

Stigi stared awkwardly down at his shoes.

'I don't even have a dog these days.'

'Poor old Stigi.'

'They won't let me keep live animals any more. They say I'm unfit.'

'We're both in a mess.'

'It could be worse, pal.'

'What do you mean?'

'Remember Midwinter? How he defected?'

'I do now.'

'Well, he didn't.'

'Didn't what?'

'According to Q-Smith he didn't defect. He didn't do anything. Perhaps one of his horses ate him. The Russians deny all knowledge of him, which isn't usual. He disappeared off the face of the earth.'

'Parr?'

'Q-Smith hinted that. But he couldn't say why. He also found it hard to swallow that Parr's murderous intent was entirely based on a desire to protect his father's war record, even if it was all the poor sod had left. He seems to think everyone was interested in your Blue Gate of Babylon. Much more than anyone would let on. Midwinter had made arrangements to take things out by air . . .'

A blackbird started to sing.

King Darius killed nine pretenders and had their faces engraved in his tomb. They died horribly. Perhaps only at the end was he satisfied no one was deceiving him.

'Do you think Parr's got my daughter?'

'I don't know, Toby. But he certainly has the answers. Q-Smith says he may have been fooling us for years.'

We sat in the cold front room for a long time saying nothing. I noticed Stigi had let his teeth go. There was dirt under his fingernails. When I suggested he go upstairs and lie down he did not protest and went with slow resigned steps. We had been talking all day and well into the night.

I so wished Maria were back with me. I wished she would run in through the door, all apologetic. I wished it under the Blue Gate of Babylon. In the old days the gods used mortals when they wanted to be revenged. Perhaps the goddess was using me? Was she angry someone had stolen the great golden statue of Bel. Angry that someone had blown her Gate to pieces . . .

I stared at the empty grate for as long as I could. I knew what would be in store for me when I looked up. My phantoms had returned. My mind was so full of Berlin and Magda and Parr, it was inevitable. I saw the figure of King Darius standing in the garden. He was by an ornamental arch over which I trained roses. The King was not now a young man. The beard was longer, infinitely curled, grey and mysterious. He looked pleadingly at me. He too was alone. But as I glanced towards the desk I realised I had another visitor. Mother was there, dressed as a priestess of Babylon. A finger heavy with rings pointed at my books. My copy of Herodotus was open on the desk. She beckoned me over. I was about to ask her what I should do but she disappeared. When I turned back to the garden Darius had gone too. Only the book remained. I had to trust in the gifts of the Greek. The Blue Gate loomed before me so I concentrated on the pages. What had Darius been searching for? The passage at which the book was open was about how the King had taken power. Of how he had put down the first rebellion of Babylon and killed Smerdus the Magus, the Chaldean pretender who had usurped the throne. The Persians hated pretenders. I had come across a cuneiform reference on a cylindrical scroll to the sixth wife of Darius being abducted. I had no conclusive evidence, of course, but suspected that years later the king's last bloody siege of Babylon, before civilisation turned its back on that city for ever, was for the love of this unnamed woman. She may have been a Jewess called Asher. Was Parr the pretender I had to dispatch? There was a very good private family reason why my mother would wish any of the Parr clan dead. But she was dressed as a priestess of Babylon, a lady of Ishtar. Had Parr transgressed in some other way? Had he committed a crime against the goddess which could not be left unpunished down the many centuries, a crime as bad as his father's against my poor mother? Was the goddess using her to be revenged? Suddenly, as I turned the pages, Herodotus gave me the clue I had been seeking. I realised what I must do. Mother stood before me again. I knew without her saying a word that I would have to go and see Parr. I had to find Maria. I had to go and face the past.

A knocking shook me out of the trance. The grey light of morning spilled through the French windows. I had fallen asleep in the chair. The room smelt of bad dreams and whisky.

When I opened the front door a uniformed policeman was smiling on the doorstep. He seemed almost surprised to see me. A radio crackled on the lapel of his jacket. I opened the door wider to let him into the hall.

'You weren't on your way anywhere, sir?'

'What makes you say that, constable?'

'Oh nothing, sir. Sergeant Ainsley asked me to call. Just a few questions. I understand from the lady at the village shop your daughter's gone mising. Don't worry, he has all the details. I expect she'll be all right, sir. Are you sure you're not going anywhere?'

'Absolutely not.'

'Then if you don't mind I'll pop in for a minute.'

'Do come in. Cup of tea? A nip of whisky?'

'Too kind, sir. A nip of whisky would go down a great. It's a nippy sort of day. I've been doing traffic down at the crossroads. Nasty business with that girl.'

He paused.

'I . . . I'm sure your daughter will be all right.'

'Water?'

'Neat's fine, sir. No point in wasting water.' He sat down and placed his helmet on the floor by an armchair and put the glass behind it, hiding the drink like a schoolboy and taking out a notebook and pencil.

'Now, what is it you do for a living, sir?'

'I teach a bit of Greek and Latin and live off my savings.'

'Not much call for the Classics now?'

'Oh, more than you'd think.'

'When did you last see your daughter?'

'She was meant to be coming for tea three days ago. She never misses. She hasn't phoned me.'

'But you didn't report it to us, sir. Why was that?'

'I thought she would turn up. I don't know. I don't like to make a fuss.'

'Busy with your Latin and Greek, sir? At the village shop they say you tend to have a lot of women callers. Ladies from Swindon.' He winked at me.

'What if I do? Are you interrogating me, constable? What exactly was it you wanted?' The man was beginning to make me annoyed. He was that older, experienced kind of bobby who liked to appear everyone's friend.

'My boss said a car like your daughter's broke down at a lay-by a few miles back. A man fitting your description was seen giving her a lift. Now that's strange. Don't you think that's strange?'

'Are you saying I gave my daughter a lift? If so I would know where she was.'

The policeman looked at me and smiled.

'She hasn't turned up then, sir.'

'No.'

I watched him slowly drain the whisky.

'Well then, in the circumstances you can expect a visit from the CID. They may want to ask you a few questions. Please don't be

240

alarmed. Common sense is the thing, sir. Don't get up. I'll show myself out. I'd be obliged if you didn't stray very far, sir. They will be wanting a word with you quite soon. Good day, sir. No doubt I will see you again.'

I was hardly listening. The only thought in my mind was of Anthony Selwyn Parr.

Dear Mother,

I feel as if someone has been rebuilding the Blue Gate of Babylon and that I am being reconstructed with it. I am sure all this is your doing. You are leading me to something I cannot possibly escape. I have to tell you, Mother, as I cannot really explain this to Stigi, bless him, and certainly not to the Mr Plod who has just left. He would send me back to The Firs.

I can see the azure tiles being fixed in place by master craftsmen as slaves hold sunshades above the artisans' heads. I can draw the exact patterns on those sunshades, Mother. I know there is a part of my life I must confront, even if it is to be destroyed again. I never really faced up to losing you, my mother. I buried the pain in work and school and would not let you go. To me you can never die. Please help me to get Maria back. She is so precious to me. I may be finished, but I want her to go on, Mother. She is my hope for the future. I'm rather glad I did not fox the village Bobby with all this. Over his shoulder I could see the figure of Darius had returned to the garden. The King is growing more impatient. He scents the blood of another pretender. Someone who has deceived me. Perhaps drunken old Daniel put in a good word for me . . .

A last thought, Mother. Babylon is not quite the same. Before I was always going back through the Gate. I was being led in procession to sacrifice at the great ziggurat, the Temple of Bel Marduk, on one of the feast days. Or I was wandering through on my own, deeper and deeper into the alleys of the market quarter, tripping over bags of spices and children with their whips and tops. I was always looking for you. As I closed my eyes just now the scene was very different. I was going out of the city to a house set aside for the new year's festivities. I feel a new year beginning in me. Please guide me.

All my love,
Toby

A noise on the stairs disturbed me. I was putting the letter into an envelope. Stigi spoke.

'Who are you writing to?'

'Oh, it's just a puzzle from the paper I forgot to post. If you get it right you win eternal happiness or at least a holiday in Majorca. Silly, really. How are you feeling, old boy?'

'Fine as ever.'

'Will you help me?' The deeply-lined face looked profoundly unsure. 'I think I know who has my daughter.'

'Parr?'

'I must confront him. I think he has Maria.'

'Is that the only reason?'

'Yes, of course.'

'I mean you're sometimes pretty weird. In the Café Babylon the girls often found you talking to the walls.'

The grin returned to his face. I walked over and poured him a glass of whisky, the hair of the dog.

'I never was really certain about the authenticity of a lot of those pieces, Stigi. But I'm sure about going to see Parr. You will help me, won't you? I'm afraid there's no angle in it this time. You will not find any yo-yo's and hula hoops on this trip. All I'm asking you to do is help me as a friend.'

'I certainly ain't got nothing to lose. After the newspaper reports the local council is very disturbed about my pets' cemetery. Besides, that happy little bastard Q-Smith said I may face charges for my old activities in Germany. All in all, my life is a bucket of shit. The only time I smile is when I think of the Café Babylon. My God, these days everyone is so scared they wear a boiler suit to fuck.'

'Please, Stigi.'

'Okay, I'm in. Do you know that bastard Parr even had Six-Shot Otto The Hound put down? He's slime.'

'I'm sorry. I didn't know.'

242

'Have you got a gun?' A certain life seemed to be coming back into Stigi Weitz. 'If you see him we should really take a piece. He used to love guns.'

'I just can't believe that monster is Maria's father. I always suspected Parr of murdering our girls in Germany.'

Stigi nodded, draining his glass. The winter sun came from behind a cloud and illuminated the room. The hard light fleetingly chased away all the dust and cobwebs, making everything new and fresh and as sharp as paint. Stigi looked capable of choice once more; a puppeteer's strings had been cut from a marionette who wanted to dance off on his own.

'What about Q-Smith?'

'Why should I trust a man who wants me to betray my own son?'

'Did you say you had a gun?'

'Sort of,' I said.

'What do you mean, sort of?'

'I've got the vicar's shotgun. He was trying to shoot the woodpeckers at the old church. I took it off him. It's still got both cartridges in it, I think.'

'Better than nothing. Have you got a plan? Look we'd better wait until dusk at least. Have you got a plan, Toby?'

'Unfortunately, yes.' I hated plans.

The afternoon was growing dark when we eventually walked over to my old Daimler. In the fields beyond I saw the chariots of Darius.

The king was smiling.

21

The powerful headlights of the Daimler caught the eyes of a hare, frozen in fear against the background of a newly-ploughed field. We were lost. We had both had a little too much whisky as we waited for the darkness.

'I thought you knew where it was?'

'Well, yes. But I'm hardly likely to have paid a call on him, am I?'

The vicar's shotgun lay on the back seat. I was now slightly embarrassed about it, about going to confront Parr at all. I mean what would one say? Ahead the road split into three by an old Saxon cross. I was about to suggest we went home when I saw the white horses. In the left-hand path, shining silver and gold through the rising mist, was the battle chariot of the king. The tall man was looking at me and smiling. Before I could collect my thoughts the chariot sped away at what was an immense speed for a heavy, horse-drawn vehicle. Everything about it from the tips of the throwing spears to the leather harness seemed to have an eerie silvery glow. I followed.

'Tally ho. We're back on the scent again.'

'You haven't got any seat-belts.'

'It's an old car.'

The chariot of the king was vanishing around the bends ahead. I put my foot down. We skidded on the next corner scraping the hedge.

'Hey, what's the hurry?'

I could see the charioteer using the whip on the horses. The king stood beside him. Darius was not even bothering to hold on. He did not move a muscle. Occasionally he glanced imperiously back. The manes and tails of the four white stallions danced and flew as they galloped full tilt down the Oxfordshire country lane.

'Toby, for Christ's sake, what if something is coming the other way . . . ?'

I laughed. If a commuter on his way for a pint of wallop at a country pub spied King Darius's gold and silver battle chariot with its spiked wheels rushing towards him out of the night, I could guarantee he would drive his polished Japanese automobile straight through the nearest hedge.

'For God's sake, look out!'

We had rounded a bend and Darius's driver had reined in, but it was all too late. I knew the dreadful feeling of queasy weightlessness in the pit of my stomach that meant the wheels were sliding on the wet and muddy road and my hands braced against the steering-wheel as the car slid sideways and we crashed into a gatepost. For a second I think I was unconscious. I wiped blood from a cut on my nose. My hands went for my legs to feel if they were all right. Steam was coming from the radiator but one headlight still scythed into the night as the car was propped half way up an ivy-clad wall marked 'Keep Out, All Callers To Main Entrance'. Beside me Stigi was groaning. My hand was shaking as I felt for the small torch in the glove compartment. I switched it on.

'My God, Stigi!'

'Let me drive next time . . .' he croaked.

'Your face.'

'Bad, huh?'

'Not good, Stigi.'

The American lay where the glass of the windscreen had stopped him and lacerated what seemed like every inch of his face. I could not see his eyes. Glass had gone through the side of his right cheek and into his mouth. As I gently moved him back he spat it out. With my handkerchief I wiped away some of the blood. As I looked around I could see Mother in the headlights. Further along the road, a quarter of a mile away were the lights of the gatehouse proper. I was sure Parr would have a guard.

'Don't worry, Stigi, I can get help.'

'I'm bleeding to death, you bastard.'

'Now please, bear with me a minute. I'm going to get you out of the car. Put you on the grass.'

'Why? It's cold and fucking wet on the grass. Get an ambulance for Christ's sake.'

'Because . . . I want to set fire to the car.'

There was a bubbling noise. Stigi seemed to be having difficulty replying.

'You want to set fire to your Daimler?'

'Yes. To attract attention.'

'Well, you've crashed it. What the hell. Why not set fire to it. I can't see, Toby. Please tell me why I can't see my hand in front of my face.'

All seemed simple to me. Mother was waiting. We were going to confront the pretender.

'Don't worry, Stigi, it's only blood in your eyes. You're not going blind. I want to attract the attention of the guards Parr's bound to have in the gatehouse up there. When they come down to help you I'll slip into the grounds. You can keep them busy. They'll just think this is a normal accident. You could even say you're a friend of Parr. I should have realised before. You're Zopyrus.'

'Look, Toby, I'm hurt bad. Get me to a hospital. Maybe this Parr thing was not a good idea. I'm losing a lot of blood. I'm cold. I want to go home. I don't want to go anywhere near Parr. Who the fuck is Zopyrus when he's at home?' Mother had folded her arms.

'Come on, Stigi. I have got to get you onto the grass. Zopyrus was a Babylonian who remained loyal to Darius after the city rebelled while the king was away fighting foreign wars. When the king came back and besieged the city Zopyrus joined him. But the city would not fall. So Zopyrus devised a plan. He mutilated himself to convince his fellow countrymen he had been tortured by Darius. The Babylonians foolishly let him back into their city. At a given moment he then opened the gates and Babylon fell . . .'

'You should be the one who's going to hospital. If I'm Zopyrus, who are you? Who's Parr then?'

'Well, I think I'm Darius and Parr is one of the pretenders to the throne of Babylon. I'm not exactly sure, of course. Come on, Stigi. Mother's waiting.'

'Mother . . . ?'

I stopped. 'Don't worry. I'll explain later.'

246

'I'm not sure if I want to know.' I leaned across and unlocked the car door and pushed it open.

'I hurt, Toby.'

With a considerable effort I pulled the small man clear of the warm car, carried him fifty yards down the road and laid him on the bank. He was groaning.

'Don't lose heart, Stigi. I'm going to set fire to the petrol tank. Don't peg out on me, old boy. It's all in a good cause, believe me. I'm sure that swine has Maria in there. When someone comes, say you staggered from your car and it burst into flames. Got it?'

'Sure.'

'Well, as Darius says, there's no Persian greater than Zopyrus.'

'What the hell were we drinking?'

I left him by the side of the road and ran back to the car. In my pocket I had a treasured blue and white polka-dot handkerchief. I did not want to part with it but reluctantly unscrewed the petrol cap and as the gasoline slopped out stuffed it into the tank to make a wick. In the boot of the car was a bottle of Famous Grouse whisky. I pulled out the cork and, after pouring some onto the handkerchief, took my cricket club tie off and pushed it down into the bottle to make an expensive Molotov cocktail. I almost forgot the shotgun and reached in and took it off the back seat. Then I walked up the road in the direction of the gatehouse and put the gun down by an ash tree. My tie went out twice before I managed to light it and with a deep breath threw the bottle in a fiery arc towards the car. The whoosh of the two initial smaller explosions was nothing to the huge bang as the reserve tank of the old Daimler went up. Swallows of fragmenting steel flew into the sky and sections of the boot clattered by me on the road. I froze.

Voices came from up the road near the gatehouse. In the distance there was the siren of a police car. But it was going the other way. Two men ran down the road. One stopped by Stigi. The other went down towards the car. One was in his dressing-gown. The man who had knelt by Stigi went to join the first watching the burning wreck.

'We got to get him to hospital . . .'

I didn't wait to hear any more. I ran as fast as I could towards the front gates. They were locked. Frantically I tried the side gate the men must have come through. But the gate seemed to be the kind that shuts automatically. Floodlights came on in the drive. I ran on past the gateway. In front of me was Mother. At a point about twenty-five yards beyond the gate there was an ancient horse chestnut. A branch extended over the barbed wire which ran along the top of the wall.

I took the cartridges out of the shotgun and threw it over. Mother floated impatiently as I tried unsuccessfully to pull myself up by a small dead branch. My arms felt as if they were coming out of their sockets. I heard shouts from down the road. Panting, I gripped the branch again and hauled myself up, my feet seeking purchase against the trunk. I found a foothold and managed to push up onto the overhanging limb of the old tree and crouched against the trunk. After using the wall as a stepping-stone I was astride the branch. I saw Mother on the other side. She beckoned me. I crawled gingerly forward. Inch by inch. I could hear another siren. It was coming closer. I was clear of the wire. I dropped gratefully down towards darkness and Mother. She moved ahead of me through the trees of immaculately maintained parkland. The house Parr had bought was not as grand as Selwyn Hall but it was certainly better maintained. A dog barked and Mother left me. It was so long since I had climbed a tree and it had been much harder than I had thought. More dogs were barking now at the other side of the house. They were getting nearer. Time to hurry. Best foot forward, Jubb.

I ran through the next coppice onto a gravel drive. It was fringed with Parr's prize-winning rhododendrons, nurtured lovingly, their roots nestling and taking nutrients from generations of bones of the criminally insane who had once been laid to rest in the paupers' graveyard in the grounds of The Firs. Now they had been disturbed, lifted and bagged for the greater good of Parr. But then, in the words of our old family cook, Mother England had always been all show and shitty knickers. I reached the front door to hear paws spluttering across the gravel at the corner of the house. I turned the handle. It was not locked. I closed it quickly behind me. The hall was hung with big game trophies. Even a giraffe looked tamely down. Every light was blazing. What could I say, standing there under the head of a giraffe, open and anxious in a tweed suit, holding the vicar's shotgun? My hands started to shake as I loaded. I nearly turned and ran. My mission seemed too bizarre. But then I caught the scent of my mother's perfume and heard the clack of billiard balls in one of the rooms off the hall.

248

'Why don't you come through and show yourself?'

The voice was Parr's.

Slowly I walked towards the open door. Would he have a gun? But when I peered around the door he seemed only intent on a difficult pot. He was thinner, almost skinny, and his face was deeply-lined. But he still had that infuriating earnestness. The same blinkered conviction. It glowed in his eyes as he made a near perfect pot.

'Doing a bit of rough shooting, old boy? I don't really encourage many visitors here. Why don't you put down that old blunderbuss and take up a cue? You used to be jolly good at billiards. Or was it snooker?'

He stood and smiled at me, completely cool. He was smoking a stubby Swiss cheroot and was dressed in a shirt and tie under an ornate silk dressing-gown.

'I have been expecting you for years, Jubb. You must hate me. You must really hate me. But please don't be silly. My men will be back at any minute.'

'First I want to know two things, Parr.'

'Always the thirst for knowledge. Being a swot hasn't done you that much good, has it?'

'Where's my daughter Maria?'

He exhaled a lungful of smoke.

'Why do you ask me? I don't know where she is. Why should I have your daughter?'

'Because you think she's yours.'

He put back his head and laughed.

'You really do have an excellent sense of humour, Jubb.'

'I know you went out with Gwen.'

'That, my dear Jubb, was purely professional and many years ago. Next question.' In that cosy Victorian billiard-room with its blazing log fire and Landseer drawings my resolve was beginning to falter. Then, around the fireplace I noticed some of the blue tiles from the Gate. Mother appeared with her arm resting against the fireplace. She was quite naked. The fire reflected on her thighs. The goddess baring all before the keepers of Hades.

'You have the fabulous golden statue of Bel Marduk.'

Parr looked at me so shocked and surprised that he dropped his cue. I was right.

'How . . . how could you know?'

'You have the statue of Bel. The golden statue made by Nebuchadnezzar and kept in the great ziggurat. The statue which Darius could not find but was recovered by Xerxes and then lost again. A treasure sought after down the millennia. Some authorities say it comprises more than twenty tons of Parsee gold. A fortune. Where is it, Parr?'

'Who told you?'

I remained silent.

'It was the Baron, wasn't it? He told you. Be careful with that gun, old man. It's not too late to come to some arrangement.'

I was icy cold. A strange feeling gripped me. At the same time as I was talking in the billiard room to Parr, I had entered a dark and forbidding citadel with a high watchtower beside the great ziggurat. I was looking for one of the Magi. I was looking for the most evil of that tribe of pretenders. Cobwebs brushed my face. My guard would not follow me.

'What did the Baron tell me?'

'About the gold, old boy. Come with me. I won't bite, you know. There's plenty for everyone.'

He edged around the table and pointed towards the door.

'Come, I'll show you. I've some things in the basement you might recognise. Come with me, Jubb . . .'

I did not hear all of his words. I was back in Babylon. I was ascending a winding staircase. Bats flew from the roof above me. Up and up I went. I knew at the end I would find great evil. A knife was hidden in my tunic.

Parr went ahead and I followed him slowly, carefully down white marble steps into the basement of his large house. I smelled chlorine. In a long room was an indoor pool. What struck me, however, was the tiles. Above a hideous American bar were the embossed ochre lions of the Processional Street. On other walls were the Bulls of Raman and the sacred Sirrush. I stopped.

'My little joke,' said Parr. 'Follow me.'

But I was back in Babylon. From an archer's window I could see the eight levels and hanging gardens of the great ziggurat of Babel. Up and up I went in that watchtower until there the pretender was, standing before me. The lines of debauchery cut deep into his face. A trussed sheep was on the floor about to be sacrificed to Bel. A young girl was tied next to the animal, her thin cotton robe caked in

250

its filth. She looked pleadingly towards me. The smell was of sandalwood, incense and excrement. A knife was hidden in my tunic. In a fold of silk.

I was back in Parr's house.

'I have a surprise for you,' said Parr, tapping a code into the digital lock of a security door. The heavy door swung back and we were in another room. The carpet was thick and over a fireplace was a collection of swords. On the far wall ascended more brilliant blue tiles from the Blue Gate of Babylon, obviously removed before the Major's demolition work, and reconstructed as part of the decorations of a comfortable room for a rich man. On the table in front of what was left of my Gate was a golden statue. I went over to the object. The figure of the god was fifteen inches high.

'But I thought . . .'

'You thought the statue of Bel was fifteen feet high as recorded in Herodotus. You of all people, Jubb, should realise that one can never trust the writers of history. Just as one should never trust a woman. My father loved your mother and it ruined him. My task has been to rebuild the family fortunes and I am going to hand it on, Jubb. Hand it on to my brother's children.' But now I could see the past clearly with another eye.

Before me in the watchtower the pretender backed away as I advanced. In the corner of the room, her hands also bound, was my beloved. The sixth wife of Darius, Asher of Ur.

In the basement, Parr retreated as I stepped towards him.

'Where was the statue?'

'Inside the Gate, your mainly false Gate, Jubb, which was in the bakery, along with a fortune in gold. The copy of the Gate was made and brought from Baghdad at the same time as the genuine article. The statue of Bel, along with other precious artefacts now lost, was inside. At the end of the Second World War, as German defeat became certain, officers who were friendly with Hermann Göring discovered the false Gate and under great secrecy had sections switched with the original in the Pergamon-Museum, to make it seem even more authentic. The top of the Gate, the plinth, was entirely hollow and they filled it with a fortune in gold they stole, mostly from the Jews. The plan was to send the Gate openly to a museum in Lugano. They told the Red Cross, whose train the Gate was to be shipped on, that it was the real artefact, while the one threatened by Allied bombs in the Pergamon was a fake. But defeat came faster than anyone thought. At the very end of the war only three people remained who knew the secret of the Blue Gate in the bakery. One of them, Göring, was executed and one died of his wounds on the Russian front. The Baron came by his information from that man. I got mine from the third, a Red Cross official turned smuggler, who mistakenly imagined the information would get him out of trouble and who was shot trying to escape. Why don't you drop that gun?'

In Parr's hand was a squat pistol.

'You were expecting me?'

'Yes, or . . .'

'You were expecting Rudi?'

'So you know about Rudi? You aren't going to shoot me, are you, Jubb? You aren't going to shoot me because of Berlin, are you, Jubb? Can you remember Berlin? Try to remember. Surely you can remember Berlin?'

I could see the past clearly.

The room in the watchtower was darkening. In front of me was the figure of the pretender. A priestess was standing at my side. She pointed at the knife in my silken tunic. She chanted a litany of his sins. His chief sin was that of pretence. Of pretending he was doing those vile things for honour when all the time he only wanted money. He had wished to possess the precious things of the temple for gain. The gods would damn him. More than that, the goddess would never forgive a man presuming to take her divine lover's image and turn it into base coin.

'You killed my girls, Parr.'

'Are you sure, old boy? Are you sure about anything to do with Berlin? I mean, in my brief encounter with that Welsh slut you married I was able to talk to your doctor. He said that every time you try to remember Berlin you find yourself back in Babylon. Now put that gun down. The Baron was after the gold, too. But I beat him to it. Thanks to you, Toby. The Baron was even prepared to gamble that he could advance those few hundred yards over the border in his tank to get the Gate without causing a world war, so great was his greed. He was completely crazy. But then, for that much gold . . .' Or was it for Magda?

I laid the shotgun down on the sideboard.

'Mene, Mene, Tekel, Peres . . .'

'Ah good, Jubb. Are you safely back in Babylon? How many miles to Babylon, Jubb. Can you take me there by candlelight?'

He pushed forward the safety catch of his automatic pistol with his thumb and slipped it into the pocket of his cavalry twills.

'I'll see you and your daughter never want for anything while you are back in the hospital. Without you cavorting about Berlin and causing endless diversions I could never have pulled it off. I was never very good at pretence. No hard feelings. There's a good chap.'

'You did it for money?'

'The family were penniless. In a way it was for a little piece of England. Come on, Jubb. Sit down. Do cheer up, there's a good fellow. Just drift on now. Safely back into Babylon. Come on now . . .'

'You did it only for money?'

'Be careful, Jubb. Stop. No!'

In the watchtower of the Magi I held the pretender by the throat and raised the knife, concealed as it was within the folds of silk. The manner of death was appointed. Babylon was finished, but a pretender does not die quickly.

22

I woke to the sound of a robin. My wrists were encircled by metal bracelets which I instinctively attempted to pull apart, then gazed at in wonder. I was on the couch in my own drawing-room. A policeman stood by the French windows, another by the door. Across from me was a smiling Quibell-Smith trying relentlessly to eat a bacon sandwich. He was dressed in a neat suit and tie.

'Maria? Have you found her?'

He paused in the middle of a mouthful.

'She's outside, old boy. So is young Rudolph. But first things first.'

'Is she all right?'

'Not a scratch.'

'How did I get here?'

'If you mean, how did you come to this point on life's journey, that I can only begin to guess at, Toby.' He nodded to the policemen. 'Please wait outside. Take off the cuffs and wait outside.'

'But sir, Mr Bryant said . . .'

'And get some more coffee and bacon sandwiches. You have no objection to bacon sandwiches?' I shook my head. Reluctantly the policemen left. One reappeared, much to Quibell-Smith's annoyance, outside the French windows.

'Do they think I'm dangerous?'

'You always were a card, old chap.'

'What do you mean? Is Stigi OK?'

'Your Mr Weitz is fine. He'll have a few scars, but there are no serious internal injuries. He put on a fine performance at the car wreck you staged. Like his old self. He kept Parr's men occupied. Probably the first time hypochondria has been used as a weapon. He must have put on a wonderful show. Every time they tried to move him he cried blue murder. They completely forgot about his nibs. You were able to pay Parr a visit. I was able to solve my puzzle. I had my suspicions, but when I got to that basement all became clear.'

'Where's Parr?'

'I'm afraid you killed him.'

'Killed him?'

'Well, that's something of an understatement.'

'Killed him?'

'Yes, correct me if I'm wrong, because it's only since I came across the Blue Gate of Babylon file that I really started to mug up on Herodotus and Persian history, but it seems Sir Anthony Selwyn Parr suffered the death usually reserved for Babylonian pretenders to the throne in the reign of King Darius the Great.' I groaned. 'Let me read this to you. The notes of a police sergeant who accompanied me. I think it explains why the officers don't want to leave me alone with you.' He cleared his throat.

'" . . . the smaller of the two men was dead amid signs of a considerable fight in the strong-room by the swimming-pool. The victim's nose had been cut off, as had his tongue and his ears. Using a sharp knife . . ." But then, as a Classics student, you know the rest. He must have died just about the time we came in. What you did to him was more or less what King Darius did to any pretender. Of course, he impaled three thousand people when he retook Babylon. Not a chap to cross.'

'I'm sorry.'

'Sorry? Sorry, old boy? Don't be. I doubt if anyone will miss Parr. Anyway his death is my fault if anything. I knew you would pop over and see him. I was using you as an excuse to go storming into his house. I had my suspicions, you see. I was just a bit too late.'

A policeman brought in the bacon sandwiches and went out again, closing the door.

The description of what I had done to Parr left me speechless.

'Well, as any schoolboy who reads the newspapers will have

noticed, there have been many calls to review the Secret Service. To ferret out yet more traitorous queens and lunatics. For my sins I was put in charge of the latest review. I am sure they wanted to be rid of me. I offend the eye.'

He grinned broadly and took a sloppy bite out of the sandwich. I had completely lost my appetite.

'After the Wall, Parr did very well. He rose within the Service. He didn't quite get as far as he wanted to. But he became deputy head of MI6 in Europe; the glamorous away team. Parr really was a superb phoney. All his success was based on the lie that he uncovered a top German espionage ring which included you and poor Midwinter. He also became comfortably wealthy. You on the other hand were in a loony bin and MI6 was being run and staffed by people who had far more of a right to be finger-painting and weaving baskets. In fact you continued to do MI6 a good turn. Every time someone in the Douglas-Home or Wilson Governments said "We must reform those spy chappies" their attention would be drawn to a thick file marked The Blue Gate of Babylon. Most Tories took a look at your sexual shenanigans and knew electoral death and the rank whiff of Profumo when they smelt it. Labour politicians get excited and then go very quiet indeed when they learn who some of your customers were. The socialists also have a tiresome tendency to see foreign affairs as a serious business. Bright young ministers start off wanting to muzzle the maniacs at Cambridge Circus and Vauxhall Bridge Road but always end up participating in the cover-up of The Blue Gate of Babylon. After losing their innocence under those illustrious portals they suddenly develop a passionate interest in something harmless like rabies or reforming the constitution. All your fun in Berlin has ended up classified for a hundred years. I'm surprised they didn't give you a knighthood. Instead, they sent you round the twist. Very British . . .'

He was looking longingly at my bacon sandwich. I handed it to him. He continued as he ate.

'Naturally, the Blue Gate of Babylon file was the first thing I read. Everybody hopes that one day they will be senior enough to see it, though not in the circumstances it was given to me. It was a way of telling me I could not get any further. But as I read about Parr and the Baron and you and Magda there were certain things I couldn't swallow.' Tomato sauce was smeared on his protruding chin. A look of triumph was in his eyes.

'While it was easy for me to believe in your love for Magda, I couldn't quite accept the Baron's infatuation. Cripples are seldom romantics. We look at things coldly. Parr also puzzled me. I proceeded as Goethe advises, without haste but without rest. Parr admitted in debriefing that he had been motivated in trying to catch the Baron in order to protect his father's war record. A thing so stupidly admirable that no one questioned it. I dug further. I discovered that the old General died penniless after your mother perished in that fire. Strange to die from a fire in a summer-house while your father was away. She and the General had both had a lot to drink that night. It could have been an accident. But it was found the summer-house door was locked from the outside. Still, it may have been a prank. The General could have locked your mother in to sleep it off. They were having an affair and he was spending his money like water. Whatever the reason he blamed himself and had an accident cleaning his shotguns a few days later. Parr made your life hell at school, of course, blaming you for his father's suicide, while you never really acknowledged your mother's death. But when I talked to Parr's masters at the school he did not seem to have a particularly strong relationship with his father. He did not seem to have a relationship with anyone. The thing that really made him tick was rebuilding the family fortunes. Order and tradition he understood. But I came to a dead end. I then recalled certain things you had said at the hospital when I had gone there as a junior all those years ago. I began to think about Babylon. Do you know what I did?'

'No.'

'I read, Jubb. Silly of me really, but I had a hunch that somewhere in your dream world was the answer to my quest. A better explanation. The answer, I believed, lay in Babylon. My suspicions were confirmed on that trip on the roundabout. I knew I could not ask you directly about things that happened in Berlin. I had to puzzle out who you were in Babylon. Who was Parr. What secret was being covered up. I played the archaeologist scraping away the sand with my brush and trowel. I was sure, you see, you could help me. I came across the story in Herodotus about the hidden statue of Bel and then I began to think it all could have been for ugly profit. I read your letters to your mother. Whatever it was you did not suspect. At least not consciously. You had to repress the dreadful death of your mother. English society can be so cruel. But I never expected my hunch to turn out right. All books are seditious, Jubb. Every single printed page. When you can tease out the secrets of a traitor like Parr by reading the travels of a Greek fibber who lived five hundred years before Christ, it's come to a pretty pass. We shall probably get to the truth about MI5's poor Roger Hollis by reading Muffin the Mule. How frightening to think books have such power. It's the ideas, you know. Our only solution is to burn the libraries! Burn the bookshops!' He sat looking at me, chuckling. My knee felt stiff.

'I've got pins and needles. Could I get up for a minute?' He nodded and I walked to the French windows. Over the wall to the right in the direction of the village I could see the church. Someone seemed to have pushed it flat against the ground, crushed it like a mushroom under a gumboot. Babylon had fallen.

'The church?'

'Fell down last night. Went over and took a look at it. Foundations are completely rotten.'

'I thought so. You expected me to go and see Parr?'

'Yes, old boy, it was naughty of me. But my suspicions had been partly confirmed in interviews with Weitz who didn't think the Baron entirely a straight bat. What could the Baron and Parr both be after? What could Midwinter be in on too, and disappear from the face of the earth for knowing? Why were you set up as a spectacular decoy? I then ran into a remarkable woman.'

'Surely not Magda?'

'No, Betty. Betty Bethlehem. Chaps in my position have lusts the same as the next man. By chance I was given a telephone number by an acquaintance I trust. It's so hard finding someone who specialises. Someone who understands. She had a nice set of rooms on the seafront at Brighton. Betty Bethlehem is a saint. She has dropped the second name and is in a wheelchair, but I recognised her from the pictures. She said she smelt a rat from the start. But one night she and a girl called Ulrike heard the Baron and Wolfgang arguing. They were arguing about gold. She never told a soul. I couldn't help wondering what a partial original of the Gate was doing in an old bakery. I knew you'd confront Parr when I

258

cast doubt on Maria's parentage. I then telephoned him and told him to expect a caller.'

'You did what?'

'Well, Parr was such a pompous man he imagined he could get away with anything. I felt sure he'd reveal his secret to you. But never in my wildest dreams did I think we would find literally tons of lucre as well as the statue. Of course the bullion wasn't from Babylon, was it?'

'Parr said it was put in the Gate by Göring and his friends. They wanted to ship it out of the country as an ancient artefact. The entire lintel was solid gold . . .'

'My God! Imagine what awesome power Göring had to ensure a secret like that was kept. What fear he must have inspired to overcome men's greed for gold. How else could the gold have remained untouched in the bakery years after the war? Imagine that power, Jubb. We're clumsy children today by comparison. Parr must have had to carry it out in his diplomatic bag and military vehicles. But it was cursed. My, it was cursed. Parr could not realise you were quite such a slave to Babylon. That you were all part of an ancient drama. God, Jubb, you are a card! But then it was Parr's trickery that exiled you to Babylon in the first place. He got what he deserved, one might say. My, it was cursed. All the curses of Babylon were on that gold.'

'He killed the girls?'

Quibell-Smith pursed his lips.

'Those murders were fascinating. Yes, I think Parr was responsible. He must have been reading about Babylon at the time and got the idea from an obscure Chaldean form of sacrifice to purify a new town or city. I must say it's an academic black mark that you didn't notice the connection. I noticed.'

He beamed at me.

'But I'm not exactly sure about Ulrike. I suppose that could have been the Baron. Or just a copycat murder.'

'I don't believe that. What about the murders here? Surely those were Parr?'

Quibell-Smith sighed.

'You know the last murder? The girl at the crossroads?'

'Yes.'

'The forensic boys suggested that could have been you.'

'Me!' I steadied myself against a chair.

'They think it may have started with your wife. I have discussed the matter with the doctor at The Firs. He says that you transformed any woman you were attracted to into your mother. Unable to bear the taboo, you then strangled them. Then I found Herodotus says the Babylonians strangled all women when they were besieged. All except their mothers . . .'

'I'll plead guilty.'

'Oh, I couldn't allow that, Jubb. Coming up before twelve good men and true with all their own sordid little secrets to bury? A jury of one's peers? I wouldn't do that to a pet dog.'

'But you think I did it?' I felt life had spun totally out of control.

'I don't know. It could be on the cards, old boy. You certainly were able to kill Parr. Of course, he liked to give the impression he was so brave; that he almost had a death wish. He may have wanted to go. But not quite in the way you dispatched him. In some ways he was as fake as your Gate.'

'But . . . in Berlin. I saw the image of the goddess above the Gate. I felt the Gate move under my hand . . .'

'Dear boy, if the entire lintel of the Gate was solid gold underneath the tiles, it's a wonder you didn't get a far nastier shock from the static electricity. I don't know about the goddess . . . with the general mood of the Café and what you were all taking I'm surprised you didn't see the heavenly host.' He looked at me sympathetically.

'Aren't you frightened that I'm mad? That I might kill you?'

'Absolutely not, old boy. I'm not a pretender. Anyway, Babylon has fallen, hasn't it? Your mother has been avenged. We'll have to send you away. But I've decided that Parr should be buried with full military honours and the Blue Gate of Babylon file will remain in its original form and be kept top secret. You see I've been promoted, after all. Don't worry, Toby. I'm a grateful man. Things are much clearer now from the top of the tree. Would you like to see Maria?' I nodded. He got up and knocked twice on the door. A second later it was unlocked.

The door opened. I was staring at a face I had previously only seen on film. But he was unmistakable.

'Son.'

'Father.'

'Daughter.'

'Papa.'

I hugged Maria to me. I couldn't believe I had her back. I blinked back the tears.

Behind Maria and Rudi, a woman in a black mink coat trundled into the room in a wheelchair.

'Betty Bethlehem!'

'Toby, love. You poor dear.'

'Maria, darling. Are you sure you're all right? I've been so worried.' Her blue eyes were also full of tears and her blonde hair peeped from the corners of a black French beret.

'Papa. You look so absolutely exhausted. Don't worry. There's no need to explain. Rudi has told me everything.'

'Everything?'

Quibell-Smith almost imperceptibly shook his head.

'I told her about the golden statue.'

'A pity it was only fifteen inches,' I said, without thinking.

'Many would be quite satisfied with that,' smirked Betty. She looked radiant.

Rudi was smiling ingenuously. He was recognisable as my son but he was far more handsome. His nose was perfectly straight and he had his mother's skin and fair hair. There was a constantly amused twinkle in his eyes and a dimple at the right-hand corner of his mouth. If he knew the real history of his family, which as a spy he should, then he played the perfect gentleman.

'Mother sends you all her love. It's so good to see you, father. I never expected to. But I have a confession to make. I am afraid I told Maria I'm your son but that we are not brother and sister by blood. My mother kept a careful watch on you. She learned of your wedding and had the girl investigated. She is terribly nosy. But you must know that. She misses nothing. She misses you.'

'I thought it was a cruel joke at first,' said Maria. 'Now I don't care about it one bit. I don't want Rudi as a brother. I like it better that we are not family.' She gave him a withering look which spoke volumes. My heart jumped. I was so grateful they did not like each other.

'Did your mother send you over to see me?'

Rudi glanced at Quibell-Smith and I knew I was not going to get the truth.

'Oh yes, dear father. I hear stories of the great gold statue from my other father the Baron when he is drunk and raving about going to Lugano. He spends most of his time in a hunting-lodge in Silesia. When Mother realised she had been tricked and it was the Gate my papa, the Baron, wanted and she could not get back, she made his life hell. He must be one of the most, how do you say, chicken-pecked generals in the Warsaw Pact. I never intended to meet Maria.'

I had said that once to myself about Magda.

'Rudi thinks he's my white knight, Papa. I was broken down by the side of the road coming to see you ... my little car had overheated. When he said who he was I thought he was crazy. Then he began to tell me the fantastic story. Oh, Papa, it's so sad. Well, he took me immediately to see Betty Bethlehem, who confirmed it all. I was going to telephone, Papa, I really was. But then Mr Quibell-Smith and his men arrested us all and made us stay in a luxury hotel near Bicester. Rudi and I ... well, we're no longer talking to each other. Poor Papa.' She rushed over and kissed me passionately on the cheek. Rudi came over too. I put my arms around them both. Somehow I didn't believe a word about her car breaking down.

'I suppose I'm not equipped to play Cupid,' said Quibell-Smith.

'These two aren't in trouble?'

'Absolutely not,' said the secret civil servant. 'Anyway, your son has diplomatic immunity. Now I think we had better talk alone. Don't worry, you'll have plenty of time to see your chicks again.' For a whole minute Maria would not let go of me. She always did that as a child. She turned and blew me a kiss at the door. Rudi gave her a wide berth. I hated to think what he had done or suggested. But another part of me felt such pain at that moment I longed to be back under the Blue Gate of Babylon with the smell of old dates and ditchwater, of sandalwood and cheap incense and sweating bodies and sacred herbs.

'Are you going to march me back to The Firs? Are you going to forget me in prison? You said you were going to send me away.'

Torrential autumn rain started to sweep the garden. Quickly it turned to hail. The policeman outside pressed close to the window. Quibell-Smith made no move to let him in.

'Ah yes, we thought about the alternatives. Or rather, the problem of your continued physical existence was mooted by one of my subordinates. We can't have the great unwashed getting to know your story, Jubb. Hundreds of ignorant busybodies are sniffing about the Service. Of course, no one would believe it; as no true scholar believes Herodotus. But it would create a bad impression. We required a permanent solution. To protect your family, you understand. A more lasting silence. I don't think you'll be writing to Mother any more, Jubb. I am afraid there is no other way.'

Epilogue

'Dr-e-e-eam, Dream, Dream, Dream,' sing the Everly Brothers. Sometimes our dreams turn out in the most unexpected ways.

Dear Mother,
I could not leave forever, Mother, without a last note to thank you. You came down into Hades and held my hand. Now you have left me. I felt the same sadness when I left Maria and Rudi, but they promise to come and see me where I am going. I do not think it makes any difference that she is not really my daughter. The bus is starting and I must close, mother. I hope you get this card. I hope I have not lost your address,

All my love,
Toby

The tour bus was parked in the Kurfürstendamm. On the seat beside me sat a grim man in an expensive raincoat. More grim men in expensive raincoats sat in front and behind.

'You must fill the front seats first,' said the tour guide in faltering English. The grim men did not move. I gave one of them the postcard. They had already taken my passport away. To them I was a traitor. I had finally become too big for England.

We halted on Schöneberger Strasse at a road-works. To me it seemed the coach had stopped on purpose. I was able to look across the still neglected district to where the Café Babylon had been. In the distance was the Wall they were now talking of taking down. We arrived at Checkpoint Charlie and took our place in a queue of cars and buses. A party of Mexican gynaecologists in the city for a convention on the diseases of the womb complained bitterly at having to wait an hour for no apparent reason. As we started off again one lady's comments became quite shrill when she learned we were not going to stop in the Alexanderplatz. 'But I pay . . . I pay,' she screamed. The cars in the East and the people looked small and shrunken. They blinked at the morning as if just emerging from an air raid shelter. Yet I felt strangely happy. They reminded me I had left Babylon.

'Here is the Pergamon-Museum. Here we will be allowed one half-hour exactly. Please do not be late. Please remember there are to be no flash pictures.'

Without a word Quibell-Smith's praetorian guard got off the coach with me. We climbed the steps to the glass-fronted building that was spewing tourists. A woman in uniform was erecting a sign. It said 'Closed until further notice'. We pushed against the crowd. The attendant tried to stop us as we made our way in. A crocodile of schoolchildren was being shooed out by a teacher with a depressingly positive manner. A man joined our little band.

So here in a museum was where Jubb was to be swapped like a stamp.

'I am to come with you,' the man said eagerly to my captors. 'He is to accompany that comrade,' the defector added in English looking over at me, and then nodding towards an attendant. I strode after the hurrying museum worker past the Pergamon Altar, through the Roman marketplace and up a wooden ramp. At last I stood in the Processional Street of Lions. I was marvelling at the genuine Blue Gate of Babylon when a figure moved out of a recess to the left.

'Magda. Oh, Magda!'

'Do you still love me, Toby?'

'Always.'

'Would you die for me?'

'I think, in a small way, I did.'

'No regrets?'

'None. Well, almost . . .'

We kissed passionately, deeply, and to me she did not seem to have changed so very much. No hint of that straw stale smell of age clouded her breath. But was I pretending?

'Come, we have a party ready in a private room. Many of the girls are still here. I managed to rescue them. Now we have rescued you. Cindy will be so pleased to see you. I love you, Toby. Come. We have all become wickedly respectable but can still be respectably wicked . . .'

I looked back at the Blue Gate of Babylon. On the battlements I thought I saw the smiling figure of a woman. Perhaps it was my imagination. But I no longer had to pretend. The powers-that-be who had stolen my pride, had also taken away my fear. Now, the gods willing, I could be happy. Darius discovered his beloved wife in the citadel after slaying the pretender Smerdus. I had rid myself of Parr. Wishes do come true under the Blue Gate of Babylon; thank you, Mother, thank you so very much.

Gratefully, I took Magda's elegant hand.

Best foot forward, Jubb.